TRACEY MARTIN

I0524676

DARKEST MISERY

MISS MISERY

BOOK FOUR

DARKEST MISERY

TRACEY MARTIN

CITY OWL
PRESS

DARKEST MISERY
Miss Misery, Book 4

CITY OWL PRESS
www.cityowlpress.com

Cover Design by MiblArt. All stock photos licensed appropriately.

Edited by Danielle DeVor.

For information on subsidiary rights, please contact the publisher at info@cityowlpress.com.

Print Edition ISBN: 978-1-64898-250-7

Digital Edition ISBN: 978-1-64898-251-4

Printed in the United States of America

PRAISE FOR TRACEY MARTIN

"The action in *Wicked Misery* was great, as was the suspense. Each character felt authentic, and the dialogue had me laughing. I definitely want to continue this series."
– Bad Bird Reads

"Readers of *Wicked Misery*…will surely be turned into fans, and will find themselves eager for the next installment."
– RT Book Reviews

"*Darkest Misery* is recommended for paranormal romance readers who enjoy a high-stakes story."
– Library Journal

"This world is rich, it has a lot of non-human, mystical elements in a human setting… I also loved the plot. A nice murder mystery with twist after twist."
– Fangs for the Fantasy

"Jess is finding out it's not so easy to let go of her past as she discovers the terrifying truth behind the Gryphons' treachery in this riveting urban fantasy romance, *Misery Loves Company*."
– Evampire

"The action was intense and the danger and mystery behind Jess's case brought along lots of drama and suspense in *Dirty Little Misery*."
– Urban Fantasy Investigations

For everyone waiting for the light to break through.

THE MISS MISERY SERIES
BY TRACEY MARTIN

Wicked Misery

Dirty Little Misery

Misery Loves Company

Darkest Misery

Misery Happens

ONE

GRYPHON AGENT TOM KASSIN MIGHT KNOW MORE ABOUT WHAT I was than most people on this planet, but he totally didn't get *who* I was. Which is how I ended up on a plane taxiing down the runway at Phoenix Sky Harbor International Airport.

Passengers shuffled in their seats, clearly antsy to get to the gate and impatient for the *Fasten seat belt* light to go off. I shared their impatience—literally. It tasted to me like bitter almonds. But that was as much as I shared with my fellow passengers. Though I wanted to stretch my legs too, I had little else to look forward to when I got off the plane.

"I still think this is a bad idea," I muttered, stuffing my water bottle into my duffel bag.

I could sense Tom was just as eager to get off this flying deathtrap as everyone else, but he hid his irritation better than most. Which was to say he was one of the few who hadn't actually made a move toward his phone yet. "You're too hard on yourself, Jessica. I truly think having you along will do a lot to reassure Mr. Johnson."

"See, this is why I keep saying you don't get me. You used my name and 'reassure' in the same sentence."

"I get you better that you think." His disconcerting accent, part

Southern twang and part butchered British, always seeped out when his emotions were heightened. And they'd been heightened a lot lately.

Tom did not like me challenging his authority.

I could no longer keep from rolling my eyes. "Just because you have my magical profile and rap sheet memorized doesn't mean you understand my psyche."

In light of a looming apocalypse I could no longer ignore, I was willing to work with Tom and his secret Gryphon group of expert magic workers and highly trained fighters to prevent it, but it killed me a little inside to do so. The Brotherhood of the Wing, aka *Le Confrérie de l'Aile*, had created me to become a super pred-fighting warrior against my will and without my knowledge. Those actions had made my life hell for a multitude of reasons, and regardless of the Brotherhood's intentions, I had a hard time forgiving them for it.

If that made me petty or short-sighted or even vindictive, I could live with it.

After several torturous minutes, the plane reached the gate, and I stuffed my brand new Kindle into my bag. Lucen had given it to me a couple days ago, just as Tom was starting to make noise about the value of having me along on his Arizona mission.

Over the years, Lucen had given me lots of things—a reason to live, a safe place to hide, all the free booze I could drink, and more recently, the best sex I could ever imagine. But this was the first present-like thing he'd given me.

Despite his bar recently being destroyed and his alliances turned upside down, Lucen had been in remarkably good spirits lately. Apparently, me screwing around with his best friend Devon did that to him. For Lucen, it was a sign that I was becoming comfortable in my sorta-satyr skin, and we could make our relationship work. While I was glad he was happy, and as much as I did like Devon, I couldn't kill my hope that one day Lucen and I could have a normal, human-style relationship that did not involve some form of ménage. I just wasn't about to tell either of the men that.

Missing Lucen already, I watched Tom worm his way into the aisle. After he grabbed his bag from the overhead compartment, I adjusted my grip on my duffel and followed his blond head into the terminal. There, I breathed deeply and stretched my cramping muscles, rejoicing in leaving behind the plane's odors of sweat and stale coffee. The airport was done up in shades of neutral, and through the wall of windows to my left, a line of majestic mountains jutted into a blue sky dotted with perfect fluffy clouds.

I gazed at them in delight. Although I still believed my presence on this trip was superfluous, maybe I wouldn't end up hating it so much. Dragging my longing gaze from the window, I turned to Tom. He was only my height, and with a disarmingly cherubic face, he inadvertently hid the extent of his magical and political power well.

"So." I yawned. "Do we have an actual plan, or are we simply going to knock on this guy's door? And do I have time to use the restroom before we do?"

Tom had his phone out, and he was staring at it. "We have time," he said, choosing to ignore what I thought was some obvious hyperbole in my question. "Mr. Johnson just got home."

"Good." I immediately took off toward the restroom signs, and Tom trailed behind me. I had a feeling he didn't intend to let me out of his sight. Lack of trust was one of the few things we had in common. "So you've been calling him?"

Tom shook his head. "Given the sensitivity of the situation, I've had someone at the local Gryphon office keeping an eye on him. This is a conversation we need to have with him face-to-face."

I merely nodded. Tom and the other members of our little apocalyptic prep group had all been in agreement about the need for discretion. For some reason, the furies were interested in me, and that meant they'd likely be interested in Mr. Johnson too if they found out we shared some traits. It was best, therefore, to keep our mission hush-hush.

"What does he do for a living?" I asked, thinking about Mitchell Johnson's strange talents and what sorts of occupations they might lend themselves to.

Tom stuck his phone away. "He's a psychiatric nurse."

I couldn't help myself. I snorted. "Oh well, then I think his job would have been the perfect place to tell him the truth. It's exactly the sort of story that makes people want to check themselves into a psych ward."

"Actually, I expect he'll want to commit *us*." Tom smiled grimly. "That's one of the reasons you're along."

Right. Because I was so mentally fucking stable.

I headed into the restroom, enjoying the image of Tom strapped into a straitjacket.

In theory, whether we accosted Johnson at his work or at his home or at the local McDonald's, it shouldn't matter. Our mission was simple: convince Johnson to come with us, both for his personal safety and because the Gryphons thought he would be instrumental in saving the world. But first, we would have to explain to Johnson what he was and find out what he could do.

The what-he-could-do part interested me greatly, but although I'd asked lots of questions, Tom only shared information with me when he felt like it. For all of his "we're in this together" BS, it was clear where he and his fraternity saw my place in the pecking order. I was their tool, a weapon they'd created to be used as they required, and no more. If I were feeling generous, I'd say they expected me to be a foot soldier to their commanding officers, but I rarely felt generous given what they'd done to me.

All I could do, therefore, was wait until Tom decided to spill his guts about the Brotherhood's experiments and those of us who'd survived them this long. We were three now. Two of *Le Confrérie's* test subjects were dead. Kyra McNaughton had committed suicide years ago, and Victor Aubrey was a twisted serial killer who'd been murdered in prison.

That left me, Mitchell Johnson, and another woman who lived in Chicago. After we convinced Johnson to come with us, we were supposed to swing by the Windy City and pick her up.

When I finished washing my hands, I pulled my mess of brown curls back in a ponytail. Whether it was the early flight or the horrible bathroom lighting, I couldn't tell, but my face seemed paler, and those circles under my eyes should not have been there. No way to deny it, I was stressed and tired. I felt like I'd been running on nothing but adrenaline for weeks.

But there was no backing out now. No getting off this roller coaster. I was the person who'd clued the Gryphons in to various parts of this prophecy, and I was the one who'd brought together the unhappy alliance of Gryphons, magi, and preds to deal with it. For the sake of everyone I loved—and maybe the world—I had to suck it up and act like something I didn't feel. A confident, competent warrior.

Too bad I couldn't shake the feeling that I was just a misery-sucking freak in way over her head.

Neither Tom nor I had any checked luggage since this was supposed to be a short trip, so after we picked up our rental car, we were on the road. Rubbing my tired eyes, I kept silent as Tom navigated us out of the airport morass. Once we hit the highway, however, I adjusted my sunglasses and seized the silence. "Tell me about Mitchell Johnson."

Tom was quiet a moment, frowning. "I can hardly tell you a lot about someone I've never met."

I glared at him, but the gesture went unnoticed because Tom kept his gaze focused on the road. "You said you'd tell me more about the experiments if I came to Phoenix. Well, I came to Phoenix. So tell me—how were we selected? Is Johnson also a satyr?"

"You're not a satyr." Tom's frown deepened.

I narrowed my eyes at him. "Really? Because the satyrs in Boston seem to think I am. They said I'm a rare subspecies." Thinking of myself that way still unsettled me. Mentally un-conditioning yourself to believe you're human was about as difficult as it sounded. Particularly when you grew up thinking the creature you truly were was evil.

Tom said nothing for a moment, but his grip on the steering wheel tightened. I waited him out. "You shouldn't listen to your satyr *friends*."

"Aw, and I thought we were all on the same side now. The enemy of my enemy is still my enemy then, as far as the Gryphons are concerned?"

They sure were as far as the satyrs were concerned. Lucen and others had made it quite clear to me that though we were all working together on this apocalyptic problem, the satyrs trusted the Gryphons not even half as far as they could throw one.

Tom sighed. "At best, the enemy of my enemy is my casual acquaintance. Nothing more. Something you'd do well to keep in mind."

It was my turn to stay silent. Neither Tom nor any other Gryphons knew just how close my current relationships with some of the satyrs were, or how far into my past those relationships extended. The animosity between all the pred races and humanity—especially the Gryphons— probably went back until the day the two groups had met thousands of years ago.

All pred races had to feed on human misery, after all. And they all had to "addict" some humans to survive. That is, the preds created a magical bond between themselves and a human whose emotional barriers— usually referred to as their soul—were worn down. Then the preds dumped their negativity on their addicts and fed on the suffering it caused.

As a result, the small pool of magically gifted humans who formed the Gryphons had always sought to defend humanity and fight preds. But centuries of laws and treaties codifying how the groups should behave around each other to avoid bloodshed couldn't overcome the natural fear and loathing between predator and prey.

"So back to my question—will Johnson share my lusty skill set? Or did you shake it up among the five of us?"

A muscle in Tom's cheek twitched. "Satyr magic was used on all of you."

"Well, that doesn't seem particularly experimental. Why?"

I was testing Tom's patience. I'd always suspected he wore some very strong charms to damper his emotions, which made sensing them difficult for me, but I was picking up on them now. "As far as pred races go, satyrs were deemed the best option. The Brotherhood felt the side effects of lust magic were less likely to cause issues."

I mused on this, twisting the water bottle cap around. "I don't know. The ability to wound a person's vanity doesn't seem so scary as far as things go. Although I'm just as glad to not be part sylph."

"The blow to the self-esteem faced by a sylph's addict is exceptionally detrimental to a person's mental health," Tom said. "Physically, too, satyrs appear more human. If there were any side effects with regards to appearance, we figured they would be easier to manage."

Okay, that made sense. Aside from the small horns on their heads, satyrs were indistinguishable from humans, something none of the other four races could say.

Tom preemptively hushed me so he could concentrate on the GPS, and I stared out the window, sucking up the view. Phoenix was so unlike Boston, I might as well have been in a different country altogether. I was used to shining steel façades and lush green trees, to peeling houses whipped raw by the Atlantic, and tall buildings crowded together on narrow, winding roads that became other narrow, winding roads without warning until outsiders were hopelessly lost.

Here, it was as though someone had taken a city and squashed it flat. The buildings oozed away from the core and spread thin across the landscape. Everything was wide and open. Everywhere I looked was a palette of browns and oranges and subdued reds, except for the sky, which was a singularly amazing blue.

Lost in my thoughts, I only returned my attention to Tom as the car slowed. He parked along the street and waved at an unmarked SUV on the opposite side of the road. The driver, a Gryphon in uniform, returned the gesture then pulled away. Once she was gone, we headed up the stone path to a ranch-style house in what appeared to be a middle-class neighborhood. Even out of uniform, Tom looked every bit the professional in his button-down shirt, tie, and khaki pants. Me? I looked like exactly what I was—an unwilling recruit.

Tom knocked twice, then let the screen door creak loudly on its hinges as it banged shut. Someone must have been home because it sounded like a TV was on.

When no one answered after a moment, Tom knocked harder. I closed my eyes and stretched out with my gift, trying to sense the emotions of whoever was inside. They came to me faintly—irritation, confusion, sadness maybe. Or more likely weariness. All emotions had their unique taste, but within those tastes were variations. Sometimes the variations gave me useful information, but just as often my interpretation depended on my own mood. I could well be projecting my own weariness and making unwarranted assumptions.

"Someone's home," I said to Tom.

He gave me a funny look, then his eyes widened in understanding. "You're sensing him. Interesting."

I crossed my arms, wishing I could make Tom sense what it felt like to be a lab rat. "Yes, Doctor Frankenstein, I am."

Tom ignored the jab and knocked a third time. At last, I heard footsteps, and the door was thrown open. Startled, I straightened and wiped away my pissy expression.

On the other side of the screen door stood a guy about my age. Tall and thin, he wore a faded gray T-shirt that stood out in stark contrast to his dark skin. His black hair was shaved close to his scalp, and a heavy five o'clock shadow covered his chin. His dark eyes swept over us. Though they were small, they were expressive. You didn't need to be an empath to figure out what he was feeling.

"Can I help you?"

"Are you Mitchell Johnson?" Tom asked.

Johnson's irritation morphed into suspicion in my mouth. "Yeah, I'm Mitch. What's this about?"

Tom flashed his badge. "I'm Gryphon Agent Tom Kassin, and this is…"

I didn't hear the rest of Tom's speech because the strength of Johnson's panic almost knocked me over. The emotional rush left my head spinning.

Then the door slammed in our faces.

TWO

I pressed my fingers to my temples. Behind the door, I could sense Johnson's racing emotions. He was a jittery mess, but fear was a pure emotional response as far as I was concerned. The most potent sort of hit, aside from lust.

It enabled me to get a good read on his intentions. "He's going to run."

Tom yanked open the screen door and knocked again. "You can't possibly know that."

"I know what he's feeling."

"We startled him."

"Yeah, that's part of it." I bounded off the front step while Tom called Johnson's name.

He turned sharply to me. "Where are you going?"

Good question. The tiny backyard was fenced off, but I found a gate to the left. "There."

Without a glance back at Tom, I ran toward it. He wanted to bring me here? He could let me be useful.

Johnson was on the move. His panic was ebbing, though a heavy current of key-lime fear ran though him. His confusion was lifting too. I couldn't tell for sure what this meant, but I could make guesses, and one of those guesses was exactly what I'd told Tom. Johnson was preparing to run, and I suspected I knew why.

Maybe Tom had been right to bring me here. Wasn't that a depressing thought?

I darted through the gate. Keeping low, I crept into the backyard, which was barely big enough to hold a gas grill and a cheap plastic patio table.

Keep positive, I told myself. Believe helpful things.

Not being a ray of sunshine under the best of circumstances, I cringed at my own pep talk. But if Johnson was like me, and he probably was, then he could sense any negativity in me as well as I could sense it in him, and I didn't want him to figure out I was lying in ambush.

Whether my attempt at forced positivity helped, I'd never know. The back door crashed open, and Johnson came flying out before I was ready for him. He wore a backpack and an expression like that of a cat trapped in a corner. Yet there was nowhere to go except through me if he meant to get to the gate.

"Wait!" I reached out for him, moving slowly, doing my damnedest to project a calm I wasn't sure I felt. "You're not in any trouble. This isn't what you think it is."

He should have been able to sense I wasn't lying, but maybe he was too far lost in his distress to notice. Judging by his eyes, I wasn't even certain he'd heard me.

I took another tentative step forward, thinking I could subdue him if necessary. I had the training. Alas, Johnson apparently had training too. I held out my hand, and unprepared for his response, I screamed as my feet flew out from under me. My backside smacked the stone patio.

Luckily, I managed to keep my head from colliding with the ground, but dragon shit on toast. Throbbing pain shot up along my spine from my tailbone all the way to my shoulders. Stunned motionless for a moment, I thought I heard Johnson mutter "Sorry" before his long legs disappeared from my peripheral vision.

Sorry? Was he fucking kidding?

I rolled over and crawled to my feet. Beneath the hair that fell in my face, I caught a glimpse of him opening the gate. Yelling Tom's name, I hobbled after Johnson.

Tom flew around the corner just as Johnson reached the same area. I clutched the gate with one hand and my aching butt with the other, but before I could warn Tom that Johnson wasn't going quietly, the men clashed.

Groaning, I pulled myself together, ready for round two, but Tom was quicker on the uptake than I was. He'd gotten to see my old-lady-with-a-bad-back act, and he must have figured out what to expect. So although Johnson had about six inches on Tom, the grappling didn't last long. And when it was over seconds later, Tom had Johnson on his knees on the path, hands pinned behind his back. Smooth, efficient, and I hated to admit it, but impressive.

For the second time today, I blinked at Tom in surprise. Well then. I'd known for a while that Tom carried a small arsenal of rare weapons. I suppose I should have expected he wouldn't be a slouch in hand-to-hand combat.

Feeling foolish, I walked over while massaging my tailbone. "I'll consider your apology if you'll cooperate now."

Johnson's confusion was heady. If only I had some super healing powers I could activate with the juice he was feeding me. Instead I was stuck with a useless head rush and a sore butt.

"I want a lawyer," he said. The annoyance was gone from his tone, his voice quiet and resigned.

"Why? What did you do?" Tom asked. He hadn't loosened his grip.

"Nothing."

Tom didn't get it, but I did. So yeah, this was why I was here.

I sighed and knelt in spite of the pain. "No one's arresting you because of your gift."

Johnson's dark skin seemed to turn a couple shades lighter. "I don't know what you're talking about."

I almost laughed at his denial. He'd rather run and make us think he was a criminal than admit to being a misery junkie.

For a fleeting second I considered whether there was a reason for that. Wouldn't it be just our luck to come all this way to find a guy who I believed was screwed over by the Gryphons, only to have him turn out to be another murderous Victor Aubrey? Then the second passed and I knew better. Face-to-face with Johnson, I couldn't sense any evil in him. Victor, on the other hand, had reeked of it—a foul, burnt-oil taste that set off my gag reflex.

"Mr. Johnson, listen to me. I know what you can do because I can do it too. I can sense negative emotions, and no one is here to arrest you. We're actually here to help and explain, and to apologize." I glared at Tom as I spoke the last word, and he returned the expression.

Whatever. Just because he didn't think *Le Confrérie* needed to apologize for screwing up our lives didn't mean they shouldn't. An apology had been part of my condition for coming along. Though, to be fair, I was glad now that I had. Johnson needed my reassurance. Tom had been right about that much.

I wet my lips. "Tom, let him go. He knows I'm not lying." I hoped so anyway.

Tom wasn't happy, but he released Johnson's arms.

Johnson stretched his shoulders a few times, looking between us but mostly at me. "I'm really not the only person with this curse?"

With an achy effort, I climbed to my feet. "It's not a curse, and no. Agent Kassin here is going to explain a lot of things to you after he apologizes, but we should have this conversation indoors."

Johnson stood, clearly dubious. Although I couldn't sense curiosity, I felt confident we'd gotten his attention. He picked up his backpack and gestured for us to follow him into the back. "All right. If the two of you can really explain things, I'm all ears. I've got a lot of questions."

"Be prepared to have your mind blown," I said, adopting a falsely cheerful smile.

A SHORT TIME LATER, MITCH SAT ACROSS FROM ME, CRADLING a beer bottle in his hands and probably wishing he'd opted for something stronger. "So let me get this straight. The Gryphons are the ones who made a mess of my gift, and they did it because it appears a prophecy about some really old preds escaping from a magical prison is coming true, and I'm supposed to be able to fight them?"

Condensation slid down Tom's water glass and dropped onto his perfect pants. "That's the gist. If we'd known the experiments had worked—"

Mitch laughed the slightly insane laugh of someone who can't believe what he's hearing. "This is bullshit. I've lived with this curse for the last ten years, and only now are you seeking me out?"

"Sorry," I muttered. "All my fault for alerting them to our existence."

Mitch rubbed his chin. "I guess I should thank you since I have an answer finally. But I don't get this part about actually being a kind of satyr. If that's the case, I'd think my dating history wouldn't suck so much."

I shrugged. "I always figured it was hard to date when other people's misery makes you feel good."

"There's that." He swigged his beer thoughtfully. "But I don't have any satyr-like abilities besides emotional feeding. Do you?"

I cast a wary glance at Tom, but he already knew this much about me. I merely disliked reminding him. "I can create addict-like bonds of lust in people and use the lust to influence them. I wouldn't be surprised if you can too. Maybe no one's ever showed you how."

Mitch blinked at me over his beer. "No, definitely no one has ever shown me how. I've never even told anyone what I can do. You have?"

Tom was staring at me. "So that ability didn't come naturally, Jessica? I assumed it had."

I reclined in my seat, trying to act like none of this was a big deal. "Nothing about this power is natural, and it's not like I could have discovered it by accident. I'm not giving off a cloud of lust-inducing pheromones wherever I go. A satyr taught me."

Tom chewed his lip thoughtfully, but Mitch gaped at me. "You talk to satyrs?"

"Sometimes." Talk to them. Sleep with them. Live among them.

Tom cleared his throat. "Jessica's example isn't one we advocate following. In fact, given the situation and the gravity of what we believe is on the horizon, we'd like you to return to Boston with us. We want to provide you with the training you never received and make you part of the alliance we're forming."

Mitch set his beer down and stood, shaking his head. "I can't just pick up and leave. I understand what you're saying, but the Gryphons dumped me. After that, I moved on. I have a life here. A job. I'm a nurse. I can't forget my other responsibilities." He paused his pacing in front of the window. "Unless you're going to arrest me, after all. Force me to go."

"We'd rather not force you," Tom said, also standing. "But this is a matter of global security. Whatever you need the Gryphon World Office to do in order to make it possible, we can and will."

And did.

Over the next hour, Tom persuaded Mitch to come to Boston, at least temporarily. A few phone calls later and the phrase "global security" tossed around like it actually meant something, Tom had also made sure Mitch's leave of absence from his job was not only approved by the hospital, but encouraged.

It wasn't surprising, but it was rather infuriating. The world was full of people who believed Gryphons were saviors. If only they knew what I did.

By the time Mitch was ready to go, darkness had settled outside. He dumped his small suitcase in the living room and scanned the place. Worry lines were deeply etched on his face, and anxiety rolled off him in great spearmint waves. I understood the sentiment and tried to forgive him for it, but I hated that flavor.

"So this is it?" He sounded like a man who expected never to see his home again.

"I've booked us on a red-eye to Chicago," Tom said. "We should get going."

"I thought we were going to Boston." Mitch stuffed his phone in his back jeans pocket.

"Detour first," Tom said.

I hung back while Mitch locked up his house. "Remember what I told you earlier? There are three of us left. The third is in Chicago. Tom's plan is to pick her up on the way."

"So I get to tail along for the ride, like you." Mitch nodded uneasily. "You're pretty calm about all this."

I forced a smile and got in the car. "I've had longer to live with the knowledge. Besides, the real danger won't come until we're stuck in a room with a bunch of preds, some arrogant magi, and a few zealous Gryphons. It'll be amazing if no one dies."

"We're not zealous." Tom's annoyance flared, and I smirked. "Not unless you mean about protecting humanity."

"Oh, so much is obvious."

Tom ignored my sarcasm as he turned off Mitch's street. Sighing, I reached for my water bottle, and as I did, something silver flashed in the corner of my eye. I had just enough time to think *Car!* before the object slammed into us, and we went spinning off the road.

THREE

SHOCK REDUCED MY WORLD TO COLORS AND SOUNDS. THE car's gray interior. The crunching metal. Tom swearing. And a single, errant and silly thought—huh, that might be the first time I'd ever heard Tom swear.

My seat belt strangled me, and before I could adjust to what was happening, a second impact followed the first. I flew back against my seat this time, grunting and gasping for breath. My head rolled to the side as the car rattled, and we finally came to an abrupt stop.

Warily, I opened my eyes. A pole. We'd been knocked into a utility pole.

Wasn't that lovely. My brain didn't seem to want to work. Some part of me was aware this must be what shock felt like, and I squeezed my eyes tight to snap out of it. Where was the pain? Where were my emotions? My reasoning?

I found my voice if nothing else. "Tom? Mitch?"

"Yeah," came Mitch's voice from the backseat.

I tried to look around, afraid of what sort of pain would hit when I did, but adrenaline had me covered. I felt nothing. No physical pain, that was. Mental clarity was coming, and I didn't like it.

"Tom!" Blood dribbled down his forehead, but he blinked and

murmured something I couldn't make out. Shit. Phone. I needed my phone. Forcing down the panic that came on clarity's heels, I undid my seat belt.

"Um, Jess?" Mitch's voice hardly registered with me, but the sudden spark of his orange fear cut through my fog.

I twisted in my seat. "What?"

"Look out!"

The front passenger door flew open, and before I could see who was there, something dark obscured my vision. A sack or bag had been thrown over my head. Strong hands pressed my shoulders into the seat. Uselessly, I flailed against my attacker and whatever was over my eyes, but I got nowhere. Then I felt a prick on my arm, like a needle, and my scream died on my tongue.

I couldn't move. Couldn't yell. My lungs worked—I breathed barely—but that was all. More doors opened and shut. Mitch was yelling. He was being attacked too. Then he also fell silent.

Careless hands yanked off my seat belt and grabbed me from under the arms. I mentally shrieked and strained with every molecule of my being, every sour orange hit of Mitch's and my collective fear, but I couldn't break the paralysis. Just as frustrating, I couldn't sense who the attackers were. Not a single emotion registered from them. I couldn't even count their number because they didn't speak. I was completely helpless, trapped with my rage and fear, my heart thrashing against my breastbone.

Internally, I recoiled in horror as more hands grabbed me about the legs. Being unable to move added an extra layer of revulsion to my attackers' touches. As if being abducted wasn't terrifying enough, knowing they could do anything to me and I'd be helpless pushed me into panic territory.

I heard a whooshing noise, like a van door opening, and my arm banged into something. Someone swore in a low voice. I could tell I was being loaded into a vehicle, but that was all. A car door slammed, and a man shouted, "Go." As I was stuffed into a seat with an unknown person pressed against me, we began to move.

I'd like to say I counted the seconds we drove or memorized the turns, but I couldn't. Panic left no room for anything so intelligent. All I could do was focus on being paralyzed. All I could do was think what these people —men from the sound of it—might do to me.

When the vehicle stopped, I was carried down a flight of stairs into a room blissfully cooler than the place I'd just left. Dumped on the floor, I held my breath, waiting for what was to come.

Nothing did. A door shut, and I got the sense I was alone.

After what felt like hours but was probably mere minutes, my right eyelid twitched. Little by little, more motion came to me. Soon, I could blink fully and shrug my shoulders.

Come on, I willed my body. *Get it together faster. Before they return.*

But whether I could will myself to heal quicker became irrelevant a second later. The unseen door opened again, and multiple sets of heavy footfalls approached. Shit.

"You sure you got the right ones?" a man with a Spanish accent asked.

"Of course we got the right ones." The second guy, who had no accent, sounded offended. "How stupid do you think we are?"

Someone, presumably the first man, snorted. "Very."

Suddenly the bag over my head was yanked off. I sucked in a mouthful of air and found myself face-to-face with a fury addict. I should have known that's who these guys were, but it made no sense. The furies in Boston had been protecting me, so why would fury addicts in Phoenix snatch me?

The addict held up his phone and glanced between it and me. The stink of cigarette smoke wafted off him. "Yeah, looks like her. Let's go."

"That's it? All this work to grab her, and we got to leave her?" The guy behind me lifted my hair. I tensed, and as pleased as I was that I could manage that much, I couldn't do more. My heart beat a death march as I waited for what would come next. "Seems such a waste when I could do with—"

"You'll not do anything," the first guy snapped. "Not if you want to keep your guts on the inside. Now shut up, and let's get going."

The second thug grumbled, and I caught sight of his legs as he walked around me. Furious but relieved, I watched the men leave through a rickety wood door. One of them flicked off the light switch before they left.

In the dark, I lay there, trying to think of a way out of the situation while I tested my muscles for movement. Also, trying not to think about spiders or scorpions or anything else that might be scurrying around the floor.

Once I could move a finger, I could move an arm soon after. Soon after that, I was back to normal. Whatever they'd drugged me with wore off almost all at once. I sprang to my feet, feeling surprisingly not too bad.

Slivers of light seeped into the room through a high window. Using it to guide me, I fumbled my way to the far wall and ran my hand over the spot where I thought the switch should be.

With the light on, I simply appraised my location for a moment. The room was small, more like a glorified closet than anything else, and the floor was dirt. Huge boxes were stacked floor to ceiling against one wall. Against another were metal shelves piled high with linens, sacks of onions, and braids of garlic. Was I stuck in some restaurant's storeroom?

Wetting my lips, I inspected the aforementioned window more closely. Beneath the block cloth draped over it, it was high and narrow. I might just be able to fit through the thing. If I could open it. If I could reach it.

But if I did, what about Mitch? It was no wonder we'd been separated since there wasn't much room in this closet for more than a single person, but where was he?

Just to be certain my captors hadn't done something stupid, I tried the door, but it was definitely locked, and I had nothing on me to try picking the mechanism with. I put my ear to it next but heard nothing.

Until Mitch called my name.

I spun around because his voice hadn't come from the other side of the door. Rather it sounded like he was on the other side of the wall with the shelves. I shoved a bag of onions aside and searched in vain for another door that I didn't honestly believe would be there.

I was right—there wasn't one. "Mitch, are you okay?"

"For the moment. You?"

I breathed a sigh of relief. "For the moment too. Do you know where you are?"

A clunking noise came from behind the wall. "Some kind of closet, I think. The door's locked, and there's no light."

Shit. Well, that wasn't helpful.

My gaze landed on the giant boxes, and hope sprang to life in my chest. Lowering my voice just in case the addicts were nearby, I rested my forehead against the wall. "I have a window. I'm going to see if I can open it."

The boxes were sealed, and the first one I tried moving was ridiculously heavy. The second was no less so, and I resorted to pushing it with my back. I was certain I was banged up from the accident, but adrenaline prevented me from feeling much pain. If I got out of here though, I suspected I was going to be in a world of hurt soon.

At last, I positioned the box beneath the window and crossed my fingers that whatever was inside could support my weight. Pushing aside the heavy black fabric, I discovered the window opened onto an alley. A dumpster sat across the street with several bags of trash next to it.

The window had an easy latch, the kind that popped the glass out, but the box didn't provide me with quite enough height. Somehow, I'd have to pull myself up at an awkward angle with not much to use for grip.

But first things first. Could I even open the window? My fingers trembled with anticipation as I went to work on the metal latches. They were sticky, but the glass came out easily once I defeated them.

Setting the glass on the floor, I tensed. Assuming I could get through the window and run, I hated leaving Mitch. Of course, odds were I wouldn't get far. I had nothing on me. Not my cell, not my ID, not even money to pay for a ride if I could find one.

I patted my jeans pockets to affirm my hopelessness and discovered a small bulge. Thinking it was a hair tie, I reached in and discovered two curse grenades. Peachy. That was much better than a hair tie. The two weren't the most useful items right now, but they were something. Vaguely, I wondered how airport security hadn't caught them.

"Jess? You still there?"

I leaned up against the wall again. Curse grenade or not, Mitch still should have been the one with the window. This was his city, and although I'd wanted to go sightseeing, this was not what I'd had in mind. "Still here, but I got the window open. I think I can get out. If I can, I'll get the Gryphons and be back soon."

"Okay. Good luck. Be careful."

"Thanks." I started to add something else, but voices outside the door stopped me cold. People were coming. I had to move faster.

Legs shaking, I climbed onto the box and pulled myself halfway into the alley. Hot grit dug into my hands, and I had to be careful to avoid broken glass. Across the street, a dragon poked its red nose out from between a couple trash bags and stared at me. I rested on my forearms and tried to will it away. Behind me, the voices grew louder.

The window frame and the concrete scratched my stomach and thighs as I pushed through the rest of the way, and I scrambled to my feet. The dragon snorted smoke at me then scampered. Good idea.

The building I'd crawled out of was a simple two-story, done up in the same muted color scheme as much of the city. But where was I, and where were all the people? It was hot as hell out here, sure, but why wasn't I picking up on any negativity? I could really use an energy boost.

Shadowtown. The answer came to me all at once, making my predicament even more precarious than I'd originally thought. Obviously, this wasn't my familiar Shadowtown, but it had to be Phoenix's neighborhood equivalent. Shit. The fury addicts had brought me to their masters' turf. I wasn't going to find friendly help around here.

On cue, shouting emanated from the open window behind me. I'd been spotted.

I put on a burst of speed, heading toward the street. Heavy air settled in my lungs. I had just enough time to catch part of the name over the restaurant's door before the door itself burst open. Three of the addicts, including one of the ones I'd met earlier, spilled onto the street.

Without a clue where I was going, I took off.

"Remember, don't hurt her!" It sounded like the guy with the Spanish accent was yelling after his friends.

Peachy. Don't hurt me. That ought to give me some advantage, right? I would have no such qualms about hurting these men if it came to that.

The street was mostly empty, strange for an evening in pred territory, but it was wicked hot. Every step I took felt like I was running into a wall of heat. That also meant I wasn't going to be able to keep up this pace for long. Sweat had beaded on my skin the moment I crawled out of the building's air conditioning, and it ran down my face and chest.

The few preds out and about merely looked on in amusement—goblins, a harpy. No furies, thanks goodness, but that couldn't last.

Gasping for breath, I retrieved one of the curse grenades from my pocket. My pursuers were getting close. Their footsteps grew louder. Frantic, I scanned the area for ideas. Up the next block, a lust addict was getting out of an Uber. If I could only get to it before the car pulled away...

I smelled the guy behind me before I felt him. Fingers snagged my hair. I put on an extra burst of speed, drawing from reserves I didn't think I had, and activated the curse grenade. They must have been in my pocket for ages, so I had no clue what kind of spells they'd been filled with.

Hoping they were good ones, I spun on my heel and threw the sphere at the nearest guy. Soon as it touched him, it exploded in a bang of black powder.

It was some kind of general anti-magic then. Not nearly as effective on a human or an addict as a disorientation curse would have been. Damn it. Nonetheless, the confusion the grenade caused was better than nothing. One of the three was down, at least temporarily.

Another man swore, and I turned, waving frantically at the cab ahead. The lust addict was getting his belongings out of the backseat.

More fingers reached for me, digging into my shoulder. I wasn't going to make it. The remaining two men had overtaken me, and one of them darted ahead, tripping me up.

I dodged, and he blocked my path, giving his partner a second chance to grab me. I could scream for help, but this was unfamiliar pred territory. Judging by the audience who was enjoying the show, I'd get no assistance. That left only one option.

There was no time to consider how close I was to my targets. I slammed the curse at the guy in front of me, and it exploded with a bang and smoke. The force of the blast sent us both flying in opposite directions. I crashed into a lamppost, hitting my head, but I felt no magical effects other than the acrid air singeing my nose. The addicts, however, yelled as the anti-magic probably disrupted their bonds with their fury masters.

Now the street seemed to erupt in chatter. People were yelling, and preds poured onto the sidewalk to see what was going on. I launched myself at the Uber, pushing the stunned lust addict out of the way.

Fortunately, the driver was human, which meant he didn't want to be in his neighborhood either. "Drive. Please. Quickly."

He took in the chaos with wide eyes and did just that.

FOUR

THE PHOENIX GRYPHON OFFICE WAS JUST AS QUICK AND efficient in an emergency as the Boston Office. Within an hour of me stumbling through the doors and yelling for help, a team was on the move.

Like Boston, they had a more-than-passing knowledge of their local pred neighborhood. Between my description of the building, the little of the restaurant's name I'd seen, and the fact that it was connected with the furies, they figured out where I'd been held.

I was reunited with Tom almost immediately once I arrived too. He'd sustained a nasty hit on the head, one that was currently bandaged, and he had a thick scab on his lip. In order to begin a search for us, however, he'd waved off medical treatment when the EMTs had shown up at the accident scene.

A quick scan from a Gryphon healer told me the attackers had used fire-scorpion venom on me. The local magical fauna produced a toxin that caused temporary paralysis, but it left no lasting harmful effects. Nonetheless, the Gryphon agent who was leading the rescue team wanted both Tom and me to stay behind, seeing as neither of us was in the best shape.

Like that was happening. Some water and a pain-relief charm later, and

I was ready to get the assholes who'd abducted me. No reason for me to sit on my butt while others had all the fun. To his credit, Tom felt the same way despite his own injuries. Of course, finding and protecting Mitch was his responsibility, so that wasn't surprising.

"You sure you're ready for this?" Tom asked as the SUV swerved to the curb.

"I'm fine." I tapped my fingers against the hilt of my knife, which I'd named Misery, impatiently. I'd been reunited with my belongings at Gryphon Headquarters. Thank dragons someone had found my phone, which I'd dropped in the crash, and my knife had been in my duffel. I'd have sorely missed both if they'd been taken along with me, particularly after I'd been so excited that Tom had gotten me some kind of special clearance so I could carry Misery on the plane with me.

Although I wanted to be on the scene and was eager to charge ahead, I held back like instructed while Phoenix Gryphons swarmed the place. I had no training for this sort of mission, and I didn't want to do anything that could endanger Mitch.

In the end, that turned out not to be a concern. I jogged into the restaurant after Tom, listening to the Gryphons yell "All clear." The place was empty. No addicts. No furies. No Mitch.

I pounded the door to the room where I'd been locked up not even two hours ago. "Damn it. I told Mitch I'd come back for him."

I hit the door again because I could feel frustration pressing against my skull, the result of a hundred insecurities. Was I wrong to have left him? Should I have tried to take him with me somehow? And why? That question plagued me most of all, and it was soon followed by another question that turned my stomach—who had told the fury addicts about what we were doing?

I held all the questions in while the Gryphons searched the restaurant for clues. Then I held them in longer while a Gryphon agent gathered all the information I could share, including a description of the addicts.

While I waited for Tom to get off the phone, I paced incessantly, and my thoughts wandered to Lucen and what he was doing tonight. A hollowness opened in my chest, and out of it poured sadness and longing. I missed him, and more. I craved his company. How ridiculous was that?

I'd been gone for what—twelve hours? Eighteen? Surely I could live without him for that long.

But my hands trembled, and when I closed my eyes and my memory played back the spinning car and the rush of fear when the addicts grabbed me, it was an entirely different sort of terror that chilled my veins. The thought of never seeing him again, or touching him, or hearing him call me "little siren." I couldn't lose that.

Damn. I wanted to go home. I wanted to crawl into his bed and pretend I was safe because his muscular arms were locked around me. Yet even if I were in his bed right now, I knew better. Safety was an illusion. Whatever happened to me and Mitch was proof. I couldn't know for certain if our abduction was related to the prophecy, but it was too big a coincidence to assume it wasn't.

Pain-relief charm or not, if I kept up with this line of thought, I'd have a headache soon.

Speaking of headaches, on cue, Tom finished his call. "The car that hit us had been reported stolen about an hour before the accident, and none of the people who witnessed the accident were able to get a plate number on the van that grabbed you."

"Fabulous."

"It could be worse. Knowing they took you to that restaurant should help narrow things down considerably. The Phoenix Office is going to coordinate with the local PD in the search. They'll find Johnson."

I finally quit pacing and plopped into a chair across from Tom. "I shouldn't have left him."

"You did the right thing, Jessica. You got an opening and you took it, and now we have a better chance of finding Johnson."

"Do we?" I rested my head in my hands, my unasked questions seeming to slither around in my gut like worms.

"We do." Tom pressed his lips firmly together as he assessed me. "What are you thinking?"

I asked the less problematic of my questions first. "Why? The Boston furies have been interested in keeping me alive for some reason. They have had plenty of opportunities to grab me there. I don't understand why they tried it now. Here."

"Perhaps they're trying to discover if Johnson shares your abilities." Tom sounded like he was guessing. "Perhaps they've always intended to grab you and were waiting for a convenient time."

"A very convenient time." I sat up straighter, finally getting to the question that was bothering me the most. "How did they know? This was supposed to be kept quiet. So how did furies on the other side of the country know to set up a kidnapping? Or that they could grab both me and Mitch?"

Tom rubbed his chin, his eyes wide and annoyingly innocent. "It's a good question."

"It's a damn good question. How many people knew what we were planning?"

"A handful of us in the Brotherhood are working on this mission. Unless you told people."

I crossed my arms. The only person I'd told where I was going and why was Lucen, and he would never betray me to the furies. "No, this wasn't leaked on my end. This was a Gryphon. One of your people."

"Not possible."

"Not even as an accident? Somebody let something slip?"

Tom's expression was as disdainful as his tone was curt. "We do not let classified information slip. I'll look into it when we get back to Boston." He stood to make it clear this discussion was over.

Feeling defensive, were we? I didn't sense any deception from him, which didn't mean much, but I didn't suspect Tom would have let the information slip deliberately or otherwise. From everything I'd learned about him, he was the perfect Gryphon warrior—dedicated, competent, and a true believer. But those traits would also blind him to the possibility that one of his own could have betrayed us.

My jaw clenched with thoughts of the future. If the furies hadn't found out via an accidental slip, then we had a big problem. And if Tom wasn't willing to consider that the Brotherhood might have a mole, then it was going to be up to me to find out the truth. As today had proven, it was my ass on the line.

Mine and Mitch's.

"So now what?" I said, giving up the argument for the time being.

"Now we get on a flight back to Boston."

"What about Chicago?"

Tom stretched. "I'm not taking chances and waiting another day to reach our last recruit. I notified the Chicago office while you were giving your official statement, and Ms. Park is being taken into protective custody as we speak. Once they have her, she'll be escorted to Boston."

It made sense, but I couldn't see it going over well. "I hope she takes Gryphons at her door better than Mitch did."

"It doesn't matter. If this is related to the prophecy, then there's no room for niceties or arguments. We're at war."

"No, you're not zealous at all."

"You might want to take this more seriously, Jessica."

I jumped up and just managed to keep my voice low. "Take this seriously? How much more serious do you expect me to take things? I am the one in Olef's damn visions, and it's my friends who have already suffered for whatever twisted end-of-the-world mumbo-jumbo you and yours are going on about. I do not want a single other person to become a victim, but I don't have any idea what you actually expect me to do, and you don't have very many details on what needs to be done. Plus, now I have to worry that you have a leak in your super-secret organization. So forgive me if—given how many unknowns we're dealing with—I'm not taking all this nothingness seriously enough."

I stood practically nose to nose with Tom in my effort to vent. All I needed to do was reach out one finger, poke him in the chest, and he'd probably fall over. His entire posture was so rigid it was amazing the force of my breath alone couldn't knock him down.

Tom stared at me for another moment. Then he placed a surprisingly gentle hand on my arm. "We do not have a leak, but I will look into what happened later. Meantime, you need to calm down. We're both shaken up from everything. It's normal."

Right. Normal. I took a deep breath and nodded.

Tom's penetrating blue eyes fixed on my face for a few more seconds while I attempted to project calm, then he let go of me. "Good. So let's figure out what we have to do to get out of here so you can go home and rest."

I swallowed, trying to shake off my fear of the future. "What about home for you?"

"Until I get word from my superiors that we're moving this operation back to World, Boston is my new home."

"Sorry about that."

He shrugged. "It's part of the job, and this is the job I wanted."

Dully, I clomped along the brightly lit corridor with him, wishing I could say the same. But all I could think was that I didn't sign up for this shit.

FIVE

I MUST HAVE BEEN MORE EXHAUSTED THAN I THOUGHT because I somehow managed to drift off to sleep on the flight to Boston. I woke as the plane began its descent and early-morning sunshine pierced the window and fell on my lap.

Mornings. Ugh. My head felt like it was stuffed with cotton. My eyes were like raw wounds. Before we left the airport, I bought an enormous coffee, but my head throbbed by the time we reached Gryphon Headquarters downtown.

Tom had been on the phone since the moment we landed, and he clearly had plans. Whatever sort of energy pills or charms he was taking, he was being completely unfair by hogging them all.

"Anything you intend to make me do," I started as we entered the building's lobby, "I don't see why it can't wait until—"

"Jess!"

My heart barely had time to skip with relief. Lucen must have been waiting right by the doors. His arms enveloped me in a hug that crushed my face against his hard chest.

Oh, yes. I breathed deeply and filled my lungs with the scent of his clean cotton shirt, the heady leather from his jacket, and the luscious cinnamon of his skin. Lucen's distinctive pheromone smell was like a drug. The tension drained from my muscles, and my nerves sizzled with his body heat. I didn't need sleep. I needed him. Now. So what if it was false comfort? I wanted to feel the safety of his body on mine.

I also wanted to forget I was in the middle of Gryphon Headquarters, getting hot and wet while pressed against a satyr. The so-called enemy. Fuck my life. There was no way Tom or any other Gryphons watching were going to forget this happy reunion for one second. The ruse I'd maintained —the distance I supposedly kept from the satyrs—was now worth salamander spit.

Cheeks flaming, I pulled away from Lucen, begging my brain to find a way to salvage this uncomfortable moment.

If such a way existed, however, it didn't matter because Lucen didn't let me go.

"Um, you're crushing me?" I whispered into his neck.

His blue-green eyes contained none of the mischievous humor that had originally drawn me to him. They were hard as stones. "Better me than a car or a fury addict."

"But the end result might be the same. Flattened Jess. Not pretty." My body betrayed me to him though. I'd dropped my bag and put my hands on his waist to push him away, but my fingers curled around his shirt. They wanted to tear it off, expose more of the skin that drove me wild, and Lucen definitely knew it. I swallowed. "I have a job here. Need to be professional."

"I hate your job." He practically growled the words, and yeah, no kidding. It was the wrong argument to use on him.

Still, he loosened his grip enough that I could finally turn around and discover that yes, in fact, most of the lobby was staring at us. My only saving grace was the early hour. It was mostly empty, and none of the inhabitants, besides Tom, were Gryphons. My witnesses were only the security guards and a couple people in business suits going through the metal detectors.

Tom's face revealed nothing, but I could sense his surprise. "Jessica, you seem to have neglected to mention just how close you are to the satyrs."

I winced. I was going to kill Lucen, who had to have realized what coming here would mean. Well, maybe sleep with him first, then kill him. At least maim him a touch. If I were truly mean, I'd withhold sex, but we both knew I'd be the one to cave first, so that was out.

I realized Tom was waiting for a response, and I had to stop thinking about tying Lucen to his bed and doing unspeakable things to punish him. "Uh, this isn't what it looks like?"

Lucen's muscles twitched behind me. He must have repressed a laugh. "Actually this is exactly what it looks like. Jess is one of us. You can put your uniform on her and call her a consultant, but she will always be one of us because you made her one of us."

Tom didn't flinch. "It's Lucen, correct? We made Jessica into a warrior capable of fighting your kind. What she is is a human with enhanced magical abilities, but that's a discussion of magical properties I'd rather have with one of your own who's an expert in the topic. Not a bartender."

This time Lucen did laugh. "I don't think there's anything you could contribute to the discussion, Agent Kassin, that I couldn't handle. Although I'm not sure the reverse is true. But that's beside the point. I'm here to take Jess home before you can do anything else to almost get her killed."

I should have known when I'd told Lucen what happened that this would be his reaction. I simply hadn't expected him to show up at Gryphon Headquarters so early in the morning when all good little preds were tucked in bed.

Exerting a bit more force, I extricated myself from his tight grip. "If it's all the same," I said to Tom, "I was about to ask if my next move could be delayed for a few hours while I got some sleep."

Around us, the lobby was slowly starting to return to normal, though the non-Gryphon guards who monitored the security checkpoints continued to watch us with uneasy expressions. Tom glanced over his shoulder toward the elevators. On the flight, he'd sprouted dark circles under his eyes. If I were him, I'd be thinking about my own bed.

But I wasn't. Because Tom was dedicated, and I apparently wasn't taking things seriously enough.

"You should continue your training today," he said. Then, with a pointed look at Lucen, he added, "And we need to discuss getting you a security detail."

"What?" I demanded.

"Given what happened to you and Johnson, we can't be too careful. I know you'll refuse protective custody, and I don't think it's a good idea for you anyway, but a couple Gryphons to serve as guards at all times would be wise."

"No." I shook my head violently. "I don't want babysitters."

Lucen cleared his throat. "Actually, Jess, much as it pains me, I agree with the Gryphon on this one. You should have some protection, but *our* people will provide it."

I poked him in the chest. Hard. "No, they will not. I can take care of myself." Spinning around to Tom, I stuck my hands on my hips. "If you want to help me concentrate on my training, don't sic babysitters on me. Send them to my family and maybe to Steph. I can't think straight if I'm worrying about their safety."

"That's not really—"

"I don't care if it's protocol or whatever. I do not need babysitters." I glared at both the men. "But I do need sleep. I'll be no good at training if I don't get some, and you should get some too. You look like crap."

To my surprise, Tom sighed. Then he yawned, and maybe that was his deciding factor. "Fine. Check in with me this evening."

"Of course. I hope you'll have an update on Mitch by then."

He nodded grimly. "So do I. But, Jess, a word first?"

Tom walked away without waiting for an answer and flashed his badge at security. I started to follow, but Lucen grabbed my arm. The fierce set of his jaw was one part protective, one part rage. No question which emotion was aimed at which person.

"I'll be right back." I gave his hand a squeeze.

Scowling, he let me go.

Tom had stopped by the lobby's centerpiece—a massive reproduction of Michelangelo's *Triumph*, which depicted magically gifted humans fighting a bunch of furies and satyrs. I neither loathed nor loved classical art, but I despised that painting, and I purposely strode by Tom so I could keep my back to it while he got in his last word.

"Yes?"

Tom's face filled with disapproval. "Really?"

"He's a friend. An old friend. I don't need your judgmental attitude."

"My attitude stems from concern for you."

Sure it did. At best, it was concern for the Gryphons' alleged ultimate warrior. Not the same thing. "He's saved my life a couple times."

"For purely selfless motives, I'm sure."

I closed my eyes, too weary to match sarcasm with sarcasm. I simply wanted to go home. I wanted to crawl in bed and wrap my legs around Lucen's naked body. Not deal with lectures from a baby-faced, annoyingly righteous Gryphon who didn't understand the first thing about me.

"Does it matter? Look, he can't hurt me. There's a reason I'm your weapon."

Tom bit his lip, seeming to debate something internally. "Leaving the threat he poses to you out of it, it's still a question of loyalty and appearances. Other members of the Brotherhood should be arriving in Boston tomorrow. If you want them to treat you as an equal and not like the lab rat you call yourself, give them cause to respect you."

Though I hated to admit it, Tom had a point. This was why I would have yelled at Lucen to stay away from HQ if I'd known he intended to show up.

But I was tired and cranky and, frankly, I didn't need Gryphon approval of my love life. "After what your fraternity did to me, I have a very hard time respecting them. I'm not one of you just because you made me into what I am. I give my loyalty to those who earned it. Lucen's earned it."

"Trusting preds gets people killed and worse. Even if you're correct about Lucen, which I doubt, the ranking members of the Brotherhood are not going to trust you if they find out how close you are. Instead of an asset, you become a liability. If he gets into your head—"

"He can't." I raised my arms in exasperation. "That's the beauty of me. I can't be addicted."

"What do you mean 'can't'?"

My mouth fell open. Shit. Something else to blame on exhaustion—I'd just played my last card. The one last secret I'd been keeping from the Gryphons.

Tom had known I was immune to pred power, that their pheromones didn't affect me, and that was mostly true. Lucen's magic did work on me, and so did Devon's, presumably because I was attracted to them both. But my ability to flip the pred-addict bond, to addict a pred instead of the other way around... Well, that was something else.

There was no logical reason I'd kept it a secret. No reason at all except my anger over what *Le Confrérie de l'Aile* had done to me and my determination therefore to exclude them from my life as much as possible. In the end, though, I'd always assumed I'd have to tell them. It could be important.

This just wasn't how I'd planned to do it. Then again, it felt appropriate somehow that my relationship with Lucen would be the thing to bring it into the open. I was tired of hiding that too.

"I meant exactly what I told you," I said finally. "No pred is going to addict me, not for long. I can explain later, but I need sleep."

Tom's eyes widened, but he wisely nodded. "Fine, but I want to know more. In the meantime, be careful."

Yeah, no kidding.

Lucen slipped on his sunglasses and a baseball cap as we left the building. The cap served the dual purposes of concealing his horns so people didn't freak out and protecting his sun-phobic head from the morning light. I also thought it made him look silly, but I kept that opinion to myself.

"What did your Gryphon master want?" he asked, stuffing his hands in his jacket pockets.

My hip bumped my duffel bag, which Lucen insisted on carrying, and I stepped away. "What do you think? Look, I'm happy to see you again too, but I didn't need an escort home."

Lucen grunted and pulled me closer as we traipsed down the stone steps to street level.

"This isn't an argument you're going to win."

We'd see about that. But one thing was certain—it was an argument I was too tired to have at present. So I let it go.

Instead of taking me home, Lucen brought me to his place, which was never a bad choice since it was nicer than mine. For starters, he had furniture.

After making it clear how much I'd missed him, I fell asleep next to him, my legs entwined with his and my head on his chest. I didn't stir until two in the afternoon. Although this was around the time Lucen usually got up, it was also a testament to just how tired I must have been.

Blinds and heavy light-blocking curtains kept the room shrouded in the dark, but the glow from the bedside clock gave me enough light to see. Lucen's chest rose and fell in a steady rhythm under my hand, and I trailed my fingers through the fine blond hairs that ran down his stomach. They were one of my favorite things about him. Partly because of where they led, and partly because it amused me how soft they were. Fine silky hairs on a body that was otherwise the very opposite of soft.

Half asleep, Lucen reached out a hand and placed it over my arm, holding me lightly in place. He had new glyphs. I'd noticed them vaguely earlier, but I'd been too fixated on other body parts to pay much attention.

Propping myself more upright, I checked them out. Heavy black lines and mysterious symbols snaked up the length of his arm from just under his elbow to his shoulder.

I knew so little about these sorts of spells—they were one of the things I was supposed to be learning about with Tom—but they looked complex. Many were linked together into some larger pattern. Lucen had always had a couple drawn on him, usually around his shoulders or on his back, but they'd never been so extensive. Were these magical preparation for the apocalypse? I couldn't imagine another reason he'd suddenly be sporting such heavy charms.

The assumption sent a shiver of unease through my contented brain, and Lucen—probably sensing it—shifted beneath me. "Little siren?"

I buried my face against him, a move that not so coincidentally allowed me to shift more of my weight on top of him. His arms wrapped around me, one hand sliding down my back to rest on my butt. Beneath me, I felt his body stiffening with my movements.

"Just not happy to have to get out of bed soon," I murmured into his neck. His skin was salty sweet with sweat as I planted kisses at the crook of his shoulder.

His grip around me tightened, hands slipping beneath the thin fabric of my underwear and shoving it off. "Not that soon."

SIX

WHILE HIS BAR WAS CLOSED DURING REPAIRS, LUCEN COULD afford to set his own schedule. We stayed in bed for almost another two glorious hours, and by the time I emerged from his shower, I was starving. Fortunately, he had the cure for all kinds of hunger. I found him in the kitchen, the coffee already brewed, bacon cooking, and a selection of croissants on the table to tempt me.

I grabbed a chocolate one, and he set a mug in front of me. I closed my eyes blissfully, inhaling the steam. "This is why I keep you around."

"This is just one of the many reasons you keep me around." The microwave beeped, and he added a plate of bacon to the decadent goodies on the table. "You also do it for my body, my ability to keep you supplied in free booze, and my keen intellect. The last reason is why you're going to trust me when I say you need bodyguards."

I sighed. "So the chocolate croissants are bribes to get me to give in and be treated like some helpless little girl?"

He narrowed his eyes at me over his mug. "We both know you're capable of putting up one hell of a fight. We also both know you're only one person, and you have one hell of a knack for getting yourself in trouble." He held up one finger. "Victor Aubrey." A second. "Lucrezia." A third. "All the goddamn sylphs in Shadowtown. And now there's this slight matter of what happened in Phoenix. See where I'm going?"

"That's not fair."

"No? And why not?" He waved a piece of bacon around as if to say *get on with it.*

I delayed by ripping off more delicious flaky bread product. "Because I handled Victor and Lucrezia, and I escaped from the Phoenix addicts." I just couldn't save Mitch too, and a fresh wave of guilt washed over me.

"You didn't do it on your own—not with Lucrezia. You figured out her scheme, true, and you *held* your own. But you didn't handle her on your own. See the difference?"

I did, and the sweet croissant turned bitter in my mouth. If Lucen and Devon hadn't come to my aid, Lucrezia probably would have succeeded in killing me and my Gryphon partner who was helping me bust her. That pissed me off.

I grunted my acknowledgment because saying it out loud annoyed me.

Lucen was smart enough to know my silence was acquiescence. "Good. Because whatever is going on with this prophecy, little siren, you're someone important. And if you're right and someone in the Gryphons leaked information to the furies, then the situation is even more dire than we first thought."

This was what I got for sharing my thoughts with Lucen earlier. He'd agreed that what happened was, at the very least, suspicious. "Fine. For the sake of the world, I consent to bodyguards."

"Don't consent for the sake of the world. Consent for me. The prophecy doesn't even make the top three reasons why I want you protected."

"Oh, yeah? And the top three reasons are?"

"I. Love. You."

Three words. Three reasons, and my world ground to a halt.

I forgot to breathe. Forgot *how* to breathe. All my brainpower was fixated on replaying and analyzing those words. He'd never said them before, and neither had I—not in a non-joking manner. And the reason for it was because I wasn't even sure Lucen could feel their meaning. So hearing them from his lips struck me dumb, and my God if it didn't turn my annoyance with him to some kind of mushy goo.

Lucen had never lied to me. When he didn't want to tell me something, he simply didn't. Thus if the sincerity on his face couldn't convince me that he meant them, his past behavior did.

I set down my coffee and sat on his lap. Wrapping my arms around his neck, I sank into him. "Damn you. I'll suck it up with the babysitters for you because I love you too."

He grinned, fingers weaving through my wet hair. "I know you do and knew you would."

"Are you manipulating me?"

That got a laugh out of him. "For years. Do you have any idea how hard you've made me work to get you here like this? To get you to a point where I could tell you I loved you and you'd believe me?"

I rested my forehead against his so he couldn't see me flush. It hadn't been all that long ago that I'd been calling him evil and telling him not to touch me. But once I'd let him under my skin, once I'd had no choice but to trust him and allow him to prove himself to me, I'd fallen hard and fast.

"By the way, that reminds me." Lucen loosened his grip on me, and I slid off his lap. "I have something for you. I meant to give it to you before you left." He popped into the living room for a moment while I finished my coffee. When he returned, he produced a narrow box from behind his back.

I gaped at it, my head spinning. "Unless this holds a really tiny dagger, this looks to be a jewelry box."

"You can stop guessing and start opening."

I wasn't sure why I was so nervous, but my hands trembled as I pulled off the ribbon. Inside the box, a pendant rested against the black velvet interior—a delicate silver fox curled around a fiery opal, both beautiful and whimsical.

I fumbled for words. "This is... It's gorgeous...but..."

Lucen laughed at me and pulled the necklace from the box. "I met you on your eighteenth birthday, if you'll recall. And for ten years, I've never been able to give you a birthday present. I even distinctly remember offering you a free drink when you turned twenty-one, and you refused because you accepted nothing from me back then. So consider this several years of delayed birthday presents."

I snapped the box shut, and the sound jolted my nerves. "I've never given you a birthday present either, and my birthday was over a month ago."

"We don't celebrate birthdays, and you wouldn't have accepted a gift over a month ago." He motioned me closer so he could put it on. "The fox represents you. Over the next few days you're going to be surrounded by my kind, goblins, Gryphons, owl shifters, falcon shifters, and who knows what else. You're going to need to be clever and sneaky and potentially deadly to make this alliance work. Like a fox. So there." He let go, and the cool metal settled against my skin. "It looks good, and now you have some grownup jewelry."

I ran my fingers over the fox's tail. "Grownup jewelry? Really?"

"You're right. I should have said now you own *some* jewelry. The next time you make me take you on date, you can wear it."

"I have a huge collection of earrings."

Lucen didn't look impressed.

"Fine." I reached up and kissed him, pressing my body close. "Thank you. I don't understand you but thank you."

He wrapped his arms around me, blanketing me in his sweet scent. "I'm easy to understand, little siren. I want to keep you alive."

Before I could respond to that, his phone rang. From the way he answered it, I could tell it was either Dezzi or Devon calling. And from the way his happy expression fell, they weren't calling with good news. I tensed.

"Got it." Lucen hung up, and he hurried into the living room and turned on the TV.

I jogged after him. "What is it?"

The answer was evident as soon as Lucen flipped to one of the twenty-four-hour news channels. The purple smoke of salamander fires drifted across the sky over what looked like a small war zone. Buildings had been reduced to rubble, and in places the debris still smoldered. Among the ruins were telltale signs of curse damage. Behind the reporter on the scene, Gryphons could be seen talking. My gaze flashed to the bottom of the TV where the news graphic informed me I was looking at parts of Sydney.

"Details are sketchy for now," the reporter was saying, "but it appears the fighting started after a series of murders targeted several sylphs' addicts."

Lucen crossed his arms. "Sounds suspiciously like what almost happened here with the furies and Aubrey."

Whereas a moment ago I'd been warm with Lucen's touch, a chill now settled in my blood. "Yeah, it does. If at first you don't succeed… Shit."

There was no way this was a coincidence. The furies needed to gather power, and they were trying Plan A again.

Over the past week, a small group of us had been working hard to confirm my theory about what the furies were up to. What we believed for certain was this: the current furies were attempting to channel enough power to fill five containers called the Vessels of Making. Once they'd accomplished that task, they could release all the power from the Vessels in a complicated spell that would rip open the magical prison, called the Pit, and release the original furies from captivity. In other words, they would bring about the apocalypse Tom and I had warned Mitch about.

The furies had managed to gather enough power in Buenos Aires recently to possibly fill one Vessel, and now it would appear they'd done it again in Sydney. Our meeting with the Gryphons and the magi was growing all the more urgent.

Lucen continued to watch the news, but while I stood with him, my thoughts strayed to matters closer to home. I was stuck in an endless loop, replaying the scene in Lucen's kitchen. He loved me.

Loved me.

This was both wonderfully good and horribly scary, and for the first time since I heard those words, it was the scary that dominated my thoughts. Lucen had been hurt before because of people trying to get to me. Lucen could be hurt again.

I loved Lucen. I needed to keep him safe. How could I do that when the world was going to shit?

SEVEN

THERE WAS STILL NO WORD ABOUT MITCH BY THE NEXT morning or even by the afternoon, although I bugged Tom the moment I got to Gryphon Headquarters.

"I spoke with the Phoenix Office just a few hours ago, Jessica." He swiped his ID through the card reader, allowing us access to another part of the building. "We'll hear something the moment there's something to hear. I do have some good news though."

"Oh?" The pendant Lucen had given me bumped against my chest as I matched Tom's pace. I had it tucked under my shirt, feeling silly for wearing something so fancy when I was dressed in my usual jeans and sneakers. But Lucen hadn't wanted me to take it off, and neither had I if I were to be honest.

Tom paused to pick some papers off the printer near his office. "Grace Park is here. Her flight got in this morning."

I tried and failed to catch a glimpse of what the papers were about. "Good. So Chicago didn't have any problem finding her? No attacks?"

"Nothing of the sort. Just some legal issues that needed to be sorted out."

"Legal issues?"

Tom made a noncommittal noise, looking slightly uncomfortable.

"She's been in and out of treatment for substance-abuse issues. Currently, she's in court-ordered counseling. Taking her into protective custody provided some challenges."

"Wait a second. Substance-abuse counseling?" I held up my hand before he could open the conference room door. "Let me guess why. Are you paying attention to any of us? Really?"

He didn't answer, and I wasn't sure if it was because he didn't understand what I was getting at or if he was choosing to ignore me. Either way, the door had been opened. I had to bite my tongue temporarily.

Warily, I followed Tom into the conference room and discovered a petite woman sitting at the table, sipping coffee and reading through a stack of papers. Grace appeared to be of some mixed heritage, and the faintly blonde hair she'd pulled into a ponytail was clearly bleached. Although I knew she had to be about my age, the lines around her eyes and lips made her look older.

She smiled when she saw us, but it wasn't a happy smile. More like that of a trapped child who's hoping to appease her captors. I couldn't blame her, but I wished I'd been there when the Chicago Gryphons came knocking on her door. Maybe I could have helped.

Then again, maybe she'd have gotten abducted too.

Tom dumped his papers on the table. "Ms. Park, this is Jessica Moore. She's the other woman who was part of the program I was telling you about."

"Program?" Such a benign word. I raised an eyebrow at Tom, then remembered to smile at the newcomer. Any ire I had at the Gryphons needed to wait for a better moment. "Nice to meet you."

"Nice to meet you too. Call me Grace." For a small woman, she had a deep, commanding voice.

I took a seat. "You can call me Jess. Agent Kassin's suggested I might be able to…" *Help you*, is what I meant to say. But realizing how foolish that was, the words dried up in my mouth. How could I help anyone when I was in the dark about most things myself?

Tom cleared his throat. "Jessica can answer some questions, and I'm sure she'll be happy to fill you in on what her experience has been like."

Grace entwined her fingers. Anxiety radiated off her, potent and unpleasant, yet understandable. "Agent Kassin said you could help me control these abilities I have. I'll be honest with you. I hate them. It's why..." She grimaced. "It's why I started drinking all those years ago. The alcohol and the pot—they numb it. Make me feel less so I can live with myself."

I closed my eyes, hoping Grace didn't misinterpret the anger surging through my veins. *This is what you've done to us, Tom. This is what your damn "program" did to us.*

Tom wisely chose that moment to leave the room.

Over the next half hour, I found myself in the strange position of feeling well-adjusted. Oh, I'd acted irrationally, and I'd made terrible choices, but I'd been lucky. I'd never had to deal alone like Grace had. Perhaps if I had, I might have done the same things she did to cope. Or maybe I wouldn't have been able to cope at all. Maybe I'd have been like Kyra McNaughton and have committed suicide to alleviate my guilt.

But I'd had Lucen, and once more I had to silently thank him for everything he'd done for me. For saving me, teaching me, and giving me a purpose.

A fierce protectiveness gripped my chest, stealing the air from my lungs. I was not going to let that man get hurt again because of whatever load of flaming salamander shit I'd fallen into.

Grace and I talked until a Gryphon arrived to take her down to the labs. They wanted to put protective glyphs on her, but she didn't look too happy about the idea. She knew even less about her abilities than Mitch had, and while he'd expressed an interest in learning more, Grace was frightened of them.

Still, I didn't know if being addicted to mundane substances would affect her magically. For all I knew, it could weaken her will to resist pred power or mess with her brain chemistry so that she couldn't resist at all. It was therefore best to let the Gryphons charm her up if they thought it a good idea. To that end, I gave her an encouraging nod, told her I'd talk to her more later, then stalked off to find Tom. He'd returned to his office and left the door partially open.

Taking that as an invitation, I stormed in. "Are you paying attention to what your people have done? Never mind my own issues, your so-called program created a serial killer, drove a teacher to kill herself, and turned another woman into an alcoholic. Go ahead and justify it all you want with the prophecy, but the bottom line is that two of your would-be warriors are dead, one is missing, and another one is in absolutely no condition to fight anything except maybe her own demons." I leaned over his desk. "And this is all your fault."

"I think it's fair to say Victor Aubrey would likely have turned to murder without our interference." The voice was unfamiliar and heavy with a German accent.

I spun around.

The speaker was a woman. She wore a Gryphon uniform with the same red pin on her collar as Tom had, identifying herself as a member of *Le Confrérie de l'Aile*. She was older than either of us, possibly in her sixties, with a touch of gray showing at the roots of her short hair. "You are Jessica Moore?"

"Yes, and you are?"

Tom stood, not appearing the least bit moved by my outrage. "Jessica, this is Agent Ingrid Blecher. She's come to take part in the meetings."

I took the hand she offered. "Nice to meet you."

If I could taste my own emotions, I was fairly certain I'd be experiencing the burnt-toast flavor of a lie.

The way Ingrid smiled at me, I suspected she was aware of it. "Tom warned me you were very opinionated, but I think your blame is misplaced. Aubrey's tendencies were likely something he would have acted on regardless, and the suicide case—well, we cannot know what her motivations were. Attributing them to what we did seems premature."

"And Grace Park? She's pretty articulate about what drove her to drink and drugs."

"Her situation sounds unfortunate, but I have not met her yet. I'll reserve judgment."

Of course. Because she was a good Gryphon, and I was the surly test subject, leaping to heap blame on people.

Speaking of which, now seemed like a brilliant moment to bring up a possible leak within the Brotherhood. Ingrid was the first member I'd met

—besides Tom, obviously—and I wondered if her opinion on the matter would be the same as his. Besides, I didn't know what Tom meant by "looking into it," so if I was going to have to investigate myself, I might as well start questioning people now.

I cleared my throat. "Have you made any progress on finding out how the Phoenix furies learned about me and Mitch?" I aimed my question at Tom, but I kept my senses focused on Ingrid. While I was fairly certain Tom had nothing to do with it, I considered everyone else in the fraternity suspect.

Ingrid's emotions, however, registered very little with me. Like with Tom, it was wicked hard to read her, and my stomach sank. If that was going to be true of all members of *Le Confrérie*, then the task I'd set myself would be a lot more difficult.

Tom sighed. "No, I haven't. Between making sure Grace Park got settled, and with what happened in Sydney yesterday, I've been preoccupied."

"What is your concern?" Ingrid asked me.

I turned to her. "If the only people who knew about our trip to Phoenix are part of your group, then one of them must have tipped off the furies."

I could have phrased my response in a less accusatory way, but I'd been hoping to needle a reaction out of her. It seemed the only way I could read Tom's emotions was if I annoyed him, so possibly that would work on her too.

But alas, although I did clearly annoy Ingrid, judging by how she stiffened, I still couldn't get a clear taste of her emotions. "Impossible. No one is invited into the Brotherhood without an outstanding service record and thorough background checks. Everyone knows the seriousness of what we're up against."

"And yet the furies found out what we were doing." I almost added *and even the CIA has moles* but didn't bother. Unless I could catch Ingrid in a blatant lie, I obviously wasn't going to pick up on deception from her. Her emotions were as well muted as Tom's were. I'd need a new tactic.

"How is your training going?" Ingrid asked, abruptly changing the topic.

"Slowly."

Tom lifted his chin a touch higher. "I've made sure Jessica's been given access to all the materials she needs to start catching up. We're fortunate that she already has some physical self-defense training, but we've had little time for her to take up weapons work."

Ingrid tapped her fingers against Tom's desk. "Have you spent any time in a charm lab learning to create your own? Learned basic detection and disarmament charms? Sparred with Agent Kassin so he's seen exactly how much more training you need? Have you finished your reading about the theory surrounding how the pred prison was created? Did you—?"

"No." I gritted my teeth. "We've been busy trying to track down your other victims, and you've given me a lot of reading material."

"Then you should get to work."

I was happy to take that as a dismissal, but Ingrid stopped me before I could leave by laying a hand on my arm. "Have her charms been updated?" She asked the question of Tom, as though I weren't there.

"Not yet," Tom said.

"I would suggest making that a first priority." Ingrid let go of me. "I will call Theo and have him take care of it. It will take several days."

I squeezed the pendant below my shirt. *Necklace give me strength.* "I don't need my magical defenses upgraded. I'm sure Tom's told you what I can do."

Ingrid got her phone out. "These are not just defenses we will give you. These are charms that will help blunt your emotions from preds. They will make it easier for you to be concealed. They will provide protection should you get hurt. You should also have the usual speed, strength, and energy increases."

Okay, I had to admit that didn't sound so pointless, particularly after what happened in Phoenix. Some speed and strength charms might have served me well. And charms to conceal my emotions from preds? Well, there was one mystery explained. Probably everyone in the Brotherhood had them, confirming for me that my talent as a human lie detector was unlikely to get me far in my search for a leak.

EIGHT

AFTER A COUPLE HOURS OF LETTING A STRANGE GRYPHON draw all over me with magical inks, I understood why this was a multi-day process. Who wanted to sit longer? Especially when the guy doing the drawing was not very talkative. I made multiple attempts to get Theo to tell me more about *Le Confrérie*, thinking I might learn something useful in my leak-hunt, but he primarily answered in monosyllables.

Finally, I gave up and turned my attention to worrying about my evening. The satyr from the Upper Council had arrived, and he'd asked to meet me.

Around eight o'clock, with my back itching from the half-finished glyphs, I paused outside my apartment building. True to his word, Lucen had arranged with Dezzi for two satyrs to guard me, and they'd be arriving in about forty minutes to escort me to the restaurant where I was supposed to meet everyone for dinner.

I still felt somewhat ambivalent about having babysitters everywhere I went, and so I was enjoying my last solitary trip between home and office. My last time feeling like an adult. I opened the door as I caught sight of a familiar figure out of the corner of my eye, and my hand clenched around my keys.

The fury I'd nicknamed Mace-head had come out of the drugstore down the street, and he was cutting across the sidewalk. I swallowed, watching him, and a ridiculously bad idea formed in my head.

Mace-head—technically, his name was Nyles—was the local fury lieutenant. And, as someone had once explained to me, everything a Dom knows, their lieutenant would know too. In fact, it was Nyles who'd saved my ass just last week and had hinted at big plans for me. Taken together, I had to assume that whatever was going on with the furies, Nyles had information. About me. About Mitch. Possibly, even about how the furies were tipped off to the Phoenix trip.

I wanted that information.

No, I *needed* it.

I patted my hip, reassuring myself that I carried my knife, and I took off after him. Lucen would kill me for this, but I wasn't about to pass up the opportunity to dig for information. Besides, with Misery at my side and heavy charms covering my skin, I'd be fine. Right? Surely I could question a single fury in a public place without worrying about being kidnapped again.

Nyles turned a corner, and I put on an extra burst of speed. The sun was creeping below the tallest buildings, and dusk further dulled Shadowtown's muted colors. Dressed in his usual all black, Nyles blended in with the scenery. Thank dragons for his unmistakable hair.

A few preds gave me funny looks as I hurried past. Nyles wasn't running, but he was walking like a man with a purpose, and he didn't seem to realize I was following him. I called out his name as he paused at an intersection for a truck to go by.

His face lit up when he saw me approach. "Well, lookie here. So glad to see you're okay, girlie. I heard you got in an accident in Phoenix."

If I'd needed confirmation that Nyles knew anything, I guess I'd gotten it. "Where's Mitch Johnson?"

"Who?"

"You know who. The guy your people kidnapped in Phoenix. Where is he?"

Nyles shook his head, a bemused smile on his face. "Do I look like I'm in Phoenix?"

"You look like someone who has answers about Phoenix."

His half smile broke into a shit-eating grin. "But, assuming you're right, do I look like someone who'd share them with you? Sorry, girlie. Whatever you're asking about, you've got the wrong guy. If you don't believe me, get your friends to ask. It's been a while since I've been treated to an all-expenses-paid trip to Gryphon Headquarters."

I started to retort that I'd do just that, then I bit my lip, suddenly uncertain. Nyles clearly knew something, but maybe I'd been mistaken about how much. I mean, I hadn't expected him to give away secrets, but I'd hoped he might inadvertently spill something I could use. Or something the Gryphons could if I gave them reason to bring Nyles in for questioning. Now, I wasn't so sure. If Nyles did know something, I was confident he'd be flaunting it. Instead, his cluelessness when I mentioned Mitch's name seemed genuine.

A couple furies on Harleys roared by as I debated my next move, and the noise temporarily killed my ability to think straight. Of course, I wasn't sure how straight I'd been thinking moments ago anyway. Chasing Nyles through Shadowtown had been reckless. And for what? I wasn't going to follow him into a deserted alley and threaten him for details. Although if I thought for a second that would work, I'd probably try.

"You're stressed, that's what you are," Nyles said. "But I hope we can still be friends."

I shuddered back into the present. "Thanks, but your friends have a habit of ending up dead, if I recall."

"Harsh." He pretended to wince. "After all I've done for you."

"You mean have your addicts kidnap me?"

Nyles placed a hand over his heart. "Those weren't my addicts, girlie. Believe me, you're in no danger from us."

Believe me. Yeah right. I was more likely to believe Lucen's dragon, Sweetpea, wouldn't bite me if I put my fingers in his mouth. "Why do you keep saying that? What do you want from me?"

"Patience, girlie. You'll find out soon enough, and when you do, it will be magnificent. Now if you'll excuse me, I'm late for an appointment."

Unfortunately, there was nothing I could do but grind my heels into the pavement as I watched him go and wish I hadn't confronted him. His gleeful promise of a magnificent purpose was even more terrifying than potentially being kidnapped again.

Bodyguards—yeah, maybe they weren't such a bad idea.

As luck would have it, they were waiting on my stoop when I returned to my apartment. The first satyr, Gi, had acted as one my guards during the whole Victor-framed-me fiasco. The other introduced herself as Melissa. They waited while I changed clothes, and they kept pace with me as we made our way to the restaurant where this shindig was going down.

The restaurant's interior was dimly lit, and candles flicked on all the tables. A goblin maître d' arrived to show me the way. My stomach knotted as we navigated between tables of preds who all eyed me curiously. Though I was pretty used to being surrounded at this point, I tended to avoid places like this where my outsider status was obvious.

I exhaled slowly, reminding myself I had nothing to fear from these people. No one was feeing aggressive, as evidenced by Theo's glyphs not activating. Besides, any anxiety I felt would be known to everyone here, and the first rule of meeting someone powerful was "show no fear."

Or maybe that was my first rule of meeting anyone. It sounded like good advice.

"Jess." Lucen stood as I approached the table, and I swore I saw apprehension in his smile. That didn't bode well.

Three of the table's other occupants remained seated. Dezzi nodded, and Devon winked. Another woman was present too—Sonya was Dezzi's recent addition to her inner triad, taking the opening left by Lucrezia's betrayal. She was every bit as beautiful as Lucrezia had been, with tan skin and long, black hair. But whereas Lucrezia's features had always been marred by her haughtiness, Sonya seemed practically demure. I didn't know her well enough to determine if that was just her natural expression, or if she was feeling the weight of her new promotion and the current, tense situation at-hand.

As for Dezzi, the Boston Dom seemed strained, as did Lucen. The fine laugh lines around her eyes were more visible than I'd ever seen before, and her eyes themselves were a touch bloodshot, like she hadn't been sleeping. Despite that, though, Dezzi looked as unflappable as always.

The fourth satyr at the table stood too. This had to be Claudius. He was built much like Lucen—tall and broad-chested—but he had dark eyes, and his honey-blond hair spilled down past his shoulders. He was pretty, in a manly way. He looked like he'd stepped out of some medieval painting, or he would have if not for the perfectly modern shirt and jacket he wore.

Also, and more importantly, power clung to him. My body was awakening with it. Although it was hard to tell how much of my reaction was caused by him and how much was due to my proximity to Lucen and Devon, I could smell his pheromones across the table, and that was enough to let me know they were working on me. His scent reminded me of the forest, filling my head with images of classical paintings. The sort that depicted satyrs of the mythological type playing pipes and frolicking with naked wood nymphs next to clear pools of water.

Alluring and dangerous.

So was the way Claudius's gaze swept over me, as though he were evaluating me, and he likely was. I did my best not to squirm at the heat coming over my skin, but I could sense his magic brushing my mind like imaginary fingers running through my hair. My nipples hardened, and I was glad I wore a slightly padded bra so he couldn't tell. This whole experience was icky enough without him getting to enjoy my reaction.

From the corner of my eye, I could see Lucen and Devon both stiffen, but I held still and met Claudius's gaze with every ounce of composure I could muster. Finally, his power withdrew, and he made a soft sound of satisfaction.

Yup, I was being evaluated. Fuck that.

"Are you going to introduce yourself or just mentally molest me for the rest of evening?" I faked a smile.

Someone stifled a laugh—probably Devon—but I kept my attention on Claudius.

To my surprise, he smiled. "I had to investigate you for myself. My apologies if you felt molested. Most people, I'm told, enjoy the experience."

"Your magic overpowers most people, and I'm not them. I'm a satyr."

Claudius rubbed his chin. "So I've been told, as well."

He sat back down, and the goblin pulled out a chair for me at last so I could do the same.

"So I've been told too." I gave Lucen's hand a squeeze under the table.

Claudius leaned back, continuing to study me, but at least doing so less obtrusively. "I admit, I expected something more. You seem very human."

"I consider that one of my positive traits."

He didn't respond directly, but he may have made a noise of derision. It was hard to tell, particularly since a waiter appeared with wine at that moment.

Conversation turned to boring small talk while everyone ordered food. Polite questions were asked about Claudius's flight, the local weather, and the usual topics people discuss when they have nothing better to talk about. No one seemed to expect me to do much speaking, which was a relief. I sipped my wine and tore off bits of my dinner roll without tasting much.

I was wondering if Lucen had been mistaken about the necessity of my presence when the conversation changed again with the arrival of the food. Dezzi brought up that tomorrow's meeting would start at three in the afternoon.

Claudius frowned, and something very weird happened. It was almost as though I felt his displeasure. Not tasted it, like I did human emotions, but felt it, like it had been planted in my mind. I could tell it was foreign, that it didn't belong to me, but my body reacted to it all the same. Disconcerted, I picked up my utensils, hoping I was imagining things.

"You agreed to meet at such an early hour?" Claudius's unhappiness was as evident in his tone as it was in my head.

Dezzi set down her glass. "It is not an ideal hour for anyone. Such is the nature of compromise."

"Neither an ideal hour nor an ideal arrangement." Claudius's gaze fixated on me again, and I cursed being seated directly across from him. "Will you be running this show?"

I swallowed. "Not precisely. There's no one in charge. We're all on equal footing because we all have the same goal."

"Assuming you believe this prophecy or that recent events are related to it."

"You don't?"

"Consider me skeptical. I'm not saying it isn't possible, just as I'm not saying you aren't a satyr. But on both accounts, I think people might be misinterpreting facts."

I blinked at him, and I wasn't the only one. Lucen visibly tensed, and Devon paused with his wineglass in hand. Sonya said nothing, but her eyes were alert, cataloguing the table.

Dezzi folded her hands. "There are stories of such people as Jessica in the lore. When you consider her talents—she feeds on human emotion, she can make humans lust, she can bypass wards designed to keep out anyone who is not a satyr—it seems entirely reasonable to assume she is one."

"Plus the Gryphons told me the other day that they used satyr magic on me." Did I sound defensive? It had to be Claudius's attitude pissing me off. I'd been in denial about what I was for so long. Defending my screwed-up biology was laughable.

Devon grinned, though it looked as forced as his smile had been earlier. "Well, there you go."

"There you don't go." Claudius's glance at Devon could have withered a dandelion, but Devon just cocked his head to the side, questioning him. "Gryphons could not possibly have done anything of the sort. It takes a satyr to make another satyr."

So I'd heard before, but I didn't know what that meant. "You assume they couldn't have convinced one to work with them?"

"No satyr with sufficient power for the task would do it."

"People will do a lot of things when you don't give them other options." I shrugged, but I really wanted to hurl my steak knife at Claudius's perfect head. "Or, you know, maybe a very powerful satyr became physically damaged, was kicked out of his domus for it, and helped the Gryphons out of spite. Sounds like the sort of thing I'd do."

Satyrs valued physical perfection to such a degree that they'd ostracize anyone without it, a fact that had bugged me since I learned of it. Dezzi had taken in one such satyr, Angelia, who—in spite of some issues I had with her—seemed like a lovely person. It was one reason I had some respect for Dezzi.

But it was probably something Claudius would disapprove of, and I was starting to get an idea about why everyone was so on edge. I made a mental note not to mention Angelia's name in his company.

My answer seemed to prove some sort of point with Claudius. "Another reason why I have my doubts as to whether you're truly a satyr or some other creature. You don't understand us or think like us."

"So we're back to my positive traits?"

Lucen stepped on my foot.

"Regardless of what she is, Jessica has been useful to our domus." Dezzi motioned toward me with her wineglass. "And there is certainly enough evidence before us to make this meeting worthwhile. It would not do to be like some races and become too self-absorbed to pay attention to the events surrounding us."

Claudius inclined his head her way. "Certainly not. If I didn't believe the discussion was worth having, I wouldn't have made the trip."

At once, the errant displeasure in my head lifted. Startled, I dropped my fork, and it clattered against my plate. I winced as everyone turned to me. "Sorry."

"Did you feel it?" Claudius asked.

I pushed my hair aside, no longer able to hide being flustered. "You in my head? Yes."

"Interesting." He gave Dezzi a pointed look. "More evidence, I think."

More evidence of what? That I wasn't a true satyr? I didn't ask, not wanting to give him the satisfaction of my curiosity. He might mistake it for caring.

So I wasn't a normal satyr. So what? I wasn't a normal human either, and as long as I knew why I wasn't normal, putting a name to myself didn't matter. It had once, but no more.

We finished dinner with more uneasy conversation, and I wondered how much worse it would have been without the wine.

When we got up, two humans did so with us. I hadn't noticed them before because they'd been sitting at another table. They were lust addicts, and it didn't take a genius to figure out whose. Claudius linked arms with the women, both of whom could have been—and quite possibly were—models. They were tall, leggy, and dressed in what I could tell were very expensive but also very short dresses.

"He brought addicts?" I said under my breath to Lucen.

"Travel isn't easy on us. The bonds weaken over the distances, even for someone as powerful as Claudius."

"Lovely. He could at least let them wear clothes that cover their asses."

Lucen shook his head at me, silently laughing.

Sonya took off as we left the restaurant, and Dezzi stayed behind to continue talking with Claudius. With my bodyguards behind me, I left with Lucen and Devon, glad to get away.

"So what did you think of our benevolent Upper Council overlord?" Devon asked once we were well out of earshot.

"Do you want honesty or diplomacy?"

Lucen nudged me in the ribs. "I think the chance for diplomacy is well past, little siren."

"So I blew that, huh?"

Devon smirked. "He's a right arse, isn't he?"

"Arse?" I raised my eyebrows at him.

"It's his accent."

I had to consider that for a moment before realizing Claudius did have an accent. I must have been so intent on taking in the rest of him that some of the details had gone completely over my head. "Arse, indeed. He called me a creature."

"Did you prefer when the goblins called you an abomination?" Lucen asked.

"Yes. Abomination gives me an edge. Creature makes me sound like a science experiment gone wrong. Which I suppose I am."

Devon looped an arm around one of mine. "I think you came out fine."

"So do I." Not to be outdone, Lucen took my other arm.

The sidewalk wasn't big enough for the three of us, but neither let go as we meandered down the street. Being so close to them both, feeling their power sliding over my skin, wreaked havoc on my nerves. I was warm all over again and growing hotter, my imagination teasing me with ideas.

I pushed these thoughts away for later. "What did Claudius mean when he said I felt him? I did feel something, like he was planting his emotions in my head."

"Very old satyrs," Lucen said, "far older than either of us, or even Dezzi, cannot just sense the emotions of humans. They can make *their* emotions felt."

"It's another way to influence people," Devon said.

I bit my lip, not liking the sound of this at all. "So they can stir lust in people, and other emotions? Peachy."

Lucen tightened his grip around my arm. "It's one reason why the idea of the original furies being released is so deadly. Someone like Claudius would have nothing on them. According to legend, they inspired anger, obviously, but also bloodlust and sadism and everything evil you can imagine."

"Oh, fabulous."

Finally, a thought that could kill any desire I'd been nursing for a threesome.

NINE

ACCORDING TO TOM, INGRID BLECHER WAS THE
Brotherhood's Big Boss in Boston. Although, being Tom, he called her
something far more boring, like Director of Special Project Research. Title
aside, the upshot meant that Ingrid was the person in charge of all matters
related to the magi prophecy and the Gryphon-magi-pred tentative alliance
we'd been putting together. Perhaps that was why she alone of the
Brotherhood members who'd arrived for the meeting had been granted an
office. The rest were stuck sharing a conference room.

Ingrid's position made her my most logical target if I wanted to poke
around for information on the Brotherhood and the source of the potential
Phoenix leak. Therefore, the morning of the meeting, I dragged myself
into Gryphon Headquarters several hours earlier than necessary. I'd
overheard Tom and others planning a pre-meeting meeting yesterday, and
I intended to snatch what might be my only opportunity to do something
incredibly rude and invasive.

I intended to search Ingrid's office. Possibly while laughing at the
comical horror of pre-meeting meetings.

I ducked in the tiny, borrowed room about ten minutes after the pre-
meeting was supposed to start. And sighed. When I'd formed this half-
brained plan yesterday, I wasn't sure what I might find, but the

possibilities were less than I'd imagined. Ingrid hadn't brought much with her. Unlike Tom, who'd stuffed his office with a veritable library and armory, Ingrid had only a laptop and whatever she'd packed in its case.

Mentally crossing my fingers, I checked the laptop first, but though it was on, it had been locked and was password protected. Not surprising.

I rummaged through her laptop bag next, not expecting to discover anything either. Aside from an odd assortment of pens, a pack of breath mints, and a phone charger, however, I also discovered a bunch of papers in an outer pocket. Trying not to get my hopes up, I rifled through them.

Ingrid had printed out several emails regarding her trip. While the content of those emails wasn't enlightening for the most part, the one on the bottom of the pile contained a single comment from Tom—a reminder of the dates that he and I would be traveling to Phoenix and Chicago.

Jackpot. My heartbeat sped up. Besides Ingrid and Tom, eleven other people had been included on the cc line at various points along the chain. I recognized Theo's name as one of them, and so I assumed the other people were also members of *Le Confrérie*. It wasn't much, but it was a start. In my not-so-copious free time, maybe I could do some digging into these people. If nothing else, the list narrowed down the number who I wanted to question. Although, since only five had come to Boston, questioning everyone on it seemed impossible.

In fact, when I was being honest with myself, all of it seemed impossible. Rubbing my eyes, I sighed again from the futility. I had neither the position within the Gryphons, nor the training, to do any serious investigation. As with the prophecy ordeal in general, I was in way over my head. Nevertheless, I took a photo of the names and email addresses, then I tucked everything away and got out before I further complicated my life by being caught snooping.

To make my day better, I found a package on my desk when I got back. Ripping it open, I discovered a neatly folded Gryphon uniform inside. What in the world? I held it up, noting it appeared to be my size.

With a groan, I tossed it on my chair. When I'd first been blackmailed into working for the Gryphons, I'd asked for a uniform. Asked, and been denied. So giving me one now? That meant one thing—the Gryphons were aiming to show they owned me.

That wasn't going to happen. This move was way more in-your-face than offering me bodyguards. If the Gryphons wanted to throw some of those into the mix, they were welcome. But I wasn't donning the black-and-gold uniform. No way could I claim neutrality if I did.

Surely, this would go over well when I refused.

My cell rang before I could kick off an argument with Tom, replacing my apprehension with a different sort of anxiety. It was my mother calling.

"Jess, honey, do you want to explain to me why the cops are keeping an eye on me?"

"Huh?" Shoving the uniform aside, I sat and turned on my computer. "What happened?"

Sirens wailed in the background. Given the time, my mom was probably on her lunch break. The doctor's office she worked at was adjacent to a hospital. "An officer stopped by the house this morning before I left. He said they'd been contacted by the Boston Gryphon Office and instructed to be alert. They were letting me know why I'd be seeing more frequent patrols or something to that effect."

Wow, so Tom must have actually done something when I'd told him I wanted my family protected. It wasn't Gryphons watching over her, but Gryphons were in short supply. This was better than nothing.

"It's a cautionary thing. I'm working on a..." How did I explain this quickly yet honestly? "A kind of high-profile case."

She sighed. She hadn't wanted me to be a Gryphon because of the danger, so to be putting her in danger too... "What sort of case? Have there been threats?"

Oh, just the end of the world as we know it. There was nothing she could do to protect herself from that. "No threats. I asked for the precautions because I'm paranoid. The case is kind of hard to explain." Or to believe, for some people.

"I see. I need to get back to work. Is there anything else you should tell me?"

I rested my head on my hands. Only that the Gryphons had turned me into a satyr and I'd been lying to her about my life since I turned eighteen.

I'd done it to protect her. I mean, who wanted to hear these things about their daughter? She'd be horrified and outraged, and she'd probably cry if she knew half of what I'd neglected to mention over the years. Yet as I ran my fingers over the uniform, I feared my time to come clean and tell her everything was running out. I guess I'd assumed I could lie to her my whole life.

Only now, my whole life didn't feel like it might be as long as I'd once believed. And it might well end in a way I could never have predicted. Suddenly, perhaps because of that, I felt like I owed it to her to confess. She deserved the truth.

Except here and now weren't the time. I just wished I knew when I'd get another opportunity.

"Jess? You there?"

"There's a lot I should tell you." My voice quivered a touch. Damn it. I grabbed a sip of water and sat upright. "I'll call you when I get a chance. Maybe this weekend."

"All right. You do that. Take care, honey."

"You too. Love you."

The hairs on my neck rose as I hung up, and I jumped, sensing someone was watching me. It was Tom. Figured. He must have been in a decent mood because I couldn't detect any negativity.

"So you do have a softer side?"

I flipped him off. "Even I have a mother who worries."

"Oh, yes. Did the police contact her?"

"That's why she called. Thank you."

He nodded and motioned toward the uniform, which was sitting in a heap. "You should change before the meeting this afternoon. In the meantime, why don't you meet Theo to finish your glyphs, then come find me and Ingrid."

"About the uniform? I'm not wearing it."

Tom's decent mood drained away, and I could taste annoyance settling in its place. "Why not?"

"I'm not a Gryphon. Seems disingenuous for me to wear a uniform."

"You are a Gryphon. You might not have been formally inducted into the organization, and Director Lee might have only hired you as a consultant, but we can fix that. You and the others were always intended to be Gryphons."

"Then how come you never mentioned this before? Why am I only finding out about it before we go marching into a meeting with preds and the magi?"

Tom ran his fingers through his blond hair. "If you'll recall, you weren't overly receptive to what I had to say prior to this. Just trying to get you to talk to me and read about the prophecy was, shall we say, an ordeal."

"You could have started off your spiel with this information." Not that it would have made a difference. Tom might be telling the truth. It was hard to know with him, but even so, the timing of this all felt extremely convenient.

Either way, it was too late. I was convinced the only way I might be able to hold the meeting together was if I showed no glaring loyalties to any one side.

"I doubt you'd have listened," Tom said, and he was right. I was certain I wouldn't have.

"Whatever. I'm not wearing it. I'll go get those glyphs finished, but we're done discussing the uniform."

Scowling, Tom stepped aside so I could leave my cube. "Don't count on it."

I wouldn't, and it was just as well. The argument resumed a couple hours later when I met up with Ingrid, Tom, and some other members of *Le Confrérie*.

Ingrid got straight to business. "Agent Kassin informs me you do not wish to wear the uniform we brought you."

I scanned the room, expecting to see Grace sitting around the table, already in a uniform, but she wasn't there. "No, and I explained why to Tom. Where's Grace?"

Ingrid rubbed lint off the reading glasses she wore around her neck. "After meeting her yesterday, we came to the assessment that she is better off not attending these meetings. Her time will be spent beginning her training. As for you, the uniform—"

"Is a no. I explained why. You're not marking me."

Ingrid and the others, whose names I'd mostly forgotten, exchanged glances. "It's not a question of marking. It's a question of demonstrating your authority, of making sure these other people listen to you."

"If that's all, give me some Gryphon-issued weapons. They'll listen then." I smiled, assuming I had them. Salamander fire-forged blades were expensive and not handed out lightly by the Gryphons. They required serious magical skills to produce. Preds wouldn't make them for others because they were extremely deadly to preds, so that left the magically talented magi as the best source. All Gryphons on duty carried knives, but no way would the Gryphons rise to the bait.

Or so I thought.

"Well yes," Ingrid said. "I thought it went without saying that you should be armed at all times."

"I…" I snapped my jaw shut. "Yeah, it makes sense."

"I see you already have a knife."

I patted Misery at my hip. The knife was one of my favorite possessions. "Yes, but I still don't think I need a uniform."

"Jessica has a jacket," Tom said, sounding resigned. "She should wear that if nothing else."

Ingrid shrugged. "It's a compromise then. Jessica, how much training do you have with firearms?"

"Uh, not much. Tom's made sure I've gone to the shooting range recently, but I wouldn't call myself proficient."

"Then you must continue to work on your skills. We have special bullets that are effective against preds."

I'd seen them before while snooping in Tom's office. Bullets with casings made of the same salamander fire-forged metal as Gryphon blades were. They were even rarer than the blades. So rare that I didn't realize such things existed until I'd found them.

A pred could bleed out from a single nick of a salamander blade if they didn't have access to magical healers. You didn't need to be a good shot to kill one if you had bullets made of the same. It was efficient, and it made fighting preds—usually a dangerous proposition—a whole lot easier for the person with the gun.

Before we left for the hotel, Tom supplied me with my new weapon. "This is exactly like the gun I've been training you on. They're made just for us to be able to accommodate the salamander-forged casings."

He set the gun and a holster, stamped with the Gryphon insignia, on his desk. Cautiously, I picked it up. Much as I'd been eager to goad Ingrid into arming me, I felt uneasy holding a firearm. Swords and knives were different. I'd studied how to use them for years as part of my martial arts training.

"Eight shots," Tom said. "I don't expect you'll need them anytime soon, but in case you do, there you go." He watched me load the gun and nodded his approval.

"You know, I was thinking you might give me a sword instead." I attached the holster next to Misery's sheath.

Tom slammed closed the case in which he kept the special bullets. "And I was thinking you might wear a uniform."

"Touché."

"It's not a game, Jessica. You of all people should know what we're facing. You're the one who linked Boston's furies to this prophecy."

I tied the windbreaker around my waist, and it covered up both my weapons. "I'm aware of that, and I understand you don't think I'm taking it seriously. But just because we don't agree on how to best handle the situation doesn't mean we aren't on the same side. That's something you should probably keep in mind as we go into this meeting. However different our opinions are, you can bet your ass the magi and satyrs and goblins are going to have even more different ones."

That, at least, I was certain of.

TEN

THE HOTEL CHOSEN FOR THE MEETING WAS ON THE OPPOSITE side of the city from Shadowtown. For the satyrs and goblins, this made it less convenient, but they'd agreed for the same reason I'd suggested it. We didn't want the furies to know about this meeting. The longer we could hide what we knew from them, the greater the possibility of finding a way to counteract their plans.

It was great in theory, but I couldn't help but think it was also pointless if the Brotherhood had a leak.

Tom and Ingrid hurried us to the hotel, but in spite of the urgency to get us there first, we weren't. Four goblins milled about the conference room. Gunthra, Boston's goblin Dom, was one of them. One of the others I knew by sight but not name. The final two were unknown to me. All four of them wore their own uniform of sorts—fancy suits that made them appear quite at home in the room. Like we'd wandered into a goblin executive meeting.

The goblins turned their large eyes on the Gryphons with suspicion.

"Miss Moore," Gunthra said, inclining her head the slightest.

Well, didn't I rank highly to get a personal greeting? "Gunthra."

An uncomfortable silence descended on the room. Tom opened his laptop and began typing. Ingrid, and those who came with her from

World, spoke in hushed voices outside the door. And the two strange goblins paced along the far wall. I was about to pull out my phone and ask Lucen where he was when the satyrs arrived.

They brought a surprise too—harpies. Eyff was the harpy Dom, tall and twiggy like all harpies with bright yellow feathers for hair. I didn't know him or one of his companions well, but the third harpy was Lei. She was a master charm maker. Back when I'd been in hiding from the Gryphons, she'd made me a potent glamour to disguise myself.

Ingrid followed the harpies and satyrs into the room, consternation on her face. "I did not realize more would be joining us."

Dezzi waved a hand in Eyff's direction. "We spoke of what was to be discussed here. This is an issue that affects us all. I thought their input might prove useful."

"Are we all assembled then?" the tall goblin asked.

I set my phone on the table to check the time. "We're waiting for the magi."

"Xander will, no doubt, be late," Tom said. "In my experience, he expects everyone to follow his schedule."

I smiled to myself, pleased that Tom didn't seem to care for the politically powerful magus any more than I did. "But Olef shouldn't be."

"They'll probably arrive together. On Xander time."

But Tom was soon proven wrong. Fifteen minutes later, Xander—along with his two usual thuggish bodyguards—arrived at the meeting. There was no Olef in tow.

"We can start now," he announced, and everyone glared at him.

"Where's Olef?" I asked.

Xander removed his jacket and didn't answer. Of course not. Xander had disliked me from the moment we met. I would never forget the way he compared my gift to a spider or how he'd told me I had a corrupted soul.

Okay, so ultimately he might have been right about me not being entirely human, but his attitude had been one of disgust and his treatment of me—and humanity in general—had been one of disdain. I'd seen no reason since to forgive or forget.

Perfect example of why? He continued to ignore my question until Tom repeated it. "We need Olef. He was supposed to be gathering research. We won't get very far until he arrives."

The red and white feathers on Xander's head fluffed in irritation. Magi and harpies were both birdlike, but magi had more variation in their appearance. Falcon shifters, like Xander, sported reddish plumage and a narrow frame. As an owl shifter, Olef had brown and white feathers, and the typical shorter, broader body.

"I don't know where Olef is. He was supposed to come by my office, but he didn't and he's not answering his phone. Knowing him, he's lost in his books, and when he emerges, he'll be most apologetic about being late." Xander made a show of checking his phone. "My schedule is extremely busy, so if you don't mind, I'd like to get started. I have some serious questions about how this situation is being handled."

I didn't like the sound of any of that—not the part about Olef, nor Xander's attitude. But the latter was to be expected. It was time to put Xander in his place. He might rub feathery elbows with senators and grace local magazine covers, but here, this was my show. If he didn't like it, he could kiss my spider-gifted ass.

"Let's get started then," I said loudly, cutting through the satyrs murmuring to my right. "I think we should start with introductions so everyone knows who everyone else is."

Introductions went smoothly, allowing me to re-familiarize myself with the names of Ingrid's companions. The two unknown goblins turned out to be members of their Upper Council—only they called it a High Council —and I learned Lei was Eyff's lieutenant. Sonya, I realized, wasn't in attendance. Dezzi had only brought Lucen and Devon, and of course Claudius. Claudius, in turn, had brought his addicts. Charming. He at least had the sense to make them wait elsewhere in the hotel once the meeting started.

Usually these sorts of intros went on for a while because everyone wanted to talk about themselves, but this time no one did. Olef still hadn't arrived when we finished, and my gut twisted uneasily. I really needed him here. Unless the preds from their uppity councils were carrying around lots of secret knowledge they were willing to share, Olef was our best resource.

"Until Olef arrives..." I hesitated for a second, letting my thoughts gather, and that was all it took.

I lost control of the meeting.

"I want to know in excruciating detail how this woman could have stumbled upon such a far-reaching and highly unlikely idea," Xander said.

At the same time, Claudius jumped in. "What sort of proof do we have for any of this? Some magi mumbo-jumbo? The word of a girl with no magical training?"

"Girl? Really?" I threw him a sharp look across the table.

The room erupted in accusations and arguments. Xander wasn't convinced of the seriousness of the problem. The goblins accused the Gryphons of holding out on key information. Claudius was obsessed with my role, and in disbelief that I should be involved in any way. Meanwhile Lucen defended me and tried explaining my past, and as for the Gryphons, they volleyed with the goblins and urged Xander to cooperate.

Only the harpies were mostly silent, but their heads swiveled from speaker to speaker like they were watching a tennis match. Soon enough they too would pick sides, most likely that of the satyrs who they'd historically allied with.

I felt a headache coming on. This was why I needed Olef. He was one of the magi whose visions of me surrounded by burning cities gave credence to the old prophecy. He was the one who could explain everything in a calm, logical manner.

The throbbing in my temples worsened until I smacked my hands against the table and stood. "Enough!"

I yelled so loudly that everyone on this floor of the hotel must have heard me, but it worked. In the momentary shocked silence that followed, I seized the floor again. "We're here to share what we know and discuss strategies. So let's start by reviewing what we know so everyone knows what everyone knows. If you have questions, save them until the end."

I paused for breath, and Dezzi passed a water bottle my way. "Go on."

I appreciated the support, regardless of why she might have offered it, but I didn't miss the way Claudius narrowed his eyes at her in disapproval either.

Taking a deep breath, I sat. "So, since the last time some of us met, a few facts have been confirmed. Every couple hundred years, a magi has had a vision of cities burning. Olef is the most recent magi to have done so, and he's recognized me in his vision. Enough of these visions have occurred that the magi call them a prophecy, and as of today, two cities have burned in magical fires caused by nonhuman riots—Buenos Aires and Sydney. Boston was almost a third."

"Parts of Boston did burn." Xander stared at me accusingly, as though what the furies had done were my fault. "Millions of dollars in damages. Lives lost. Are you forgetting that?"

My hands balled into fists, but Lucen responded before I could. "No, but it could have been a lot worse if Jess hadn't stopped the furies."

I let out a breath, imperceptibly I hoped, although the preds would all be well aware of my frayed temper. "Yes, what happened in Boston is a tragedy, but it never reached the scale of Buenos Aires or Sydney. Moving on. The Gryphons took the prophecy seriously, and they created me, and four others like me, with rather unique satyr-like powers in response."

Claudius snorted at the satyr-like part.

Temper, down.

More deep breaths. "There are two of us left."

"Three," Tom said.

"Oh? You've found Mitch?"

He frowned. "Not yet."

"Then I stand by the two." I took a sip from the water bottle, wishing fervently that it contained coffee. Preferably coffee spiked with whiskey. "I'm assuming everyone here knows the Vessels of Making were basically containers used to channel power into creating a magical prison called the Pit. According to lore, there were five Vessels used in making the Pit, and the Gryphons recently confirmed that the lore also states all five would be needed to open it."

Ulan's ears twitched. He was the tall High Council goblin, and he glanced between me and Gunthra. "The theory, as I understand it, is that you believe the furies are destroying these cities in order to channel enough of their brand of power to fill the Vessels."

"Yes."

Ulan made a noise that sounded like "Hmph." I couldn't tell if he didn't approve of Gunthra talking to me, the theory, or if he just didn't like the sound of this.

No one should like it. According to Olef, the creatures that had been locked in the Pit weren't even as human-friendly as modern furies, and modern furies were probably the least friendly of all the pred races. The descriptions I'd read of the originals in Tom's history books made them sound like demons straight out of a horror movie.

"This is all very speculative," Xander said, waving a four-fingered hand dismissively. "I don't discount Olef's vision, but I'd like to see some proof that these visions are related to the Vessels."

Gunthra's ears flattened. "One of my people saw the object, felt its power. It matches the description of the Vessels."

"I'm hardly about to trust the word of a goblin any more than I would trust her word." He motioned to me.

Peachy.

"So long as we're voicing our concerns," Claudius said, "I'm not sure I trust a magi's hallucination. But even if it is true, what are we supposed to do about it?"

"Find the rest of the Vessels before the furies do." Ingrid's tone was remarkably controlled under the circumstances. "Exactly what we spoke to you about earlier."

"A lot of work based on sketchy speculation." Xander jumped up, the feathers on his head rising with him. "And what if the furies already have the others?"

Tom smacked his hand against the table. "That's what we need to find out, ASAP. The sooner we stop bickering, the sooner we can make progress."

"And assuming all this is true," said Eyff, speaking for the first time, "where do we find these missing Vessels?"

"They can't." Xander raised his arms in defeat.

Tom sighed. "The Vessels have been lost for over a thousand years. The lore suggests each group involved in creating the prison took one with them, ensuring they would never be reunited. We don't know how the furies might have gotten their hands on the one or two they did."

"It seems unlikely they did then." Claudius's face was strained, and as I had last night at dinner, I felt a stirring of something in me that wasn't my own. I wasn't even sure what it was. Not lust, and not anxiety exactly, but something that made me suspect Claudius might know more than he was letting on. Interesting.

Lucen had said Claudius controlled whether he inflicted his emotions on others, and maybe that was usually true. With pureblooded humans. But I was something else, and pred power affected me differently sometimes. In his agitation, could Claudius's control have slipped? Was I feeling an emotion I wasn't meant to feel?

Or was I the one having emotional hallucinations? Goodness knew I was stressed enough for such a thing.

Lucen tapped his fingers on the table. "Then there's the mystery of the furies' interest in Jess."

I groaned. Here came more inexplicable weirdness to be met by everyone's disbelief.

"What interest?" Xander yanked out his chair and sat back down, looking pissed off.

"One of the furies, the local lieutenant, said he didn't want me getting hurt. He's protected me on more than one occasion."

The magi crossed his arms. "And you don't know why, naturally."

"I was hoping we could discuss theories."

"Frankly, all we have here are theories supported by only the flimsiest of evidence. Without Olef, I'm not sure what there is to discuss."

The shorter of the High Council goblins finally broke his silence. "I hate to concur with the magi, but he's right."

Gunthra paled. "I trust what my informant saw."

"I'm not doubting your informant," the goblin said. "Just the rest of this information."

Devon leaned around Lucen toward me. "Are we having fun yet?"

I closed my eyes and silently swore, trusting Devon would gather the gist.

Him, and everyone else, making me long for an entire bottle of Jameson's to drown out their noise.

And what noise it was. The arguing continued, much of it surrounding me and my role in everything. I wasn't the only one starting to tune it out either. Tom's phone buzzed, and he got up to take the call.

I watched him walk outside the room, envious of his excuse to leave and amused that he seemed glad for the chance. So, for that reason, when his emotions went into a tailspin, I noticed right away. Whatever news he'd received on that call couldn't be good if I felt his frustration and anger so clearly.

I caught his eye and silently left the table to join him in the hall. He hung up as I approached. "Are you okay?"

Tom rubbed his eyes. "I'm fine, but we have a problem. Jessica, Olef is dead."

ELEVEN

THE FLOOR DROPPED OUT FROM UNDER ME. THAT'S WHAT IT felt like. I actually pressed against the wall for support. I thought my spinning head might fly off in a million directions.

"Dead? No." Olef couldn't be dead. It wasn't just that we needed him here—his knowledge and his calming presence—although we did. But I counted Olef as a friend. Not one I knew well, but one I'd known for a long time. He was a good person. Always kind, invariably helpful, and damn it—a good tipper too.

Of all the ridiculous things to remember. Shit. I felt sick to my stomach.

"The cops are on the scene already," Tom was saying as he punched numbers into his phone. "Hold it together. I need to get us over there before they mess things up."

Cops? Mess what up?

Before I could ask, the answer came to me like another blow to the head. It was obvious. Olef wasn't merely dead. He'd been murdered, and quite possibly—likely—because of his involvement with this meeting. Had someone found out about it and tried to silence him?

That line of thought opened up a hundred new questions and problems, none of which I could deal with in my current state.

Olef. Dead. I was stuck on that, and my emotions seesawed between nauseated grief and searing rage in a way that totally did not help my head.

"Jess?" Lucen appeared in the hall, and he put a hand on my arm. "What happened?"

"Olef was killed," I whispered, only belatedly wondering if Tom would be upset with me for sharing the news.

Swearing, Lucen wrapped his arms around me, and at the moment, I didn't care how many Gryphons saw as I collapsed against him.

"He was a friend." A friend, and we needed him. Though my chest hurt, I couldn't overlook the cold practicality of the situation. Even with my head buried against Lucen, I could hear the arguments continue inside the conference room.

Without Olef, we were toast.

I took a shaky breath, realized Tom was watching me, and released Lucen. I had to get my head back in the game fast. "I want to be part of this investigation," I told Tom.

He nodded slowly, sticking the phone away. "A team is heading over now. You should join them with me. Olef was searching for materials. It's possible whoever did this might not have found them."

Lucen didn't let go of my wrists. "You're certain Olef's death is related to this?"

"I can't be one hundred percent, but it seems likely. It's clearly homicide from what I was told."

I closed my eyes, hoping however Olef had died, it had been quick. Fear of the answer kept me from asking, but I'd find out soon enough. "First Mitch and I are kidnapped. Now Olef is killed. If we're trying to be discreet, I'd say we failed."

Tom's frown deepened, but he didn't disagree. "I've got to let Ingrid know. They can finish the meeting today without us."

Lucen laughed mirthlessly. "Oh, I think they're finished already." He grabbed my hands as Tom returned to the room. "Are you sure you want to go?"

"Positive. I liked Olef, and let's be realistic. We needed whatever he was researching. I have to go."

He bit his lip. "I only ask because you're upset, little siren. I don't want you more upset by visiting the crime scene."

"I can handle it. I want to be a part of this. I want to find whoever did this, and I want to kill them."

Before they could kill anyone else involved. Like the satyr in front of me.

———

SINCE I WAS LEAVING WITH TOM, I WAS SPARED THE annoyance of being tailed by my satyr bodyguards. We said very little on the drive. There wasn't much to talk about yet, and I didn't have much to say regardless. The nausea and dizziness of shock had worn off, leaving me with the awful empty numbness of grief and a slow, simmering anger.

Just as all preds lived in Shadowtown, the magi grouped together in their own neighborhood known as The Feathers. It was the very opposite of Shadowtown in every conceivable way, from the bright colors to the overwhelming filth.

Tom had to find parking a couple streets away, and we traipsed down the crowded sidewalks. The cacophony of bike bells and car horns and the cheery flags flying from the streetlamps got under my nerves. It was all too happy and normal. My emotions had been easier to control in the sterile, bland hotel, and again in Tom's meticulously clean, gray car. I had to refrain from snapping at the people who brushed by me as we walked.

Thanks to the Gryphon SUVs outside, and the cop car that was pulling away from the curb, it was easy to figure out which building was Olef's. It stood smack in the middle of a row of enormous Victorians that had been converted into apartments, a green-and-purple monstrosity complete with a turret.

It was also too garishly cheerful.

The front door was propped open, and I counted three mailboxes next to it. A cop met us in the tiny foyer. We flashed him our badges, and he pointed past a beat-up bike into a set of dimly lit stairs that had seen better days.

"Second floor. Your buddies are already here."

The stairs creaked mood-appropriate background noise as we climbed, but voices soon drowned out the plaintive sound. The door atop the landing had been propped open, and I slipped inside the apartment after Tom.

Sadness hit me anew. This place was quintessentially Olef. Exactly as I'd have imagined it. Bookshelves lined every foot of wall space in the living room, each overflowing. More books cluttered the small tables, one of which was overturned, and still others were spread across the floor.

Overturned.

I paused, taking a closer inspection. Magi were generally a slovenly lot, but this seemed very not Olef-like. The books weren't neatly stacked, but strewn everywhere, lying open, spines bent upside down, pages crumpled. Olef was a librarian, and he loved books too much to treat his in such a way, even if he shared the magi predilection for untidiness. "Whoever did this was searching for something. But did they find it?"

"Let's hope not," Tom said, and it was the last word he got out before two new Gryphons and an unknown woman appeared around the corner.

I ignored the woman, who was either plain-clothed PD or from the coroner's office, and my eyes settled on one of the Gryphons. My unhappy stomach sank further. As if this situation wasn't unpleasant enough already.

"Jess." Agent Andre Pagan gave me an awkward smile. "Good to see you."

Andre had been the Gryphon assigned to train me when I'd first been blackmailed into working for them. Tall, sexy, and an all-around good guy, I once thought he'd be a great catch if I hadn't had Lucen. But the case we'd worked on had nearly gotten us killed, and—perhaps worse—dealing with curses and satyr aphrodisiacs had gotten us both naked and into a very, uh, interesting situation.

I'd had to hit a naked Andre with a chair in order to save his life. That sort of behavior made things uncomfortable after the fact. To put it mildly. No matter how well we'd worked together until then, I'd known it would be the last time. I hadn't gone out of my way to avoid him since, but I hadn't searched him out either. Andre, I suspected, had been avoiding *me*. Blaming him for it wasn't possible.

I returned the smile as best I could, and mine came out more sad than awkward. "So you'll be the one investigating?"

"I'm usually one of the go-to people for magic-related homicides." He sighed heavily. "I'm not necessarily seeing why we're here though. This looks like a case for the regular PD."

Tom held out a hand and introduced himself. "I requested your involvement because we have reason to believe what happened is related to a larger case."

While introductions and other formalities were taken care of, I found a pair of gloves and slipped them on. A half wall to my right separated the kitchen from the living room, and I wandered over.

The kitchen wasn't the same disaster as the living room. The sink and some of the appliances could have used a good cleaning, but I'd seen plenty of people with housekeeping skills just as poor. Nothing struck me as amiss. A bowl sat in the sink, and a soggy, used teabag remained in a mug next to an electric kettle. Dregs of tea water coated the bottom of the mug, but it was cold, the contents drank a while ago. So Olef had been alive and well this morning.

Andre watched me as I made my way back into the living room. "The real mess is in the office. Come on."

The three of us squeezed down a narrow hall, past a dingy bathroom, and Andre gestured to the door on the right. "That's the bedroom. It's also been torn apart. But this is where the body was found." He pushed open the left door.

"Olef," I muttered. "His name was Olef."

"Jessica was friends with him," Tom said.

Andre grimaced. "Sorry, Jess. He's already been taken away if that helps."

I wasn't sure if it did, but I couldn't help but feel relieved not to see Olef lying dead on the floor. "How did he die?"

"I'm not sure what the official medical term will be, but my term would be a very hard blow to the head."

"So over quickly? Good." I braced myself and approached the doorway where Tom was standing.

Andre held up a hand before I got close enough to see past Tom.

"Actually, I'm not so sure. Were you working on whatever case you think this is connected to?"

I glanced at Tom. "Yeah. Why?"

Tom inhaled sharply and darted inside the room. "I think Olef left you a message."

Andre removed his hand, and I rushed forward, heart beating faster. Tape marked where Olef had been found, but even if it hadn't, his location would have been obvious by the pool of drying blood near his desk. I closed my eyes momentarily, fighting to maintain my grip.

The room had been torn apart, like Andre said. More books were tossed everywhere, drawers flung open, and paper and pens scattered across a space barely big enough to hold three people. With shaky breaths, I knelt next to Tom. He moved aside so I could see he was looking at imprints of dried blood. They covered a spot on the bottom of the wall, right above the molding. Through the mess was a message, scrawled in an almost illegible hand.

JESS USE KEY

If Olef had time to leave me a message, he hadn't died quickly. The dizziness washed over me again, and I waited for it to pass.

Focus, focus, focus, I demanded my brain. This must be important. I just wished I had a clue what it meant.

"Key?" I raised my eyebrows hopefully at Tom.

I could see his answer before he shook his head. His expression showed him to be as lost as I was.

Tom took out his phone and snapped a photo of the message, and I stood, scanning the room. So many books. What were the odds any of them held the answers we required? What were the odds that whoever did this hadn't taken what we needed?

"So you don't understand it?" Andre asked.

I wondered how much I was allowed to share. "Olef was researching stuff for our case. I guess he found some answers."

"You tell us what you're looking for, we can help you go through his belongings to see if we can find it."

"It's probably not going to be that simple," Tom said. "But let's start with what we do know so we can track down whoever did this. It's possible the killer took the information we need."

We made our way back into the living room. More uniformed Gryphons had arrived and were conferring with the remaining cops.

Andre pulled out a notebook, and we stepped onto the landing to get out of the newcomers' way. "Here are the facts as originally taken by the PD before we arrived. Olef was found by his landlady when she went to deliver a package to him. She also saw him come home from work last night, which means there's a good chance that makes her the last person to see him alive, but we'll follow up on that. Landlady says she was home all day, but she was in her back room most of the time. So if someone came to Olef's apartment via the front door, she wouldn't have seen them."

"How else could someone enter?" I asked.

"Fire escape." Andre pointed toward the window. "There's also a roof entrance—standard in The Feathers. And, you know, we're dealing with magi. Olef's bedroom window was open. Someone could have flown in."

I crossed my arms. "If we're dealing with a magi murderer."

"True." Andre gave me a pointed look. "I'll get to that in a moment. But first, back to what I just said. The landlady claims she didn't hear a thing all day except for the usual footsteps. That seem strange to you?"

I rubbed my sweaty neck. It was getting wicked hot up here with everyone roaming about. "But there was overturned furniture, and the books—shouldn't she have heard that?"

"Exactly. You'd think anyway. So either she's lying, or the mess upstairs was carefully and quietly staged."

"To make it look like a robbery. Why?"

"Throw us off, perhaps," Tom suggested. "Make us think this isn't connected to the other case. Hide the fact that something we need was stolen."

I groaned and turned to Andre. "You're suggesting the cops think we're dealing with a magi killer?"

It would definitely shake things up. I couldn't believe for a second that Olef's death wasn't related to the prophecy, but there was no reason for another magi to have killed him in that case. Was there?

Andre flipped the page in his notebook. "A magi is possible at this point. The cops found a bright red feather under Olef's body. It's clearly not Olef's."

"Falcon shifters have red feathers." They were the only magi with colorful plumage. "So do many harpies."

Tom scratched his head. "Or it could mean nothing. Another fake clue to throw us off."

"Yeah, well." Andre stretched and stuffed the notebook away. "We're sending the feather to the lab and hoping they can tell us if it's magi or harpy in origin. Whether it's just a red herring—er, feather—that's another story."

Tom got his phone out. "We'll be here. Let us know as soon we can get in there and start taking control of Olef's belongings."

I collapsed to the stairs as Tom wandered off to make his call and Andre headed into the apartment. All I wanted was to run back to Shadowtown. To hold Lucen and make sure he was safe. And Steph. And my mother. And hell, add Devon to that list, and anyone else I remotely cared about.

Maybe whoever had done this was just trying to prevent us from learning what Olef found out, in which case, the others were safe. Or maybe they were trying to keep us too distracted to stop the furies, in which case they weren't. I couldn't take the risk. If the furies were behind this—and I couldn't believe anything else—then everyone connected to me and that damn prophecy might be in danger.

So as much as I wanted to run home, I didn't move. I had to get my hands on Olef's research. I had to find out what this mysterious key was. And I had to make sure Olef didn't die in vain. It was the best I could do to protect everyone.

TWELVE

It was late by the time we called it quits for the day. Tom and I had boxed up every promising book and scrap of paper Olef had accumulated over the years. We'd even obtained the package his landlady had tried dropping off earlier. Alas, the package only contained tea he'd ordered.

Andre was reluctant to give us first crack at going through Olef's computer, but he'd been forced to relent because Tom outranked him. He was smart to realize, however, that Tom didn't share his investigative background, and Tom's interest in catching the murderer was only secondary to some other interest in Olef's files.

I tried to explain to Andre that everything was related, but by eight o'clock I had a pounding headache. I gave up on talking to anyone and kept to myself, organizing Olef's books and choosing any that looked promising to take to Headquarters to study.

I was pumped up with painkillers, uptight because of copious quantities of coffee, and vaguely aware I was starving when I returned to Lucen's. He yanked open the door before I could fish out my spare key.

"Why didn't you call before you left?" He pulled me inside. "You have no bodyguards."

Though I'd been fretting over his well-being all evening, I was also cranky, and his tone didn't improve my mood. "I'm fine. No one's going to attack me on the subway."

"In Phoenix, you were attacked in a moving car, and you think someone can't hurt you on the T?" He crossed his arms.

I grumbled something that didn't even make sense to me because he was right. "I'm sorry. I'm tired, and once we got everything, I just wanted to go home."

Lucen ran his hands through his hair in obvious exasperation. "I want to keep you safe, little siren."

"I know. You do tend to be a little overbearing about it though." I wandered into the kitchen for a glass of water.

Lucen followed me in. "Overbearing?"

"You're doing it now. You're hovering." I turned around with my glass in hand to make my point. He stood only inches behind me, a solid satyr wall. Protecting me from what—his pet dragon?

"Sometimes you like me close."

I poked him in the chest to get him to back up. "When you're not being overbearing, and loud, and doing things like threatening to lock me up for my own good."

"When have I ever done that?"

I sat at the table with my water, wishing for that spiked coffee I never had. "There was a time, if you'll recall, when we were hunting Victor Aubrey."

Lucen must have read my thoughts because he set two glasses and a half-full bottle of wine on the table. "I don't quite remember it like that, but if you're referring to the time you ran headfirst into a fury bar, you could have gotten yourself killed. It was not one of your best moves."

"And you yelled at me in the middle of the street. Not one of your best moves either."

"I didn't yell at you."

"You got agitated and loud."

He glared at me. "You ran. Into a fury bar. Chasing a serial killer."

"And survived."

Lucen shoved the wine bottle toward me. "Forgive me, Jess, if I'm the only one who realizes that might not always be the case."

I poured myself a glass while he stormed into the living room. *I love him*, I reminded myself. Was that why we were both acting irrational? "Do you want some?"

"No. Yes. I think you're driving me to need some."

I emptied the rest of the bottle into the second glass. "What happened after we left?"

Lucen had flopped on the sofa. "Not much. The news spread, and the meeting dissolved pretty damn fast. Fair to say, expect tomorrow to be a regular shitstorm if anyone bothers to show up."

"Damn." I handed him his glass and sat.

"What did you find at Olef's?"

Wearily, I filled Lucen in on my past few hours. Whether it was exhaustion or the lack of food, the wine was going straight to my head. Alas, it wasn't giving me a happy buzz, just cloudy thoughts and a dreary outlook.

"You're sure it's the furies?" Lucen set his glass down.

I yawned. "Who else would it be? Olef doesn't strike me as the sort to have enemies, and he scrawled my name on his wall."

"The message could be unrelated to the cause of his death. It could simply have been his last attempt to convey information he thought you needed."

I put my glass next to Lucen's and pulled my knees in. "Possible, but you can't really believe that. He's dead because of me."

"Not because of you."

"Yes, it is." My inebriated brain pulsed with the logic headache. "It all goes back to me. I should have figured things out sooner. I should have stayed away from the furies way back when. This is all my fault."

Lucen pushed hair out of my face. "You're not making sense anymore. The only fault here belongs to the people who are orchestrating bad things. You, apparently, are part of the key to stopping them."

JESS USE KEY

I winced. *Olef, what the hell did you mean?*

"Tom suggested Olef might have been killed because he knew stuff, or simply because whoever did it knew it would disrupt our momentum."

Lucen continued to play with my hair, draping it behind my neck. "Could be."

His touch felt so good that my eyes closed involuntarily. "If the furies are interested in me, and they want to torment me, they could come after other people I care about next."

"I thought the cops were keeping an eye on your family."

"They are, but no one's keeping an eye on you."

"I can take care of myself."

I grabbed his hand, and he let go of my hair. "So can I."

"So we're back to this?"

I didn't have the energy to respond, so I settled into the cushions. Olef was dead, Lucen was being a stubborn pain in the ass, and I should not have had that glass of wine no matter how badly I wanted a drink. I'd been reduced to an emotional disaster. All I wanted was to curl into a ball and wish for everything to go away.

IN A WAY, I GOT PART OF MY WISH. UNFORTUNATELY, THE BIT that disappeared was my hope—hope of accomplishing much at the meeting the next day.

I'd slept poorly and spent the morning paging through the books we'd collected from Olef for anything about a key, but I discovered nothing. My mood was as dark as the sky when I arrived at the hotel.

Peeling off my rain-soaked windbreaker, I clomped down to the meeting room with the other Gryphons. The preds had all beaten us there today, which was a relief after Lucen's worry that people wouldn't show up. Eyff had come alone this time, and Devon was missing, taking care of other business for Dezzi.

"How do we proceed at this point?" Ulan asked. "Without this magi who supposedly had all the answers, it doesn't seem we have much to do."

I flung the windbreaker down on a chair. "We find the answers he left us clues about. Olef must have gone through a great deal of trouble to write something about a key. Does that mean anything to anyone?"

Judging by the blank faces, the consensus was apparently no.

I rested my head in my hands. "Does anyone know anything, or did you all just show up here to antagonize each other?"

Ingrid cleared her throat. "Jessica, perhaps you want to let someone else do the talking today. You are still upset."

No shit. I bit my tongue.

"We came here to discuss information and credible theories," the goblin said. "I've yet to see sufficient proof that would induce us to share anything."

I raised my head. "One person's been kidnapped. Another murdered. You don't think that's proof enough that something is up?"

The conference room door flew open, and an irate Xander stormed in. Every tiny feather on his head stood on end, and his gold eyes shimmered with emotion. "Why has she been released?"

His question was directed at the Gryphons, and I frowned in confusion.

The answer to Xander's question, however, came not from the humans but from Eyff. "Because she's innocent."

"None of you are innocent, harpy."

Xander's language was so similar to what he'd once told me in regard to my magic that I almost snorted. Perhaps luckily, I was too confused to find his comment funny.

Lucen took my hand under the table, questioning me with his eyes, but I could only shrug.

It was Tom who finally answered, cutting off Eyff and Xander's verbal sparring. "She was brought in for questioning only. There's not sufficient evidence to hold her."

"Hold who?" I demanded.

"Lei."

Xander pointed at Eyff. "That monster's lieutenant murdered Olef."

Eyff's feathers were as ruffled as Xander's. "If you had any proof of that, she wouldn't have been released, would she? Her feathers are the same color as yours, magi. Take a look in the mirror. Maybe it was you who killed Olef."

"You're going to turn this around on me?" Xander laughed

incredulously, and his thugs shifted position uneasily behind him. "Lei was seen in The Feathers yesterday morning. Now, I ask you, why would a harpy be out so early in the day, and why would she be in The Feathers unless she had a nefarious purpose?"

Eyff took a couple calming breaths. "Why would she be so stupid as to allow herself to be seen if she were there to commit murder, you bombastic asshole?"

I glanced between the Gryphons, who were trying futilely to calm everyone down, and the satyrs. Eyff's logic was sound, and goodness knew Xander had a history of baseless accusations, but they both raised good questions. Why was Lei in The Feathers?

Also, why had no one told me she'd been brought in for questioning?

"Eyff, let him rant," Dezzi said in her typically soft but firm way. "You accomplish nothing by slinging insults with him here."

I heard the slight emphasis she placed on "here" and winced internally. Dezzi might argue for better sense to prevail, but far be it from a pred not to seek retaliation for a believed wrong or slight. I'd known today wasn't going to be easy, but my control over the meeting was more fleeting than I'd feared.

When Dezzi's subtle suggestion was ignored and more insults went flying, I couldn't take it any longer.

"Enough!" I raised my hands in exasperation, for all the good it did. It required several more attempts by multiple people before Xander quit ranting. "We need to move on and start considering how we might find the remaining Vessels before the furies get to them."

Xander sat, glaring at me. "This isn't over. You of all people should be aware of what was lost with Olef's death."

Mental note: next time, bring a hip flask to this meeting.

"Oh, I'm sure it's far from over," Claudius said, far too cheerfully. "As Jessica has pointed out, one abduction and one murder so far. I'm sure we have much more—dare I say it?—*foul* play to look forward to."

I slammed my hands on the table. "Are you seriously making jokes about this?"

Xander, Eyff, and Ingrid were all on their feet again, but it took me a moment to realize the screaming I heard was my own. The thread of composure that had been holding me together had snapped.

"A good, intelligent person—which is obviously more than I can say for you—is dead." My hands trembled, and I balled them into fists. "Hundreds of people died right in this damn city. Thousands in Buenos Aires. Maybe thousands in Sydney too. And who knows how many more will follow if we can't find a way to stop what's coming—something we needed Olef for. So if you're not going to contribute anything useful, then you can get out."

My voice died away in the silence. I could feel everyone's gaze pressing down on me, but my eyes were locked on Claudius.

Feed on that anger, you smirking asshole. I hope it gives you indigestion.

"Jess." Lucen placed a hand over mine, but I was beyond being calmed.

Once more, Dezzi tried to be the voice of reason. "We are all stressed, and we all cope with stress in different ways. I think it would be good if we all assumed helpful intentions."

Both Xander and I snorted.

Great. Now I had something in common with that birdbrain.

"Jessica." Tom cast a pleading look at me. "Please sit. We all need to do our best to get along."

"I do not get along with people who make jokes about my dead friends."

I'd lost it. Even as I spun around and stomped out of the room, I was well aware what a bad idea it was. I mentally yelled at myself to stop, but I couldn't. Like the day I'd found out what the Gryphons had done to me, I moved on autopilot, pushed too hard by my temper to regain control. I saw what I was doing, knew it was a bad idea and was powerless to prevent it.

A couple chairs lined the deserted hotel corridor, and I collapsed on one of them. Footsteps approached a moment later. I hoped for Lucen, but when I raised my head, I saw Tom.

"You need to get your temper under control."

"Yeah, well, you'd know about it, wouldn't you?"

Tom stepped away and leaned against the opposite wall, studying me.

"I have had the misfortune of being on the receiving end of it before. Between you and Xander—"

"Do not ever lump me in with Xander."

"Then stop acting like him."

I jumped up. "I am not. He's making baseless accusations. I'm pissed off about some satyr jackass making jokes about dead people. It's not the same."

"Not in the specifics, but you're both derailing the meeting."

I couldn't argue with that so I ignored it. "Why didn't anyone tell me Lei was brought in for questioning?"

"Can we discuss this later? We should go back inside."

"I cannot go back in there yet or I'll punch Claudius. So why not?" I crossed my arms.

Tom pushed off the wall and paced, hands in his pockets. "I spoke about your involvement in the investigation with Ingrid, and on further reflection we agreed that it wasn't the best use of your time. You should be training. At the most, your part in the investigation should be focused on reviewing the information we obtained from Olef to decipher his message to you."

I opened my eyes wide. The angry adrenaline that had been dissipating in my blood was refreshed. "She convinced you to take me off the case? I want to be involved."

"We agreed together. You have more important things to do."

"No, you have things you want me to do. Whether they're more important is debatable. We have no idea what role I might play in this prophecy. Therefore, learning how to make charms or read glyphs might be a complete waste of my time. The only thing I do know isn't a waste of time is finding out who killed Olef and bringing them to justice."

I could sense Tom's annoyance with me seeping past his emotion-dampening charms. "We can discuss this more later. Jessica, please go back inside and calm down."

"Has the lab figured out what kind of feather was in Olef's room?"

"We're still waiting on results."

"Why was Lei in The Feathers? Xander's got a point. It's very strange."

"Jessica..." Tom closed his eyes, and I got the sense he wouldn't mind bashing my head in. "Can we discuss this later?"

I stared at Tom, utterly lost. Why was he deflecting? What could Lei have been doing in The Feathers that he didn't want me to know about? Dragon shit on toast, nothing was making sense anymore.

"Fine, I'll go ask her myself."

"Jessica, please. You need to work with us right now."

I jabbed the elevator button, and when it didn't appear immediately, I opened the stairwell door. "In case you've forgotten, I don't trust any of you. If I have to do this on my own, I will."

I feared for a moment Tom would charge after me, but the door slammed shut, and then all I heard was my feet on the concrete stairs and the sound of blood rushing by my ears.

THIRTEEN

Tom didn't follow me, but apparently my satyr bodyguards had arrived at the hotel sometime after I had. Gi and Melissa were hanging out in the bar, disguise charms in place. I had to pass by them to get from the stairs to the front door. Gi downed the rest of his beer, and they rushed to catch up to me as I left.

I rolled my eyes as I opened the door. The rain had gotten worse. It was pouring. "How effective are you guys supposed to be if you've been drinking?"

Gi grinned. "We're still the biggest badasses this side of the Charles."

"Uh-huh. Let's hope my potential attackers don't hail from the Cambridge side then."

Melissa tucked her extra-large umbrella under her arm. "Your meeting was scheduled to go on longer."

"I stormed out ahead of schedule. Everyone else is yelling at each other."

Gi's phone rang as we gained cover under the parking garage roof, and from his expression, I gathered the caller was talking about me. He hung up, shaking his head. "Sounds like you caused a scene."

"Me? Never."

"Hit anyone with a chair lately?"

In spite of everything, I laughed. "No, but I'll keep it in mind for next time."

"So where are we going?" Melissa opened the car door.

"Shadowtown. I need to talk to Lei."

I WASN'T READY TO ADMIT IT TO LUCEN, BUT OCCASIONALLY, having bodyguards was useful. Melissa dropped me off in front of Lei's shop and went to park while Gi escorted me inside. The rain had lightened, but I was just as glad not to have to walk in it.

In fact, being away from the meeting had lifted my mood considerably. Everything felt hopeless, but I no longer wanted to hit people.

Lei's shop was neither fancy nor particularly inviting, but it didn't need to be. Her work and reputation spoke for itself. She had no need to lure people in with decorative charm vials in the window or a fancy sign over the storefront.

People, be they preds or humans, came here because they wanted complicated or powerful spells, and they paid a lot to obtain them. The ones humans came here for were probably illegal or else they would have bought them from a magi, and no doubt they paid for them with their souls. There was a time not so long ago when I'd have been disgusted by that, but I had bigger issues.

Besides, I had to admit the information Devon had shared with me about why preds needed addicts had softened my attitude a bit. I could tell myself that as long as the pred treated their addicts well, it wasn't too terrible a situation for the humans.

I told myself that again now, although I still couldn't force myself to entirely believe it.

A harpy with cascading yellow and blue feathers down her head was mixing some sort of concoction in an obsidian bowl. "Can I help you?"

"I'm looking for Lei."

The harpy paused her mixing and cocked her head side to side. "She's busy."

"I need to talk to her about why the Gryphons questioned her this morning."

"You are a Gryphon. Ask them."

I groaned, and Gi tapped me on the shoulder. "Might not want to wear your jacket 'round here or carry so many weapons."

The Gryphon windbreaker. I'd forgotten I had it on, and I pulled it off. "Would you tell her Jessica Moore wants to talk to her? She should—"

"In here, Ms. Moore," Lei called out from the back room.

I smiled.

The other harpy returned to her concoction. "Go on then."

Gi stayed behind, commandeering one of the plush chairs in the shop's corner while I headed into the work area. I'd been back here before. When Lei had created her glamour for me, I'd had to spend several hours in her back room as she taught me how to use it. It looked much like the charm labs I'd since seen at Gryphon Headquarters, and much how I'd imagine a mundane chemistry lab might look. Only with more vile ingredients and stranger-smelling brews.

Lei gestured me to the small metal table in the corner, and she sat across from me. "I assure you, the Gryphons questioned me quite thoroughly this morning. I don't have anything left to tell."

I twisted my fingers together, thinking I should have approached this in a better way. Of course Lei wasn't going to enjoy explaining herself a second time. "The Gryphons are locking me out of the investigation about Olef."

"And what does this have to do with me?"

"I don't like being locked out. If they won't tell me what you told them, then I figure it's got to be important."

Lei stared at me a moment, then she laughed, a high cackling sound that once would have made the hairs on my neck stand on end. These days, I was able merely to consider it an unfortunate personality quirk. Lei wasn't nearly so sinister anymore. "The Gryphons chose well when they made you to be one of their elite, didn't they? You have to do everything on your own."

I wasn't sure if she was being sarcastic. "The Gryphons got lucky with me, but they don't appreciate it. They also chose Victor Aubrey."

Lei laughed again. "Point taken. I like you. Since you're the one responsible for setting this odd coalition into motion, I'll play along. I was in The Feathers the morning of Olef's death to meet with him. I am, unfortunately, probably the last person to have seen him alive."

I sat up straighter with surprise. Of all the reasons I could have imagined why Lei might be in the magi neighborhood—and admittedly, I couldn't imagine many—meeting with Olef was not one of them. Yet I wondered if I should have suspected something. There had to be a good reason why the Gryphons had released Lei so quickly, especially if she'd seen him the morning he was killed.

I made a guess. "Were you talking about the prophecy?"

Lei folded her fingers together. "Not quite. I'm not sure what path Olef was going down with the research he was doing for you, but he was asking me questions about magic. I went to his apartment so he wouldn't have to lug his books around. You find this odd?"

She was reading my emotions, and I could only hope she didn't think I was being rude. "A bit, yeah. No offense, but why would Olef ask you? Plenty of magi are skilled in magic even if Olef wasn't."

"I wouldn't say plenty. It's only plenty compared to humanity's lack of skilled charm makers." She looked so smug I was tempted to point out that a harpy's weakness was supposed to be jealously, not vanity. But Lei continued. "Magi are as different from our races as they are from yours. Magic is inherent in them. It's a force within them since they are born. With us, that's not true. Do you follow?"

I followed. Preds were made, not born. They were once humans with not a hint of a magical gift in their bodies. "So do you mean you work magic differently than magi?"

"Essentially. We react to it and can use it differently, which is why Olef wanted my perspective."

My phone buzzed, and I ignored it. "About what?"

"I'm honestly not entirely sure what he was getting at. He was keeping his motives secretive, but he was asking me about how we channel power. It made some sense because of what Dezzi told us about the Vessels, but Olef was asking about alternate ways we can do it. I don't think I was much help."

Alternate ways to channel power didn't make sense to me either. We weren't trying to channel anything. Our goal was to prevent the furies from being able to open the Pit, and to do that we needed to find the Vessels.

I bit my lip. "Did Olef ask you anything about a key?"

"A key? No. Key to what?"

"I have no clue. It was a long shot, but I was hoping you could tell me."

Lei looked at my phone, which buzzed again. "A key to the prison?"

"I had that thought, but he was telling me to use it. If the prison's locked, why would I want something that could unlock it?"

"Perhaps you need to find this key and the Vessels to prevent it being unlocked."

Tom and I had brainstormed the same thoughts yesterday, but the fact remained—he'd never heard of a key either. And next to Olef, Tom was the most knowledgeable person we had about any of this lore. "I guess I need to keep searching Olef's research."

"I do wish you luck, Ms. Moore. I'd have returned to the meeting today, except Xander." She grimaced. "Neither Eyff nor I thought it would be wise."

"Good call."

After I left, Gi and Melissa escorted me to Lucen's. I had to promise them I had no plans to go anywhere before they took off. Finally alone, not counting one grumpy pet dragon who was snorting in his cage, I plopped on the sofa.

I wanted to nap. Maybe eat some ice cream. But I also wanted to find Olef's killer and stop the furies, which meant no nap for me. I decided to compromise—make coffee, check if Lucen had any ice cream, then return to Olef's research. I had a couple of his books at the apartment. It wasn't much to work with, but it was something.

Before I could move from the couch, though, I remembered my messages. Both were from Tom and annoyingly uninformative. *Call me.*

Grumbling to myself, I did as asked. "Yes?"

"Have you calmed down?"

Ooh, moose tracks. Trust Lucen to only buy the good stuff. I pulled out the ice cream carton. "I'm about to eat ice cream. Does that sound like I'm calm? Why wouldn't you share what Lei told you?"

"You're still hung up on that?" He sighed. "It wasn't the time. Lei's information raised a whole lot of new questions for us to consider. I didn't want you getting sidetracked. I was going to tell you later."

I relegated myself to only taking a couple spoonfuls in a dish because I could probably stress-eat the entire carton if I wasn't careful. "So you weren't blowing me off?"

"Do you have to take everything in the worst possible way?"

"When it comes to your fraternity? Do you need to ask?"

Wisely, he ignored my comment. "I take it you spoke to Lei. Where are you?"

"Home." Close enough. "How's the meeting going?"

"It's not. I'm confident both the satyrs and the goblins have information about the Vessels that could be useful, but none of them are willing to share what they know."

Gooey chocolate melted on my tongue. My muscles seemed to melt with the ice cream. "How did you find that out?"

"I overheard the goblins from the High Council talking to Gunthra."

"Sloppy of them."

I could almost hear Tom smile. "They weren't aware of my presence."

"So you were spying? I approve."

"I'm so thrilled to have finally earned some respect from you."

I grinned and ate the last spoonful of ice cream. "Every now and then you manage, but don't think I'm happy about being removed from the investigation. I'm not done arguing."

"I wouldn't dream I'd be so lucky. Are you returning to the office?"

I stuck the dirty dishes in Lucen's dishwasher and wandered into the living room. "I have a couple of Olef's books here, and more to go on from Lei. So no. It's enough to keep me busy. Unless you plan to let me in on more secrets if I go in."

"Not today. Keep researching."

"Fine." I hung up on him and tossed the phone on the table.

A banging noise from behind alerted me that Sweetpea was up to no good. The dragon had apparently decided he was sick of being caged and was butting his head against the bars. "That makes two of us," I told him. "I feel like I'm doing exactly the same thing."

FOURTEEN

ALTHOUGH I CONSIDERED SWEETPEA AND MYSELF TO HAVE shared a bonding moment, the dragon didn't agree. Biting was more his style than bonding, but he eventually calmed down when he realized I wasn't going to let him out of the cage so he could sink his teeth into me.

"Hush, you," I muttered as he attacked the poor chew toy Lucen had given him.

My stomach rumbled, and I flipped the page in Olef's book. Since the meeting had broken up, I expected Lucen home soon, and I was trying to be good and wait for him to arrive so we could eat together. As he enjoyed pointing out, he was the better cook.

Alas, Olef's book was dry reading and therefore a poor distraction. Thanks to my conversation with Lei, I had an idea why he'd been reading it, but the content—magical theory—was mostly over my head. The Gryphons wanted me to study the topic too but at a much more basic level. As such, my eyes glazed over as I scanned the pages in hopes of finding words like "channel" or "key" or anything that would induce me to stop and read more thoroughly.

I was about to give up and text Lucen when someone knocked. Warily, I set the book down and traipsed to the narrow entryway that was squeezed between the living room and kitchen. Lucen had no peephole on the door, but he had a chain lock, which I made sure was in place.

Despite my caution, I'd been hoping for a friendly visitor. Maybe Devon coming by to tease me for storming out of the meeting, or Dezzi stopping in to express her displeasure.

I got Claudius. Fuck.

"Lucen's not home yet." I went to shut the door, but it never made it all the way.

The Upper Council satyr smiled down on me, and the effect was dizzying. My head clouded with his pheromones, and my lungs constricted.

At the meeting this afternoon, he'd been working none of his power on me, and I'd seen him as just another satyr. Another arrogant satyr. Someone I could have decked for his terribly timed sense of humor.

That man was gone. Too late, I realized Claudius had only been toying with me the first time we'd met. Now, when I gaped at him, my body was overwhelmed by his beauty and the primal lust he aroused. It seemed to settle on my skin like dew.

My tongue swept against my teeth, and my knees trembled. I wanted to kneel before him. Take him in my mouth. Already, I could taste the salty sweetness of his skin. Picture myself closing my lips around his cock, feel his hands pressing me closer, deeper, hear myself moaning as I pleasured him.

And even though some part of me knew he was inserting these images and desires in my mind, I couldn't fight them off. My immunity to pred power was shot to hell. I ached for him something fierce.

"Let me in, Jessica." He notched his head to the side. "I came to apologize for offending you earlier."

"So apologize." The protective glyphs the Gryphons had drawn on me warmed, but their magical shield proved thin.

Wet wind gusted outside, and Claudius's dark eyes gazed at me endearingly. "I thought I just did. Are you going to let me in?"

No. Absolutely not. Yet my traitorous right hand was releasing the chain lock, and my left was sliding over my breasts, clutching the fabric of my shirt and rubbing my hard nipples. I shivered.

The chain fell against the door, and I stepped back to let Claudius in. He shut the door behind him.

Realizing what my left hand was doing, I dropped it back to my side. My heart pounded, burning lust mixed with increasing fear. I should not have let him in. This could go bad so very fast, and I'd enjoy every second of it right until he left and I had to deal with the fallout. Lucen wouldn't care if I had sex with Claudius, but I would. No matter what my body was telling me, I did not want him touching me.

For the first time in a long while, I remembered very clearly why I'd been scared of preds. Why I'd stayed away from Lucen and denied my feelings for him for so long. When you couldn't tell a person no, you had no ability to tell them yes.

Backed against the wall, I inched away from Claudius. "Since you think you've already apologized, you can either give me another reason for staying or you can leave."

He chuckled. "You think you could kick me out?"

"I'm willing to try."

"Someone needs to teach you manners. That's not how a satyr speaks to her superiors. This is the second time today you've been insulting."

I crossed my arms in front of my chest, sensing he'd been staring at it. "Second time you've been too. Don't be a jackass, and I'll be nice."

Claudius turned his back on me, but I could see his shoulders shaking with amusement as he wandered deeper into Lucen's apartment. He'd changed out of the clothes he'd worn to the meeting earlier, opting for a tight black shirt and a pair of jeans that hugged his ass nicely.

Bad Jess. Stop staring at his ass. You're as terrible as he is.

"How am I being a jackass?" He stopped in front of Sweetpea's cage, and I was pleased to see the dragon growl at him.

"You're messing with my head."

He tossed me a glance over his shoulder. "Messing with it sounds very unsystematic. I'm testing you, Jessica. I want to see how much of a satyr you are."

"Not enough for you. You made that clear."

"No. And yet your very human reaction to me does intrigue. I've been alive a long time, you know. I've fucked kings and queens, heroes and villains, Gryphons and priests, and so many boring satyrs. But never someone with your unique magical signature. I'd like to remedy that."

Oh, God. My body wanted to remedy that too. Traitor, I silently cursed it, but it didn't care. Liquid heat pooled between my legs the moment Claudius uttered the word *fuck* like some erotic and terrible Pavlovian response.

If he was determined, there would be nothing I could do about it. My body didn't want me doing anything. My brain was screaming, *Oh, hell no*, but the stupid cluster of nerves between my legs was yelling, *Oh, please yes*.

The nerves got the better of my legs, and I shuffled forward then grasped the stairwell baluster, breathing hard. With one hand I reached under my shirt and grabbed the pendant Lucen had given me, clutching it tight, as though it could drive off these thoughts. All it did was up the aching in my breasts as my skin brushed them. My stance widened as I leaned against the railing.

Way to go, body. Just spread your legs for him.

Luckily, my brain had better control of my mouth than my limbs. "I don't think it's a good idea."

Okay, so maybe its control of my mouth was lacking a little force.

Sweetpea's cage was near the stairs, and it only took Claudius a couple steps to reach me. "You don't think? I'm doing you an honor."

I laughed shakily. "Why am I not surprised you believe you're that good?"

"You are feisty." He came up behind me, his body heat enveloping me. "I'm going to enjoy listening to you come and begging for more."

I held my breath as his hands lifted my shirt and slid around my waist. His touch was light and cool, and his fingertips sent sparks down my skin into my groin. I squirmed in his grip. Though I wanted to tell him to stop, my brain was disassociating from my body. And when he leaned over me and inhaled deeply at the crook of my neck, I actually moaned.

"Again," he whispered in my ear, and his breath was fire. His lips brushed my earlobe, and his hard body and a massive erection pressed against my ass. My legs spread wider, begging to take him in, and I was helpless not to do as he commanded. "Good girl."

Claudius pulled me away from the railing and shoved me against the wall. His fingers dug into my hips, slipping under the waistband of my jeans. My hands grabbed hold of his shirt, but I couldn't decide whether to push him away or rip it off.

"A true satyr wouldn't be fighting me," he whispered, bending in closer. I closed my eyes, intoxicated by his scent and enthralled with the sensation of his cock on my stomach. I rubbed myself against him, and he licked my collarbone and up my throat.

I gasped, struggling for words. "A true human couldn't fight you either."

That seemed to give him pause. "Your resistance is unusual, I admit. But I never said you were a pure human."

He withdrew suddenly, and I thought I might have won. Feared I might have too. My body was flushed from head to toe, and my breaths were nothing but a series of jagged gasps. Looking at Claudius's hard stomach muscles and the teasing bulge in his pants was going to drive me insane. I had to kick him out while I had a chance, but I couldn't do it.

He smiled slowly. "Dezzi told me what you could do. Let's see how strong you are, shall we?"

"What are you...?"

I crumpled to the stairs, and a horrible reality swept over me. Claudius hadn't just been working his wickedly tempting mojo on me. He'd been arousing me enough to have laid the groundwork for a pred-addict bond.

My nerves danced, and Claudius watched me writhe with an expression of such hunger that it fed my desire. I had to close my eyes, and only then could I sense his grip around my soul. It was surprisingly— or maybe unsurprisingly—pleasant. When the furies and sylphs had mentally assaulted me, it felt like a vise squeezing my head. With Claudius, his magic felt more like a pair of very skillful hands playing with my body.

But he was still a pred, and I knew what to do with preds who tried to addict me. *Test this.*

I stopped resisting and let him in. All at once, the whole of his power flooded me. I cried out, grasping at the stairs as it crescendoed through me, and I exploded in the least satisfying orgasm ever. My body felt like it rocked forever, but the release lasted a mere second.

I opened my eyes to see him wetting his lips in triumph as he watched me. My need for him was unabated. If I had the ability to stand, I'd have gone straight for his jeans, torn them off and taken his erection for myself. There was almost nothing left of me but pure, animal instinct.

Almost.

So instead I grabbed at his power. This was my test, after all. He wanted to see how strong I was, so I'd show him.

In my mind's eye, the bond connecting us was a circuit, a river of power with a current flowing almost entirely from me into him but for one measly tributary that closed the loop and connected us in the other direction. It was on the tributary that I focused my attention and yanked.

I felt the tug instantly, letting me know I'd snagged something. But unlike when I'd used this trick on Red-eye the fury or one of the sylphs, the circuit didn't reverse so easily. Claudius's pull was stronger. Much stronger. And my body didn't want to fight him or the glorious desire that immersed it. I wanted to give in and give up, let this struggle go and let him have his way with me.

Seething, I fought against myself as much as against him, and I tightened my grip. The current faltered and slowed, but it didn't reverse. Yet even that much effort made my head shriek in pain.

Clenching my jaw, I tried again, and I got the distinct sense that Claudius wasn't fighting me. This time when I pulled, a new tributary split off and more of his power slammed into me. The throbbing in my head picked up tempo. As good as my body felt, my head felt awful—a splitting pain like my skull had cracked open.

Then he released me.

I gasped, and my eyes watered in agony as I hunched over. "What the hell?"

"I have to say that was disappointing."

I winced as I raised my gaze to meet his. "I hate you."

Claudius threw his head back and laughed. "Why? Because you can't keep me out of your head like you do the others? That's hardly my fault. You're not as powerful as Dezzi led me to believe, nor—I'm guessing—as powerful as the Gryphons think you are. How do they expect you to stand up to the originals if you can't even fight me?"

I whimpered and rubbed my temples. "I have no clue what they expect me to do."

He knelt next to me and placed his hands on my arms. The desire that had grown cold in me, overpowered by my splitting head, returned. His warmth crept up my arms, and my pulse quickened once more. "You fear me, don't you? I can sense it. That's good. Fear goes a long way toward engendering the respect you owe me. Plus it can make other undertakings much more exciting."

Claudius ran his thumb over my lips. I was tempted to bite it, but that would likely give him the wrong idea.

"Can't tonight, honey. You gave me a headache."

"I could make it go away."

"You could. It's called leaving." The apartment door opened, and I breathed a sigh of relief.

"Jess?"

Claudius stood as Lucen appeared in the living room entryway. "You missed our tête-a-tête, Lucen. Jessica was showing me what she could do."

"Was she?" His voice was cold.

I glanced up at him, wanting to throw my arms around him but too weak to move. His face softened.

"Unfortunately, she's not as impressive as I was hoping," Claudius continued. "Being a strange human does not make her a satyr. More like an imperfect imitation of one. Though I imagine she has uses, that's hardly a reason to claim her as one of our own. I'll need to speak with Dezzi about her."

"Her is here, you know," I said through gritted teeth.

Claudius blew me a kiss. "We can try again another time." Then he nodded at a stunned-looking Lucen and left.

I flipped him off as the door shut.

Lucen dropped the bag he'd been holding and rushed over to me. "Little siren, are you okay? What did he do to you?"

I launched myself forward and fell onto him. Wrapping my arms around his neck, I felt better although I wasn't sure what throbbed worse —my head or the residual lust Claudius left behind. Either way, for the love of dragons, it was a terrible and unnatural combination.

"He said he was testing me." I burrowed my face against Lucen's shoulder. "First he seemed intent on sex, and when I resisted, he decided to test how strong my resistance to his magic was. He addicted me."

Lucen lifted my head and clasped my cheeks. His eyes burned green. "He did what?"

"I couldn't reverse the bond. I tried, and that's why my head is killing me. It didn't work on him."

Lucen's whole body shook with rage. He pulled me closer, hands entwining in my hair. "I'm going to kill him. If he didn't let you go…"

I'd have been screwed. The fear Claudius sensed in me rose to the surface, and I clutched Lucen tighter. "And you wonder why I used to be so afraid of you all."

"I'm going to kill him," Lucen said again. He took my mouth in his and kissed me hard and slow.

A moan climbed up my throat, all my unfulfilled need begging for his touch. I pressed myself closer, slipping my legs around him. When he released my lips, I nibbled at his chin, rubbed my face against his throat. "He started this. I want you to finish it. Make what I'm feeling yours."

Lucen set me back on the stairs, his hand trailing down my face and coming to rest cupping my breast. I inhaled sharply as he drew his thumb across my aching nipple. "Are you hurt?"

"A headache, but I'll live."

His hand moved on, sliding down my stomach and pausing at my waistband. "Let me get you something for the pain." He bent over, lifted my shirt and gently kissed my bare stomach.

My whole body quivered. "You'd better hurry. And then maybe carry me to a better spot because stairs are ouch, but I don't think I can move on my own yet."

Lucen unbuttoned my jeans and kissed me lower, eliciting more heat between my legs. "Remember how I once said that I don't care who you fuck? I've changed my mind. If he ever touches you again, I'm going to feed him his genitals."

Belatedly, I wished I hadn't taken off my weapons when I got to Lucen's. Maybe they would serve to deter Claudius next time. He might be too powerful for me to resist magically, but I was fairly certain salamander-forged steel could still kill him.

"I'd like to see that," I told Lucen, struggling upright. "Better yet, I'd like to be the one who does it."

FIFTEEN

THE PAIN-RELIEF CHARM LUCEN GAVE ME AFTER MY encounter with Claudius worked faster than any human-made remedy. When added to his own brand of spectacular sex and the Thai food he'd brought for dinner, I'd recovered my strength.

Or I thought I had. When I took off the charm later, my head still ached. Sleep helped some more, and by the next day I was back to normal. That it had taken almost twenty-four hours for me to get there didn't bode well for future confrontations.

I had a lot of time to dwell on what my weakness meant. Theo finished my charms the next morning, and I didn't object to as many protective or defensive spells as he felt compelled to add. My torso and arms were covered in a series of glyphs by the time I put my shirt on. After yesterday's encounter, however, I felt less than reassured by them.

As usual, I met with Tom, Ingrid and the others before the meeting, and I gave them a not-very-graphic rundown of what happened with Claudius. Their disappointment was palpable. Apparently, given how easily I'd flipped the bonds on other preds, they'd thought I could do better.

At least one good thing came out of my dismal failure. Because of my inability to fight off Claudius, I spared Grace the tedium of attending the day's meeting. Ingrid was growing eager to get her involved, but thanks to my difficulties, she opted to hold Grace back a while longer to better educate her.

I questioned Tom about Mitch and Olef, and predictably learned nothing useful about the former and only more confusion about the latter. The lab had positively identified the red feather found in Olef's apartment as belonging to a magi. But which magi, and did it matter?

I couldn't believe Olef's murder was unconnected to the prophecy, and I suspected the feather was a false clue. Tom didn't disagree, but the Gryphons had to be thorough and investigate every lead just in case.

With some trepidation and no small amount of dread, we arrived at the hotel for day three of the meeting from hell. Gunthra inquired after my health while the Gryphons set up the one thing certain to horrify humans, preds, and magi alike—a PowerPoint presentation on the Vessels.

The High Council goblins watched me curiously, and now that I knew enough to fear them, I stayed as far away as possible. "I'm fine, thanks," I said to Gunthra, hoping she only asked out of politeness and not for a more sinister reason.

The satyrs arrived next, and I dug my nails into my palms, hoping the completed glyph Theo had drawn was powerful enough to hide my anger and disgust from Claudius. Somehow I suspected not.

Devon had returned with them today, and the way he and Lucen circled around me like a couple of guard dogs was enough to let me know Lucen had shared what happened with his best friend. While I appreciated their protective instincts, it all felt rather suffocating. Especially since if Claudius wanted to harass me, all their hovering wouldn't actually do any good.

And then we waited. And waited some more. I sipped my increasingly cool coffee, more convinced with each passing minute that, after what happened yesterday, neither the harpies nor Xander were going to attend.

Ten minutes beyond the agreed-upon start time, Ingrid gave up and called for the meeting to begin. The tension in the air settled a bit while Tom reviewed the information we knew about the Vessels, including where some of them were rumored to have been hidden, but once he finished and asked for others to share their knowledge, an uncomfortable silence descended on the room.

Claudius was the first to break it. "You're asking me to share secrets, which I can't even say exist, on the basis of a flimsily held together theory and the vision of a dead prophet."

My hands clenched into fists beneath the table. Though at this point, all it took was hearing Claudius's voice to set my teeth on edge.

"We've been over the evidence," Ingrid said. "It is much stronger than you make it out to be. If you do not want to share what you know, then it will be on your head if the furies succeed in opening the Pit. If the histories are believed, you will regret it."

"Perhaps." Claudius stroked his chin, adopting an expression of the unconcerned. "But it occurs to me there might be a simpler solution than scouring the world in search of artifacts that may well have been destroyed centuries ago."

I felt his amusement blossom in my mind, an ethereal buzzing in my skull like an imp's wings. And like an imp, I wanted to smack it away. Instead, I gave his emotions a mental shove, but it didn't help. Claudius's brown eyes sparkled with amusement.

"What did you have in mind?" Dezzi asked, voicing the question everyone was clearly wondering.

Claudius stretched his arms. "You are all certain Jessica is tied to this prophecy, and Jessica is convinced the furies have been trying to keep her alive. Therefore, it stands to reason that they need her for something. If we killed her, they can't have her. Game over."

The room exploded. This time, I wasn't one of the people yelling. I gawked at Claudius, and the asshole smirked at me.

The smirk knocked the shock right out of me. I seethed, focusing all my fury and hate at him. Devon had once told me being around too much lust could make a satyr queasy, like gorging on a high-fat meal. I sincerely hoped too much negativity could give Claudius an upset stomach.

"We will not tolerate comments like that." Tom's face was red with anger. "If you can't keep it civil..." He trailed off, at a loss for a useful threat.

"It wasn't a pointless comment," Claudius said. By all appearances he was unfazed by either the furor he'd caused or the emotional punch I kept trying to throw at him. "It was a serious suggestion. You created Jessica to be a warrior. Perhaps this was meant to be her battle. A sacrifice."

I inhaled deeply, noticing that Lucen was hovering over me. I could forgive him for it this time. "You're an asshole," I told Claudius.

"The satyr has a point," Ulan said, and everyone's heads swiveled in the goblin's direction. "If the woman is somehow the key to all this, then her death could put an end to it."

"Could." Lucen gripped the back of my chair, his knuckles white. "You have no proof."

"Lucen, sit down." Dezzi spoke quietly, but her tone was firm.

Claudius turned a very critical eye on Lucen. The amusement I'd felt was gone, replaced by something cold. "You have little proof of anything. Why deny this but believe the rest?"

Dezzi's hand shot out, and she grabbed Lucen's wrist. "Sit. Now."

"Do it," I whispered. He was drawing Claudius's wrath. I could feel it. I didn't give a damn what Claudius thought of me, but I suspected Lucen could be in real trouble if the Upper Council was displeased with him.

Lucen sat, but his face was hard. The cinnamon scent of his pheromones was as potent as I'd ever noticed, but I was too angry and worried to register any lust. Throwing off power was simply what preds did when their emotions were heightened.

Tom also returned to his chair, but his hand hovered near the hilt of his sword as he did. "We are not entertaining this idea. End of discussion."

I reached toward my own waist and patted my knife for good measure. "No, we're not."

"I thought you were serious about stopping the furies." Claudius raised an eyebrow. "Dezdemona, what do you think?"

Dezzi looked as though she'd swallowed something foul, and she fidgeted with the bracelets around her wrist. Her gaze flickered once toward Lucen, or maybe toward me. "It at least deserves discussion."

My stomach sank, but what could I expect? Openly defying Claudius was a terrible move for her, and besides, I had no reason to believe she had any true loyalty to me. Maybe if I'd accepted her offer to join her council, things would be different. She'd have reason to defend me. Then again, perhaps not. I doubted such a move would have helped my case with Claudius. His feelings toward me were clear. Having joined the satyr council would probably only have lowered Claudius's opinion of Dezzi.

A muscle in Lucen's jaw twitched, and he flexed his fingers on his lap. The cords of muscle in his arms flexed with it, and I could only guess what he was thinking. Thank dragons, though, he kept his mouth shut.

I couldn't even look at Devon. He sat on Claudius's far side, so it would have required seeing Claudius too. Devon's silence could mean anything, but I had no reason to believe his opinion would differ from Dezzi's.

Gunthra cleared her throat, and her gaze met mine across the table. She was curiously unreadable. "I'm not sure it's wise to discuss anything so drastic while some members of this alliance are absent."

"On the contrary," Ulan said. "There is no need for the harpies to be involved at all, and if that pompous magi can't bring himself to attend the meeting, then he abdicates responsibility. Time might be of the essence. We should be willing to discuss all possibilities and ideas, not just those the Gryphons wish to put forth. The woman's full potential should be on the table, dead or alive."

"The woman is right here." My words came out like a growl. "And she is not going to sit around and listen to you discuss killing her as a solution when the only reason he brought it up—" I pointed to Claudius, unable to spit out his name, "—is because he considers me an imperfect satyr and is looking for an excuse to get rid of me."

Lucen reached for my hand, and I shook his off before he did anything else reckless. "Jess."

I stood. "You know what my opinion is. Have your talk without me."

For the second day in a row, I got up and stormed out of the room.

Someone hurried after me as I approached the elevator. Hoping it wasn't Lucen, I turned, and my shoulders sagged in relief at seeing Tom. "Don't expect me to go back in today and listen to this."

"I don't."

The elevator arrived, and Tom stepped inside with me. The blood had faded from his face, and his stress was evident in the dark circles beneath his eyes. For a moment, I felt bad for him. Tom was as much a pain in my ass as Claudius, but I was starting to accept that his intentions were good even if his methods left much to be desired.

"You following me?" I asked.

He shook his head. "I need to go back. More voices of reason are required. You should go to Headquarters and continue your training."

"I should go to Headquarters and help find Olef's murderer. We need the magi's involvement, and that means we need to get to the bottom of it. Even if we can't point fingers at a specific fury, pointing to their race would help."

"I agree, but especially in light of what's going on in the meeting, I think it's more important than ever that you prove how much more useful you are alive than dead." The elevator stopped on the ground floor. Tom held the door open with his hand but stayed put. "Skip reading about laws and regulations, and practice your magic and how to kill things."

Actually that didn't sound like a bad idea. I knew exactly whose head I would imagine during target practice.

SIXTEEN

Instead of heading straight to the shooting range when I got to Headquarter's training facility, I changed into my workout clothes and went to the gym.

Until Tom had showed me this place a week ago, I hadn't known the building housed any such thing in the basement. But house a gym it did, and a nice one too. It made sense that the Gryphons would want training and exercise space nearby for their use.

Stepping into the gym, I stretched my arms over my head and inhaled the scent of rubber and stale sweat. Gross, yet comfortingly familiar. The gym was divided into two sections, half given over to your standard equipment—treadmills and weight benches and the like—and the other half to more combat-style training. The latter side contained two punching bags and several large mats. On the walls, an array of practice weapons had been hung, along with body padding to facilitate sparring.

My gaze rested on the punching bags. They sounded about right for my mood. I'd been wanting to punch someone for days, and if I couldn't actually hit Claudius for what he'd done, I could pretend to.

Besides me, the gym was mostly empty. A Gryphon who had on a pair of headphones was using a treadmill, and she ignored me. I adjusted my ponytail, did a series of light stretches, then began whaling on one of the bags.

The rush of endorphins did wonders for my mood even though I suspected my muscles weren't going to be pleased tomorrow. I should have been holding back, focusing on technique and good form. But naturally I wasn't. With every punch I threw, I envisioned the bag as Claudius's face, and the only thing that mattered was power. I wanted to smash his perfect nose into a pancake, and so I grew sore and tired way too quickly.

"Whoa there, ex-partner. You're going to hurt something."

I dropped a roundhouse kick on the bag in frustration and spun to face Andre. "I didn't see you come in."

"I don't think you've been seeing anything. Someone having a bad day?"

I bent over, catching my breath and flexing my knuckles. "Let's just say that right now a group of preds are calmly discussing whether they should kill me for the good of all living creatures."

To his credit, Andre didn't ask why. "I suppose that would be a no. I'm also thinking this isn't the first time preds have pondered killing you."

"No, but it is the first time the word 'good' has factored into their decision."

Andre set his phone down on his sweatshirt. "Since when do preds care for the good of anything except themselves?"

"Well, as was once pointed out to me, dead humans make for lousy food, and the end of the world as we know it would leave lots of dead humans."

"I guess that's true. So you're planning on bringing about the end of the world, are you?"

I just smiled and silently cursed my slip-up. Andre didn't press.

Sweat ran down my nose, and I wiped it away, listening to the rhythmic sound of the treadmill. Memories of the night Andre and I had almost died played through my head, unbidden and unwanted. Andre half-naked, straddling me, the sweat running down his taut stomach. Me clawing at his pants zipper and wrapping my hands...

I remained bent over longer, pretending to pant for air that I no longer needed so I didn't have to look at him. Damn Lucrezia and the way she'd cursed us.

Judging by the potent pickled-olive taste of Andre's embarrassment, he was having similar flashbacks.

Had events gone differently, I might have slept with Andre anyway. I'd certainly thought about it at the time, and I could tell he had too. Ultimately, though, there never would have been anything between us except friendship. I was done contemplating normal—aka human— relationships, but Lucrezia's schemes had made even my memories a challenge.

"How's your head?" I asked, biting my lip.

"Good," Andre said, a little too enthusiastically. "My head healed fine. My psyche is another story, but that's not your fault."

I offered him my best attempt at a smile, but it came out more like a cringe. "I look forward to testifying at Lucrezia's trial."

Assuming I lived long enough.

"Honestly, I can't say the same." Andre gave me a look of disbelief as he started stretching. "I am not ready to have everything that happened that night become public knowledge."

"I was assuming we wouldn't have to delve into the more salacious details."

Andre's expression suggested I might be assuming too much. "Let's hope not. By the way, I could use a sparring partner, and I do believe someone told me you're supposed to be doing weapons training."

"You want to spar?"

Andre smiled hesitantly. "So long as no chairs are involved. Let's go for it."

The longer we talked, the weaker his emotions tasted, and consequently, my own discomfort eased with his. It was about time. My life could be going to hell everywhere else, but if I could salvage a friendship, the day wouldn't be a total disaster.

Some of my gloomy mood lifted. "Let's."

Andre picked up one of the practice blades that imitated a standard-sized Gryphon sword. "You game?"

"Sure." I grabbed a matching one and swung it around a few times, loosening my wrists. "So any movement on Olef's case?"

Andre pulled on a pair of gloves. "Not much. We've started interviewing neighbors and associates, gathering financials, all the usual. You still think the case is connected to what you're working on?"

"Positive. I don't think you're going to find a motive by interviewing people."

"Uh-huh." He strolled to the center of the nearest mat, swinging his arms. "Yet there's obviously a motive. What is it? If you suspect something, I don't get why I haven't been told."

"Talk to Tom."

Andre grunted. "That's like talking to a wall."

I laughed and started to make a joke about walls being friendlier, then changed my mind. A new idea was occurring to me. If my assumption about why Olef was killed was correct, it meant the furies had found out he possessed crucial information. And how would they have done that? It was certainly possible they'd managed it on their own, but it was also possible—perhaps even likely—they'd found out the same way they'd found out about Phoenix.

What if someone in the Brotherhood had clued them in to Olef's research or the many visions he'd had?

I lowered my voice. "This might not be related to your case exactly, but then again. I think someone in the Gryphons might be leaking sensitive information to the furies, and that might be what got Olef killed."

Andre stared at me a moment, and I hoped he'd be curious enough to take the bait. "That's a serious accusation."

"Against a potentially very powerful Gryphon, which is probably why the people I've mentioned it to are reluctant to do much investigating. But I'd bet my life that Olef's death is due to the furies, and that could make it the second time confidential information has reached them. I don't believe it's a coincidence."

Andre raised his practice blade. "You have suspects?"

I adjusted my stance, mimicking Andre's form. While I'd taken martial arts since I was a kid, the Gryphons had their own unique fighting style, one that relied heavily on speed. With short, quick strikes, they danced in and out of an opponent's immediate range. It would minimize the length of time a Gryphon needed to get close to a pred, and since all it took was a nick with a salamander fire-forged blade to do serious damage, they didn't need any fancy moves to disarm or disable their opponents.

"I have a list of possibilities, but not the means to investigate them myself." I batted my eyelashes in an attempt to lighten the seriousness of what I was suggesting.

Andre snorted, but he looked thoughtful too. "Send it to me, and I'll see what I can find out. No promises."

A heavy weight lifted from my shoulders. Although I knew checking out my list of names couldn't be Andre's top priority, it was more than I could do on my own. I'd take what I could get. "That would be awesome."

To thank him, I lunged at Andre, and he easily countered.

For the next forty-five minutes, we jumped and skittered around the mat, him offering tips and me occasionally sharing some of my own while we smacked the crap out of each other.

Sweat rolled down my back, and Andre's tan skin gleamed with it. Given his skill and greater size, I felt good knowing I'd made him work. Not only would I be sore tomorrow, I'd be bruised. But it would be worth it. With every hit or laugh, the past dissipated. We weren't just beating each other up, but our awkward memories as well.

In fact, the exercise had been exactly what I needed to soothe the edges on multiple areas of my life. Endorphins were wonderful. Claudius's threat and the meeting's lack of progress hung over my head, but I was able to ignore them temporarily, lost in the need to dodge, block, and attack.

When we called it quits, I chugged some water and hung up the practice blade, breathing hard and thinking about next moves. A good first one would be to call Lucen or Tom and find out what was happening at the meeting. If the meeting was still going on, that was.

Andre wiped his face with a towel. "Look at that. I think it's beer o'clock."

As I checked the time, my stomach growled. "A beer sounds pretty good."

"I'm not surprised. You looked like you needed one, or three, earlier."

"More like a six-pack."

Andre grinned. "You got time?"

Biting my lip, I checked the clock again. Why not? I liked hanging out with Andre, and I especially liked things between us returning to normal. Nothing said I couldn't text Tom or Lucen from a bar. "Sure."

Showered and changed into my street clothes, I met Andre in the lobby fifteen minutes later.

"I've rounded up a few more people," Andre said as we headed outside. "They'll meet us in about ten minutes."

The bar Andre had in mind was one I'd gone to with him once before. It was a few blocks from Headquarters, squished between a chain restaurant and an office supply store. Around this time of day it would be packed as businesses emptied for the evening and happy hour turned into hours, plural.

Yesterday's rain had lifted, but the air felt ripe with a storm, and the dark clouds to the southwest and falling pressure suggested more bad weather wasn't far away. Over my shoulder, I noticed with mild amusement that Gi and Melissa were following us. They wouldn't run up and flank me with a Gryphon at my side, so instead they literally watched my back.

Andre had been talking about Olef's case again, but halfway down the block he paused abruptly in mid-sentence, frowned and scanned the street. "We have company somewhere. Funny place for it."

"Company?" It dawned on me what he meant as I asked. Gryphons trained their magical senses to pick up on preds. Once, back when I'd gone to the Gryphon pre-training Academy, I'd been able to do the same. I could have detected a feeling of cold, unnatural power radiating from a pred yards away. I'd lost the ability ages ago, but Andre wouldn't have. "The funny case I'm working on has funny implications. I have a couple satyrs acting as my bodyguards. They're behind us."

Andre snorted. "Satyr bodyguards. Only you, Jess." He resumed walking, but his frown returned almost as quickly. "Do you literally mean a couple. As in two?"

"Yeah, why?" My phone buzzed and I pulled it out, hoping it was Tom or Lucen, but it was an unknown number sending me a text. I almost ignored it, but my gut told me not to.

We think you have tails. A brown jacket and a blue shirt. Disguise charms.

I swallowed, checking the street's reflection in a storefront window as I passed. I saw nothing amiss, but Gi and Melissa had increased their pace, closing the distance, and Melissa had her phone out. She was the one who'd texted me.

I tucked my phone away and carefully adjusted my bag so that my hand brushed Misery's hilt at my hip. The gun from Tom was in my bag, but I wasn't about to whip that out on a busy street unless I had no other option. Alas, without knowing what I was dealing with, the knife might not be the most useful weapon either. Andre carried a similar blade, at least. Not all Gryphons did when off-duty.

"How many do you sense?" I asked, my voice low. "My bodyguards think I have tails."

"Great. I sense three preds behind us, possibly more."

We passed another large window, but I couldn't make out who Brown Jacket or Blue Shirt might be in the crowd. Who or what, for that matter. And while I was at it, why? Was I merely being spied on, or was something more sinister afoot? I wanted to find Mitch, but not by being another kidnapping victim.

We were almost at the bar. The best plan I could come up with was to take shelter inside and get a good look at my tails from within. If they followed us through the doorway, even better. Then we could grab them in the confined space.

I touched Andre's arm lightly. "I think—"

The opposite side of the street suddenly lit up like a camera flash. Blinding white burned my retinas. Instinctively, I dove low, but the explosion my reflexes anticipated never happened. Instead, everything went pitch-black a second later. Holding my breath, I stayed down. People screamed and tires squealed, followed by the unmistakable sound of crashing cars.

"Jess!" Andre's voice was right in my ears, but I couldn't see him. The light had temporarily blinded me, and now the darkness along the street was absolute, as though someone had flipped a switch from day to night.

Though it was a night without stars or streetlamps, an eerie, thick darkness that could only be the result of magic.

I could hear chaos spreading all around me, the street shuddering to a panicked stop. People shouted and sirens wailed. Pounding feet beat against the sidewalk.

No, that made no sense. The darkness was complete. No one should be running in it. But someone—or someones—was, and I sensed no emotions tied to those feet.

My tails. They must be wearing some sort of anti-magic to protect their eyes.

I grabbed Misery as Andre yelled my name again. He'd sensed them too. Blindly, I spun around with the knife, hoping to keep whoever approached far enough away to prevent an attack. Dark lines and blurry shapes shifted before my eyes as my pupils struggled to readjust. The immediate area was magically black, but pinpricks of light were reappearing. Headlights and phone lights sliced through the darkness, and the curse itself was slowly fading.

One of the tails was on me. Blue or brown, I couldn't see well enough to distinguish, but he carried a knife of his own. The switchblade's sheen caught the light from Andre's keychain flashlight.

Heart pounding, trying not to think how close that blade might have come to my ribs, I lashed out again, driving my attacker back toward the street. Where was the other one? Melissa had said two. And if there were two here, then how many more were across the street? Someone had to have set off the curse.

"Drop it," I warned the guy. "Maybe you can't see the black blade, but my knife's bigger and will do more damage."

The attacker hesitated. Clearly, he could see the blade, or he was sensing that I wasn't lying about it.

Then Andre was there, behind my attacker, flashlight in one hand, his knife in the other. "So is mine."

I squinted as the street lightened some more, and fresh sirens—the distinct sound of Gryphon ones—grew louder. The guy with the switchblade glanced between me and Andre. His eyes widened farther when he stared down the street. His hand twitched, then cursing, he dropped his knife.

Doing my best to hold steady, I took a cautious step forward. To my left, I heard more cursing and Gi's voice telling someone to shut up. Trusting that meant the satyrs got this guy's partner, I kept my eyes on him and Misery near his throat. Andre pulled out a zip tie and bound his hands.

"You got another of those?" Melissa asked, appearing at Andre's side.

He gave her an odd look, and I could taste the lust spreading through his core thanks to her proximity. "You helping us arrest goblins?"

Melissa made a noncommittal noise and took the tie. "I'd rather kill them and be done with it, but they should be questioned."

I re-sheathed my knife. "Goblins?" Now that Andre had mentioned it, I could sense the goblin's greedy effect on his emotions too. That must have been how he figured it out.

"Sure feels that way to me." Andre shoved the attacker forward.

As the blackness gave way to a heavy gray that dulled the block like a photographic filter, I could tell we'd nabbed Blue Shirt. Gi and Melissa had captured Brown Jacket, and they marched him over to us. The goblins, who weren't looking very goblin-like at the moment, glared defiantly at us.

"Satyrs working with Gryphons." Brown Jacket spit by Melissa's feet.

She backhanded him.

Andre got out his phone, muttering something about how he'd pretend not to see that.

"Why?" I asked the goblins as Andre called in to HQ.

"Orders," Blue Shirt said.

The satyrs exchanged confused expressions, but a chill ran through my blood. "The satyr has a point," Ulan had said. "Her death could put an end to it."

But that was only a couple hours ago. Could he or Gunthra have ordered a hit so quickly, and while the meeting was supposed to be in progress?

I stuffed my hands in my pockets, but I couldn't hide my nerves or the despair that was hitting me anew. All my exercise-induced endorphins were gone. No beer or renewed friendships were going to make this day any better.

If Gunthra had gone ahead and ordered some of her people to take me out, then this alliance was already over. Any hope for salvaging the truce and forestalling the prophecy was gone. We were well and truly fucked.

Naturally, it was a satyr who had started it all.

SEVENTEEN

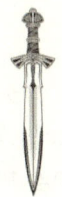

The unnatural darkness had vanished completely by the time I returned to Headquarters. The block was awash in the blue, red, and golden lights of police cars, ambulances, fire trucks, and, of course, Gryphon emergency vehicles.

But dealing with the innocent victims and the fallout from the goblins' attack was someone else's problem. In the bland hallway by the Gryphons' interrogation rooms, I paced and waited. The two goblins we'd arrested had been stripped of their disguises, separated, and were in the process of being questioned. Meanwhile, Gunthra, Ulan, and their big-eared company were being hauled in. The satyrs, or Lucen anyway, would be right behind them. He'd called immediately once news had broken at the meeting.

Andre shut one of the doors then banged a fist against the wall. "They're waiting for their lawyer. How are you?"

I forced my feet to quit moving, but that resulted in me swaying in place. I was too jacked up on adrenaline, my own misery and Andre's anger to hold still. "I'll be fine. Not the first time someone's tried to kill me in the past week. I'm just furious because…"

Because any progress we'd made was gone. Any hope of working together was over. I should have known better. Known it couldn't and wouldn't work. But I'd given over to hope—that most vulgar of four-letter words—because I couldn't imagine how to tackle this problem on my own.

I was going to have to start imagining, and fast.

"Jess?"

I snapped out of it and pushed my hair from my face. I couldn't vent to Andre. "It's a complicated case, and this is related to it."

"I could help if—"

"You knew more. Yeah, I know. I could use all the help I can get, but it's not my call." If it were, I'd tell Andre immediately. I'd tell lots of people. The more heads working together, the better, especially if nonhuman heads were going to be unreliable at best and dangerous at worst.

Unfortunately, I also understood *Le Confrérie's* reasons for keeping quiet. Most Gryphons would have no prior knowledge about what we were dealing with, so lots of education and explanations would be required. Word getting out to the population at large could lead to panic. And, most importantly, we'd originally thought we could keep a low profile so the furies wouldn't discover we were working against them, thus buying us time.

The last reason might no longer apply if my theories about Mitch's abduction and Olef's murder were right, but I'd defer to Tom and the others to make the call about sharing information. Much as I loathed it, I needed their support like they needed mine. If that meant letting them make some decisions for me, I'd do it. For now.

Commotion elsewhere broke up our conversation, and the double doors into the hallway flew open. Four seriously pissed-off-looking goblins, each with their hands bound, were marched toward us. Behind them strode Gryphons and satyrs, also livid. Well, except for Claudius, who appeared unable to remove the smirk from his face.

My hands clenched into fists behind my back. I'd been kidding myself if I thought punching an inanimate object was anywhere near as satisfying as punching him would be.

Ulan refused to look at me as one of the Gryphons stuffed him inside an empty room, but Gunthra did the opposite, watching me until a door closed behind her. Of all the goblins, her face was the least hardened, her expression almost contemplative. Since those were her goblins we'd arrested, I wasn't sure what to make of it.

Lucen reached for me, but I drew back, not letting him touch me while Claudius was nearby. His jaw tightened.

The last interrogation room door shut, and Tom spun around. "Everybody out."

"Are you talking to me too?" I asked.

"Yes, I'm talking to everyone. Everyone get out while we question people." The Southern twang in his accent was thicker than I'd ever heard it. So I wasn't the only one losing my shit. Peachy.

Andre pointed back through the door. "There's an empty meeting room that way."

I pushed through the crowd, brushing Lucen's hand with a single finger as I did, hoping the gesture would go unnoticed by his evil overlord yet let him know I was thinking of him. "This way, come on."

Surprisingly, the satyrs followed, but perhaps that was only so they could have some relative privacy in which to argue. Ingrid, Theo, and the other Gryphons from World came along. Tom remained behind with Andre, presumably to question the goblins.

As soon as the door slammed, Lucen turned on Claudius. "This is all your fault."

I sucked in a breath, willing him to shut up.

"Lucen, calm down," Dezzi said. It was clearly an order, not a suggestion.

"With all due respect, Dez, we're supposed to be okay with him nearly getting one of our own killed?"

Dezzi pulled out a chair and gestured to it. "She's not one of our own."

Lucen ignored the chair. "Are you forgetting—?"

"I am not forgetting anything." Dezzi's dark eyes seemed to glow, and I could have sworn at that moment she grew several inches to tower over Lucen. Power leaked off her, and I inadvertently pressed myself against the wall, heart hammering. "You are forgetting your place. If you continue to forget it, you will lose it. Understood?"

Lucen held her gaze for a moment, and I prayed he did understand.

Dezzi hadn't forgotten she'd offered me a council spot, but she sure didn't need Claudius finding out about it. She also didn't condone what had been done, but she was stuck in one hell of a nasty position—trying to protect herself, her domus, including Lucen, and appease Claudius at the same time.

Across the room, Devon loosened his tie. Unless he'd spoken up after I left earlier, he was being uncharacteristically quiet. A smart move since there wasn't much good to be said.

Claudius's smirk finally disappeared. "Dezzi, if you're having trouble controlling some of your council members—"

"I am not having trouble."

Lucen took the cue and sat, but his face was so dark and tight that my jaw clenched for him.

"Good." Claudius tossed his hair behind his shoulders. "Then we all acknowledge there is no fault here except for that which belongs to the failed goblin assassins. I simply made a suggestion for discussion."

"There will be no more discussion of anything resembling cold-blooded murder," Ingrid said.

I started, so caught up in the satyr power struggle that I'd forgotten the Gryphons had joined us.

Discussion circled the drain for the next half hour, if it could even be said to get that far. Our drain was clogged with suspicion, disgust, and dislike, and though we circled, there wasn't so much as a trickle of progress.

After five minutes, I'd tuned out the conversation. The way I saw it, the chances of getting anything useful accomplished were over. My best bet was trying to figure out whatever Olef had meant by using a key and going about searching for the remaining Vessels alone.

Make that a Vessel. One. Logically, that was all we needed. The furies couldn't open the Pit without all five, so if we got our hands on one, we'd have thwarted them. The Gryphons must have information on the one left in their care, even if Tom hadn't found it yet.

There was a flaw in this plan, naturally. The furies had two, possibly more. One of the ones they had might have been the lone Vessel the Gryphons had information on. Because of that, it would be ideal if I could get my hands on the information the satyrs and goblins had brought too. But that meant going through Claudius and Ulan.

Yet there had to be a way. I simply needed to figure out what it was, preferably including a plan that didn't involve Lucen. Being kicked off Dezzi's council was probably the least terrible of all the things that could happen to him if he kept challenging Claudius.

Tom stuck his head through the doorway and beckoned me over. "Come on."

I wasn't thrilled to have my thoughts interrupted, but leaving the tense room was a relief. "What's up?"

"Gunthra wants to speak to you."

"To me? Why?"

He paused outside one of the interrogation rooms, his hand on the doorknob. "Couldn't tell you. Feel free to share when you find out."

My stomach twisted as he opened the door. I'd already had way more dealings with the goblin Dom than I'd ever wanted, and since she'd tried to have me killed, I was less inclined than ever to talk to her.

Gunthra sat with her hands folded at the metal table in the center of the room. I shut the door behind me and faced her.

"I'm pleased to see you are unharmed," she said.

Goblins liked to stare at people without blinking. Whether it was normal behavior for them or merely a trick to unnerve humans, I couldn't say. But I did the same to her now, letting the silence drag out before breaking it. "Yeah? Then next time don't order a hit on me."

She toyed with the pearl buttons on her sleeve cuff. "I've denied having anything to do with that."

"Which isn't the same as telling me you had nothing to do with that. I'm getting better at playing your word games, and I'm not interested in making any deals."

Gunthra spread open her hands innocently. "No deals. I owe you, Miss Moore, for this unfortunate situation."

I crossed my arms. "Meaning?"

"Meaning..." She paused, glancing up at the camera in the corner. Her shoulders sagged. "I believe my superiors are acting rashly. Fear and mistrust do not engender wise decisions."

I couldn't help but think of Xander and his unfounded accusations. "Tell me something I don't know."

"Four-fifty-two. You didn't know that."

"What?"

Her large eyes widened farther. "That is the room number for the High Council goblins. You've proven to be a clever woman. Do with the information what you see fit."

My mouth went dry, and I snapped my lips together. It was as though Gunthra had been pondering the same things I'd been pondering several rooms down. Either that or she'd been reading my mind and not merely my emotions. Creepy.

But damn useful. Part of me whispered that I'd been too quick to condemn Gunthra. Her hands might be as tied as Dezzi's were with regards to having her superiors breathing down her neck, but she'd been on to the furies from the beginning. She'd studied the situation and had been driven by desperation and her convictions to make deals with me to learn more information.

Gunthra would not act rashly. Neither by trying to kill me, nor by handing over Ulan's hotel room number. She'd thought this through and come to the same conclusion as I had—the only way to get shit done was for one of us to say "the hell with it" and just do it.

Tom believed the goblins had brought information with them. Gunthra had given me a push in the direction to finding it.

My pulse hammered in my ears. "I will."

"Good, and good luck."

Head spinning, I left the room and crashed into Tom, who must have been standing right by the door.

"What did she want?"

I checked up and down the hallway. Andre had disappeared, but a few other Gryphons roamed about. "Any of these rooms open?"

Gathering I wanted privacy, Tom headed down the hall away from the interrogation rooms and led me into one of the dull beige conference rooms not far from where the Gryphons and satyrs were butting heads. He closed the door and blocked it with his body. "So?"

I fingered the pendant beneath my shirt. "First, tell me your opinion. Do we really need the goblins and satyrs to find the Vessels?"

Tom's eyebrows shot up. "Honestly, I don't know. I thought so, but we haven't begun to scratch the surface of everything at World's archives. All I can tell you is what the texts I've found say, and they say each group in the original alliance took a Vessel with them. So we probably don't have everything we need without their cooperation."

"Okay, but think about this. We only need one, right? Just one is all it takes to prevent the furies from opening the Pit. Is it possible information about one of them is buried at the archives still?"

"Anything is possible. I have a researcher working on it full-time, but she hasn't discovered much yet. When I say the archives are huge, Jessica, I mean enormous and not necessarily well-organized. Very few Gryphons are interested in becoming librarians, and Gryphon policy isn't to allow non-Gryphons a lot of access because of the magic involved."

I closed my eyes and took a deep breath. "So what if we went and dug some more ourselves? Both for the Vessel and for more information about this key Olef mentioned."

"We never did search the archives for anything about a key because we had no reason to." Tom scratched his neck. "What are you thinking exactly, and what does this have to do with why Gunthra talked to you?"

I released my grip on the pendant before I accidentally yanked it off. "I'm thinking this alliance is a failure. Neither the satyrs or goblins are going to share willingly, and I don't much feel like hanging around and waiting for the next batch of assassins or the furies to make their move on me. I want to take what these people know and disappear. Specifically, disappear to France and go through the archives using Olef's key and their information as a starting point."

I held my breath while Tom seemed to debate internally. "How will you get their information?"

"I have a plan, which is where Gunthra comes in, and you're better off not knowing it."

With a great exhale, Tom's interest collapsed. "Forget it. You need to tell me what you're up to."

I gripped the table behind me in frustration. He was so close to going for this. "Later. We still don't know how the furies found out about Phoenix. The fewer people who know anything, the better. I'll tell you all when you come to France with me, but we leave Ingrid and the others here without them knowing what I'm doing."

Tom groaned. "I still don't believe there's a leak within the Brotherhood, but I'll concede the possibility since I haven't had time to investigate. Just tell me how illegal are your plans?"

"The less you know, the happier you'll be. But I do need you to help. I need someone here to run interference for me. Let me know when Ulan and the other goblins leave since I'm guessing they can't be detained forever." I hadn't thought of it before, but that was another reason not to bring Tom into my immediate plans.

He chewed on his lip, then raised his hands in surrender. "Fine. But only because I agree that we aren't getting far, and I can't risk you being killed by a goddamned goblin. You're safer outside the country. I'll get plane tickets. When will you be ready to go?"

"Tomorrow." Once the goblins found out they'd been robbed, I wasn't sure France would be far enough away.

EIGHTEEN

I DIDN'T HAVE MUCH TIME. THE GOBLINS' LAWYER WAS ON HIS way, and Tom could only stall Ulan's release for so long. If Ulan and the others headed right to their hotel after leaving, I might not have enough time as it was.

Speaking of leaving, the Gryphons and satyrs were abandoning their meeting. But although they were filing out, Xander must have arrived. I could hear him telling Ingrid that he approved of Claudius's idea.

Go fly into a tree, I thought, bypassing the room.

"There you are." Lucen grabbed my arm and tugged me toward the doors. "He left already."

My spike of fear must have been enough to inform him I'd been worried about Claudius seeing us. "Good. You need to stop challenging him, or you'll get in serious trouble."

"Fuck him. He almost got you killed."

"Technically that was the goblins." Ugh, it pained me to take some of the blame off Claudius. "Never mind that. I do not want you getting killed or demoted or kicked out of Dezzi's domus, or whatever else might happen. Please. Yes, he's an asshole, but..." He was a damn powerful asshole as I'd learned only too well.

Lucen tightened his grip on my arm. "He's not invincible, Jess, and he doesn't get to come over here and threaten the people I love without repercussion."

I slipped my sunglasses on, and we stepped outside. "You are badass and wonderful, and I understand you want to protect me, but you're not invincible either. And while if you got into a fight with Claudius, I'd root for you, no sane person would bet money on you. It's not a slight. He's older, more powerful, and he is definitely the biggest dick. Doesn't mean he has the biggest dick, but he can hurt you."

Lucen scowled. The summer sun was high in spite of the hour, and he pulled a jacket on to cover his arms while we stood in the shade of the granite gryphons. "Yeah, well, Dezzi has ordered me not to attend the meeting tomorrow. Officially, I've been tasked with some menial duties for her and supervising The Lair's rebuilding."

"Good. I'm not going to be at the meetings anymore either."

"Why not? They seem like the safest place. No one's going to try to take you out when you're surrounded by Gryphons."

I took off down the street, conscious of the time. "No one's going to take me out if they don't know where I am. I'm leaving, but first I'm on a mission."

"Leaving? What mission?" His voice was heavy with wariness.

I filled Lucen in en route to my apartment. Not surprisingly, he insisted on coming along. Not just to the goblins' hotel, but also to France. I didn't have time for an argument, so I ignored the bit about France and agreed to take him with to the hotel. He'd likely be useful.

Everyone was on high alert when we reached my apartment, but no one was waiting to ambush me. I snatched one of my remaining containers of the glamour Lei had made for me, and Lucen met us with his car.

While he drove, I used the potent disguise spell to alter my appearance. It didn't need to be a great job, just something sufficiently capable of making me look not like myself. Alas, the glamour was keyed specifically to me, so it wouldn't work on Lucen or the guards. Instead, Lucen had grabbed a cheap, generic charm of his own, but since Gi and

Melissa only had ones that hid their horns, I wanted to keep them out of sight in case things went badly.

They refused to play along.

"We already had one close call today," Gi said. "We're not waiting in the car."

Melissa inspected her knife in the backseat. "Dezzi will have our hides if something happens to you."

"I'll have your hides," Lucen growled. "Jess, you do realize you're putting a lot of trust in Gunthra."

"It has occurred to me."

He turned into the hotel's parking garage and removed his sunglasses. "This whole trip could be a trap. She could have more of her people waiting in the room to ambush you."

I shifted uncomfortably in my seat. "She'd have to have expected the first attempt would fail. Once it did, and she discovered it did, the Gryphons arrested her. She wouldn't have had a chance to set this up."

Lucen shut off the engine, shaking his head. "Let's hope not."

"One thing at a time. We've got to get a keycard if this is going to work."

"The keycard is easy. It's the rest that makes me nervous."

Our timing was lucky. We got out of the car as a couple exited the hotel via the garage entrance. Hiding my grimace, I hung back initially while Lucen and the others approached the people.

I didn't like this part, but when Lucen suggested it, I had to admit it was the easiest method anyone had come up with. Besides, it wasn't like the people were in real danger. Lucen, Gi, and Melissa would bowl the couple over with their magic while I rifled through the woman's purse and stole her keycard. When it was all over, the couple would be scared shitless by what happened, and yes, the woman would be a bit inconvenienced by the missing room key, but no one would get permanently damaged.

For a hastily thought-out plan, I'd done far worse.

Part one accomplished, we entered the hotel a few minutes later with me holding the stolen keycard and neither human any wiser about what they'd lost. They'd continue on their way to dinner, squirming with the aftereffects of lust and trembling with nerves.

"You sure you're the best person to do this?" Melissa asked.

We stopped at the lobby periphery. A group of flight attendants had arrived in their bright red uniforms, and the area around the front desk was crowded.

"If you do it, it'll be obvious to anyone nearby what's going on. They'll feel your power, and who knows what they'll do. If nothing else, you'll be memorable. If I do it, no one will know. Not even the person I'm using my gift on."

Lucen nodded. "She's done this enough."

Yup, I had, though the circumstances were usually different. Not so long ago, Steph had accused me of acting too pred-like for using my gift on innocent people. It hadn't been a fun conversation. Nor had the follow-up been when I'd finally admitted to her what I truly was.

Steph and I were good now, but I couldn't rid my mind of her voice as I crossed the lobby. Under the circumstances, I hoped she'd be willing to overlook this abuse of my power.

"Can I help you?" the desk clerk asked.

I smiled and pushed the stolen card toward her. "My room key doesn't seem to be working anymore."

"We can rekey it, no problem. I just need your room number and ID for verification."

"Room 452. Thanks." As I exhaled, I channeled my power into my breath. Like a fog, I envisioned it slowly encompassing the clerk's body and binding her to me. My gut clenched, informing me the bond was solid.

Solid, yet weak. This was nothing like a true addict bond, but for the moment, she'd be highly suggestible.

The clerk's eyelids drooped under the weight of the spell, but her breath hitched in her throat. When she glanced up at me, she wet her lips, and I tasted her lust like a dense chocolate mousse. "Do you have ID?"

I pretended to root around in my bag, and I let my face fall. "I must have left my wallet in my room." I bit my lip in what I hoped was a seductive way. "You can trust me. I'm a good girl."

I threw every ounce of suggestive power I had into those sentences. I couldn't force the clerk to do something she didn't really want to do. All I could do was make her want to please me. Usually that was sufficient.

"I'm not supposed to..." Her face was a perfect apology, but her tone was wistful.

"Please." I raised my finger to my lips, as if to say our secret.

Her cheeks turned pink. "All right, just this once."

"I won't tell anyone, and neither should you." There was another suggestion in there, one she'd probably want to heed even if I hadn't put any power into it.

"Absolutely not." Her fingers grazed my hand as she gave me back the card.

Though I wanted to pull away, I let her touch me and reveled in the huge hit of lust the sensation provided her. When this was over, I wanted chocolate.

"You should forget about this if you can." Taking the card—and my hand—back, I broke the connection between us. "Thanks so much."

She blinked at me, slightly dazed. "Uh, you're welcome."

As I left the desk, the chocolate I tasted turned to butterscotch confusion. If I was lucky, she wasn't sure what I was thanking her for.

Gi and Melissa split up, with Melissa staying in the lobby to watch for the goblins in case we ran out of time, and Gi accompanying Lucen and me to the room in case a threat was lurking. He insisted on being the one to open the door, and the men swept the room while I remained in the hallway, feeling superfluous.

"Clear?" I asked, unable to keep all traces of sarcasm from my tone. I mean, yes, I had been attacked by goblins earlier, but I didn't see this as a likely ambush for the reasons I'd already explained. Plus, I couldn't get over the feeling I was being babysat.

Gi tucked his gun back under his jacket. "Clear."

I strode into the meticulously clean room. Maid service had already come through, but preds being preds, everything about the place was neat and tidy regardless. It was a large room, with two beds against the far wall and a partition wall separating them from the seating area. The drapes were open, spreading sunshine around the place.

Lucen unzipped one of the two suitcases. "Do we know what we're looking for?"

"No." I grabbed an outer pocket zipper on the second suitcase. "Tom overheard them saying they brought information, and I'm assuming Gunthra didn't send me here on a wild-goose chase. If we can't find something obvious, then my guess is the information is electronic."

At my apartment, I'd also grabbed a spare USB key to download files if it came to that.

"Let's get started then." Lucen flipped open the suitcase.

We worked in silence, methodically checking every pocket in every travel bag, and going through drawers and closets. Lucen even cracked the room safe, but it was empty. My phone went off with the arrival of a text as I opened the last possibility—the laptop bag.

Couldn't hold them any longer. Left 5 minutes ago.

I swore. "Tom just let me know they're out of Gryphon custody."

"I'll check the bag, you boot it up," Lucen said.

The goblins' laptop was old and heavy, which was rather surprising. Such powerful people should have been able to afford the best equipment. But then I remembered Gunthra's old-fashioned house and the few goblin-owned businesses I'd done soul-swapping deals with. Those goblins tended to keep their records on paper, as had the goblin we'd busted not long ago in the Marshall case.

Given how old these goblins were, maybe technology wasn't their thing. It gave me reason to hope their electronic security wasn't so good, but alas, once the damn device finally finished booting, it turned out to be password protected.

"Any ideas?" I asked.

Lucen was rifling through papers he'd found in the bag. "Not a clue. There's nothing here. It's only their flight and hotel information, and a three-day-old newspaper."

"Damn it."

"Just take the laptop."

I tapped my fingers against the keyboard. "I was hoping to keep them in the dark about any theft until I was out of the country."

"Given how clunky it is, I doubt they're the sort to regularly use it." He pulled out a pocket knife and popped the screwdriver attachment. "Be glad it's so ancient that the hard drive is removable. We can take it, and maybe they won't notice the laptop is missing right away."

I twirled the screwdriver between my fingers. Take the hard drive, it was.

NINETEEN

WE WERE BACK IN THE CAR AND I WAS STRIPPING AWAY MY disguise when Lucen returned the conversation to France. "Do you have your ticket yet? Where are we going?"

I ran a finger down the edge of the hard drive. Gi and Melissa did not need to hear us arguing. "Tom is getting the tickets, and I assume he knows where we're going. Gryphon World Headquarters is in Grenoble."

"You always wanted to go to France, didn't you?"

I forced a smile. "Yeah, but not like this."

Lucen mused a bit about Paris and various things French, and I refrained from explaining that he was not coming along. My anxiety must have been evident, but goodness knew I had a lot of reasons to be anxious. A brewing argument with Lucen over international travel was unlikely to be the first explanation either of my bodyguards jumped to.

Before leaving the hotel, I'd called Steph and explained I needed to talk to her in person. So her apartment was where Lucen drove me, and I insisted he drop me off.

"It's not that Steph wouldn't be thrilled to see a group of satyrs appear in her doorway, it's just that, well, she'd probably slam the door in your faces."

Lucen rolled his eyes. "I thought the couple times Steph and I met, we got along great."

"Meaning you didn't kill each other?"

"You set a low bar, little siren. If I recall, Steph shook my hand once, which was more than you were willing to do at the time."

I stuffed the hard drive into my purse. "And now I sleep with you. Your point?"

He scratched his scruffy chin. "If I had one, it's lost because now I'm thinking about you in my bed."

Grinning, I kissed his cheek. "You're adorable. Don't pick any fights with Claudius, the goblins, or anyone else while I'm gone. Oh, and don't book your plane ticket yet. We'll discuss it when I get to your place. Okay?"

Lucen's eyes narrowed. "Why do I get the feeling this is not going to be a fun conversation?"

"Because you're a misery-sucking fool for spending time with me?" I opened the car door and hitched my bag over my shoulder.

"Watch her!" Lucen called to my guards as I headed toward the apartment building.

I waved as he drove away, then turned to Gi and Melissa. "I'm going to be a while."

"Yeah, yeah." Gi pointed to the fast food place across the street. "We'll be getting lunch. Call us if you need us."

Promising I would, I buzzed Steph then entered the building. She met me at her door with a beer. I took it gratefully and followed her inside. Had it really been only two weeks since I'd last been here? Two weeks since she told me she didn't care that I was a satyr, and I told her the end of the world might be upon us? Something like emotional vertigo washed over me.

Steph turned down the music and pointed toward the bathroom. "Jim's here. It's going to be the three of us for dinner. He's in the shower."

Translation: if there was anything I didn't want to say in front of him, this was the time.

"Right." I took a swig of the beer and plopped the hard drive on her table. "The problem I told you about a couple weeks ago with the furies? This might have some information I need on it."

Steph grimaced. She'd changed out of her work clothes and, ironically, was wearing a T-shirt that said *Yes, I work in IT. No, I don't want to fix your computer.*

"Your shirt goes great with those pajama pants." I gave her my biggest please-don't-kill-me grin. The pants were covered in pictures of beer bottles.

Steph picked up the hard drive and waved it in front of my face. "You gave me those pants years ago."

"I remember. Now I'm giving you a password-protected hard drive. Early birthday present?"

"I get to help you for my birthday? How sweet."

I spread my arms. "When we save the world, you'll get some of the credit."

It wasn't as funny as I'd intended. Steph froze, and I got a blast of her fear that tasted like the straight citric acid I'd once eaten on a dare. Foul, especially with the taste of my blueberry beer.

"This really has something to do with..." she glanced toward the bathroom, "...that?"

I exhaled heavily. "There could be information on the drive that would help us stop it. I stole it from a goblin's hotel room."

Her laugh was one of dismay, and she set the drive down. "Your life has gotten way too exciting. I miss the times when our biggest adventures were tracking down potential rapists in sketchy corners of Chelsea so you could mug them for their souls. I mean, that was way more excitement than I needed in my life, but by comparison, it was like playing with puppies."

"I didn't choose this."

"Nobody ever does, do they?" Steph opened her oven and peeked inside. "I'll see what I can do. If I can't do, do you want me to take it to Ben?"

Ben was the hacker Steph had found for me several weeks ago when I needed someone to decrypt files we'd stolen from the Gryphons. He'd gotten the job done—barely—and so far the persuasion I'd used on him had kept his lips sealed about what he'd discovered. That was good to know. Once the goblins found out what I'd done today, they'd be pissed and set on vengeance. Although I was certain someone in Dezzi's domus could crack the encryption on their drive, I didn't want the goblins starting fights with the satyrs. The more I could insulate them, the better. Both for Lucen's sake, and potentially my own.

"Yeah, we can bring Ben in if needed. Thanks, Steph."

She shut the oven, and a delicious-smelling wind rushed over my nose. "Don't thank me. I haven't accomplished anything yet, and you know—the way you said that has a certain deadly seriousness to it I don't like. Just keep up that tab of how many favors you owe me and be sure you live long enough for me to collect."

"I'm putting you in my will for my steel-toed boots."

"Well, yeah, you'd better. But I don't want to inherit them until I'm at least eighty. 'Kay?"

I crossed my heart.

Jim joined us a few minutes later, and I spent the next couple hours with them, eating dinner and drinking beer and pretending I didn't have a long night ahead. Around eight thirty I left so they could destroy each other in whatever computer game they were currently playing, and I met my bodyguards in the parking lot.

"Back to Shadowtown?" Gi asked.

"Not yet. I've got another errand. Want to go dancing?"

GI AND MELISSA DID NOT, IN FACT, WANT TO GO DANCING. They were okay, however, with getting to sit at a bar and having a beer.

Devon met us in the back of Purgatory, and while my bodyguards chilled in a private lounge where no one would look twice at them for not being dressed for the club, I prepared to put part two of my plan into play.

Devon flopped on one of the many sofas decorating his office above the dance floor. "You want me to what?"

"Find out what Claudius knows about the Vessels. Am I speaking English?"

"Not proper English," he responded, cranking his British accent up about a hundred degrees. "Do you think he's going to tell me if I ask?"

I pulled my knees in, and my butt sank deeper into the soft leather. "I don't know. Does he dislike you as much as he seems to dislike Dezzi and Lucen?"

"Ah, so this is why you're asking me and not Lucen."

"I figured Lucen was already in deep enough trouble without drawing Claudius's attention."

"Yes. Yes, he is. Lucen needs to keep his mouth shut and stay below Claudius's notice." Devon scowled. "Dezzi gives us a lot of leeway to speak our minds and do stupid things, but she's not typical. It's why we like her."

I played with the fraying fabric on my jeans. "Kind of like how she didn't kill either of us when Lucen put me under your protection while I was hiding from the Gryphons?"

"Exactly. And we're used to that sort of freedom. Claudius..." Devon seemed to be searching for the word. "Claudius would not approve."

"Obviously. He hates me."

"He doesn't hate you. He thinks you're inferior and defective. There's a difference."

"He's an asshole."

"True, but a genetically perfect specimen of one."

I rested my head against the sofa. "Back to my question—does he hate you too?"

"No, he seems to like me because I've been kissing his ass since he arrived."

"Literally?" I shrugged when Devon narrowed his eyes at me. "Hey, with you guys, I figure it's a fair and reasonable question."

In a blur, Devon's hands snaked out, and he yanked me over to him. I half landed on his lap and struggled to retain my balance. Those hands grabbed me by the hips and held me in place.

Sitting nose to nose with him, I had no choice but to gaze into his blue eyes. "I need to stay away from Claudius, and I can't ask Lucen to do this. I'm afraid Claudius might..."

"Kill him?" Devon sighed. "So am I. But Claudius isn't going to open up to me. I'm suspect because I'm here."

"Are you sure?" I loosened his tie and unbuttoned the top of his shirt. "You can be very charming."

"You only admit these things when you want something from me."

"But I am admitting them. Still counts." I batted my eyelashes, which earned me a derisive snort. "Look, I even have a plan for you and all that charm. You can tell Claudius you don't approve of Dezzi defending Lucen or something to that effect. Make him think there's dissension in the ranks. That you're an ally of his. You'll be his spy to keep Lucen in line."

Devon took my hands and placed them on my legs. "I could do this, and if Claudius finds out I'm playing him or that I sent you the information he shared, Lucen won't be the only one of us on his shitlist. So, with that in mind, do you still think I should do this for you and your half-baked plan?"

I snatched his tie again, only this time I yanked it tight. "No, I think you should—and will—do this because you're not a fool. You don't want to be standing around jerking off when the apocalypse is coming."

Devon took a deep breath once I let go of the tie and he could breathe again. "Fine, but you're going to owe me."

"Seriously?"

"Three favors."

I tried to get up, but he pulled me back down by my waistband. He was grinning, and the scent of his clove pheromones was stronger. I fought to maintain my annoyance, but damn. That mischievous expression of his was disarming. The lust he'd been stirring up since he tugged me on top of him was overpowering my better sense. My breaths quickened.

Responding to my mood, Devon slid his fingers against my bare hips, and I tensed further. "One, for asking me to risk my ass for you. Two, for choking me with my tie. And three, for taking offense when I said you owed me."

I laughed. "You're a jerk."

"I'd be offended if you meant that. But since we both know you don't, you can pay off one of those favors now." He slid his hands across my skin and unfastened my jeans button, and my laughter dried up, giving way to need. Honestly, exercise had nothing on a flirty satyr when it came to stress relief.

It ended up being two favors by my estimation, but who cared when you enjoyed it so much?

LUCEN WAS STEWING WHEN I GOT TO HIS APARTMENT. HIS posture and the aura of darkness that hung around him reminded me of Sweetpea, who was pacing about in his cage. I half-expected Lucen to snort smoke along with his pet dragon any moment.

In a normal relationship, he'd be stewing because I'd been screwing his best friend for the past hour, and I—in turn—would be feeling guilty about it. But I wasn't allowed a normal relationship.

No, Lucen was stewing because he'd started realizing I didn't intend for him to come to France with me, and the guilt I felt was due to discussing the situation and how best to argue my case with Devon.

He was hunched over his laptop in the living room. "I'm going with you, and that's all there is to this discussion."

"No, you're not, but I'm fine not discussing it any further."

"Jess."

"No."

"I'm not kidding. The goblins tried to kill you today. The furies are... Well, fuck-all knows what the furies might want with you, but they did abduct you in Phoenix. For sin's sake, you are in danger, and if you think for a moment I'm about to let you prance off to another continent without me, you've failed to consider—"

I pressed my mouth to his and pushed him back on the sofa with my body. Strong arms pulled me against his chest, and his hands groped at my hair. In spite of my mood, my day, or what I'd gotten up to with Devon, a needy moan escaped my throat.

Part of me knew this was my fault. I'd tried to derail him, and he'd turned the tables and was derailing me instead. Oh, it wasn't that I didn't crave his touch normally, but I could sense he was blasting me with his power too, undoubtedly believing he could seduce me into agreeing with him. Or, failing that, convince me I couldn't live without him.

Such was the curse and the blessing of having a relationship with a satyr. Er, satyrs. Their magic left them constantly needing sex, and the same magic made anyone with them receptive to the idea. Never mind if she might not be able to walk normally the next day.

Lucen pulled back when he had me pinned to the cushions, and I gasped for air. "I'm coming."

"Yes, eventually, but not to France."

"Funny."

Just as it had been hard to stay annoyed at Devon when he was holding me, it was hard to remain focused while Lucen was pressed against me. The intensity in his eyes was alarming in a too-sexy manner, and the way his chest rose and fell against mine was making me far more interested in wicked ideas than the issue at hand.

I pried my fingers open and released his shirt. "You can't risk going with me. Claudius is not pleased with you for rushing to my defense or threatening him."

"All the more reason I should come with you. It puts an entire ocean between me and Claudius."

My hands trailed up his torso like they couldn't help themselves. He was sweaty beneath his shirt, the ridge of each ab like silk beneath my fingers. I wanted to lick each one, graze my... *Stop it, Jess. Focus.*

"How does Dezzi spin that? Think about her. If I disappear, and you disappear at the same time, do you honestly believe Claudius is going to jump to some incorrect conclusion? He might be an asshole, but I doubt he reached his current position by being a dumbass."

"You are more important to me than Claudius's opinion, little siren." Grunting, he pushed himself up, and my body deflated at the loss of his touch. "If he pressures Dezzi, we'll deal. I'd much rather be kicked out of her domus than lose you. Don't you get that? After everything we've been through?"

I did. I got it completely, but why didn't he see that I was trying to protect him as much as he was trying to protect me?

Tears of frustration burned behind my eyes, and I closed my eyelids, holding them in. "After everything we've been through, don't you understand that I will not let you get hurt? You need to distance yourself from me, for both our sakes." I grabbed his hands. "Claudius considers me disposable. You heard him earlier. If he thinks the fury threat can be neutralized by killing me, he'll do it. If he thinks he can get to me through hurting you, don't you think he'd use you that way? And if he did, understand that I will do anything to protect you."

Lucen squeezed my hands. "Claudius wouldn't hurt me to get to you."

"No? Devon would disagree."

Lucen swore and flung my hands away, but he didn't argue the point. It was as good an admission as I was going to get that he knew I spoke the truth.

It hardly made me feel better. Some part of me must have been hoping he'd pull a wildly perfect plan out of thin air, some argument that would convince me, and I wouldn't have to leave him behind after all. He'd done as much before.

Elbows on my knees, I watched him pace the living room. His jaw was set, and his eyes glowed with the fierce determination I loved. He would either think of something, or he would see reason. There was no other outcome.

Finally, he stopped and stared at me. "Forget it. I'm coming with you."

TWENTY

We argued the rest of the evening. I used logic. Lucen resorted to outlandish accusations.

"You can't protect everyone by pushing them away, Jess. This is my life. If I'm willing to risk it and my position for you, that's my choice."

I tossed pillows at the bed in frustration. "You're missing the point."

He picked up the pillows and re-fluffed them. "You've got this backward. You're the one missing the bigger picture. You cannot do this alone."

"I won't be alone. I'll have Tom."

"You and Tom do not an army make. The whole point of this alliance, which was your idea I might remind you, was to—"

"The alliance failed spectacularly." I snatched my phone and headed into the bathroom. "The alliance is now me, me alone, or me with Tom. Olef is dead, Mitch has disappeared, and no one knows who's next. I will not have you risking or ruining your life over this. It's not necessary."

From the privacy of the bathroom, I texted Devon. *Lucen insists on going with me. Stop him.*

With Claudius, he wrote back. *Will handle Lucen next.*

I collapsed onto the toilet seat and kissed my phone. Devon might be the only one who could talk sense into Lucen. I guessed that made four favors I owed him.

You excel at driving people mad, he wrote a moment later. *Lucky for you, I excel at saving your lovely ass.*

Never mind. I'd leave it at three owed, one of which was paid.

Lucen banged on the bathroom door. "I hear your phone. What are you planning?"

"I'm not planning anything."

"Have you forgotten you can't lie to me?"

I threw open the door. "Have you forgotten you can be a pain in my lovely ass?"

"Never. I take great pride in torturing you. I have ten years of experience."

I tossed my phone aside and fell on the bed. Exhaustion and anxiety nibbled away at me from within. All I wanted was to curl up against Lucen and sleep. I was done arguing and would just have to hope Devon could convince him not to be such a dolt.

I GOT MY WISH FOR SLEEP, BUT ANY ACTUAL REST WAS questionable. The clock on Lucen's nightstand taunted me, and the only reason I knew I slept at all was because I woke up twice from nightmares. Bleary-eyed, I crawled out of bed the next day while Lucen slept on.

Tom must have been up for hours already, and he'd sent me several emails. One of them included my flight information. I read through them all before showering then fretted in the steamy water. Having my schedule was good, but it also raised logistical questions I hadn't thought of yesterday.

I had a passport and a suitcase, but no way to use my phone overseas nor even an adapter to charge it. Both of those were necessary since I needed to stay in contact with Steph and Devon about what they learned. While these and a hundred other issues were fresh in my mind, I shot emails to Tom and got dressed.

Lucen had woken up and was staring at me while I put my boots on.

"Where are you going so early?" Even half asleep, his voice was laden with distrust.

"To Headquarters." I'd thought everything through this time. He wouldn't catch me so unawares and upset that I'd lie. I was going to Headquarters, after all. It just wouldn't be my first stop.

"For what? Yesterday you said you wouldn't be in the meetings anymore."

"I won't, but the Gryphons expect me to train, and I have a lot of training to do." Also a truth.

Lucen slid his arms around his pillow, his blue-green eyes appraising me and his tousled hair and naked torso calling to me. "You're not sneaking away, are you?"

"Do I look like I'm sneaking?" I kissed his forehead. "We'll talk more later."

"We will, and don't forget Gi and Mel."

I shut his bedroom door partway. "Already called them. They're on their way."

I met my two sleepy bodyguards on Lucen's front step. The Shadowtown street was quiet and the air thick with humidity. Today would be a scorcher. Not even noon and it was hard to breathe outside. Above, a thin cloud cover blanketed the city, not heavy enough to block out the sun, but enough to keep Shadowtown its usual gloomy self.

A lone delivery van rumbled by, but most preds were like Lucen, asleep in their beds. The two with me were clearly not pleased to be among the exceptions.

Melissa unlocked the car remotely as I trudged down to the curb. "To the damn Gryphon building, I assume?"

I climbed in, grateful for the remains of the A/C-chilled air inside. "Eventually. First, I need to stop at my apartment."

It was a quick jaunt over the couple blocks, and driving was a waste of gas, but it would be handy to have the car when I was done. Melissa parked illegally by the door, and she and Gi did their whole bodyguard routine of checking the entry and clearing my apartment. After yesterday's attack, I didn't feel foolish letting them.

Bemused, they stood around while I pulled my ancient suitcase from the closet.

"You're leaving already?" Gi asked.

I didn't have a whole lot of time to be picky about what I packed. A couple pairs of jeans, some shirts—I cursed, remembering I'd left my hoodie at Lucen's. And what about weapons? Was the special clearance Tom had procured for me before the trip to Phoenix still good, or would I have to leave my knife behind? He hadn't answered my emails yet.

I counted out a week's worth of comfortable but not particularly attractive underwear. "Yes. I'm sure you heard me yesterday. I'm going to France with the Gryphons."

"And Lucen?" Melissa idly picked up Misery and examined the blade.

I found my passport and a bag of travel-sized bath supplies that I hoped were still good, and I threw them in the suitcase too. "No, so don't you tell him anything. He hasn't figured it out yet."

Gi shook his head and wandered into the galley kitchen that connected my bedroom to the living room. "We answer to Dezzi, not him."

"Good." I shut the suitcase, feeling anything but.

The day flew by once I got to Headquarters. It started with weapons training, then searching through Olef's books, updates on Olef's case from Andre's team, updates about Mitch's kidnapping from Tom, and finally—just when the lack of progress on any of those fronts was getting to me—I was presented with gifts.

I opened the shopping bag Tom handed me. "What's this?"

"Supplies so your phone will work overseas," he said. "I'll take care of it for you later. Don't tell me what you did yesterday, but when do you expect you'll hear about progress?"

"It could be a couple days. Ste..." I cut myself off so as not to incriminate Steph. "I had to borrow stuff from the goblins. A friend is working on some of the details. Another friend is going to question Claudius."

Tom's lips might have twitched into something resembling a smile, but it faded quickly. "Check in with them once we arrive."

"I assume you know where we're going?"

There was no mistaking his happiness this time. "Home. For me, that is. I've booked you a hotel room within walking distance of World."

"Thanks."

I checked my phone for new messages, expecting to have heard from Lucen, but I had nothing. His silence nibbled away at me over the next couple hours, and eventually all those nibbles turned into a huge chunk of missing confidence. By the time we left for the airport, I felt as though part of me had been stranded at his apartment.

Everything had gone smoothly until this point. Everything except saying goodbye to him properly.

I swallowed as the security line inched forward, my unease growing with every foot of progress I made toward the scanners. What had I been expecting? I had snuck out, just like he'd said. I'd been intending to leave him behind all along.

So had I believed he'd show up at Headquarters or the airport to give me a last kiss goodbye? To tell me Devon had convinced him to stay after all? That was ridiculous. Yet I didn't like the uneasiness in my gut. The worry that I'd seen the last of him this morning.

"Ticket and ID?" The TSA agent held out her hand.

Numbly, I passed them over and made my way through the security checkpoint. With my shoes back on my feet and the scanner behind me, the unlikely possibility of Lucen arriving had passed.

Guilty and nervous, I took out my phone when I reached the gate. Time was running out. We boarded in thirty minutes. If he was angry or upset or even on his way, I had to know. Bracing myself for what I assumed would be furious silence on the other end, I dialed.

Lucen picked up on the second ring. "Was wondering if you'd call or if that would be too overtly friendly."

I winced at the hurt in his voice. "I'm trying to protect you from Claudius. I thought you might call when you had the chance."

"Believe it or not, I've been busy. I don't like this, and I'm not happy. I think your determination to run off on your own is misguided."

"I'm not on my own."

"You're pushing away the people who care about you. How is that not on your own? Me, Steph, and did you ever talk to your mother like you'd planned?"

I wound my carry-on's nylon strap around my hand in frustration. "I'm not pushing them away, or you. I've been preoccupied. As I explained, I'm trying to protect you. Why are you taking this so badly?"

"Because I know you, Jess. You hate asking for help, you don't trust other people, and you don't listen to my good advice. This is not a problem you and one other Gryphon can solve."

"But it's one I have to try to solve before anyone else gets hurts." Pain stabbed me right between the eyes. I was not continuing last night's argument in the airport terminal when all I'd wanted was to hear Lucen's voice. "Are you planning on joining me anyway?"

I heard voices shouting in the background, and something that could have been a motor. The Lair's reconstruction must be underway. "No. I had a meeting with the triad earlier. Plans are changing here, and Dezzi wants me to stay."

"Plans are changing—what does that mean?"

"You'll find out." His voice softened, and the noise faded in the distance as he must have entered a different room. "Please be careful, little siren. I hate not being there with you, and if there's a traitor in the Gryphons..."

I forced a laugh as Tom returned to the seat across from me. "Yeah, I know. I'll be careful."

Not wanting to finish this conversation in Tom's presence, I pointed to his coffee and wandered away once he acknowledged my intention. Lucen no longer sounded angry when we hung up a couple minutes later, more like resigned and unhappy. That made two of us, but I could get on the plane with less stress knowing I hadn't left a furious satyr behind.

FRANCE—THE COUNTRY I'D BEEN WANTING TO VISIT SINCE THE Gryphon's New England Academy for the Magically Gifted made me choose between studying French, Spanish, or Latin when I was twelve. Finally, after a long flight during which I'd been squeezed between a woman wearing too much perfume on my left and a guy who snored half the time on my right, I'd arrived.

Tired, hungry, and dazed, I'd arrived.

This was not how I'd once anticipated arriving. But then I wasn't here to sightsee or drink wine and eat cheese at the foot of the Eiffel Tower. I barely knew where I was going, and I didn't have high hopes of being successful when I got there. The best I could say was that the odds of anyone here trying to knife me on a busy street were low.

"I can read that sign and that one." I gawked at the airport signage, testing my fading memories of high-school-level French.

"Of course you can." Tom yawned. "They have the English written beneath them."

I rolled my eyes. "Can you let me enjoy something about this trip? If the world's going to end in a blaze of fury fire, I'm going to speak French and gorge on chocolate croissants before it does. My bucket list has a whole lot of French wine and pastries on it."

In response, Tom spouted something in rapid-fire French.

I scowled. Naturally, he spoke it fluently, or fluently enough to get by while living here. "I think I caught every other word. Something about my life being backward?"

His regularly scheduled smirk appeared, and he pressed on, leading me toward the train ticketing counter without bothering to translate.

Deux billets et trente minutes later, I was seated next to Tom on a high speed train heading south. After explaining it would take two to three hours to reach Grenoble, he closed his eyes and went to sleep. Tired as I was, I couldn't join him. I had a window to gaze through, and my brain was determined to soak up as much of the foreign countryside as it could.

Even I couldn't stay awake forever though apparently. Sometime after visions of farmland passed by, I was woken up by Tom shaking my arm. "We're here."

Rubbing my eyes, I stumbled off the train with my luggage, thankful that *excusez-moi* was an easy to remember phrase.

"My research assistant, Marie, is coming to pick us up," Tom said, as we stepped outside. "We'll get you checked into your hotel, then get to work. Jess?"

I lifted my sunglasses to take in the full effect of the sun bouncing off the sleek buildings and the Alps rising in the distance. "Yeah, okay."

I expected Tom's research assistant to be a young Gryphon, but Marie was older than either of us. Short and olive-skinned, she greeted me enthusiastically in French, then switched to perfectly fluent but accented English for the rest of the drive. I searched my memory for her name, but I couldn't recall it being on that email chain I'd discovered, and I relaxed a little. She probably wasn't the leak.

Marie played tour guide, explaining to me how to use the tram and where I might want to go if Tom ever gave me time to leave the building. At last, we stopped in the shadow of a glassy high-rise bearing the Gryphon seal over the doors. A large plaque to the left sported a smaller version of the seal, and beneath it, the words *Siège International*.

World Headquarters. Oh yeah, I'd finally arrived.

TWENTY-ONE

WORLD'S INTERIOR WAS AS FLASHY AS THE EXTERIOR. SLEEK, dark marble floors mixed with lots of glass, blue-tinted walls, and modern curves to give the lobby an impressive air that was like neither Boston's stately nor Phoenix's southwesterly style. The high ceiling over half the room opened up to a balcony on the second floor, and all those windows let in a refreshing level of sunlight.

For some reason, I'd expected World to bask in the Gryphons' long, historical roots. Perhaps because I expected everything in Europe to be older than the U.S. Instead, the building and its inhabitants gave the impression of a cool, thoroughly modern and efficient magical police force.

Beyond the architecture, however, the layout of the ground floor was all too familiar. After presenting my ID and being waved through the mundane and magical security checks along with Tom, he showed me the floor directory hanging by the elevators. Titles and place names were written in both English and French.

"This building houses the Grenoble Office as well as World Office." He gestured to the directory. "Upper floors are World. My office is on the seventh if you ever need to find me there. Basements One and Two are the archive levels."

Tom pressed the button for basement level one, and down we went.

The doors opened into a small, well-lit room filled with tables and computers. A partition-like desk ran most of the length of the far wall, and behind it was a set of modern glass doors with a very obvious electronic lock.

A young guy in a wheelchair sat at one of the tables, running a handheld scanner over a book. He glanced up and waved. "Tom, *vous revenez.*"

"With a coworker," Tom replied in English, apparently deferring to my ears. "Jessica, this is Umut. He's one of our guardians."

"Guardians?" I asked once I said hi to Umut.

Umut grinned. "Fancy way of calling us librarians. They like to make us feel special."

"You are," Marie said. Turning to me, she added, "They go through a rigorous process to be hired."

I noticed Umut was wearing a T-shirt and khaki pants, not a uniform. Tom wasn't wearing his at the moment either, considering we'd only arrived a few hours ago, but I hazarded a guess about Umut. "So guardians aren't Gryphons?"

"No," Umut said. "I am a magical deficient, but an interested one. Must do something with that history degree, yeah?"

"Nice to meet you, magical deficient. I'm a magical anomaly."

Tom's cheek twitched with disapproval. "One of three."

"We assume there are still three." With every day that passed since Mitch's abduction, my hopes of the Gryphons and FBI locating him grew dimmer, and the statistical likelihood of ever finding him grew smaller.

Tom had to be as aware of the grim outlook as I was, and he chose to ignore my comment. "Jessica is a Gryphon consultant from Boston. I need her to be given permission to access the archives. It falls under my clearance."

Umut nodded and beckoned us behind the desk. "Do you have a badge number?"

I pulled out my ID to check since I'd never looked closely at it. "No number."

"You can use one of the *Le Confrérie* guest ones," Tom said.

"Off-hours access for the guest." Umut sounded amused. "Part of that special project you two have been working on?"

"Exactly." Tom grabbed white cotton gloves from a container on the desk and handed me a pair. "All Gryphons who work for World have access to the archives during open hours. During those hours, there will always be a guardian, like Umut, here to record visitations and provide entry. The doors are always locked. Umut will take biometric data from you today, and you can choose a pin code. If you want access during off hours, those will get you in."

I twisted the gloves around in my hands. "Off hours? You really are planning on working me into the ground, aren't you?"

"The computers are a card catalog of sorts," Tom continued, ignoring me. "Put in keywords, dates, whatever it is you think will help with your search. It will spit out a list of possible items that could apply. The code next to each item will tell you where it's located. You can access basement level two once you're inside the archive itself."

"Yes, sir," I muttered.

Marie smiled.

Umut called me over so he could scan my fingerprints, and I entered a five-digit pass code into a machine that resembled the sort banks use to encode ATM cards. Afterward, Tom led me to a computer so he could explain how to use the system in more detail, and he showed me the notes he and Marie had been keeping so I didn't replicate searches they'd already performed or waste time looking up objects they'd already dismissed. The whole process took far longer than it seemed like it should, and by the time I was finally allowed to enter the archive itself, my energy had plummeted.

A whoosh of cool, temperature- and humidity-controlled air rushed over me when the glass doors opened. The archive turned out to be nothing so much as a giant warehouse filled with row after row of shelves, each section of which was labeled. It was indeed much like a library, only the shelves didn't just contain books.

Tom gave me a rundown of how the shelves were ordered, and took me into the back where several additional rooms were sealed off. They were unlocked, he explained, but the items inside them had to be stored in unique environments.

"The more dangerous magical objects are on the floor below us," he said, stopping by the staircase down. "No one will stop you from going in there, but removing items from their rooms does activate the security system. You'll have to explain why you need to do it."

"Odds of finding a Vessel in one of those rooms?"

He shook his head. "First places I thought to search. There is nothing in the archives labeled as a Vessel or any variation thereof."

The next couple hours were spent with Tom and Marie, going over what they'd researched, how they'd done it and what new strategies we might want to try. My eyelids continued to droop, and finally Tom either took pity on me or realized he wasn't getting anything else useful out of me today.

"It's about eight," he said, closing the book we'd been staring at. "Maybe it's time to take a break."

"Eight? No wonder I'm beat and starving." Even as I said it, I yawned. "It's been…" I attempted to do the math in my head and gave up. "Way too many hours since I last slept in a bed. I'm missing most of a day, or is it a night I missed?"

Tom rubbed his temples. Though he feigned wakefulness well, his eyes were bloodshot. "I should get home. It's been a while. We can get dinner first if you like. I don't have anything to eat at home at this point."

I wasn't sure I wanted to spend more time in Tom's company, but I wasn't up for exploring on my own when I was exhausted. Better to let him direct me to a decent restaurant.

Marie bade us good night, so it was just the two of us. The place Tom took me to must have been popular with the Gryphons because the owners recognized him even without his uniform. Sadly, I barely tasted my food, and the wine Tom insisted I have with it only made me sleepier. After deciding on a time to meet tomorrow, I practically crawled my way to my hotel room.

Tossing my phone on the bed, I groaned. I hadn't unpacked a damn thing, and I knew I should contact both Steph and Lucen before I went to sleep. Hopefully, the time difference meant it was earlier there. My brainpower had been sucked dry, and I could no longer be sure how these pesky time zones worked.

I yanked my boots off and flopped on the bed. I hadn't been able to get a signal in World's basement, so I'd put my phone in airplane mode to avoid the battery draining. When it reconnected, I discovered several emails and missed texts.

One of the emails was from Steph, and I opened it first.

Those goblins and their 20th-century computer were using 20th-century encryption. I'd have expected better from them. Doesn't greed extend to technology these days? Got a bunch of files for you. I'll assume you know what they mean. They're attached.

Don't get dead, you owe me.

XO, Steph

"You're a genius," I told her. Then, because I wasn't so tired that I'd forgotten she couldn't hear me, I emailed her with the same praise.

Rather than try opening the files on my phone tonight, I sent them to Tom and prayed the information we needed was in them. Tomorrow, I'd find out.

Next, I went through my texts and responded to those from Lucen asking me to let him know I'd made it safely.

He wrote back almost immediately. *Took you long enough. Talk later. Meeting started.*

So that was that. By the time he got out of the meeting, I planned to be asleep. Might as well get on with the plan.

I found my toothbrush and started to the bathroom when someone knocked on my door. I froze, and fear trickled down my spine. The other side of the door was an emotional void, meaning either preds, magi, or addicts. But that shouldn't have been possible. The only people who should know where I was were Tom and Marie.

The hairs on my neck rose. Putting the Atlantic between me and any potential goblin assassins was supposed to keep me safe. So much for that. I dropped my toothbrush and reached for my knife.

"Jess, for sin's sake, I can feel you in there. Stop contemplating ways to kill me, and open the door."

The fear left me in whoosh of breath, replaced by annoyance. Cursing, I chucked the knife away and threw open the heavy door. "What are you doing here?"

Devon stuffed his hands in his pockets, looking smug despite his hair not lying in its usually perfect black waves or his shirt remaining wrinkle-free. "All in good time. But honestly, when someone knocks on your door, consider asking who it is before you begin contemplating ways to dispose of their bodies."

"I have reason to worry, or did you forget I was attacked yesterday?" I frowned. "Wait, was it yesterday anymore? I'm so lost and tired."

He rested his head against the doorframe. "Please tell me you're not too tired. I spent the last hour tracking you down. I need you."

"For what?"

He gazed at me with pleading, puppy-dog eyes, an expression that suited his face far too well when he wanted it to. "You remember the conversation I had with you a couple weeks ago about how the pred-addict bond works?"

"You mean how you need to dump your excess emotions on your addicts? I'm not likely to forget. Your point?"

Devon cleared his throat. "When the bond gets stretched thin, say by distance, say by an entire fucking ocean, using it becomes challenging."

"You traveled here without an addict?" I hated myself immediately for thinking of a human being like a travel accessory, but clearly from Devon's point of view, one should have been. Even Claudius had brought two addicts with him to Boston.

"I left on short notice. Bringing someone would have delayed me. Besides, they could have gotten in the way while I was here."

"So you need...?"

"A good fuck. Probably several. I'm starting to lose my mind, and since you know what that's like thanks to Lucrezia, I thought you'd be sympathetic."

I wasn't sure whether to laugh or cry. "There's a whole city of people out there."

"And yet I sought you out." He smiled pitifully. "Don't make me remind you that you owe me two favors."

I wanted to bang my head against something, preferably before collapsing in my bed. Yet I couldn't deny there was something endearing in the fact that Devon had looked for me instead of finding a random stranger. It wasn't as though a random stranger would—or could—turn him down. A satyr with as much power as he had could magic the vestments off a priest.

"Fine," I said, wondering if anyone in the close-by rooms had heard this conversation. "But this counts toward one of those favors."

The charming mask slipped from his face. "Come on, that's mean. It's not like you don't enjoy it."

"Yes, but I'm exhausted." I grabbed his shirt and pulled him into the room.

Devon didn't bother to argue. He barely bothered to close the door before pressing me up against the wall and kissing me so hard I forgot to breathe. His power didn't gently roll over me. It nearly bowled me over with its strength and ferocity. My exhaustion didn't stand a chance. I went from painfully tired to unbearably wet in seconds.

Good thing because Devon gave no hint of letting up. He kissed me like a man starved, and in a way, he was. But he clearly hadn't been exaggerating about the effects distance from his addicts had on his body.

Unbearable and excruciating were how he'd once described what it was like to be a pred with no addicts on which to dump emotions. Unfortunately, as he'd noted, I had a good idea what it felt like to have a body raging with insatiable lust. Lucky for him, too, that I could empathize because this was not going to be the best sex of my life.

Devon was too needy, too desperate for release to do more than pay cursory attention to my body. He knew it too. I could see in his eyes how genuinely distressed he was. Whatever his faults, not striving to please me had never been one of them.

"I'm sorry, Jess," he murmured into my ear. His hands fumbled with my jeans button, and I sucked in a breath as he shoved my pants and underwear to the floor.

In spite of the strangeness of the situation, my body didn't care. I could feel myself growing wetter, my skin begging to be touched and my ache longing to be filled. He didn't have to tease me to make me as hungry as he was. The clove scent of his power was intoxicating, and his lack of restraint more so. Our roles were always reversed. It was satyrs who drove people mad with lust. To see one driven wild by his own was a surprising turn-on.

Fingers, one then two, slipped inside me. My knees shook, and I moaned, dying for more than that, but Devon's breath hitched. "Damn it, Jess. I'm sorry. I need you now. I can't..."

"Shut up," I told him, grabbing his head and pulling him closer.

Devon's hands worked to unfasten his own pants, and every time his knuckles brushed my bare stomach, I tensed in anticipation. Then finally he was free, the heat of his erection splitting me in two and sliding inside me, backing me harder against the wall.

I wrapped my arms around his neck for support, trying in vain to taste his skin and being stymied by the shirt he'd never removed. I bit his shoulder and figured it was his fault if I stained his clothes.

Devon thrust harder, his cries growing louder and more guttural until he gasped for breath. "Jess, I'm sorry."

I held him as he shuddered over and over, and my body let out a silent scream of frustration. I was certain Devon could sense it. Even if I'd been prepared to do so, there was no such thing as faking an orgasm with a satyr. Not when unfulfilled lust was their meal of choice.

My distress only increased when he pulled out, and he brought me close and buried his head against mine. "I'm so sorry. I feel like a teenager all over again. I'm going to make this up to you."

I patted him on the back and relaxed my body against his. The warmth of his skin, especially the heat of his still-hard cock, had my nerves singing with a beautiful agony. I wanted to wrap my fingers around him and plunge him back into me, and I didn't think he'd mind if I did.

But being held by Devon was a weird phenomenon. Weird enough to distract me. He wasn't usually the hugging sort, and although the first time we'd had sex I'd spent the night in his bed, that had been the only time. And we hadn't exactly spent the waking hours there cuddling. Our sex had always been hot, but never particularly emotional.

Really, the whole point of sex with Devon had been to help me separate sex from emotions. With Lucen, I could let my feelings be involved, even if I knew his weren't in the same way. Devon, however, was the friend with benefits, a Lucen-endorsed treatment for my human outlook on relationships. There was no hugging or holding and rarely any kissing.

As if in response to my thoughts, Devon wrapped his fingers through my hair and took my mouth in his. A hint of the same desperation underlay the languid brush of his lips, but he seemed better in control.

I couldn't help succumbing to the gentle touch of his tongue or running my fingers over the hairs on his chin. "So this is why you sought me out, huh?" I removed my hand from his face, disturbed by the intimacy of the gesture and its effect on me. "Of all the people in Grenoble, I'm the one you thought it would be okay to leave hanging?"

Sarcasm—the best defense against confusion.

Devon swallowed noticeably. "I'll have you know, if you were a normal person, I would still have gotten you off."

"Uh-huh. I'm supposed to believe you?"

"It would be the charitable thing to do." He slid his arms down me and carried me over to the bed. "But I'm going to make it up to you. I have it under control."

I pushed myself backward so he could climb onto the bed, and I ran my hand along his stomach. Devon closed his eyes and nearly fell on top of me, shuddering. "Yeah, you're under control." I smirked.

Cringing, he placed his hand on top of mine. "Okay, fine. It might take a little more time," he said, clearly struggling for words. "That's all."

So I gave him time, and when Devon finally worked off enough of his overloaded lust to return the favor, there was no denying it had been worth it. I was more exhausted than ever though as I lay on the bed, and only the power of my curiosity kept me from falling asleep.

I wrapped my arms around my pillow and stared at Devon. "How are you going to survive if you're like this after only a few hours?"

He waved his hand idly. "As you said, there's a whole city of people. Worst case, I'll cut off someone in Boston and..." He caught me frowning. "You should be happy. I'd be setting someone free."

"And addicting someone local in their place. No net positive there."

"It'll be a temporary move only. If it makes you feel better, I'll find someone unattached. Someone who might enjoy it." To make his point, he ran a finger down my spine, and I shivered. "Unless you want to make yourself available every few hours?"

Alas, part of me was tempted. "I'll be busy, covered in dusty books and mysterious artifacts at World."

Devon flopped on his back. "Pity."

"So spill it. Why are you here, and how did you find me?"

Instead of answering, he picked up the pendant Lucen gave me and examined it. "He has surprisingly good taste in jewelry for someone who spends all his time in T-shirts."

I removed the pendant from Devon's hand. "Not everyone has a job that goes with wearing designer suits. Stop changing the subject."

"Fine." He grinned. "It wasn't hard to find you. I knew you were heading to Grenoble, and it made sense that you'd be in a hotel close to World. This one is the closest."

And then he probably bashed the hotel clerk over the head with his magic and got them to give up my room number. It was easy enough to fill in details. I couldn't judge, having recently done something even more devious.

"And you're here why?" I raised an eyebrow.

"You have to ask? Part of convincing Lucen not to go chasing after you was promising to find a way for us to protect you."

Right. I should have figured it out. Lucen had told me how plans had changed. Apparently this was what he'd meant. "And you got stuck with bodyguard duty. Why not Gi or Melissa?"

Devon rolled on his side and began playing with my hair. "A couple reasons, but the main ones were Lucen trusts me, and since arrangements had to be made fast, they required someone able to act without taking the time to bring an addict along. I could handle it."

"Oh, yeah. You handled it great."

"You go ahead and make fun of me, but I lasted hours. Gi or Melissa would have broken down on the flight and joined the mile-high club."

"And you didn't want to?"

He looked at me aghast. "Have you ever used an airplane bathroom? Some of us have standards."

While I laughed silently, Devon took the opportunity to stop messing with my hair and rub his thumb over my breasts. White-hot heat shot through my core, burning off the giggles.

"So that's why Lucen's back at the meeting today." I managed to get the words out between heavy breaths, determined not to be distracted.

Devon was just as determined. He nudged me over and lowered his lips to my skin. "Yes. Dezzi doesn't want either of you dead, but Claudius has put her in an awkward position. As her lieutenant, I can be sent away on domus business for her without Claudius raising an eyebrow. Meanwhile, you escape, and she keeps Lucen close to her side, and hopefully he does a decent job of pretending not to be concerned about your disappearance. It might placate Claudius."

My skin sizzled where he grazed his teeth over me. Without meaning to, I grasped his hair, holding him in place and teetering on the brink of leaving my rational self behind to indulge once more in the sensations he aroused. But I couldn't yet. There was some problem with this plan of his. Something he was making me forget...

It came to me all at once, and I yanked Devon off me. "What about the information I asked you to get from Claudius? If you're here, you're not helping me."

Devon sighed, hovering over me, and for a moment I thought he might ignore my question. His breathing was hard, and his body was very clearly ready for more. It took a lot of effort not to reach up and reclaim all that glistening skin.

Then he bounded off the bed. "Your resistance to my charm is disheartening."

"I've let you charm me enough for one night, don't you think?"

"Not at all." He pulled his cell phone from his pants pocket and tossed it to me before flopping back on the bed with a smug smile. He'd referred to himself as a teenager earlier, and he was acting like one, far too obviously pleased with himself.

I sat up, barely catching the phone. "And?"

"I decided your plan, while clever, wasn't the best idea. We didn't need Claudius believing there were more issues in the domus than he already thinks exist. So I forewent the idea of lying to him and straight up raided his possessions."

I overlooked his casual use of "forewent" for the more important issue. "You raided his possessions?"

"In a manner of speaking. I caused a distraction, got him to leave his room, and searched it before he returned. I got the idea from Lucen, who got it from you. Anyway, he didn't appear to bring anything tangible with him, but I found a file on his phone and sent it to myself."

I frowned at the image, which was hard to understand in such a small size. "It looks like a scrap of paper with some words on it. Or maybe those are glyphs?"

"Both, I think." He pointed to a couple spots. "I also think that's real parchment, not paper. It's old, whatever it is, and odd. I honestly have no idea if this was what you were hoping to find, but it's the only thing I thought might be related. The time period appears to be on target."

I swore and zoomed in on the photo for a better look, but I could make no sense of it. "I don't know if it's what I need either, but thank you." I leaned over and kissed his cheek. "Can you send it to me?"

Devon held out his hand, and I returned the phone. "What would you do without me?"

Happy but yawning, I dropped back to the pillow. "Get some sleep."

TWENTY-TWO

I WASN'T SURE HOW IT HAPPENED, BUT WHEN I WOKE UP, Devon was still in my bed. Vaguely, I remembered falling asleep while he rubbed my back, but shouldn't he have left? He must have his own room somewhere because he didn't have any luggage with him, and it had been far too early for a pred to fall asleep when I'd finally lost consciousness.

Not that I entirely minded his presence. Sleeping around other people made me feel vulnerable, but I'd already done it once with Devon and survived. Plus, there was something nice about having a familiar person so close when I was in such unfamiliar territory.

It was just confusing. Again.

I gazed at him a moment as he lay on his back, dark hair fanned out across the white pillowcase. His breaths were a steady rhythm in the otherwise quiet room. Amazing how innocent people appeared when they slept.

Along the nearby wall, thin strips of daylight outlined the drapes, providing just enough brightness to see by. Whatever time it was, I could tell it wasn't late enough for me to have gotten sufficient rest. Alas, sufficient probably wasn't happening.

The clock on the far side of the bed was blocked by Devon's body, and when I shifted to check it, he snaked an arm around me. I fell back to the mattress and let him press us together. Warm skin, hard muscles, and a heavy erection met me, rousing me further awake, though Devon's eyes remained closed.

This wouldn't do. I was on a timetable. But as I went to poke him in the chest to wake him up, my gaze was drawn down the length of him, and my will buckled slightly. Devon lacked Lucen's broad physique, but his narrower shoulders and chest were solid muscle. Rather than poke him, my finger traced the line of dark hairs between his pecs. I could afford to be nice and ease some of his emotional distress before I left him for the day, right?

He must have sensed my feelings. His eyes opened, and he smiled, wrapping his other arm around me too. "This is not a bad way to wake up. We should do this more often." His voice lacked the telltale signs of grogginess, suggesting he hadn't been sound asleep after all.

"That seems..." I floundered for the right words, but all I could think of was *disturbingly intimate.*

Devon could sense it too. "Relax, Jess."

"I am relaxed."

"Which is why you tensed down to your toes."

I rested my head on his shoulder because it was better than letting him see how my cheeks burned. "Is this what being away from your addicts does? It makes you act funny."

"No, this is what facing the possible end of the world does. It makes me think about priorities." He lifted my head. "How many nights a week do you stay with Lucen?"

"Before recent events, you mean? About three." That was the schedule we'd set anyway, but we hadn't had much opportunity to test the feasibility of it. The idea was to give Lucen plenty of time to see his addicts without me accidentally running into one of them. Although I'd had to accept this was part of life with satyrs, I didn't need more reminders of it.

Devon ran a finger over my lips. "Tell me honestly that you wouldn't like spending one or two of those free nights with me."

I couldn't, but it scared me regardless. I could feel my heart beating against my chest. "So a quickie in your office at Purgatory is no longer enough for you?"

There I went again, hiding in the jokes.

"Not all of them were quick, and no. Last night reminded me of the joys of extended get-togethers."

"So you want more sex?" And those kisses and the sleeping here last night—that was nothing? I couldn't tell how I wanted him to answer. His behavior and my emotions were tangled in a knot that I feared to pick. My love life was complicated enough as it was.

Devon's cool eyes seemed to be searching me for something. "This has no impact on you and Lucen, Jess. You love him, and I'm glad. He loves you, and I'm glad. But I have more fun verbally sparring with you than I do with anyone else, and I have even more fun fucking you, and I *like* you. You're smart and sexy, and you make me work for every time I've managed to leave you speechless. I've tried to keep my distance emotionally, but it gets harder the more time we spend together. And the more time we spend together, the more I want to spend. You can't tell me you feel differently."

My mouth went dry. Devon's speech didn't do much to ease my confusion or chase away my fear. If anything, it made the confusion worse. My head swam with emotions I couldn't sort out. "I don't understand how I can do both—love Lucen and like you. Or how either of you are okay with both."

"We're not like most people you're used to." He coughed dramatically. "You're even less like most people, which is probably where your confusion comes from. In your head, you're a normal human. Oh, I know you've accepted you're not," he said, cutting off my objection, "but years of acculturation aren't unlearned in a couple weeks."

No, they couldn't be, and Devon excelled at pointing out things I didn't like to hear and making me listen. I hung my head, gathering my thoughts, and got a nice view of the man beneath me for my troubles. Damn, he complicated things, but my body didn't care.

"Okay. I mean, yes. I mean, I like the idea of spending more time with you too."

He grinned. "So, are we good?"

My head spun, and I really wished Lucen were here to give me his opinion on what happened. Logic told me he'd agree with Devon, but it would have helped to hear it from his lips. "We're good."

I was merely very, very confused.

And late. Very, very late.

As it turned out, Devon hadn't stayed up much later than me, his internal clock as messed up by the flight and time zone changes as mine had been. While I showered, he got dressed and planned to spend a few more daylight hours sleeping in his room, which was conveniently located in the same hotel. Apparently he trusted I'd be safe locked up inside Gryphon archives during the day.

Someone knocked on the door as I was finishing drying my hair. Before I could yell at Devon not to answer, I heard the door swing open.

Dragon shit on toast. I was going to be late even if I skipped breakfast, and there was only one person that could be.

"Agent Kassin," Devon exclaimed. "How unpleasant to see you as always."

I dropped the hairdryer and hurried into the room. The scene was worse than I'd feared. Devon was only partially dressed. His shirt was unbuttoned, and he was wearing no shoes. Tom did not look amused.

Flustered, I ran my fingers through my damp curls. "Devon was just here to..."

"Make sure no one tried to knife Jess in the middle of the night." He smiled as he finished buttoning his shirt. "I'm disappointed there were no Gryphon guards outside her door."

"He brought us some potentially useful information," I said. That had been the story I was planning to spin. For all the good it would do now. What Devon had been doing in my room was quite obvious, and Tom was obviously quite disgusted.

Devon picked up his phone and gestured to me with it. "Let me know when you leave."

"Yeah." I breathed a sigh of relief as he slipped past Tom and out the door.

Tom didn't bother to disguise his contempt, and only then did I notice he was carrying coffee. He set the coffee on my desk. "What happened with the other one?"

I assumed he meant Lucen, and my cheeks warmed. Tom probably thought I was sleeping with the entire Boston domus. "He's in Boston."

"Were you paying any attention to what I told you about spending time with satyrs?"

"That was also in Boston. Look, can we agree that I stay out of your personal life and you stay out of mine?"

Tom crossed his arms. "My personal life doesn't consider me a snack."

"No, but when you get angry, your experimental coworker occasionally does."

He set a brown paper bag next to the coffee. "And I was trying to be nice. When you didn't show up at the café like we planned, I brought you breakfast."

I peeked into the bag and discovered a croissant. Damn it. Now I felt guilty, although I suspected part of Tom's motivation had been to get me working earlier. "Thank you."

I had no interest in spending more time in the room while the rumpled sheets on the bed and my clothes on the floor reminded Tom of what I'd been up to, so I ate my breakfast as we walked to World.

"I got the email you sent last night," Tom said. "Is that what Devon gave you?"

I stuffed the last piece of croissant in my mouth so I could ditch the bag before entering the building. "No, I haven't sent you the photo from Devon yet. What I sent last night was information from the goblins. Too much information, I'm guessing. We'll have to search through it and see if anything useful is there."

I emailed Tom the photo from Devon and explained in more detail on our way to the archives. Tom had already sent the goblins' information to Marie, and he passed the photograph on to her as well, in case it helped. Down in the basement, he put the photo up on a larger screen so we could see it better.

"Devon said some of the markings were glyphs, but he thought others were a language he couldn't recognize."

Tom scratched his chin, zooming in more closely on the upper right-hand side of the photo, but unfortunately, the resolution only allowed for so much detail. "I think they're all glyphs, but not glyphs in the current style. We call glyphs a magical alphabet these days, but once they were a true alphabet. The magicians and priests—the people who ended up becoming Gryphons—used it to encode spells and other magic-related writing. The magi taught it to them. They used it to send messages that only those in the know could read."

"Like a code alphabet?"

"Basically." He nodded to himself. "I'm sure I've seen this before, but we'll need help translating it. If that really is the glyph language, then this is certainly old enough to be from the correct era. If it contains anything useful, I might have to grit my teeth and thank Devon myself."

I snorted. "Start with me. It was my idea."

A shadow of a smile passed over Tom's lips. "It wasn't enough that I bought you breakfast?"

"Not when you're just going to expense it."

WHILE THE INFORMATION DEVON AND STEPH HAD PROCURED for us excited Tom and Marie, putting it to use was slow and tedious work. Translating the glyphs would take time, and Marie needed just as much time to go through everything Steph had sent. Tom and I kept busy in the archives, him continuing his search for anything related to the Vessels, and me researching the fury prison, particularly whatever a key might have to do with it.

Our first real break occurred on the second day of our efforts. Marie found a scanned photograph in the goblins' files that was very similar to what Devon had obtained from Claudius. Certain we were on the right track with these photographs, Tom used them as a new starting point in his search. If the others had pieces of this parchment, then it stood to reason the Gryphons did too, and that it was important.

Olga, the Gryphon who'd been tasked to translate the parchments, came down to the archives as we were getting ready to leave later that day.

"I'm not getting far with these translations." Her English was perfect, yet oddly accented with both Russian and French, and it struck me what an interesting mix of Gryphons came together to work at World. "This part—" she pointed to the upper left on the goblins' scan, "—is simple. Basically, someone made a note about who this belonged to. This says it's property of some goblin. The other one says it is property of a satyr. But the rest?" She shrugged.

"Nothing?" I cursed to myself.

"It's what-you-call-it—gobblegook. Meaningless."

Marie cracked open a can of soda. "Maybe it is code?"

"Code written in code?" I raised an eyebrow.

"These things you are looking for," Marie said. "The people who hid them would want them well-protected."

Tom rubbed his hands together thoughtfully. "It's not impossible. Thanks, Olga. I might bother you again if we find another one."

Olga's inability to translate the remaining text on the photos was dispiriting, but as Tom pointed out, it could also be another clue we were on the right track.

Since Tom hadn't specifically told me to keep quiet about what we found, and since Lucen and Devon had both proven themselves useful sources of information, I shared what we'd discovered with them that evening.

Devon had brought his laptop, and he set up a video chat with Lucen. While we drank French wine in Devon's hotel room, Lucen sat on his sofa drinking beer.

"Did the meeting end early?" I asked. "Why are you home?"

He raised a blond eyebrow. "You didn't hear what happened?"

"I've been buried in a basement all day. No, what happened?"

Devon muttered something that sounded like "Not good" and refilled my wineglass. I took it he'd been in contact with Lucen—or simply the outside world—over the past twelve hours. Something I hadn't been.

Lucen set his beer down and grimaced. "You want to start with the local or the national?"

"Ease me into the disasters. It'll give the alcohol more time to hit."

"The goblins figured out their hard drive was stolen. That went over as well as you can imagine."

I sipped the wine gratefully. "They accused everyone at the meeting."

"Of course. And when it was clear no one at the meeting knew anything about it—not that they could sense anyway—they became angrier. Ulan wanted to blame the Gryphons regardless, and Gunthra suspected the furies were behind it. That agitated even more people."

Nice work, Gunthra. She'd probably have been better off keeping her mouth shut, but if she wanted to keep people focused on the fury threat, it wasn't a terrible idea.

"So I take it that broke up the meeting?"

"Weeell." Lucen made me wait while he drank more beer. "I think the meeting could have survived if it weren't for the other disaster. I can't believe you didn't hear about this where you are."

Devon put his hands on my shoulders. "You've met Tom Kassin. He's fairly single-minded and is probably trying to keep Jess focused."

Lucen shook his head. "Yeah, but seeing as this concerns us."

"What?" I asked, a second time.

"Atlanta."

Lucen didn't have to be more specific. From his tone, it was obvious what had happened, and I almost jumped out of my chair, but Devon's hands got in the way. "No. How bad?"

Lucen must have brought his laptop closer to his face because his head got larger. "As bad as you'd expect. I'd say this was almost exactly the same M.O. too."

I pushed down my fear as best I could, but my blood wouldn't be warmed. "Buenos Aires, Sydney, and Atlanta. That's three. If they have the Vessels, they only need two more."

"Europe, Asia, or Africa—should we start placing bets on which continent goes next?"

"You're making unfunny jokes," I told Devon.

"Things are less scary when you can laugh at them." He leaned over my shoulder so he could see the laptop better. "In light of this, is his Supreme Upper Asshole still not saying anything useful?"

Lucen smiled grimly at the description of Claudius. "I don't know. The meeting broke up when the news came in. The Gryphons left to confer, and Dezzi went with Claudius. He doesn't like me, so she might have thought she could talk sense into him better alone. That was only a couple hours ago. I'm hoping she'll call later."

"When do we start to panic?" I mused aloud, but I was mostly talking to myself. "Three down, two to go, and we're not getting anywhere half as fast."

Lucen glared at me through the camera. "You don't panic. You keep doing what you're doing where you are. I do think we need to be more proactive on this side of the Atlantic though. The Gryphons need to lean harder on the magi. Fuck Xander. It's not as though he's the only one with connections among them. And we need to think about expanding our allies. Dezzi should talk more to Eyff. There hasn't been a breakthrough on the murder investigation, but we don't have time to wait for everyone's feathers to un-ruffle."

"Agreed," Devon said. "I'm so disappointed our people sent Claudius instead of someone more reasonable. There had to have been a better choice."

Discussing satyr politics wasn't anything I was interested in, and I drank more wine, too stressed out to appreciate the taste. It wasn't until Devon started massaging my shoulders that my attention returned to the men's conversation.

"You know what else I think? I think we need to help Jess relax so she can sleep tonight."

Lucen grinned. "Excellent idea. I even have a plan for how to do this remotely."

I held out my glass to Devon. "Fill please. Whatever you two are scheming, I don't think I'm drunk enough yet."

TWENTY-THREE

TOM DIDN'T WANT TO TALK TO ME ABOUT ATLANTA OTHER than to acknowledge the situation wasn't good. Well, no shit. He did, however, get called into a meeting with members of the Brotherhood, leaving me and Marie in the archives without him.

The silence and dreary tediousness of the work left me restless, and the hours of sitting drove me batshit. I'd regretted never going to college, but if this was what it was like to study, I couldn't help think I'd been better off. Poorer, possibly, but at least when I'd been waiting tables, I never started having auditory hallucinations or too much time to daydream.

The latter was particularly problematic as my daydreams tended to involve two satyrs, and then I became bored *and* horny. And until the evening came around, there was nothing I could do about either problem.

The ceaseless whir of the A/C droned on as I made my way down a row of shelves, searching for another book I had depressingly low hopes for. A moment of horror when I almost dropped it livened up my life for a split second, then normality returned. The book was larger than anything I'd checked out yet, and consequently it weighed a ton. But it was just as fragile as the others, and I feared what a good smack on the floor would have done to it.

I set it down on one of the tables within the archive itself, missing the gentle clicking sounds of Umut's scanner, which at least came in irregular intervals. Irregular intervals gave the brain something to notice and therefore offset auditory hallucinations. Or so was my working theory.

Taking a deep breath, I flipped open the cover. Naturally, a book like this had no index, but the archivist who'd stashed it away had said it contained information about the Pit, and one of the keywords it had been logged under was "key." Alas, I'd have to read the whole thing to find the word, and the English was as archaic as the book.

I yawned, fidgeted and occasionally twitched when I thought I heard Marie nearby, but no one else was ever there. My head was propped on my left hand, my right hand turned the pages, and my eyes glazed over. Focusing on the words became difficult.

So thank dragons the book contained interesting illustrations, one of which was a fancy key.

I inhaled sharply and sat up. With a white-gloved hand, I traced my finger over the difficult-to-decipher English. Best as I could tell, the author was merely reciting things about the fury prison we already knew, but at last I discovered a small paragraph with something useful.

I read through it several times, wishing I had an English-to-English dictionary for help, but I thought I caught the gist. Surely Tom or someone else here was more fluent in sixteenth-century verbiage and could translate.

The book had several silk bookmarks attached, so I used one to mark the page and hurried into the research room. It must have been about lunchtime because Umut was gone, and Marie was getting ready to leave.

"Is Tom still in his meeting?"

"I think so, yes." She beckoned me forward. "You want to come to lunch?"

My stomach growled. "Yeah, sure."

I'd learned the hard way that light breakfasts plus skipping lunch and a long time until dinner did not improve my research skills or my mood. The book would have to wait.

The upside of getting food was that Tom had returned to the archives before we did, and I practically dragged him out of his chair when we got back. "I found something, but I'm not one hundred percent positive I'm translating it right."

He bounded after me into the archive while Umut looked on in amusement. "Why aren't you sure?"

"Well, the English is painful, and it doesn't make much sense. But it means Olef was on to something." I led Tom to the book and pointed to the passage. "It sounds like the people who created the Pit needed to make some kind of key as part of the spell, along with the Vessels. But the key could then be used to unlock the prison. Since no one wanted that obviously, they tossed the key into the prison when they sealed it so it could never be unlocked from the outside."

Tom's brow furrowed in concentration as he read, and he flipped the page a couple times as if hoping more text would appear. None did—I'd already checked. "That's my read of it too," he said after a couple minutes. "This part right here explains the key can't be used from the inside."

I grabbed the back of a chair, my blood racing. "So whatever Olef was on to means something. But it also doesn't make sense."

"Why not?" He checked the book's covers.

"Because he wrote 'Jess use key.' How can I use a key locked inside a prison we're trying to stop from being opened, and why would I?"

Unless, that was, Olef had known more that we'd never learned. What if he hadn't merely had visions of cities burning but also of the prison opening? I shivered and declined to mention this idea.

If Tom had the same one, he also kept the gloomy possibility to himself. "Are there any other mentions of the key?"

"In this book? No clue. This is as far as I got. I searched the rest of the chapter, but then I ended up going to lunch."

Tom pulled a slip of paper from the table and jotted down information about the book, including the author's name. "We can see if he wrote anything else, but you should finish. These older scholars weren't always the most organized. There could be more in some of the later chapters."

I tried to suppress my groan but apparently failed given the way Tom glared at me. "What? I thought you had me training to be a warrior, not a researcher."

"It's true, although this was your idea. Maybe we should take a break soon so we can work on your other skills."

"Oh, I have skills?" I smiled because the thought of doing anything to get out of the archives appealed, even if it meant being lectured by Tom. My discovery, exciting as it was, could not get my adrenaline going for more than a few minutes.

Unfortunately, the archives was where I was to remain for several more hours. Tom left to follow up on whatever he was doing, and I went back to the book. Hope that it really did contain more badly organized information was all that kept me going, but the hope diminished with each new page. When I got to the end, I was ready to drown myself in a vat of coffee.

The archive rule was that anything you didn't check out had to be returned as soon as you were done. Since we'd made note of the book, I took it back to its shelf, and I swore it felt heavier this time around. If I was lucky, Tom was ready to go do that training session. My back ached from being hunched over, and my fidgeting was starting to annoy even me.

As I slid the book in place, the bright red cover of the one next to it caught my eye. Whatever you weren't searching for was always more fascinating than what you were, so I picked it up, curious about what other treasures were locked away in this vast warehouse.

A Treatise on the Nature of Transformative Magic. Idly, I opened the cover and scanned the contents. It was a more modern book than what I'd been reading, published in the late eighteen hundreds. It also seemed to take pains to treat its subject area like a science. The author described being inspired by the "flourishing field of medicine and the recent biological discoveries of Mr. Darwin" and others whose names I didn't recognize.

The chapter titles read almost as much like a medical textbook as they did a magical one. Amused, I skimmed through them until the last one made me catch my breath.

IX. Reversing the Effects of Transformative Magic

Reversing the effects. Holy shit. This was the very thing I'd been wanting to know—was it possible?

I wet my lips, bidding the guilt that bubbled up inside me to go away. Just because I wished I could make Lucen human again didn't mean he wished for the same. And my reasons for wanting him human were entirely selfish. I wanted him to myself. I hated having to share him with addicts.

I supposed I should feel hypocritical since I was sexing it up with Devon, but I couldn't. What I'd told Devon the other day was true—I liked him. But I'd cut Devon from my life without a second thought if it meant a normal life with Lucen.

My fingers trembled as I flipped the page.

"Find something new?" Tom asked.

I almost dropped the book, so lost in my thoughts I hadn't heard him arrive. "Uh, no. I knocked this off the shelf while I was putting the other one away."

Lying to Tom was a subconscious decision, one that I wrote off to more guilt. This time that I'd been distracted from my real purpose. But whatever the cause, I didn't need him knowing what I'd found so interesting in the book. I'd likely get another lecture about relationships with satyrs.

I slid the book on the shelf, making a mental note of the red cover and which book I'd found it by. I'd be back to the archives tomorrow. And if tomorrow yielded no time, the day after. Assuming the furies didn't carry out their plans by then.

"Are we going to train?" I asked.

We did for another two hours, only it wasn't physical training like I'd been hoping for. Tom took me to an empty lab and began instructing me in the finer points of defensive magic. From creating basic counter-curses to healing charms to the rudiments of how to make quick and dirty curse grenades—it sounded more exciting than it was. In fact, it all resembled chemistry too much to be fascinating in the details. I also wasn't ready to do more than learn the fundamentals, so there was no mixing magical anti-pred dust for me yet.

For the third day in a row, I had the beginnings of a headache when I left the building. Devon waited across the street at a café, same as he'd done yesterday, his horns hidden by a disguise charm. I wondered what the Gryphons going in and out of the building thought of it. They might not see the satyr in their midst, but they'd sense him and certainly wonder if one was staking out the building.

"Where to tonight?" I asked as he took my arm.

Devon had taken to playing tourist since Tom had refused his offer to help. While not surprising, the refusal was also a touch infuriating. But then, I could understand the Gryphons not wanting a satyr in their archives.

So as not to completely waste time, however, Devon also had taken to designing magic lessons for me. Lucen had suggested it, and I'd reluctantly agreed, so Devon spent about an hour each night magically assaulting me. After my encounter with Claudius, I knew I had to get better at mentally thwarting pred influence without relying on my ability to reverse the bond. I just wasn't sure it was possible to practice such a thing, nor did it help that these training sessions invariably ended up with both of us naked.

But ultimately, the vast hours of Devon's afternoons and late nights without me had been given over to his own research—choosing attractions, restaurants, and cafés we could visit in the evening. He'd be wide awake, and I'd be tired but in need of mental rest.

"There's a Moroccan restaurant I want to check out," Devon said.

"In France?"

"Honestly, Jess, Morocco was a French colony. Why not?"

Why not? Even if I were awake, I'd have had no answer.

I ordered some excellent dish with couscous and more wine, and I was feeling a little too relaxed as we exited the restaurant. Certainly too relaxed for someone in my position. The universe drove home that fact when I caught sight of two familiar-looking men down the street.

I grabbed Devon's arm. "Hold on. Did you see them?"

One of the two glanced over his shoulder the moment I spoke. Our eyes met, then he quickly spun around, and he and his partner disappeared around the corner.

"See who?"

"Two guys." I dragged Devon with me down the sidewalk. "One's wearing a jeans jacket, and the other has on a colorful scarf. They're not human. I can't sense them, but I saw them earlier at lunch and thought it was weird. They were out early for preds, and magi don't usually bother disguising themselves."

The amusement in Devon's eyes vanished, and he picked up his pace so that I had to struggle to keep up with his longer legs. If he thought I was being paranoid, he gave no indication of it. "Most nonhumans live on the other side of the city, far from the Gryphons. No idea about the magi."

We turned the corner, but the street was busy, filled with outdoor table seating and lined with trees. I strained on my toes, my vision stymied by the canvas patio covers on the bistros and a passing bus.

"I see them." Devon took off, and I followed blindly. "I think they're addicts."

I kept close behind as we weaved through the crowds. All the wine, combined with the aroma of food and the smell of perfume and sweat, made my insides regret the past hour's indulgence. It would be just what I needed, to catch up with these guys and vomit when I should be fighting.

Note to self: from now on, only one glass of wine after a long day.

"There. Damn." Devon pulled me toward the intersection, and I saw them at last. A tram stop was up ahead and the tram already there. Although we darted through traffic, we weren't going to make it. I wasn't anyway.

"Go!" I pushed Devon from behind, cursing my spinning head. He could make it if he ran.

He didn't respond, and in unison we slowed to a stop several seconds later as the tram doors shut in front of us.

I swore. "You could have caught them."

"My job here is to protect you. Not to chase after potential threats. For all we know, seeing them twice was a coincidence."

I kicked a pebble down the platform. "That guy took off when he saw me watching him. It doesn't feel like a coincidence."

Devon ran his hands through his hair, catching his breath. "No, it doesn't, but that's all the more reason for me not to abandon you. Who could know you're here?"

It sounded like a rhetorical question, and it had many obvious answers, but I responded aloud anyway. "Everybody. Nobody. The goblins know Tom and I stopped coming to the meetings. They'll have had plenty of opportunities to send new assassins after me. Or Claudius could have figured out the same thing and contacted the local Dom to dispatch me.

Or it's the furies." I gave Devon a quick rundown on my suspicions about a Gryphon leak.

"Given what happened in Boston, Claudius or the goblins strike me as most likely," Devon said. "Let's get back to the hotel. I've got a couple things to do besides magically assault you tonight."

I cringed at the choice of words. "We can skip that part. My brain is addled enough as it is. What do you need to do?"

"First, you're moving into my room. Don't argue. It didn't take me long to find you in this city. It won't take anyone else with half a brain either. Second, I've got to contact Dezzi. If it is the local satyrs, I want to find out. Dezzi should know more about their Dom. If I'm lucky, she'll actually know their Dom or know someone who does. Introductions always come in handy when you're trying to ruin someone's best laid plans for murder."

Sighing, I clomped along next to him, and I didn't feel secure until we'd moved my belongings into his room. Putting an ocean between me and Boston was supposed to keep me safe. If I wasn't, how was I supposed to concentrate on research? Goodness knew I had a hard enough time as it was.

So far, nothing about this trip had gone as planned. Figured.

TWENTY-FOUR

I DEBATED FOR A WHILE WHAT TO TELL TOM ABOUT THE MEN and ultimately decided to say nothing. My anxiety lessened overnight, right along with my blood alcohol level. In the bright glow of morning, it was harder to worry. Maybe that was foolish, but I didn't want to distract Tom, nor did I relish the thought of being stuck with Gryphon bodyguards. Bad enough that Lucen would find out, but at least I was separated from his overprotectiveness by several thousand miles.

I would simply take better precautions myself. I wouldn't stray far from World during the day, wouldn't get lunch or coffee alone, and wouldn't drink outside the hotel room. When I did go out, I'd pay more attention to the people surrounding me than the sights. It was common sense.

I was following up on yesterday's lead about the key when Marie triumphantly set a polished wood box in front of me and Tom. "I believe this is what you wanted?"

My heart missed a beat as I gaped at the box. Could this truly be it? If Marie had found a Vessel, we could all let out a giant sigh of relief. There was no way the furies could break into these archives to steal it.

Then logic squashed my excitement like a bug. The box Marie had brought didn't possibly look big enough to hold a Vessel like they were described in the lore. Though large, the box was flat, no more than two inches thick.

Tom put on his gloves and released the latch. The lid swung open, and I held my breath—logic be damned—as he pulled something glassy out of it.

Tom's gleeful smile transformed his face into something even younger than usual. "Our piece of the puzzle. Marie, excellent work."

Incased in glass was a familiar piece of paper or parchment. It was rougher than I'd have expected around the edges, but given how old Tom speculated it had to be, the ink was remarkably dark and clear. And there was a lot of it. Writing or drawings of some sort covered nearly every inch.

I pulled up the photo Devon had stolen to compare it. Although hard to say for sure, our piece must have been about the same size based on how much writing there was. The markings were comparable too, yet different. Same code hiding different words.

"We need to decipher it," Tom said, glancing between my photo and the parchment.

"How do we do that? You have a codebreaker here?"

Tom lifted the glass and ran his finger over the seal. "In a manner of speaking. It's all about magic. These were written by magicians for magicians. That's the key to understanding how to unlock the meaning. We don't need a cryptologist in the traditional sense. We need the right counter-charm."

That proved tricky enough. Concocting the right sort of anti-magic was a delicate skill in the best of situations, and it was made all the more challenging in this case because of the age of the parchment. First, we had to remove it from the glass without damaging it. Next, Tom had to defer to an expert charm maker to do the deed.

This process was further hampered by the need to construct the counter-charm in the air-quality-controlled archive as well as by the preservation charms on the parchment, of which we were informed there were many. The parchment's magic had been weakened over time. If it hadn't been so carefully preserved, both by mundane and magical means, I couldn't imagine the thing would still exist.

As for the preservation charms, they interfered with the Gryphon's reading of the spell he had to break, and there was a certain danger in trying too many times to do it. For all we knew, there could be layers upon layers of spells on the parchment, including one that initiated some sort of self-destruct if the wrong counter-charms were used.

Marie had found the parchment early in the morning, but the process to decode it dragged on well into the afternoon. At first, I'd watched expectantly, as had Tom and Marie, as if any moment our expert charm maker would succeed. When it became clear nothing was happening fast as usual, Tom sent me and Marie back to our research.

In need of coffee, I popped back into the room later where Tom was hovering over the charm maker as he prepared for another go. "I'm very glad you guys don't use the same sorts of magic on your top-secret belongings these days."

"What do you mean?" Tom asked.

I thought of the time I'd had to break a magical lock on the server room door in Boston. I thought it had been challenging, but I was beginning to see how wrong I'd been. "You're happier not knowing."

Jacques Maurice, our Gryphon magical expert, gestured wildly to us. "Silence! *Je suis prêt.*"

I wasn't sure why exactly we needed to be quiet given the hard part of what he had to do was already over, but I clamped my lips together and tiptoed closer.

Rather than spray a counter-charm over the fragile parchment, Jacques Maurice had to create a kind of wand he used to brush it. It made me think of an eraser, something to wipe across the parchment and clean it like an old-fashioned blackboard. Each wand was made after he studied the magical energies on the parchment, and each was his best attempt to negate them. Running the wand over the parchment was merely the showy half of the attempt.

Except none of the attempts so far had much to show for themselves. The parchment had remained unchanged and unwilling to divulge its secrets.

But this time was different. I could sense something new was happening immediately, and I was back to holding my breath as I'd done this morning. The hairs on my arms bristled. There was a charge in the air, like static electricity, as powerful spells collided with other powerful spells. My skin tingled with the magic.

Slowly, as Jacques Maurice drew the wand across the ancient document, the writing began to change. The ink became liquid once more, melting into the parchment in places. In others, it slithered like black snakes around itself, joining other trails, loops and straight lines, and reforming into new glyphs. The more of the parchment the wand touched, the darker it turned as the ink spread. By the time he reached the bottom, the top of the page was starting to settle. The squirming symbols stuck where they were, shortening lines in some places and lengthening ones in others until they fell still.

I might have sworn. Even Tom's jaw hung open, and Jacques Maurice rubbed his eyes in plain astonishment.

"Is that what you want it to do?" he asked, switching to English.

Tom raised an eyebrow. "I hope so. Time to bring Olga back to translate."

I insisted we get afternoon coffee while we let Olga work, and a couple hours later we were hunched around a table in the research room once more. The parchment was resealed and tucked safely away in the archive, and Olga had a large photo of the counter-charmed version on her laptop for us to look at.

She pointed to a scrawling set of glyphs in the corner. "This is like the other two you gave me. It says this is the property of someone named Daniel. The rest of this writing resembles a journal entry. Essentially, it explains how five unnamed groups split up some magical objects so they could never be united again. Each group was meant to hide whatever the objects were so they would never be found. It says Daniel wrapped his object in spells to conceal it, then he gave it to someone named Narah to keep."

As the weird symbols on Olga's screen meant nothing to me, I watched Tom's face as she spoke, searching for signs that he understood more than I did. His emotions raced, giving me the sense of being caught in a windstorm, but I couldn't discern much else from probing him with my gift. His excitement must outweigh anything else. Either that or everything was making perfect sense to him so he had no reason to be confused.

I hoped to hell it was that.

"The spell to unwrap the object is here." Olga pointed to a new set of glyphs, these in the bottom right corner. "I translated the spell, along with the full text, but it is different than any I have seen before. Daniel apparently held on to the parchment, or he planned to do so. There is nothing else."

"What's that?" Careful not to touch her screen, I gestured to a blob of ink beneath the spell.

"Ah, that." Olga smiled. "Thank you for reminding me. That..." She zoomed in on the errant blob, and it became clear instantly. It was a crudely stylized drawing of a gryphon. "Interesting, I think."

Tom thanked Olga and brought up the word-for-word translation file she'd given us to study. I read it with him, but I couldn't not feel disappointed. Though interesting, the information didn't seem to help much. And as for where the Vessel might be, we remained lost in the archival swamps.

Tom acknowledged as much when I pointed it out. "It's not as illuminating as I'd have hoped, but it gives us a new area to consider. The gryphon drawing ties this Daniel person to us, even if the Gryphons themselves hadn't formed yet. It might actually be the first reference we have to our origins. We also know from Daniel's writing that the Vessel was wrapped in some very strong magic, making it appear not to be magical at all. That's impressive."

"Impressive, and it might only make our task harder."

Someone cleared their throat nearby, and I glanced up. Umut was wheeling his chair over, his expression sheepish. "I don't know exactly what you are searching for or why, but I couldn't help overhear you talking these past few days. I have a suggestion."

"We'll take it," I said before Tom might grumble about Umut's lack of clearance.

Umut tapped his fingers together. "You're familiar with the story of Daniel the Dragon-slayer?"

I'd heard the name, but was unable to recall anything, so Tom explained. "He's one of the people credited with forming the temple that would later become the church that would later become the Angelic Order of the Knights of the Gryphon that would later become—"

"You. Us. I get it. I remember from school." I gestured for Umut to continue.

"Finally the historian gets to be useful." Umut grinned. "Daniel was known to have an apprentice, a woman. This was before the days when women were excluded from formal magical learning. Her name was Narah, though it's been butchered in many texts to Nora."

"So that could be who these people are."

Umut held up a hand. "There is more to Narah. She was an excellent magical healer, and later became known as Saint Nora when religious fervor attached itself to the magical orders. In all the drawings of her, you'll see she has a cup tied about her waist. It's called Narah's Cup, or Nora's Cup, and no one knows what it was for. But it was considered important enough to be treasured as a relic after her death."

"Worthy of being preserved?"

"For its historical value, not any magical value, yes." Umut returned to his desk against the far wall. "Daniel had begun organizing his small group of magicians by then, and though he had died, the organization kept his treasures. They still have it—meaning we have it. It's in our archives somewhere. I've seen reference to it."

I gawked at Umut, adrenaline seeping into my veins. This day had been filled with too many ups and downs. I refused to let my hopes rise, but my heart didn't seem to care.

Tom was already on the case, bringing up the archive's database. "Umut, you're a genius."

"Yeah, I know."

I laughed, but my giddiness faded as the search result for Narah's Cup popped up on the screen. "What does that mean?"

The result showed no storage number and listed the item as not catalogued.

Tom pushed his chair back from the table with a sigh. "That means exactly what it says. It's not in the proper archives."

Marie, who'd been silent for a while, got up from her chair and clapped her hands together. "It means we are going to Paris."

THERE WAS NO REST FOR THE WEARY, NOT WITH AN apocalypse breathing down our backs and the means to prevent it so close at hand.

Against my arguments about a possible leak, Tom insisted on assembling a team. After much heated discussion, I gave up and we compromised by him agreeing to share as little information with the others as he could get away with.

He also explained the Paris situation to me. The Gryphons' original World Headquarters had been located in Paris and badly damaged during WWII. Once the war ended, rather than rebuild, the Gryphons moved their headquarters to Grenoble where they were better situated to keep expanding their worldwide operations. Most of the contents of their archives had moved with it.

Priority for the move had been given to their most valuable items, usually so designated because of their magical properties or the knowledge they contained. But over a thousand years of collected books and manuscripts, weapons, art, and more had to be accounted for. At the same time, the Gryphons, always reluctant to hire non-Gryphon help for mundane tasks, had to get on with rebuilding and returning to regular work. Some objects, therefore, had been purposely left behind.

Many of those items were of no magical value, but of artistic or historical interest, and they'd been permanently donated to museums. The rest had been gathered into a secure warehouse facility for later cataloguing and organization. But life happened and priority for taking care of those items was never high on anyone's to-do list. Couple that with the lack of Gryphons willing to forgo their primary *raison d'être* and become researchers or librarians, and the warehouse's contents remained largely untouched over the decades.

It was to that warehouse we had to travel, and it amused me that the most powerfully magical item in the Gryphons' possession had been left behind with what sounded like much of their junk.

I should say it *would have* amused me because this was going to be a long trip. Tom didn't want to wait, and neither did I, but eventually good sense won out. By the time Tom prepped a team for leaving, it was approaching six o'clock. The round trip alone would take about eleven hours, never mind needing to search a warehouse that was—by all accounts—not the best organized.

Marie talked us down from our excitement-induced foolishness. After all, we didn't know for certain whether Narah's Cup was the Vessel. That was the whole reason for taking it back to Headquarters where we could attempt the parchment's spell on it and find out for certain. The trip to pick it up, therefore, could wait until morning. It had been sitting in a secured location for decades.

While I knew Marie was right, I remained eager to get my hands on this thing and bring it back to Grenoble. I was certain it had to be the Vessel, and although the warehouse was secure, it was not half as secure as World's official archives.

More to the point, once we had our hands on one of the Vessels, everything else we'd been doing should become unnecessary. Assuming, that was, our interpretation of history and the recent events that led us here were correct. The Pit couldn't be opened without all five Vessels. Therefore, no matter how many others the furies got their hands on, we'd be safe. We could turn our efforts from fighting the apocalypse to fighting the furies who'd caused so much death and destruction in their quest to bring it about.

DEVON COULD TELL I WAS EXTRA JUMPY ABOUT SOMETHING that evening, but I refrained from discussing it until we were safely locked in his hotel room.

"If the Gryphons have their Vessel," he mused, "I wonder whose Vessels the furies stole."

"Does it matter?" I stretched out on the bed, yawning. With great excitement came great energy crashes later.

"Maybe not, but it would be a bit embarrassing if ours was one of them."

I attempted to toss a pillow at him at him and missed entirely. "I don't suppose you can fire your upper management for incompetence, can you?"

Devon pulled out his phone. "There are two ways to get removed from the Upper Council, much like getting kicked off a domus council. The rest of the council votes to boot you or you die. Well, I suppose you could resign too, but I've never heard of that."

"So you're stuck with Claudius until the end of time, or until I kill him."

"You're not going to kill him."

No, probably not, but if he made a play for my body or soul again, I'd try. Fail, but try. "What are you doing?"

"Looking up rental car companies. The Gryphons aren't going to let me come with them, so I'm going to have to follow you."

I sat up and tucked my feet under me. "Your dedication is honorable, but Tom is taking a convoy with us tomorrow. It's not exactly discreet, but he wants to be ready for anything. I'll be surrounded by Gryphons."

"You'll forgive me if that doesn't inspire confidence."

I flopped back on the bed. "No wonder you and Lucen get along so well."

TWENTY-FIVE

WE LEFT BRIGHT AND EARLY THE NEXT MORNING, RIGHT around the time Devon should have been falling asleep. I hoped he came to his senses and did exactly that after walking with me to World, but I doubted it.

Once I met Tom inside, I didn't have a moment more to spare for Devon's decisions. Tom's team had been briefed yesterday, so all that was required this morning was for everyone to arm themselves and the convoy to roll out.

The sky was a gorgeous clear blue backdrop to the Alps as we drove away, the third car in a four-car caravan. Marie was at the wheel, and another member of the *Le Confrérie* rode shotgun. I was stuck in the backseat with Tom.

Ours was the only car filled entirely with members of the Brotherhood. Me, the test subject, not included. The other three cars each contained one member who had been fully briefed on what was going on, despite my objections, and three nonmembers who were along for their tactical support. They only knew we were going to retrieve something potentially dangerous. The details were forbidden.

The benefit for us, therefore, was that we could discuss strategy for searching the warehouse and what we would do when we got back to World. At least, that was the theory.

Tom and Marie were perfectly willing to include me in the conversation, but the other *Le Confrérie* member didn't seem so inclined. Mostly, he ignored any contributions I attempted to make and asked questions only of Tom. I would have written off his behavior to sexism, except the few times he did deign to address me, it was to wonder why I was along. The point of my existence, according to him, was to be a fighter. My brain was not needed for other tasks.

Annoyed, when conversation lulled, I pointedly asked Tom about the status of Mitch and Grace. As I suspected, not much had changed with either. Mitch was still missing, and Grace, though she was improving with her training, was still hopelessly slow and skittish about magic.

The *Le Confrérie* member sitting in front of me said nothing, but I could taste his bad mood and I savored it. If something went wrong today, he'd damn well better remember I was their only useful science project. I expected respect, or if nothing else, to be treated like a human being, or maybe a satyr, or a fuck-it-who-cares-at-this-point person. So long as it was an equal person.

Countryside finally gave way to civilization, and civilization to unattractive urban blight, proving that big cities were all alike in many regards. The warehouse was located in an industrial area filled with many similar-looking buildings and heavily patrolled by private security.

Marie put the car in park outside one of the ubiquitous gray façades. I reached for the door handle, but Tom shook his head. "Wait here."

I strained to see what was going on, but I was on the wrong side of the car. I could hear voices speaking French, a car door shutting once then twice. A few minutes later, Marie started the engine again and turned the car around.

The warehouse's ground floor doors were opening. We followed the first two cars in the convoy inside.

This time when Marie stopped, she shut off the engine and everyone got out. The warehouse doors closed behind us, trapping us inside what amounted to a large staging area. More doors, wide enough to admit a single car, were closed before us.

Tom and the others headed toward a set of stairs on the right, and I kept pace. Someone on the other side of the door buzzed us in, and we entered what appeared to be part security office and part old school library.

The security appeared high tech—lots of monitors showing lots of camera angles, and computers that must control all the various locks. The library side of the room could have used one of those computers to organize the papers and—you had to be kidding me—an old-fashioned card catalog.

I gripped Tom's arm. "Do we seriously have to use that? I've seen one before, but I'm not sure I know how."

"Relax, you don't need to use the card catalog." He patted one of the large books on the table. "You need to use these indexes."

Fortunately, that turned out not to be as onerous as it sounded. We only had to look up one object, and it was an easy one to describe. The challenge came with finding it once we entered the warehouse.

Unlike the official archive, where everything was neatly stored by shelf and row number, items in the warehouse were stored by section. Some had shelf numbers attached, but I was warned that disorganization reigned. Attempts to control the mess were haphazard at best.

Then there was the complication that the Brotherhood wanted to exclude their nonmembers from searching. As a result, seven of the sixteen of us entered the warehouse proper once we had an approximate location.

I'd been expecting something dark and dingy, like a giant attic filled with Gryphon junk, but I should have known better. Disorganized and neglected was in the eye of the beholder. The warehouse was climate-controlled like the archive, brightly lit and scrupulously clean, even if the shelves weren't properly labeled and items sat on them without apparent consideration for age, use, or value.

Tom led us to the correct section of the warehouse, then we split up to cover the shelves and tables within it. My stomach growled, and I pulled on my windbreaker. After the hot sun outside, the A/C within was extra chilly. For the first time since we left Grenoble, I wondered where Devon was and how he was surviving the sunny day.

Very few of the objects I came across in my search were labeled, or if they were, their labels were irritatingly vague. The Gryphons didn't know half of what they had stored, but that was hardly a surprise. It was the reason I was here.

Working my way down a shelf, I closed a box containing a stone figurine, and moved on to the canvas bag next to it. Whoever had tied it had done so tightly. I gritted my teeth, fingers digging into the leather strap and the leather strap returning the favor painfully. When it gave, I let out a breath of relief and yanked the bag open.

For a second I froze, not wanting to get ahead of myself. Then I eagerly pushed the bag down and lifted the object within. It was lighter than it looked, but wow, did it look ugly—a misshapen clay pot, no larger than my spread hand. It was nicked and lumpy, something my childhood self might have produced in art class. It also gave off no telltale signs of power. No tingles in my hands, no hairs rising on my neck.

Gingerly, I set the object on the shelf and poked around in the bag in case I'd missed anything. Some of the items had their labels stuffed in their storage containers. I was rewarded when my fingers closed around a piece of paper. The writing had faded to a barely readable purple, and I stepped into a better lit aisle to read it.

Believed to be Saint Nora's Cup. Original tag lost. Verification needed.

Verification, huh? We could do that.

With shaking hands, I carefully set the label inside the cup. "Found it!"

It would be another hour before we left. The Gryphons came running, and every member of *Le Confrérie* wanted to examine the object themselves and pass judgment. A few wouldn't be satisfied until we finished searching the area, and I got the sense that they wouldn't truly accept the damn thing until they'd searched the entire warehouse and maybe did some carbon dating on it. Fortunately, they were overruled.

While the Brotherhood fussed over packing the Cup for transport, and our support lounged around the vehicles eating lunch, I checked my phone. Devon had texted me about ten minutes ago.

Are you almost done? It's hot as balls out here.

You would know.

So would you.

I sat on the metal steps and took a sip of water. *We should be leaving in a minute.*

Good.

Indeed. I was starving, and the granola bar I'd brought along was not tiding me over, but there'd be no stopping for lunch on the drive back with the would-be Vessel. So very disappointingly un-French to skip the midday meal.

I clambered to my feet as the security door opened.

"We're leaving." Tom had won the war over who got to take possession of the Cup. He carried it inside an innocent-looking cardboard box.

We're leaving, I told Devon, then I crumpled my granola wrapper and started down the steps.

Wait.

I frowned at my phone. *What?*

Devon didn't respond immediately. Impatient, I texted him again, but my phone buzzed with an answer too late. The giant doors in front of the warehouse rattled, and an explosion thundered in my ears. The whole building shook. Dust fell from the ceiling, and I grabbed the metal baluster for support even as I doubled over.

Alarms shrieked overhead, mixing with a cacophony of English and French shouting. Though the doors remained unharmed by all appearances, I heard someone yell something about wards weakening.

Staying low, I checked the phone I'd been clutching to my chest. *Fury addicts. About two dozen.*

Shit. How was this possible?

I closed my eyes for the briefest of moments, letting the panic have its way, then I pulled myself together. "Fury addicts!"

No one asked how I knew, which was a good thing. The reason they didn't ask, however, was because another explosion swallowed the end of my words. When the doors clanged and vibrated this time, smoke began to seep into the room. The Gryphons and the security team leapt into action, but whatever they intended to do, it was too late. Seconds later, the doors burst apart in a blaze of light and shrapnel.

I wasn't the only one screaming as I hit the floor. Smoke or dust, hot and heavy, settled in my lungs, but I felt no pain. Only heat. Only panic tearing at me from the inside. Where was the cup? That was the single thought running through my mind. People might be hurt, I might be hurt, but protecting the possible Vessel had to be my focus.

I coughed and my ears rang, and it took a moment before I realized the warehouse floor had descended into bullet-flying chaos. Security had rushed out from their perch inside the office, and the heavy security door hung open. My eyes burned as I crawled up the steps and put the door between myself and the stairs in a pathetic attempt at a shield.

Below, the red-tinged smoke was lifting, informing me that was no ordinary explosion but a series of magical blasts designed to take out any magical, as well as mundane, security measures. It might have been addicts leading the charge, but with weapons like those, this assault had been planned and provided for by their masters.

This was no time to think about how it was done though. I'd come armed like everyone else, and I took the gun from its holster, not the least bit comforted by its heft. For all my shooting practice with Tom, it felt like an awkward weapon in my hand. A fistfight was far more my style, but no one had asked me.

The Gryphons had opened their car doors and were using them as cover. I couldn't find Tom or the cup from my vantage point, but I could see a couple black-clad bodies on the ground and blood.

Anger soared through my veins, and I sucked in the power it gave me. The hit drove away some of my fear, and my fingers adjusted their grip on the gun. It was unfortunate it had been loaded with those pred-killing rounds. They'd be wasted on humans.

Crouched low, I nudged the door open as far as I dared with my knee, and fired into the melee. My first target screamed something in French and dove to the floor. My second shot missed completely, but it served to alert the addict I'd targeted to my presence. I threw myself back around the door just in time. I swore I could feel the bullets he sent whizzing through the air.

Fear told my anger it could fuck off. This was not my type of fight, and I wasn't ready to find out what lead poisoning felt like. Breathing heavily, I slunk farther into the security office, wondering if there was something else I could do. Some other weapon I could use from my height advantage. Curse grenades would be handy, but I carried none.

My phone buzzed, and if it weren't for the vibration, I'd never have heard it. "Devon, where are you?"

"Jess, are you all right?"

"I'm fine for the moment. You?"

"I'm okay. I'm right behind them. I've got some grenades loaded with disorientation curses. They're enough to knock out a good number of addicts at once, but they're short range. I can't get close enough to set any off so long as the Gryphons are returning fire."

I swore. The gunfire below was ceaseless, and the Gryphons were outnumbered. It was a good bet that since the furies were orchestrating this, they were pumping their addicts full of power, giving them a preternatural ability to overlook pain and fight through any injuries. They'd also be charmed out the ass. They could go on fighting well after a normal human should have dropped.

And all it would take was one to get close enough to the cup to grab it.

I swallowed, an idea forming that I didn't much care for. "What if I can get the Gryphons to stop shooting?"

"I've got the grenades, a gun, and I'm fast. What are you thinking?"

"Nothing any of us will like. Just be ready." I hung up before Devon could protest or I could come to my senses.

Taking a deep breath, I peeked down below. More smoke had cleared around the giant doors. They'd partially collapsed, forming a convenient pile of twisted scrap metal for the addicts to use for cover. New smoke also indicated someone had set off another curse, but I found no indication of what it had done. More Gryphons were down. Marie was holding her right arm, braced against one of the cars. And there, I thought I could see Tom's blond hair.

The shooting had slowed but not stopped, and this would be my best chance to be heard. I had to trust the furies didn't want me dead and that these jackasses knew it.

I threw the door open and stepped onto the stairwell. "*Arrêtez! Je suis Jessica Moore. Votre…*" Ah, fuck. That was where my high school French ran its course. "Uh, *votre* masters want me alive. *Oui?*"

Slowly, I set my gun down. I had their attention, and one of the addicts yelled at the others to stop firing. Shock grabbed me by the throat. I recognized him. It was one of the guys who I thought had been following me in Grenoble. Damn, that meant the furies had known where I was all along. If only I'd gotten close enough to figure out what kind of addicts they were the other night…

I pushed these thoughts away. Too late now, and this was no time for self-recrimination.

I could hear a couple of the Gryphons' annoyed swearing as they expressed their confusion. What the fuck was I doing?

Good question.

I clomped down the stairs, silently screaming at Devon to get on with it. The Gryphons had stopped shooting when the addicts had, and this window wouldn't last for long. I hadn't thought beyond distracting the shooters.

I needn't have worried. A third of the way down, a dark blur streaked past the ripped-open doorway. Devon wasn't exaggerating about being fast. He had to have been wearing a speed charm. It was the only way to account for his movement.

A couple of the Gryphons saw him too, and they started to shout, but it didn't matter. He was faster than them and faster than the addicts—a combination of a pred's natural abilities enhanced by charms. Two mild bangs in quick succession shattered the silence, and a soggy fog whooshed out of the curse grenades and enveloped the nearest addicts.

While they fell to their knees, grasping their heads with a terrible case of vertigo, the unaffected others spun around. But Devon had anticipated that too. One addict went down before it registered with me who was shooting. Then another.

Attacked on both sides, the remaining addicts didn't know which way to turn. I dove behind one of the car doors and landed next to Marie. The other Gryphons were taking advantage of the confusion, and I hoped Devon got out of the way.

"Are you okay?" I asked, and I could barely hear my own voice.

Either Marie was a good lip reader or she got the gist because she nodded. Her arm was soaked in blood, but although pale, she didn't seem in imminent danger of dying.

Before I could decide what to do next, the shooting stopped all at once and gave way to shouting. Or what I thought was shouting. My hearing was terrible, my ears rang, and the space reeked of gunpowder and various unnatural smokes. My knees trembled when I stood for a better view.

The last addicts had been shot or subdued, a couple Gryphons were on the phone, and what followed could best be described as a clusterfuck. Over the course of the next hour, we pieced it together.

Local police had heard the shooting but been unable to get into the compound because the addicts had created a barricade. The addicts had also killed several of the private security guards. When I found Devon, who was unscratched, and I explained to Tom and the others who'd been responsible for taking out over a dozen addicts, they were as thrilled as might be expected.

The Paris Gryphon Office came along with the ambulances, and we spent what felt like forever taking stock of the situation while the wounded and dead were tended to. One Gryphon had been killed, and a member of the Brotherhood was in critical condition as she was whisked away. Marie had received a flesh wound, but she went to the hospital after Tom insisted.

Not quite a part of the group, I sat on the stairs, wiping away my sweat and drinking water. Devon sat with me, and his icy expression dared any Gryphon to tell him to leave. No one tried, probably because they were preoccupied with other matters, but more than one gave us wary looks, and I could taste their suspicion.

Tom approached me at long last. He appeared exhausted but otherwise unharmed, and I was strangely relieved. Not that I wanted anyone to get hurt, but it hadn't been so long ago that I was threatening to punch him or worse for what his group did to me. So much for familiarity breeding contempt. He was growing on me.

"Still don't think you might have a leak?" I asked, my voice low.

Tom frowned. "Once the Vessel is secure, it's a situation that deserves more attention. Fair enough? Are you ready to leave?"

I pressed a cool water bottle to my forehead. "Good. And yes. What's going on?"

He checked over his shoulder as one of the Gryphon vehicles pulled away. "The addicts who don't need medical care are being taken into custody locally. Some of our group are staying behind to question them. The rest of us are returning to Grenoble with the prize, and an escort from the Paris Office is coming along to make up for our lost numbers."

I rubbed my temples. "You expect another attack on the way?"

"I'm not ruling it out."

Devon cleared his throat. "Radical suggestion that you won't take, but since you are a known target at this point, why don't you give the Vessel to me. I'll be following you back to Grenoble, and—"

"No."

"My mistake for bringing in logic."

Tom's lips thinned. "Even if I trusted you fully, which I don't, do you have any idea what would happen to me if anyone found out I'd handed a Gryphon artifact to a satyr?"

"You mean like I handed a satyr artifact to a Gryphon?"

"That was a photograph."

"Which I stole for you."

"For all of us."

I spread my arms out between them. "Enough. We'll stick with the original plan. I want to get back, get the cup locked away, and have my ears stop ringing."

"The last one's out of my control, but let's get moving with the others." Tom motioned for me to follow him.

Devon grabbed my arm as I got up. "He's such a friendly guy. Can we throw him and Claudius into a ring together?"

TWENTY-SIX

NO ONE ATTACKED US ON THE WAY BACK TO GRENOBLE, BUT everyone was on high alert, particularly as we pulled into World. For a brief time, the cup was out in the open, then the building doors shut behind us and we were within the security limits.

Safe at last, I calmed down enough to become aware of my body. I needed a bathroom, food, and alcohol. Preferably in that order, but I wouldn't be picky.

The first two were managed. After the cup was tucked away within the archive's security, one of the Brotherhood Gryphons announced we needed dinner. Magic should never be attempted on an empty stomach, and it had been a long time since most people had eaten.

Soon enough, someone brought in food, but alas, no wine. While we ate, I listened to the others discuss the spell we'd found. One of the Gryphons suggested that I might want to go home and relax, and I stared at him with my best *Are you fucking kidding me?* expression.

Tom noticed and laughed silently. Maybe he was starting to understand who I was, after all.

Preparations for the spell work took time, so I checked in with Devon to make sure he'd returned safely. Then I sent Andre an email, asking if he'd made any progress with the list of names I'd sent him. If Tom really was going to dedicate some time to investigating the possible leak, then I didn't want to waste Andre's time. I just wasn't sure I believed him.

I felt more than a little superfluous while I waited for the Gryphons, but there was no way I was going to miss anything. If the cup really was the Vessel, I wanted to holler with triumph. And if it wasn't, I wanted to know immediately.

Whichever the outcome, I informed Devon to have wine waiting in the hotel room. I'd need it.

Tom came over to get me when all was ready, and he took me up to the lab where the deed was to be done. Even he was fidgeting with excitement.

"Too bad Marie and Umut can't be here to witness," I said as the elevator doors opened. "They played such a big role in this."

Tom smiled in a distracted way. "They'll both have time to check it out later. Don't worry."

The lab we entered was far more industrial than the ones I'd seen in Boston. Everything shined in brushed stainless steel and polished glass. Narah's Cup appeared more pathetic than ever sitting on a gleaming lab table amongst all the modern trappings.

Various containers of unknown ingredients sat next to it, and a baby salamander crawled around inside an obsidian bowl. Several bottles were also present, including one that contained a sprite. It pressed its watery face to the glass, its gray eyes following the salamander.

"Let's begin," said an older woman.

I felt like I was witnessing a religious ritual rather than a charm-casting, or un-casting in this case. Though, to be fair, this was magic unlike any I'd ever seen or heard of. If we were right, there were spells on the cup that somehow disguised the fact that there were spells on the cup. At first, I thought it might just have been my ignorance of magic that had me confused, but talking to Tom and listening to the other Gryphons had clarified it wasn't me. A couple of them had heard of such things, but to work this kind of magic was something else.

I wasn't sure whether to be impressed by the original magician's skill, or terrified by these current people's lack of knowledge. My gut clenched, and it occurred to me for the first time to wonder what the odds were of the Gryphons screwing up the counter-spell and getting us all killed. Until this point, I'd taken the cause of their nervous energy to be the same as mine.

These happy thoughts only increased my anxiety, and I turned my attention to the Gryphon who was actually doing the charm work. It wasn't Jacques Maurice this evening but an older man. I wondered how he'd been selected and if he'd prefer not to have an audience.

All these thoughts swirled around my brain as the minutes ticked by. I watched as inks were made, glyphs were drawn, unknown substances were sprinkled or rubbed, and yet nothing about the cup changed. Not physically. It was possible the magical energies were shifting, or just as possible nothing noticeable would happen until the end when—if—the spell was lifted and the object's power became detectable.

Gunthra's goblin, who claimed to have seen the furies with a Vessel, had said its power was unmistakable. She could sense it from some distance away. Having been created by magic, preds were more attuned to it and better able to work with it, but would we be able to sense the same? Would I, being sort of pred myself?

I checked the time. Nearly half an hour had passed, and no one but the guy working the spell or the Gryphons assisting with ingredients had moved.

"Almost done," he said at last.

He uncapped the bottle with the sprite and poured the creature into the cup. Someone timed it while it swam around, then it was returned to captivity.

I bounced from foot to foot, fingers tapping uselessly against my palms with impatience.

The Gryphon took one of the magical ink pens he'd created and drew a glyph in the center of the wet cup. A couple others peered into it and consulted a copy of the parchment.

"Looks right," the older woman said.

Then why wasn't anything happening? My fingers curled into my sweaty palms with disappointment, and the woman signaled to someone over my shoulder. I turned as two Gryphons wheeled in a cart. An object draped in a sheet sat on it. As they approached the lab table, one of the Gryphons pulled off the covering.

I blinked.

They'd brought in a dragon, and not a little one either. This dragon was fully grown and old, about the size of a large housecat—one of the rare ones you did not want to run into while waiting for the subway. Unlike most of its brethren, this boy or girl could breathe true fire.

In the wild urban jungle they called home, dragons tended to die much younger, usually taken down by other dragons since they were a highly territorial and unsociable species. Or they were killed by human exterminators for obvious reasons. But the Gryphons would have reasons for raising their own, and it appeared I'd discovered one of them.

Inside the cage, the dragon stretched its sinewy, scaly limbs. Dragons, like other magical pests, were attracted to powerfully magical things. A good reason for me not to like them. Dragons bit me and imps stung me more than the average person.

And this dragon was surrounded by magical things and people. It circled its cage, seemingly unable to decide where to focus its attention.

During the time I'd been watching the dragon, Gryphons had cleared off the lab table of everything except the cup. The dragon's cage was lifted on to it, and suddenly the dragon's attention shifted as well. Its head snapped toward the cup. Could it sense something I didn't?

"Ready?" the older Gryphon asked.

The younger of the dragon's handlers put on dragonhide gloves and opened a window on the dragon's cage. It wasn't big enough to let the creature free, but the dragon could stick its head outside. Since the window faced the cup, the dragon did just that. It sniffed the air a few times, cocking its head to the side with very humanlike curiosity.

We waited some more.

"Not going to oblige us on your own, are you?" the Gryphon asked. With a shrug, she pulled a sprig of some kind of plant from her pocket and wound it around what looked like miniature fireplace tongs with an insulated handle.

Guessing what was about to come next, I shifted a few feet around the table for a better view. People who were in the line of fire moved to get out of the way.

The young Gryphon brought the plant end of the tongs to the dragon's face. All it took was a sniff and the dragon got annoyed and sneezed. A few sparks flew from its nose. It tried to bat the sprig away with its head, but the Gryphon held it steady, continuing to taunt it with the plant. Then slowly, she lowered it in the direction of the cup. By now, the dragon was understandably irritated, and there was only one way to destroy the thing.

It let loose. Flames the color of molten gold burst from its mouth. I sucked in a breath, never having seen true dragon fire in person. For my safety, that was a good thing, but aesthetically, the real thing blew away the photographs and videos I'd watched.

But the fire faded as quickly as it had begun, a burst of shimmering, liquid light that became no more than a flash spot on my retinas.

The cup, on the other hand, began to smoke.

I rubbed my eyes, trying to rid myself of the retinal burnout so I could see clearly. The smoke coming off the cup was no more like normal smoke than dragon fire was like a campfire. It rose in an amber spiral, counterclockwise, almost as though peeling off the cup, or perhaps like the cup was releasing the smoke inch by inch. As though it was burning up from the inside out.

I held my breath, and a Gryphon near me gasped.

Faster now, the spiral spun and lengthened, and the smoke dissipated a couple feet above the cup. Like an inverted tornado, it thickened until the outline of the bowl disappeared in the cloud. And when it lifted seconds later, vanishing all at once, the cup had changed.

I let out my breath and clasped my hands to my mouth to keep from doing what, I could only imagine. I was too awestruck to swear. Too happy and relieved to shriek.

This was it. It had to be. We did it. The Vessel was safe.

A lead blanket-sized weight lifted from my shoulders. But while I was content to stand and gawk, several of the smiling Gryphons rushed forward to examine what we had.

I got my look as the crowd thinned. The Vessel held the same basic shape and size of the cup, but it was neither crude nor lumpy, nor made of anything that appeared to be clay. It had been hollowed out of rock of some sort, a blackish-brown color with glyphs carved around the outside edge. When I put my hand toward it, close but not touching, I could feel a hum of power, an electrified wind brushing my skin. It wasn't exactly pleasant, but it was stronger than anything I'd ever felt before.

"So this is it," I said.

"This is it." Tom knelt to get a better look at the glyphs. "It must be. Tonight we lock this in our most secure vault within the archives, then tomorrow we regroup and plan our next move, knowing we've handled the worst of the threat."

I withdrew my hand and yawned. "Tomorrow? How about we take a day to bask in our success, sleep in and not work? I think we've earned it, and we have time."

"Your problem, Jessica, is with your dedication." I opened my mouth to argue, but Tom laughed. "Yeah, I suppose you're right. Go do something touristy tomorrow. God knows I've forgotten what it's like to have a life too."

I DIDN'T KNOW HOW, WHEN, OR IF *LE CONFRÉRIE* PLANNED ON letting the other groups in our failing alliance know about the Vessel. The fewer who did know, the less chance we had of the furies discovering where it was, although I suspected that was a lost cause. After what happened in Paris, even Tom had to admit someone was likely feeding them information.

To be safe, however, I asked Devon and Lucen not to share this information with Dezzi yet. They wouldn't keep quiet forever, but I wanted their silence until I met with Tom again.

I finally had my glass of celebratory wine, and I slept in late the next morning. Devon had suggested a few fun things to do today, including an excursion I'd been wanting to take since I arrived—a gondola ride to an old fort overlooking the city. The views from the ruins were supposed to be amazing.

But that was for later. I had a private errand to run in the meantime.

I was certain none of the satyrs nor the Gryphons would approve of me heading out alone, but with the Vessel secured, I felt more secure too. Nonetheless, I wasn't going to be reckless. I kept my knife with me and my eyes and other senses alert as I strolled over to World. Nothing suggested any threats on the brief trip, and I relaxed as I entered the building.

Umut wasn't working today in the archives, but another woman waved me in. After consulting the note I'd made, I headed straight for the red-covered book. With it in hand, I sank to the floor to read, hoping for the best.

Alas, my good luck, such as it was, appeared to have run out. The chapter on transformative magic was about exactly what I'd been hoping it was about—the complex series of charms and the utterly bizarre process of how humans were turned into preds. I started from the beginning and read for a while, learning more about the process than I'd ever wanted to know and wondering why anyone would choose to put themselves through it. Long lives and immunity to disease and aging were nice, but the transformation, coupled with the aftereffects Devon had told me about, did not seem worth it. Of course, Devon had also told me most people had no idea what they were getting into.

Yet while the fascinatingly horrible process of it all occupied my thoughts, I never lost sight of my real reason for reading—could the pred process be undone? And there, the book had an unequivocal answer—no.

My heart sank as I read about theories and actual attempts to "save" preds by returning them to their human selves. Since the book discussed magic as though it were medicine, the author ended the chapter by concluding that becoming a pred was a terminal condition for which there was no cure. Perhaps later theorists would prove more successful.

I doubted it. Curing preds or "saving" them was not something the Gryphons cared much about.

Throughout the nineteenth century when this book was published, religious overtones had permeated the organization. Reclaiming a pred was part of it. Yet these days, with preds an accepted—though not well liked—part of society, turning a pred human would not be anyone's priority, and most preds would likely be outraged by the idea. The Gryphons were entirely secular too, and they stuck to their primary task of law enforcement and human protection.

I sighed heavily and shut the book. Yesterday's high was well and truly gone, replaced by a dim hopelessness that I knew I should feel guilty about. Lucen's life wasn't mine to wish away any more than mine was his. Hell, if he was researching ways to make me more fully satyr, I'd be pissed. And although he'd once said he wished he could stop needing addicts for my sake, he'd never said he wished he could stop being what he was. There was a difference, and I'd chosen to ignore it for my totally selfish reasons.

Yet despite that, I was disappointed.

"Dumbass," I muttered to myself, putting the book away.

I'd been making peace with what I had, and it wasn't as though I was unhappy. But I was a misery junkie. I was probably always going to be cursed to want what was out of my reach—namely, the illusion of normal.

Using nothing more than cold-hearted logic, I was aware it made no sense. What was so great about normal? Thanks to my screwed-up biology, I could never have those 2.5 kids, and I didn't want them, possibly also thanks to my biology. I did not want a house in the suburbs or a typical job or a hundred other things generally considered normal.

What I did have was pretty damn good—an amazing, smart, hot-as-hell boyfriend who loved me, even if he had to sleep around. And, uh, maybe a second since I didn't know what to make of Devon these days. Also, for the moment, I had an interesting job, good friends, and a world that wasn't about to end.

Yup, there was no question that I ought to be content. So why did I need Lucen all to myself to make me happy? I could only conclude I was selfish, and that irked me.

Maybe I needed to see a therapist. Ugh.

I banged my head lightly against the metal shelf. On my way over, I'd been prepared to follow up reading this book with more research, but my enthusiasm had faded. I wasn't sure if it was logic telling me to knock it off or disappointment, but whichever. I was done searching for miracle cures for Lucen. It wasn't fair to either of us.

My phone buzzed as I left the archive. Devon was awake and wondering where I'd gone.

I wrote back, and we settled on finding me a late lunch and him breakfast before heading to the fort. By now, I was aware that a late lunch inevitably meant either kebabs, a fast-food chain, or stopping by *le supermarché* to make our own.

Opening the main doors, I stuck my sunglasses on and tried to put the morning behind me. Devon remained paranoid and had insisted on meeting me at World, but I could wait for him in the fresh air.

That, I decided, was what I really needed—sunshine, a cool breeze, and some time to revel in my own normal. Time to relax and see what living my life was like when I wasn't being targeted by a serial killer, angry preds, or trying to save the world. Maybe, just maybe, if I could get some peace and routine in my life, this incessant need for a normal relationship would go away. Maybe that's what all this craving was for in the first place —stability.

I didn't exactly believe this theory, but hope was like a goddamn cancer. Once it got under your skin, you might think you killed it, but it had a nasty habit of returning and driving you off a mental cliff.

Here was to hope.

I sat on a bench inside the building's small but elegant courtyard and waited. Planters had been spaced around two fenced-in trees, and pansies in shades of pinks, purples, and white fluttered in the breeze. My stomach growled, a reminder that I'd only had a granola bar for breakfast. My dreams of mornings filled with buttery croissants and pastries stuffed with fruit and chocolate had rarely come to pass. I needed to do something about that.

But my plans for a day of gorging on carbohydrates were rudely interrupted. Something cold pressed into the back of my neck. I jerked out of my thoughts, acutely aware too late that I hadn't been paying attention to my surroundings. My heart stammered.

"Don't move," said a French-accented voice. "Don't scream, or your friend will regret it."

I closed my eyes, cursing myself. I couldn't sense anything behind me except the faintest tinge of anger, and the answer came to me in a rush. I was being touched by a fury.

They'd come for me again.

TWENTY-SEVEN

I EXHALED SLOWLY. THE FURY'S TOUCH MADE CONTROLLING MY fear all the more difficult. My very blood seemed to vibrate with tension.

So this was it? They must have Devon. And if so, what did they want—for me to go into World and retrieve the Vessel for them? It was the only thing that made sense, yet even if I were willing to do that, I wasn't sure I could.

"What did you do to Devon?" My hands pawed at my jeans. Screw the order not to move. I couldn't stop them. My emotions gave my energy a huge boost, better than adrenaline although that wasn't helping either. My knife was so close. I only needed to slide my hand a couple inches up my thigh and reach around my hip.

"The dark-haired satyr?" the fury asked. "Nothing. We have the one called Lucen."

For one awful second, my heart stopped beating. Then I caught my breath and winced. Oh no, not Lucen. Oh, shit. I swore a thousand times in my head, feeling sick. Please not Lucen.

And yet some pessimistic part of me had always assumed it would end up like this, hadn't it? As soon I'd admitted being in love with him, something happening to him became my biggest fear. And furies loved to feed on fear.

Maybe that was all this was. They were playing on my fear and faking me out. Lucen wouldn't be the easiest person for them to grab. For one, he was on the other side of the Atlantic. He also knew how to take care of himself.

I grasped on to that thought with both mental hands. Hope again. Fucking bitch. "Where is he? What do you want?"

"Stop moving. He's fine for now." The speaker paused, and a second disguised fury stepped in front of me. "Raise your hands slowly."

I debated my odds and decided they weren't in my favor. Yet. So I lifted my hands to shoulder height, and the second fury took my knife. I hadn't brought the gun with me today, so that was all I had.

From the corner of my eye, I stared at World's main doors. Hundreds of Gryphons were working right behind me, and not one had left the building in these past couple minutes. The audacity of these furies to approach me in this spot was astounding. I was praying it was also their downfall, but so far they were winning the round. Gryphons inside the building might be aware preds lingered nearby, but as proven with Devon hanging around recently, they didn't much care so long as the preds stayed outside.

The fury in front of me tucked away my knife, and the one behind me removed whatever it was he'd had pressed to my neck. "You have strong magic on you. Where is it?"

I gritted my teeth. "My skin, dumbass. Don't you know Gryphons write their protective spells on themselves?"

"I've never gotten close enough to one to find out before. No matter. Get up slowly and walk with us."

Well, that wasn't what I'd expected. I was certain they were going to ask me to retrieve the Vessel.

Bracing myself, I stood. My sunglasses slipped down my nose because I was sweating, but I didn't dare push them up until I had a better sense of the furies' intentions. They weren't trying to hurt me, just like the furies back home hadn't.

Just like Nyles—aka Mace-head—had promised they wouldn't.

But why not? I wished I knew what they needed me alive for because then I'd have a much better idea of what I could get away with.

"Come." The fury behind me gave me a slight shove forward. With my adrenaline flowing, I could sense his cold, creepy power as I followed his friend toward the street. An SUV with dark-tinted windows started its engines as we approached.

So I was being abducted like Mitch. Peachy. This was not how I'd wanted to solve the mystery of his disappearance.

"Get in."

"Where are we going, and what do you want with me?"

"You will find out soon enough."

I paused. The non-speaking fury opened a back door, but I refused to move. Once I got in this car, it was all over. This was my last chance. I had a building of Gryphons nearby and—supposedly—Devon on his way. The furies might have weapons, but I wasn't helpless. I'd better make my stand while I could.

"Prove to me you have Lucen."

The fury sighed. "I thought you might ask that." He grabbed my arm and came around to my side. With his other hand, he opened a video on his phone.

My hope deflated. The camera footage was dark and shitty, but there was no denying it was Lucen. He was tied up in unidentifiable location, his eyes wild but willful. "Jess, don't listen to them! Don't—"

The garbled sound cut out, and a second later the video ended.

Okay, they had Lucen. Shit. My last chance to do something crazy and heroic had been shot to hell because there was no way I was risking Lucen's life. Still. "How do I know you haven't killed him since?"

"You don't. Do you want to take the chance that you could have saved him? We have no use for him. You come nicely, and we let him go. Choose quickly."

I didn't see what choice I had. I got in the car.

The last thing I heard from outside was Devon's voice yelling my name. Then the car door shut, and the driver sped off as though the devil were chasing us and not merely one satyr incapable of catching up.

I ALWAYS THOUGHT HEAVEN WOULD BE WARM. OR MAYBE THE truth was I'd always thought I'd end up in that other place when I died. Then Steph and I would sit around roasting marshmallows and dipping our toes in a toasty lava lake.

But no, I got cold. Emptiness. And oddly enough, a massive headache.

That seemed like my first clue I wasn't dead.

I shivered and wrapped my arms around myself, strolling through the misty wherever-I-was. All my senses felt muted. I had gauze in my ears, a white veil over my eyes, and the air was empty of smells and sensations. My energy was dulled too. I was alone. Part of me had always feared I needed to be around people to feed on their misery like the pred I was. Perhaps this confirmed it.

I walked forever and nothing changed.

I shivered but never grew warmer or cooler.

I was as static as the world around me. Lost or trapped or imprisoned in my own head. It hardly mattered which if I couldn't do anything about it.

"There's my Jesse-bear."

That voice. I turned, something my feet hadn't felt capable of a moment ago, and now I was no longer certain about the not-dead thing.

My father smiled at me.

My dead father. Almost twenty years dead.

He appeared as he always did in my memories, the way he'd looked as he'd walked out the door the morning before he was killed on the job. His reddish-brown hair was slightly thinning, but his hazel eyes were bright, and the few freckles on his nose were an unfortunate mirror of the ones I'd inherited from him.

He wore his Gryphon uniform. We'd buried him in it. Threw dirt on the job that had gotten him killed. For my mother, I think it had been a very symbolic act, but not for me. At the time, I'd wanted nothing more than to follow in his footsteps.

And here I was. The job had killed me too. At least the Gryphons had. They made me, therefore anything that happened to me was their fault.

"Jesse?"

"Dad?" I hesitated for a moment, then I ran over and threw my arms around him.

Finally, I had senses again. I could smell his spicy aftershave and rub my cheek against his uniform fabric. His warmth chased away some of my chill. But as soon as he released me, the cold came flooding back. "Am I dead?"

"Do the furies want you dead?"

The furies, right. There was something about the furies I should remember. "Maybe they do, but not yet."

"Then you're probably not dead."

"Then where am I?"

His eyebrows chased his receding hairline. "I haven't the faintest idea. Listen."

"But..."

Where there had been no sound a moment ago, there came noise. Low and rumbling, then harsh and clanging. I spun in place, searching for the source, but nothing had changed.

"What is it?"

"Reality."

I frowned. "It's getting closer."

"No, it's getting louder. You're waking up."

"No." I didn't want to wake up. Regardless of anything else, I was certain of that. Being lost in my unconscious, or plain old dead, had to be better than waking up. The very notion spawned fear that ballooned in my chest, suffocating me.

He took my arms, and this time I felt it in a whole new way. My real arms, wherever they were, had been touched. Something within me knew it and struggled against it, but that Jess was paralyzed. Trapped in this Jess.

"They have Lucen," said my father, who never knew Lucen. "They have the Vessels. You have to stop them."

"What if I can't? It'll kill Mom if I die on the job like you."

He patted my cheek, but his hand was no longer warm and smooth. It was cold and rough, not a hand at all. "Then don't die. Wake up. Fight."

A THICK, UGLY SCREAM WOKE ME.

Mine, apparently. It ripped through my dry throat, and I lashed out, limbs flying blindly. My legs collided with something firm, and only then did I open my eyes.

The fury hovering above me spat out something in an unfamiliar language and jumped out of the way. Instinctively, I lunged for him, blind to any sense of self-preservation, but my body wouldn't cooperate. My legs shook, and my muscles gave out. I fell face first to the cold ground.

The fury kicked me in the arm. While I moaned, his feet disappeared from view and a door slammed shut.

I didn't move, partially because I was afraid if I tried, I'd fail and then I'd really be panicking. So I stayed where I was, a lump on the floor, and took stock of my health and situation.

For starters, I was cold. The damp air clung to me, giving me the impression I was in a basement. It sure stank of mildew and decay, but there was also an earthy smell to it that reminded me of my mother's New Hampshire home.

My eyes told me little. The room was dark, but it wasn't true pitch blackness, so light had to be coming from somewhere. Mostly, I could see the floor, which was cold, gritty, and hard. Concrete, I assumed. This told me nothing useful, so I moved on.

My headache was my most pressing concern. It was a dull, all-encompassing pain that covered my skull and could have been brought on by anything. I had no memory of being hit on the head, yet the furies must have knocked me unconscious. If I thought hard about it, I could vaguely remember being jabbed in the arm with something. Perhaps they'd drugged me. It might explain the strange dream about my father.

Gingerly, I tested my muscles next, sliding my legs straight against the floor, slowly moving my arms. I even wiggled my fingers and toes. Everything appeared to work, and aside from generalized achiness, I felt okay. No stabbing or throbbing pains plagued me. I was fairly certain I hadn't suffered any serious damage.

That was something. Not much, but something.

I raised my head next, but it clearly was too optimistic a move. The room swam, and nausea bubbled up in my gut. Okay, never mind. I didn't need to add vomit breath to my list of problems, and my throat was sore as it was.

I rolled on my back instead and hoped the dizziness would pass in time. From my back, the ceiling appeared disturbingly low. Maybe this was like the basement in my grandparents' very old Cape. Most people had to duck when they went down there.

Wait, did houses in Europe have basements? They didn't everywhere in the U.S., but this was not the sort of question normal people researched before traveling abroad. What if I wasn't in a house? What if I wasn't even in France anymore?

I closed my eyes and tried to dredge up memories, but I had absolutely none of leaving Grenoble. I must have blacked out before we reached the city's edge. For all I knew, I was still there or halfway to Siberia. Until I got out of this room, I doubted I'd find out.

On that thought, sitting up, take two.

I took a deep breath, and more slowly than before, forced myself upright. The dizziness spun me around for a moment, then cleared. I opened my eyes and rubbed my unhappy head.

The room's light was coming from the gaps around a poorly hung door. Possibly it was warped by age, as it appeared far older than me. First thought: *This place is seriously ancient.* Second thought: *I'm in a dungeon.*

That sent me into another head-spinning dizzy spell.

The walls were a mix of rough stone and old, unpainted wood. Not nice wood, but splintery, unfinished wood. Now that I could see it better, I could tell the floor was stone too. Mismatched slabs had been thrown down over dirt. All that was missing was a pair of iron shackles. Alas, I had a feeling those could be arranged.

But this was absurd. I knew there were plenty of old castles scattered throughout Europe, and presumably many had dungeons. Or did people call them basements in this enlightened age? Whichever, assuming my judgment—and years of watching medieval-set television shows—hadn't led me astray, why did I have to end up in one? This was creepy, even for preds.

Maybe this suggested I was still in Europe, or maybe not. The U.S. had freaky basements too. I'd been in my share of them.

I had no idea. My head hurt. I'd been drugged. I had to get out of here.

These people had Lucen.

Whoa. That was what I needed to focus on. *Priorities, Jess. Who cares where you are?*

I reached under my shirt and wrapped my fingers around Lucen's pendant. The metal felt strangely warm, the only thing that did. What I wouldn't give for my Gryphon jacket.

Moving would get my blood flowing. Moving would make me warm.

Gathering my courage, I climbed to my knees and paused, waiting to see if my head could keep it together. The nausea had faded, and the dizziness had followed. Right foot then, and left. I stood.

The ceiling was low, but I could stand fully upright. I shuffled over to the door, breathing heavily, my body like a sack of flour on my feet.

Think of Lucen, I told myself. Think of Lucen and what the furies are trying to do. Get angry or scared. Doesn't matter which.

My thoughts drifted to the way I'd left Boston. Was that supposed to be the last time I saw him? It was inadequate, not a proper goodbye.

I thought of my mother, ignorant of the truth because I'd been too chicken to tell her. And I thought of the Vessels, the people who'd suffered and died as the furies filled the three they had. The many more who would die if they broke open the prison.

I didn't get angry or scared. I got depressed.

In the end, it didn't make much difference. Negative emotions were fuel. My own might not be as ideal as someone else's, but in a pinch, they'd do.

My hands clenched into fists, and my shoulders straightened. My legs steadied beneath me, and I pounded on the door. "Hey! Open up! Where's Lucen?"

Screaming with a dry throat didn't work all that well. I choked on half my words, my voice weak in spite of my self-feeding. Banging on the door worked better, so I abandoned yelling and kept that up. The door shuddered and creaked, but the hinges were thick and strong and the wood heavy. It gave me only the illusion of being able to break it down.

My door was a damned tease. That finally made me angry, and I kicked it a few times. The more I beat on it, the angrier I got, and the anger fueled my pounding. I was aware this was both stupid and futile, but if I did it long enough, maybe I'd get a response.

At last, I heard a door open somewhere, and clunky footsteps approached. I banged the door once more for good measure, but my hands were sore, and I suspected splinters were involved.

Someone undid the lock, and I backed up as the door opened, expecting hostility. I got it too—in the form of a gigantic fury whose appearance was hostility personified.

Furies tended to favor outlandish dress and ornamentation, part punk, part comic book villain. Their natural appearance helped it along—their strange-colored eyes and their weird horns that could take a variety of shapes and sizes. But the rest? The tattoos, skin dye, and piercings they sported were deliberate. Like the satyrs who cultivated their appearance to maximize seduction, and the sylphs who attempted to project flawless perfection, the furies decorated themselves to instill fear. Some more so than others.

The guy in front of me didn't need to do much. He had to be over seven feet tall, and he was built like a linebacker—a virtual wall of muscle, all covered in tattoos, including his face. He glared down at me, arms crossed, and it was a good thing I'd decided not to try to rush out the door. I'd probably have ended up with a concussion where my skull met his pecs.

"Nice ink."

He grunted. "Quit your bloody banging. They want to see you anyway."

"British, huh?" First Bostonian furies had a Vessel, then French ones abducted me, then ones speaking an unknown language had dumped me in this cell. Oh, and I couldn't forget the ones raising hell in Argentina and Australia. This was turning out to be quite an international affair.

Given the mess I'd left behind in Boston with the satyrs and goblins, I had to almost admire the furies' ability to work together and get shit done. If only human governments could do the same.

"Let's go." Big Fury stepped aside so I could leave the cell. "Don't think about running."

"With you chasing after me? I'm not."

The rest of the basement he led me through was every bit as dreary as my cell, but it was brighter. Someone had strung bulbs along the wall. Naked and dusty, they illuminated more doors and lit a path up a narrow staircase.

I rubbed my arms for warmth, following the light. The steps, too, were stone, as were the walls. No way was this a normal basement or a normal house.

My theory was confirmed when we reached the top, and the fury directed me through a series of rooms, also with stone walls. Finally, after yet another winding staircase, we entered the biggest room yet. An enormous table sat in the middle, and fraying tapestries covered one of the walls. Sunlight poured in through narrow windows.

And at the table's far end, sat three furies, including a very familiar one —Raj, Boston's Dom. He smiled at me. "Hello, soul swapper. So we meet again."

TWENTY-EIGHT

It was the perfectly cliché thing to say and fitting because Raj looked like a cliché of evil. Two curved horns sprouted from his head, adding to his already imposing height, and black and red glyphs covered his face. He had more of them than I remembered, masking almost all of his skin. His eyes were so dark it was hard to tell where his irises ended and his pupils began.

His very presence unnerved me. It shouldn't have surprised me that he'd be here—he'd disappeared from Boston weeks ago—yet standing in the same room as him made my last two months come full circle.

I licked my lips, summoning the ability to speak. "Actually, I don't soul swap anymore. Things changed after you left on vacation."

Raj clapped his hands together happily. "I'm glad to see you haven't lost your wits. I remember you being quite a force of nature. Such an excellent and unexpected triumph at the Meat Match."

"You mean when I almost slit your fury's throat?"

"That too, but also when you beat up what's-his-face. That killer my people were using."

I clenched my jaw tight to keep from retorting. Too many people were dead because of this asshole, and he didn't sound the least bit upset that

I'd stopped more from dying. That pissed me off. He was the fury. Where was his rage over me thwarting his people?

Raj took a drink from what appeared to be a beer bottle. "Your anger is sadly muted. I hear the Gryphons marked you."

"Glad to know their charms are working."

He wrinkled his nose in disgust. "Gryphon magic can be effective, but it's not important. I should introduce you to people, and you should eat. You must be hungry."

Was he serious? This was getting weirder by the second.

When I didn't respond, Raj motioned to his companions and rattled off their names, which meant little to me. What I found curious was that Raj identified one as the Dom for Vienna, and the other as the Dom for Beijing. So I could now add Austria and China into the unholy international mix.

"So where are your superiors?" I asked.

The furies glanced amongst themselves, and it was the Austrian one who answered. "We are the superiors, satyr."

"Ah, you're thinking where's our equivalent of an Upper Council?" Raj tapped his fingers together. "That's who we're trying to free. Unlike those weaker races, we've vowed only to obey those who truly are our superiors. Not mere social climbers, but gods."

"None of you are gods." But a shiver ran down my spine. I'd read enough descriptions of the original preds at this point to take Raj's description seriously. When the creatures humans used to call demons called other demons their gods… Yeah, not good.

"Sit," Raj urged me.

I wanted to refuse, but it was taking an awful lot of energy to remain standing. And when a fury addict carrying a tray of heavenly-smelling food placed it at the table, my stomach overrode my brain.

I sat. But damn it, I scowled doing it.

All the furies were drinking beer, but they'd given me a pitcher of water, and I attacked it first. Only good sense kept me from gulping the whole thing down. The water was cold and tasted clean. I didn't pause to consider what the furies might be tainting my food with until after I'd finished a giant glass.

I stared at the plate, which was covered in an enormous quarter of roasted chicken, broiled potatoes, and broccoli in some kind of sauce. My stomach demanded I dive in. If these people were going to kill me, I might as well enjoy a last meal. But what else might be in the food? Poisoning me made no sense when they could have killed me easily already, but it was possible to work charms and curses into anything.

I sipped my water, holding my face steady. "What's this for?"

"You must be hungry, that's all," Raj said. "Hurting you has never been our intention. You should realize that. In fact, I apologize for the rough handling you received upon arrival. Given how you blew up a street in Phoenix, your reputation for being difficult preceded you. But I didn't expect you to be thrown in a cell." He glared at the Austrian Dom, who didn't look the least bit apologetic.

I rolled my eyes with so much force it was painful. "I hardly blew up a street in Phoenix, but why let that interfere with your pretty speech? You're obviously not above cursing or drugging me—or almost killing me in a car accident, for that matter—but throwing me in a cell was too much?"

"I don't believe we've ever cursed you, but I admit the accident was a bit of a risky move. Also, it wasn't my idea."

"Well, that's a relief."

"I'm glad to hear it. Drugging you was necessary after what you did last time. You're a hard person to make cooperate, although you should know we let you go in Phoenix."

I laughed, though my throat was so dry it sounded more like a cough. "That was you letting me go?"

Raj shrugged. "We let you go in the sense that we didn't try very hard to get you back. Now you should eat. Get the remaining drug out of your system. I promise you, the food's not tainted with anything. We need you healthy."

Only an idiot would trust a fury's promises, but Raj wanting me healthy—that I believed. Clearly it wasn't for my own interest, yet getting my strength up, regardless of their desires, was in my own interest. I couldn't hope to rescue Lucen and save my own ass if I had trouble walking.

Why the furies wanted me healthy, well, I'd deal with that later. For the moment, Raj's reasoning was good enough for me. I jabbed my fork into the chicken and tore off a chunk.

Wisely, they hadn't given me a knife.

"Why is it so important I be healthy?" I asked between bites.

"You'll find out soon enough. More than that though…" Raj got up, grinning. "You and Mitchell are rare creatures, capable of rare magic. You should be protected. We'll talk about that later."

Mitch. Chicken stuck to my throat, and I washed it down with water. It figured he'd be here too. "I assume he's okay."

"Perfectly fine. We can take you to him when you're done."

I rubbed my head. I had so many questions I wasn't sure where to start. "If you didn't care enough to come after me again until now, why did you kidnap me in Phoenix to begin with?"

The Austrian fury seemed to grow bored with the conversation and left, muttering to himself, but the Beijing Dom chuckled. He stared at me as though I were a fascinating toy.

"It was a question of resources and timing," Raj said. "The Gryphons made their move, and we had to act quickly before they tightened security around you both. It wasn't the ideal timing though, so once you got away, we figured we'd let you run. That was a gamble, but with our informant able to feed us information on you, it was an acceptable risk. Even better, you led us straight to another Vessel."

With our informant. The food turned to stones in my stomach. So nice to know I'd been right. Damn it, I'd told Tom. Maybe if he'd taken the possibility more seriously, I wouldn't be here now. "Who is it?"

Raj grunted. "Can't tell you that. They might still be useful. But to go back to your question, I promise you, *I* didn't want to grab you in Phoenix at all. It wouldn't have been as much fun." He loomed over me, a towering nightmare, and I inadvertently pushed my chair back. "We're going to succeed with our plan. But where would be the sport in crushing your hopes—and the Gryphons' hopes—so quickly? You're fun to watch, Jessica, and like in the Matches, we always make sure the people who are fun to watch live to fight another day. Life is nothing without entertainment."

I darted out from under Raj's bulk. "You're as insane as Victor Aubrey was. Now I understand where he got the idea to call us rare creatures the way he did—from you. Speaking of which, if we're such rare creatures that need preserving, why did you order your furies to kill him in prison? Why not break him out?"

Raj sat on the table, spinning his bottle around. "Victor, yes, I remember his name now. He became a liability, and he was delusional. It's true. Because of that, he was mostly useless. Even among the rare, the herd needs culling to keep it strong. I'm curious how the one you brought to Boston is faring, but we'll check her out soon."

Grace. I winced.

"So." Raj shoved the bottle away and spread his arms. "Any more questions I can answer, or would you like to clean up and see Mitchell?"

"I want to see Lucen. I want to make sure you're upholding your end of what I was promised."

Raj's face fell, and he dropped his arms. "That won't be possible."

"I am not—"

"We don't have the satyr. We never had him."

I faltered mid-stride. "What? Your French goon—"

"That was Mitchell." Raj bounded off the table, his faux-sad face replaced by a delighted smile that I wanted to punch. "Why take the extra risk to capture someone when we could easily put a glamour on Mitchell?"

My breath left me, and I hunched over, head to knees. Relief and rage left me speechless. Lucen was safe. Thank dragons, Lucen was safe. But what the hell—I'd been fooled by a damn fury with a glamour spell? I wanted to kick something. Raj. In the nuts.

I finally pulled myself together with the thought that Raj must be enjoying my silent seething. "Fuck you. You're lucky you didn't hurt him."

Raj and the Beijing Dom were laughing. "Your belief that you could have done anything about it is so...so you. It's very entertaining. I've noticed you haven't asked anything about Olef yet though."

I snapped my head toward him. Of course. I'd suspected the furies were behind his murder, but I should have guessed the details. "That was you, wasn't it? You killed him."

"Not personally," Raj said. "I only gave the order, but Olef had to go.

He knew too much. Plus, it was such an easy way to disrupt that whole silly alliance you were trying to put together. Murder Olef, point blame at both the magi and the harpies—instant chaos."

My hands balled into fists. Raj was grinning, proud of himself, and that shit-eating expression was what pulled me over the edge. No one murdered my friends and laughed about it.

I rushed him, blindly, madly, as though caught up in a fury-induced magical frenzy. Blood pounded in my ears. I wanted to make Raj hurt. Make him bleed.

But blind rage was a terrible motivator. Raj could sense it a moment before I sprung, and without coordination on my part, it was simple for him to subdue me. I cursed loudly as Raj pinned me to the cold stone floor.

"Get off me! Fuck you, you dragon-fucking son of a—" Coherence was for losers. Words spilled out of my mouth in nonsensical, unfinished phrases.

Being a fury, Raj's power did nothing to calm me down. Touching as much of me as he did, I became vulnerable to it, and it engulfed me, turning my thoughts chaotic.

It left off at once as each of my arms was grabbed out from under me. Two fury addicts had taken control of my body. I struggled in their grasp, but I was also partially relieved not to have those fury pheromones clouding my emotions.

"I will make you pay for killing Olef," I said, getting my breathing under control.

Raj laughed some more. "I look forward to you trying. It should be extremely entertaining. But for now, I think you should go see Mitchell. Get reacquainted and rested. You two have such a big role in what's in store tonight."

I fought against the addicts, but they were big guys, much like the furies I'd seen. Fighting would get me nowhere. I needed to clear my head, calm down, and come up with something useful to try.

The addicts practically dragged me into another area of the castle. Or building. Whatever it was, I no longer cared. Not all of it was so wholly medieval compared to its basement, at least.

The addicts pushed me into a thoroughly modern bathroom and slammed the door. I fumbled into the sink and caught my balance. I used the toilet because I was really starting to need it, and I washed my hands and face, both of which were covered in dirt. That done, I took advantage of the moment alone to search the room for anything I could use as a weapon.

Talk about futile. The medicine cabinet held someone's toothbrush and toothpaste, and nail clippers. The cabinet under the sink had only extra toilet paper. There wasn't even a plunger I could swing at people. There was, however, a towel bar and a shower rod.

I tried the bar first, but although I did my best to unscrew the damn thing with my thumbnail, it wasn't happening. This was what I got for preferring my nails very short. I tried the nail clipper on it next, but the clipper was too thick. The curtain rod was as big a letdown—a cheap plastic thing that would be as good as useless. I briefly considered taking the lid off the toilet, then thought about how far that would get me and opted against it. In my current state, I only had a couple good swings in me.

The nail clippers then. I slid them and the tiny file I found with them in my pocket.

I was just in time because an addict flung the door open. "What are you doing?"

"Grooming." I pretended to adjust my jeans so he wouldn't get suspicious about why my hand was in my pocket. "Did you ever hear of privacy?"

"No. Move."

I rolled my eyes and hurried out of the room before they took my attitude as an excuse to manhandle me again. We didn't go far. One of them unlocked the next door over and stared at me. My hand started to my pocket as I sensed this might be my best chance to make a run for it, then a familiar voice called out my name.

"Mitch?" I glanced in the room, and that was my mistake.

The addict stuffed me inside. I went tumbling forward, and the door shut. Damn it.

A pair of hands caught me by the arms and steadied me. I straightened, and Mitch released me with a sad smile. "On one hand, it's nice to see a friendly face. On the other, shit. They finally got you back."

I laughed once and nodded at the sentiment. "Yeah. How are you? The Gryphons have been searching for you since…"

"I'm all right. The furies are treating me well. And let me tell you, that's been creeping the hell out of me."

I scanned Mitch's cell. The lone window was narrow, like the others I'd seen, but he could have had far worse accommodations. Starting with the ones I'd had when I arrived. He had a bed in the far corner, a tattered chair, and a faded rug covering the dusty floor.

"How long have you been here?" I asked.

Mitch shook his head. "About a week? I've lost track of the days. Where is here?"

"You don't know? I was hoping you could tell me."

"All I know is I was in one place, then another, then finally I was here. It's nice here—" he gestured to the window, "—but I don't know where here is. It's got trees."

I joined Mitch at the window. We were a good two to three stories above the sloping ground. A thin clearing separated the building from a dense, primarily evergreen forest. I'd never been able to tell a spruce from a pine from a fir, and I wasn't sure it would have helped me narrow down our location if I could. The air smelled lovely though, of needles and wood smoke.

"At least you have a nice view."

"Yeah, it's gorgeous." Mitch plopped on the chair. "And believe me when I say it gets dark at night. Not a hint of light pollution. Wherever this is, it's far from civilization. I think it's some old fort, and whoever owns it must also own a huge chunk of land with it."

Peachy. This situation was getting worse and worse. Even if I fought my way out of this place, it sounded like I'd have one hell of a run to find help. And I was a city girl. Dump me in a dark forest, especially at night, and I was liable to get eaten.

I collapsed to the floor. "Do they ever let you out?"

Mitch rubbed his head and leaned back in the chair. "Yeah. Well, they let me use the bathroom next door, but if you mean out, as in outside, they have on a couple occasions. But I was on a very tight leash both those times. I think they did it because they wanted me to see how hopeless it was."

"What do you mean?"

"This place is huge, and there's only one way in or out as far as I could see. Like I said, fort. Or castle, I guess. There's also lots of cars parked nearby. It's crawling with furies and addicts. Not a single normal person. They don't seem too uptight about security either, so I'm thinking they have no reason to expect being found."

I rested my head against my knees. "Great. Raj likes to have his games. It wouldn't surprise me at all that he let you out just to get a rise from you."

"Which one is Raj?"

I gave Mitch a brief description.

"I don't think I've seen him much." Mitch suddenly darted up. "That's the weird thing about it. None of these people seem to be in charge. Each time..." Every muscle in his body tensed at once, and he collapsed back to the chair.

I quit picking at stray threads in the rug. "Each time what?"

Mitch made a miserable face and sighed. "They've addicted me. On multiple occasions. When I told you they kept me on a tight leash outside? That's what I meant. It's always been different ones though, and they've never done it for long. Just when I wouldn't cooperate with whatever they wanted me to do. This way they could make me cooperate. The feeling of one of them inside your head like that..." He closed his eyes. "That's how they got me to hold still while they turned me into your friend. If that's how they lured you here, then shit. I'm sorry, Jess."

"It's not your fault. I've had preds in my head before. I know what it's like." I started to say more, but my words evaporated as what he'd told me sank in.

Small wonder Raj had never addicted him. Raj knew what people like us could do, and he wasn't willing to risk Mitch figuring it out. But if Raj's friends didn't know, then maybe, just maybe, we had something we could use.

My excitement rose, and I did my best to bury the feeling while I considered the details. No sense giving anything away.

"What have you been doing while I've been stuck here?" Mitch asked. "Did you find the other person?"

I shook off my thoughts, but my mind continued to race. "Yeah, we have her. She's in Boston, or was. We've been hunting down these Vessels of Making. Did I explain—?"

"The things the furies were obsessed with. I've heard them talking about filling them."

"Yeah, exactly. What do you mean *were* obsessed with?"

Mitch sat up with what appeared to be great mental difficulty. It was hard to tell for sure from where he sat in the shadows, but his face seemed more lined. He also had several fading cuts on his cheeks. "They don't care about them anymore. I think they filled them all."

"Not all."

"Enough then."

I froze. "Can't be. Are you sure?"

"Not positive, no. But I've overheard bits of conversations. They haven't exactly tried to hide their plans from me." He dragged his nails over the chair arms in agitation, digging them into the holes in the fabric. "Whatever they were doing, they're done with that phase of the plan."

I let my breath out slowly. As of this morning or yesterday, the furies had only filled three. How could three out of the five be enough? Nothing we'd read had suggested that. And yet... Yet it would explain why the furies grabbed me without a care for the Vessel at World.

But it didn't explain why they went after the Vessel in Paris. Not unless that was just more entertainment for Raj. After all, they only had to throw a few disposable addicts at us, and we'd think we were getting somewhere. Then, should the addicts have been successful, the furies would have another Vessel. If not, no big deal.

If only I'd seen Tom before I'd been abducted. Had *Le Confrérie* found out anything by interrogating those addicts we'd caught?

I was starting to feel sick again because it made all too much sense. The furies had tricked me to get me here. Could they have been messing with my mind all along—keeping me distracted? Raj had let me play his game, put together an alliance, chase down another Vessel—all actions that gave the furies the time to gather the power they needed. Then, once they were ready, they came and grabbed me.

No. My hands clenched, and I buried my head against my knees. Though the logic was twisted, so were the furies. I hated to admit it made some sense.

But I refused to let this be the way the game ended. I would get us out of this, and moreover, I would stop them from opening the Pit. I had to. Failure was too scary to contemplate.

"Jess?"

I took a deep breath and lumbered over to the door. Ear pressed against it, I strained to hear any noise out in the hall, but there was none. Mitch had said security wasn't tight, so I hoped I was right. "Back in Phoenix when I explained what people like us could do, I left something out. Let's talk about addiction."

TWENTY-NINE

I TOLD MITCH EVERYTHING, FROM WHY GUNTHRA CALLED ME an abomination to why preds avoided transforming gifted humans. I told him about both times I'd used my ability to reverse the pred-addict bond and its effect on me and the pred in question. I almost neglected mentioning what happened between me and Claudius, but in the end, I decided I should be completely truthful. Mitch needed to know what we might be dealing with.

He took the information skeptically. Same as me, he'd grown up fearing preds, loathing what their magic did to him. He'd never felt powerful in comparison. Throw in the fact that he'd recently been addicted and hadn't been able to fight their hold on him, and it was understandable. If Gunthra hadn't given me enough hints as to what I could do, I doubted I would have figured it out on my own.

Alas, the only way for Mitch to try it for himself was for him to be addicted again. I just hoped when and if that time came, the visualization I used and had taught him would help. We'd only get one shot to do this most likely, and it wouldn't be a long one. We'd have to take advantage of the magical hit immediately.

Since Mitch explained the furies only addicted him when he became uncooperative, our task was simple—get uncooperative all over their asses.

Hell, I excelled at being uncooperative. I wasn't so sure about what would happen afterward, but it eased my mind to remember Mitch wasn't entirely lacking fighting skills. Despite my assurances, however, he wasn't thrilled with the plan, but he had nothing better to offer. So that decided, all we could do was wait.

Our chance didn't arrive until late in the evening. Heavily armed addicts came by once before then, dropping off more food and water. From the window, I watched the sun sink behind the trees, turning their many shades of green to gray and black. Shadows lengthened on the floor, and every noise inside and out grew louder. I didn't like it. There was no lamp to turn on, and the darkness spread without streetlights and neon signs to fight it. I wasn't used to truly dark nights. Not even a moon rose over the trees.

Mitch was confident that if we could break out of the building, we could steal one of the many cars, but the darkness made me wonder how far we'd get. He questioned my part of the plan. I questioned his. My better sense screamed it would never work, but the other option—stand idly by while the furies opened the Pit—wasn't going to happen.

As the darkness consumed our last patch of warm floor, someone unlocked the door. I sprang to my feet, and Mitch got up slowly. He'd been expecting the addicts earlier, but this was obviously not part of the daily routine.

Four of them stood in the hallway, and one beckoned to us. "Come on. They're ready."

I held still, but the fear gnawing at me all day became more insistent. "For what?"

"Showtime." The addict grinned in a way that should send shivers down the back of any mortal, and not just because he'd filed a couple of his teeth into points.

Mitch stepped forward, but I hesitated as it dawned on me that the addicts weren't armed. Perhaps we wouldn't have to deal with the furies yet. A nail clipper and a file weren't much in the way of weapons, but if they were unexpected…

I simply had to get my hand in my pocket without being noticed. Easier said than done, especially since I wasn't wearing the loosest of jeans.

"I said now." The addict's hand shot out and snatched my arm before I could respond.

I flew forward and bumped into Mitch, and the two of us plus a couple addicts jostled in the narrow hall. This was it. There was no way to signal my intentions to Mitch, so he'd have to follow my lead.

Pretending to lose my balance, I went down on one knee. Rather than get up immediately, I waited for a second addict to yank me to my feet. When he was bent over me and my arm shielded from view, I reached into my pocket.

I'd given the file to Mitch earlier, and my fingers snatched the clippers. Whirling around, I jabbed them into the addict's arm.

He screamed a curse, though I suspected it was more from surprise than damage. The damn thing wasn't sharp enough to break skin, but that was okay. His distraction would have to be enough. While he grasped his arm, I shoved him against the wall and kneed him in the groin.

Mitch caught on quickly. From the corner of my eye, I saw him spin around and deck the addict behind him.

I didn't hang around to see more. Yelling to Mitch, I dashed down the hall, searching for the stairs that had brought me here. Mitch was right behind me, calling out directions. But the addicts weren't far back either. The two unhurt ones had been temporarily stunned and inconvenienced by their friends flailing in the narrow corridor, but I could hear their heavy footsteps.

"This way." Mitch bounded by me, and we practically skidded down the stairs.

When we reached the bottom, he tugged me in a new direction. Empty rooms flew by, and I had enough brainpower left to wonder where everyone was, but no more than that. Food and water had helped my exhaustion, but they weren't enough. My muscles were tiring quickly. My lungs struggled for air, though this run should barely have taxed them.

I sucked in a deep breath, sending out my gift to feed on Mitch's fear, but though it helped, it was far from ideal. Lucen had once told me one person wasn't enough for him to feed on. Was it not enough for me either? My own fear should have helped, but maybe I was too drained for anything to make a difference.

Shouting echoed off the walls behind us, and I thought I heard new footsteps coming from the opposite direction. We were about to get cut off.

Mitch sensed it too, and we stumbled to a halt. I grabbed a nearby counter, belatedly realizing it was indeed a counter and that meant we were in a kitchen. Catching my breath, I scanned the area. Kitchen meant knives. Knives were useful. I wanted my knife back.

Damn, my brain was seriously starting to fail me.

"Knives." I gasped the word, flinging myself around the center island, certain there had to be sharp, pointy objects somewhere.

Probably there were, but I had no time to find out. Five addicts burst through the doors at either end of the kitchen, all looking seriously pissed off. Out of options, I snatched one of the pans hanging above the center island, but the nearest fury grabbed my arm before I could swing it. Then he wrestled me to the wood floor.

Rough fingers dug into my arm, twisting skin and muscle. I clenched my teeth against the pain, searching in vain for an opening. But this guy was good. He had me pinned like a pro, preventing me from using his momentum against him.

Another hand wrested the pot handle from my grip, and I was finally brought to my feet, swearing. Three on one was no fair. Though I tried to twist out of the addicts' hands, I was too weak, and they were just too much *them*.

Dragon shit on toast. Most pred races coveted addicts who could be useful for their position, profession, or skills. Furies only seemed to choose ones who could successfully wrestle bears. My best self-defense moves were rendered totally useless in their bone-crushing grips.

With much grunting on the addicts' parts, and scowling, kicking, and swearing on mine, the addicts dragged me and Mitch out of the kitchen. I had no chance to get my bearings before we entered a new part of the building. One with a view that made my breath catch in my throat.

I wasn't sure where to look first, but up was the least terrifying option, so my gaze lingered there.

A velvet-black, star-sprinkled sky twinkled over me. My first thought was that it was a trick, an illusion, but the night air was cool and damp. There was also no mistaking the breeze on my face. It blew stray hairs in my eyes.

As I traced the lines of the walls it became clear that once this room had supported a roof. Stone by stone, it appeared as though someone had removed it, leaving ragged edges and creepy gray teeth jutting into the night. The effect was stunning and otherworldly, and yet slightly sinister all the same. It reminded me of the cell I'd been in when I first woke up—old and decaying.

The walls that remained—all four of them—were tall and unadorned. The farthest of them had gaping, symmetrical holes, where someone had removed the windows. And to my right, farther down the enormous open space, the floor had been raised like a stage.

I squinted at it, the setup nagging my weary brain until it came to me. Quite possibly this space had once been a chapel. I could fill in the details in my mind. The holes were where the stained-glass windows would have been. The stage was the altar area. The arched alcove on the wall behind it had likely once held religious statues or paintings for the kneelers to gaze upon.

I stopped craning my neck and fixed my attention on the scene before me. No moon shone down, so the furies or their addicts had lit dozens of candles, and their flickering glow contributed to the eerie atmosphere. But what really set the scene was the floor.

The stones had been swept free of any natural debris and covered in glyphs. Thanks to my search for the Vessels, I'd seen glyphs strung together like sentences, and prior to that I'd seen glyphs merged to form new glyphs. But I'd never seen anything quite like what was before me—series of glyphs, lines of them making up lines of larger glyphs, like the letter A written in letter As, then looped into sentences. Maybe paragraphs. All meaningless to me, but full of meaning, no doubt.

And what the glyphs were written in? I blinked, my eyes adjusting to the low light. Some were red, others brown. White and silver. Some were like paint on the stones and others like powder. Without question, this was the most complex magical rendering I'd ever seen. And after what I'd thought of the magic used to disguise the Vessel we'd found, the shock of it left me numb.

Dazed, I closed my jaw and swallowed hard. The giant glyph of glyphs was drawn roughly in a circle, and spaced at odd intervals near the edge were three Vessels, similar in shape and color to the one at World.

"Have I actually rendered the soul swapper speechless?" Raj asked.

I shuddered back to reality, having been totally oblivious to his closeness until he spoke. "I told you, I don't do that anymore."

"You will always be the soul swapper to me, Jessica, because that night was momentous." He motioned to the addicts, and they dropped my arms and slunk off into the candlelit perimeter.

I massaged my sore skin, wondering what would happen if I darted into the center of the glyph. Could I mess it up? Ruin its power?

Mitch seemed to be having the same thoughts. As soon as the addicts let go of him, he took off. But he didn't get more than a foot closer to the target before another fury snatched him back with preternatural speed. The fury wrapped something around Mitch's neck—a charm vial on a string—and Mitch froze in place.

I tensed, and thoughts of imitating Mitch vanished. It had to be some kind of paralysis curse they'd put on him.

"Much smarter, Jessica," Raj said. "You don't want the same treatment."

"Fuck you. What do you want? To show off?"

"Not at all. Well." Raj shrugged with mock modesty. "Maybe a little. But there's a reason you're here. We need you."

I quit rubbing my arms, the dread in my stomach seeming to open into a dark pit. How appropriate I should feel such. "For what?"

Raj draped an arm around me, forcing me against him. My skin crawled with revulsion and tingled with his power. The rage his presence usually induced was oddly muted by my disgust, but my fear was ever growing—a panic building from a low wail into an ear-splitting shriek in my head.

"What I saw you do at the Match," Raj said, his grin making it clear he was enjoying his effect on me, "that's when I knew how useful you could be. It's why you'll always be the soul swapper to me. The Match was everything."

To my left, Mitch blinked a couple times, and I could sense his confusion along with my own, but he could do nothing about it. "I don't get you. Are you talking about when I attacked your fury?"

"He's talking about you," said another fury. "How he discovered what you are."

I frowned. So few furies were women it always surprised me when I met one. She was nearly as tall as the men, well over six feet, her skin astoundingly dark and her eyes yellow gold.

"And what am I? Everyone has a different opinion."

The female fury smiled. "That's because they try to place you in a box. They define you by their idea of magic. But you cannot be defined that way. You're not human, and you're not satyr. You are the proverbial 'none of the above'."

"Better that than one of you."

"Better for us. We are of magic. And humans are not-magic. So what does that make you?"

"A freak?"

"A bridge between the two. A channel." She stalked off suddenly, calling out to an addict.

Raj watched her, his eyes narrowed, and I took the opportunity to worm out of his grip. "Well, gee, that was enlightening."

Before I could demand he explain, Raj whipped a knife from seemingly nowhere and slashed one of my arms. I cried out, doubling over to protect myself from more damage. Blood seeped between my fingers. But Raj made no further attacks, and the pain vanished quickly. The knife had been sharp, the cut not too deep.

Seething, I straightened, clutching my arm. "What the hell?"

"I need some of your blood." He waved the bloodied knife in my face, and I recognized it in a fresh wave of anger. My knife. The asshole had cut me with my own knife. "Now."

Hands grabbed me from behind. Boiling-hot rage flooded my veins. I could feel it pouring through my open cut, dripping onto my hand.

Raj circled around the glyph, and I was forced to follow until he stopped between two of the Vessels. Forced to watch him coat his finger with my blood from the knife and draw a glyph with it in an empty spot in the spell space. He stepped aside then, and the fury holding me shoved me into the area.

Finally, a chance to do some damage. Ignoring my bleeding arm, I ran to the nearest glyph before they could stop me and swept it with my foot.

Or tried to. My foot collided with an invisible wall, and the force of the impact sent me bouncing back. What in the world? I kicked out a second time to no avail.

My heart seemed to beat in my throat. Frantically, I tried once more, and once more my foot smacked into some kind of magical shield. I pressed my hands against the area, banged on it with my fist.

I got nowhere. My lungs gasped for air, but there was no shortage. I only felt like I couldn't breathe because panic was setting in. I was trapped, and I screamed with rage.

Raj's face was all amusement. He smirked as I pounded on the barrier between us. "Be glad you're not frozen."

I spun around in time to see Mitch carried into a similar spot across from me. The fury pulled off the curse once Mitch was inside the trap. Released from his paralysis, he made the same mistake I did. He wailed against the walls holding him. I yelled his name, but Mitch didn't seem to hear me.

Raj shook his head. "Don't bother. Or, well, bother if you must, but all you're going to do is give the rest of us a headache, and it won't dissuade us from our purpose. Although you might get a sore throat."

"Fuck you." I threw myself at the barrier, though I knew it was pointless. For my useless rage, all I got was a banged-up shoulder.

"You become most inarticulate when you're angry."

"I said, fuck you."

Raj signaled to someone behind me. "I heard you the first time, but go on. You're adorable when you lose your shit. Did Lucen ever tell you that?"

My hands clenched into fists. Every muscle within me was contracting. "I'm going to kill you when I get out of here."

"And you'll fail, but I'll enjoy your attempt."

I felt it this time. A sharp sensation in my skull. A red-hot poker to my soul.

I screamed again as Raj's magic tried working its way into me. This wasn't like a sylph's cold, slithering breach of my defenses or Claudius's seductive, magical warmth. This was an incandescent sledgehammer to my brain.

So that's what Raj had been doing all this time. Goading me. Working me up to this moment. My instinct was to resist, to fight him, and all the protective glyphs the Gryphons had drawn on me activated at the thought. I could feel them heating up like brands on my skin, claiming me.

But why? Wasn't this what I'd told Mitch would be our advantage? This was what we needed to do. I had to let myself go, let Raj into my head. He was no Claudius, after all, though he was likely far more powerful than any other pred I'd tried my trick on. Nonetheless, I was confident I could take control of him. And he'd built this cage, or parts of it. With his power in my grasp, maybe I could break free.

Calm, I willed myself. I took a deep breath and stopped resisting. Pressed against the magical wall, I closed my eyes and welcomed Raj's power inside. Immediately, the hammer to my brain stopped. He flowed in smoothly. Hot and irritable, yes, but far more controlled than I'd have expected.

And for a second, it occurred to me to wonder why. I mean, Raj should know better. He'd even told me he'd seen what I did at the Match. Thus Raj should know the perils of making me his addict. So why risk it now?

The question vanished in a tidal wave of power that dropped me to my knees. My muscles relaxed, and my body swelled with it. The head rush left me dizzy, and oh God—the head rush.

I tried to stand, but my legs couldn't hold me. The room swayed in my vision. Raj's power didn't tingle on my skin. It crawled and sparked so heavily that I swore I could see it dancing along my arm hair. I was drunk. I was lost as though hit with a disorientation curse. I was high and yet knocked on my ass.

I tried to funnel the power into something I could grasp, to channel it and maintain my grip on my body, but I flailed and failed. I was on the cold floor, yelling before I knew what happened to me. Caught somewhere between ecstasy and pain.

And Raj's voice was there with me, in my head, and I couldn't toss him out because I couldn't break the bond. I'd never been able to break it, only to convince the pred to do so.

But Raj was not convinced.

"You know what goes into spells, Jessica?" His voice was between my ears, a disembodied intruder. My mind reeled, and I clawed at my hair, wanting to shove him out. My own will had never felt so violated, not even when Claudius had worked his mojo on me.

Was this what addicts had to deal with? Because holy shit. I'd never disparage one again. In fact, I'd smack Lucen myself if I learned he got into his addicts' heads this way.

"Dragon scales and sprite tears," Raj continued, "and salamander fire and phoenix eggs. But it's not only the lesser creatures we use, is it? It's harpy spit and satyr sweat and goblin piss and the sylphs' finest hairs. We are magic, and did it never occur to you that you are too? You are a magic like none other, so rare because you're neither one thing nor another. You're a bridge between species, and bridges are paths by which other magic can travel. Watch them, Jessica. Look to your left and see what you can do."

I didn't want to look, but Raj's presence or some sick masochism compelled me.

Three fury addicts huddled against the crumbling wall nearby. Two of the three had collapsed to their knees, and as I watched, the third fell on top of them. In the flickering candlelight, the shadows across their features grew long, and their skin turned dark and sallow. Their eyes seemed to sink into their heads, and their hair lost its color. The one in the middle's began to crumble and fall out.

"No." I gasped for breath, forcing myself to sit. I didn't understand how this was happening, but what was happening—that much I could tell. Someone was draining these addicts, turning them to ghouls, and I had a very bad feeling that someone was me. Through my bond with Raj, the power he fed me wasn't his at all. It was the addicts'. "Stop it!"

Raj laughed, and as he did, more power surged into my body,

overloading my nerve endings. I screamed again, unable to control the euphoria that sent me crashing back to the floor. "Not yet, but soon. Do you understand now, Jessica?"

I clutched my head, mentally kicking and punching Raj, for all the good it did. Once or twice, I swore I did see him flinch, but he recovered quickly. "I understand you're a murdering asshole."

I slammed my feet into the barrier, and this time it gave but only a little. I felt it stretch around my boots, no longer a hard wall but a rubbery one. Hope swelled in my chest, and despite what my brain wanted, I sucked in harder on Raj's magic. Dizziness overwhelmed me, but once I regained my balance, I pressed my advantage.

The barrier stretched but didn't break. More power. Whatever the cost, I needed more.

"Magic and anti-magic cancel each other out," Raj said. "But you're more like an anti-addict. I channel the power I get from my addicts into you, and it creates an explosion, a powerful burst of magic. Not as much, as say, what can be stored in a Vessel, but good enough."

"Fuck. You." I lashed out at the barrier again, my lungs expanding with another breath filled with power.

From the corner of my eye, the addicts toppled the rest of the way to the ground, though technically they were no longer addicts, but ghouls. Even I could see that from where I'd been trapped. They were empty shells, clinging to life.

"Just like that." Raj closed his eyes as though my cursing and the addicts' pain gave him great pleasure. "You're the one killing them, you know. I only feed their power to you, and you've given us almost enough. You and Mitchell."

I was in the middle of drawing a new breath, and I stopped, my blood turning cold. Horrified, I stared at the addict-ghouls a moment longer, then spun around and finally witnessed the activity in the rest of the room. Furies crowded around the Vessels, reciting words I couldn't hear, messing with the glyphs in ways I couldn't make out. And Mitch was curled on the stone floor, addicted like me, in agony like me.

This was my fault. I'd told him we could use the bond to our advantage, but we were being used again. Just like the furies had been using me all along. I still couldn't get the upper hand. I'd walked into yet another trap.

A scream ripped from my throat, and my mind tore into two. I wanted to expel Raj from my brain—I needed to before it was too late—but my impotent rage only fed his hold over me. While I pushed on him, he pushed right back. I flung my body over and over into the barrier. If I couldn't shake him, I could use him to fight back. But the next wave of power sent me hurtling across the invisible cell with the blowback. White light flashed before my eyes, and my nerves shrieked. My body felt as though it were flying apart.

Then everything disappeared.

THIRTY

AWARENESS RETURNED TO ME ALL AT ONCE. I WAS AWAKE. I was alive, and I was fucking terrified.

I was also back in the room from earlier, the one where I'd found Mitch. Breathing hard, I pressed a hand to my chest, feeling my eerily fast heartbeat. The open window gaped before me, and the night was dark, though brighter than the room. I had to get up, had to do something, but I took a moment to breathe in and out, trying to calm down.

Finally, my pulse slowed to something approximating normal, and my brain began to sort through what had happened. The blinding light. The rush of power that was more like being run over by a tractor trailer than anything else.

The Pit had opened. I was certain of it. Hell, when I closed my eyes, I could swear the air felt different, as though an electric charge coursed through it. It was how the air sometimes felt during a storm.

So why was the night so quiet? The death and destruction I expected— where were they?

I shoved these thoughts aside. I knew I wasn't wrong about the spell's success, and dwelling on it only increased my anxiety. Whatever the reason for the stillness beyond my window, I'd be thankful. In the meantime, I had to recover and get out of here so I could warn people.

I had to recover? I lifted my hands from my chest and stared at the spot where Raj had sliced me open, but the wound had healed near completely. In fact, I felt fine.

It made no sense. I'd lost consciousness. I should probably have a headache or dizziness or something to indicate what I'd gone through, but instead I felt good. Better than good—I felt like I could run a marathon. I felt, well, an awful lot like I'd expected to feel once Raj addicted me and I'd reversed the bond.

Like a freaking demigod.

I sprang to my feet, testing whether my emotional state was related to my physical one, and I was pleased to do so effortlessly. I had energy, and tons of it.

Yet Raj was no longer in my head. No bond remained between us. I waved my arms around, power tingling as it flowed through my limbs. It had to be some kind of residual effect. He'd pumped so much magic into me that whatever he'd done with it hadn't used it all up.

Whatever he'd done. I bit my lip, parsing through his words. He'd used me to create some kind of magical explosion. Somehow I could channel massive amounts of power and—do what? I was fairly sure I hadn't done anything myself, but perhaps that glyph of glyphs had. Just like the Vessels had done nothing but be a power receptacle, I'd been filled with magical juju, and the furies had extracted it.

I shivered at the thought. So this was why they'd wanted me alive. Had they known all along they wouldn't be able to get their hands on the five Vessels, or had they been keeping me as a backup plan?

And did it matter? They'd used me in so many ways. Since I'd failed to stop them, I had to make them pay. But that seemed even more impossible than stopping them had.

My head didn't hurt, but I could feel the pressure of these thoughts building inside me. I squeezed my eyes shut, fighting to keep a grip on my emotions. I was down, but not out. Not yet. For whatever reason, the furies still hadn't killed me. I would make them regret that.

Somehow. Eventually.

And I would not think about the Pit being open because it paralyzed me with fear when I did.

So I'd think about what I could control, like getting out of here. Warning the Gryphons. Finding out what had happened to Mitch and Devon. Killing Raj.

Yeah, that last one had moved to the top of my to-do list. If I didn't accomplish it before I left, when would I get another chance?

A bright light flashed outside the window, and I stuck my head out as a second one followed. Lightning. I gripped the windowsill, my stomach seeming to curl into a ball within me. The stars were gone, and the reddish light dancing across the sky was unlike any lightning I'd ever seen. I mean, for starters, it was red as though the clouds were bleeding. And while the flashes themselves appeared only sporadically, the overall ruddy glow remained, hovering over the grounds.

A new flash sent me ducking back inside the room, and I debated my options. Freaky as the red glow was, maybe I could use it to my advantage. Mitch had led me to believe it would be pitch-black outside, but instead I had light.

The euphoric part of me was tempted to just swing my legs over the windowsill and drop to the ground. It was entirely certain my muscles could stand it, but my better sense wasn't so sure. It was a long drop, and if I landed wrong, I could break bones. Magically sober Jess would think attempting it was batshit.

I was, however, buzzing with power and no small amount of panic.

Bad Jess. Try the door first.

The door. Of course. I spun around, utterly convinced that in my juiced-up state I could kick it down, and I tripped over something lying in front of it. Mitch.

I swore, bracing myself against the door to keep from falling over, but Mitch merely grunted. Kneeling, I poked him a couple times then checked his wrist when he didn't respond.

"Mitch?" His pulse was steady, but he was out cold. I patted his cheek then poked him harder, but he didn't stir again.

Shit. Well, I wasn't about to leave him here. Looping my arms around his shoulders, I dragged him away from the door. He seemed to weigh scarcely more than a feather. Convenient, but I suspected once this power surge wore off, I'd need to soak a week in a hot tub, followed by a good massage to get my muscles back in order. Especially if I had to carry a full-grown man out of this place, which was exactly what I was planning.

But first, I had to find out if I could actually leave.

Kicking down doors always looked so easy in movies, but I seriously doubted it would be easy in real life. And this door was solid, though the lock appeared cheap. Preparing myself for imminent pain, I envisioned directing my excess power into my leg.

Then I kicked. It was a damn good kick, maybe not in form, but in strength. The door agreed, and it shuddered as it flew open. I gaped at it for a moment, half shocked that my maneuver worked, half listening for the sound of pounding footsteps. An addict army on the way to shut me down.

I heard nothing. That in itself was creepy after everything that had happened.

Maybe the furies were busy with the next stage of their plans. And the addicts—wait. Many of the addicts were dead, or as good as. A pang of horror shuddered through me as I recalled how Raj had sacrificed three in whatever he'd done to me. Presumably, another three had died or turned to ghouls for Mitch. Just how many had been here to begin with?

Don't think. Just move.

Right. Of all the people who deserved to be mourned in this tragedy, six fury addicts weren't doing it for me. I'd say their deaths belonged on Raj and his co-conspirators' consciences, except I didn't believe for a second they had any.

I crouched down by Mitch, whispering his name, and he moaned this time. "Mitch, you there?"

One eye opened, then another. "Jess? What happened?" He darted up so suddenly our skulls collided.

I cursed, sitting back on my heels. "You're awake then? Good."

Mitch rubbed his forehead. "Yeah, I feel strange."

"But good and energetic, right?"

"Kind of. What happened?"

I bounded back to my feet. "I'll explain later, but we need to leave."

Mitch climbed upright and flexed his limbs one at a time. "How did we get here? Where—?"

"Later. Promise. We need to go."

"You really think we're going to walk out of here?"

Cautiously, I stepped into the hall and checked both directions. "Not entirely, but I don't have a better idea. And right now, I feel like I could take on a domus of furies, so I'm going to give it a shot."

Mitch snorted. "Can't say I feel the same, although I am feeling strangely awake. Let's do this then."

We did it, and we met with almost no obstacles. Mitch led the way. Though we stopped at every doorway and checked all our corners, the huge building appeared nearly empty. Mitch didn't seem to know quite what to do with his excess power, and he swore in amazement over and over again until I hushed him. He wasn't being loud, but he wasn't helping.

In the kitchen, we found two half-drunk addicts and easily got the jump on them. We took their guns, though they were largely useless against the furies. Then I paused, recognizing the path we'd been taken to get to the ritual space. It made no sense, but I had to see. To know for sure what had happened and what we were up against.

"Jess, what are you doing?" Mitch kept his voice low, but his tension was audible.

Overloaded as I was on magic, I barely noticed the taste of his anxiety. "Don't you want to see it?"

"Yes, but I don't need to go back there. What if the furies are hanging around? We're almost out. Come on."

Mitch was making good, logical sense. Yet the closer I crept to the crumbling spell area, the more certain I was that I had to see this through. Like I was craving closure.

Voices drifted by on an air current and a spicy undertone with them. More power. The angry power of furies. I could smell it. They were still here, but doing what? I needed to know that too.

The low vibrations turned to a rumble, and I realized too late that the furies could likely sense my nervousness this close, but I'd already paused by the doorway. Mitch wasn't far behind, apparently as unwilling to flee without me as I had been without him.

Biting my lip, I crept to the corner and peeked around. Over a dozen furies—possibly all the furies that had gathered here—remained in the room with no roof. I saw Raj and the Vienna fury, the fury from Beijing, and the woman. I saw others I recognized too, but not a single one glanced in my direction. If they sensed me, not one let on. Possibly, the power coursing through my veins shielded me. But the furies were also deep in discussion among themselves, standing in the middle of their glyph, which glowed a faint red, reminiscent of the sky above.

The glyph had changed too. Some of the lines I remembered were missing, and the different ingredients used to create it had all turned the same eerie crimson. I could sense its power, and there was no denying the furies seemed pleased.

But if it worked, where were the original furies they'd unleashed?

Red lightning flashed overhead, as though in answer to my question, and a spike of fear shot through me, one strong enough that at last a couple heads turned my way. I snapped back around the wall, balling the fear into my gut.

"Time to go." I grabbed Mitch's arm, and he followed without question.

No furies charged after us, so either I hadn't been seen or they didn't care. We met no more addicts either. When we burst outside, I wasn't sure whether I was more relieved or confused by their indifference.

The air was cooler and the glowing sky twice as creepy without a roof over my head. Mitch must not have noticed it before because he stopped in the middle of the grounds and gawked.

"I was wondering why everything looked so weird." He swore a few times in a very religious manner, which would have been amusing under other circumstances.

"I don't think God's got anything to do with this. We need to hurry." As I said it though, reluctance weighed on me. What if this was my last chance to go after Raj? Not just for what he did to me, but also for Olef. Damned if I was going to let that horned bastard get away with murdering my friend.

Mitch, meanwhile, had snapped out of his reverie and jogged toward the assorted cars parked along the circular drive. "We're not going anywhere without keys."

"So you can't hot-wire a car either?" Of all the skills Tom had tried to teach me, that had never been one of them.

"Actually, I can. I come from a family of mechanics, and that was my plan, but these are very modern cars." Mitch stopped in front of some fancy black sports car. "You can't hot-wire these things. It's all electronic."

"Really?" Yet another trick the movies always made look easy. Although I had my license, I knew nothing about cars beyond how to drive an automatic. I'd never owned one, and had never been interested in doing so.

I glanced toward the massive stone building we'd managed to flee. Someone in there had keys. Quite possibly the addicts we'd tied up in the kitchen. If I went back to search them, there was always the chance I'd run into Raj.

Of course, if I ran into Raj, there was no guarantee I'd run away again. I had no weapons to use against him. The asshole had taken my knife.

I gritted my teeth. Though I strongly suspected my magical high was interfering with my common sense, I didn't much care. I was the same way when I drank too much. I'd do something stupid, knowing full well it was stupid and damning the consequences. Lucen would call me reckless as usual.

Reckless, scared shitless, and really fucking pissed off. If I might not get a second attempt at Raj, no way was I fleeing like some little child. I'd go down swinging like I always did.

"I'm going back to find keys."

"What?" Mitch turned sharply. "No. I say we take off down the road on foot."

"We have no idea where we are. We could be hours from the nearest town. Do you see any signs of civilization?"

The quiet night was my answer. Somewhere in the trees something fluttered, and a pine-scented wind rustled the leaves, but those were the only sounds.

Mitch scowled, and I took that as my answer. "I'm going."

"Fine. Fuck." He caught up to me, and we ran to the door.

I could taste his fear once more, stronger than the first time. Briefly, I wondered if I was coming off the high and prayed not yet. Just in case, though, I needed to move fast.

"Someone's out there," Mitch said suddenly. "In the trees."

My heart leapt into my throat, and my mind immediately jumped to the conclusion that it was the furies—the real original furies, not Raj and company—but it was a ridiculous fear. The original ones were monster or demons, yet that didn't make them fairytale creatures who lurked in the woods.

Still, my hand trembled as I reached for the door handle. "This is all the more reason we need a car. We are not walking through the darkness."

Mitch nodded, and as he did, I saw the same thing he must have. Movement in the shadows of the trees. Then someone, dressed all in black, stepped into the clearing and waved frantically at us.

"You've got to be kidding." For a moment, I forgot about Mitch and my fantasies of snatching my knife from Raj and jabbing it through his gut. I dashed across the grass and threw myself at Lucen.

THIRTY-ONE

I MIGHT HAVE CRUSHED THE LIFE OUT OF HIM, BUT THAT WAS okay because Lucen did the same to me. The strength of his grip, his cinnamon scent—everything about him felt so good, so comforting, that I was tempted to fall to pieces and let him put me back together. Preferably somewhere far away from here.

But that thought led to a hundred questions, including how he'd found me and how he'd gotten here. Whatever was going on, it wasn't over yet.

To confirm it, someone deeper in the woods hissed our names. Lucen released me and half dragged me under the tree cover. Mitch had raced over too, and I motioned for him to follow.

"What in the world?" Mitch's bewilderment spoke for both of us.

Even with the reddened sky, it was so dark under the tree canopy that I could do no more than make out a few vaguely human shapes. No one spoke. The only sounds were of insects and my feet crushing the needles beneath my sneakers, releasing a potently woodsy scent.

Then something cool was shoved in my hand. "Put this on."

I recognized Tom's voice and draped the cord around my neck. Instantly, the world brightened. I rubbed my eyes, more from the shock than to adjust to the light, and discovered I stood among a group of at least twenty people. Most appeared to be Gryphons dressed in serious body armor. They were all heavily armed, and they were joined by a sizable number of satyrs, who were also literally dressed to kill. Besides Lucen, Devon was among them, and his expression when I made eye contact with him was as relieved as I felt.

"How did you…? What…?" I didn't know where to start.

Mitch did. "What is this thing? I can see in the dark?"

"It's a charm," Tom said. "More convenient than night-vision goggles."

I started to ask why he'd never taught me about this, but I shut my mouth. We had more important issues to deal with, and besides, the number of things Tom could teach me could take years. Saying my training was woefully incomplete was an understatement of epic proportions.

"So they opened the Pit?" Tom's voice was matter-of-fact, but his expression was wary as he glanced skyward.

"Yeah, they opened it." My hand sought out Lucen's, and he gave it a squeeze that lacked any ability to reassure me.

"How?" Devon asked sharply. "I thought you had one of the Vessels."

I was about to answer, but one of the unknown satyrs cut me off. "Who is that?" He had a French accent, and he motioned to Mitch. Devon or Lucen must have rounded up a local posse.

I could sense Tom's irritation with the delay, but he also seemed genuinely relieved to find Mitch alive and well. After a brief explanation of who Mitch and I were, he turned back to us. "What happened? Quick version."

Quick was too optimistic, but I did my best to recount the highlights. I could feel Lucen tense when I described what Raj did to me, and Devon's face was hard. The Gryphons' emotions were all so heightened too that I was getting a secondary hit from their anxiety.

When I finished speaking, a few of them exchanged heavy glances. "We go in," one said. Like the satyr who'd spoken, she had a French accent.

"We go in," Tom confirmed.

"What?" Mitch shook his head. "Jess and I were only heading inside because we needed to find car keys so we could leave. They opened the goddamned prison. We need to get out of here before the inmates discover us."

Tom took a bag from one of the Gryphons and tossed it at me. The shifting heft as I caught it told me what it contained—weapons. "What we need is the Vessels they used to open it. We have no way to close it without them, and we're unlikely to get a better chance to grab three at once."

"Jess and I might have been able to sneak in and steal keys, but there's no way the furies aren't going to notice a small army trying to run off with their supplies."

"That is true," said the French Gryphon. She appraised Mitch with a cool eye. "Which is why you will stay here. We are trained for this. You're not."

Mitch's mood darkened. He clearly didn't like being told to shove off by a woman barely half his size, but she had a point. Hell, I had no business going with them either. Not that I had the good sense to let it stop me.

I pulled a sword from the bag Tom gave me and smiled grimly as I imagined cornering Raj with it. Just a nick. That was all I needed with this blade. Fuck yeah, I was going with the others for this chance.

"Where are the Vessels?" Lucen asked.

His question jerked me back to reality. Getting revenge on Raj was not my primary focus, no matter how good it would feel. Tom had our priorities straight. We'd grab the Vessels and go.

Mitch and I did our best to sketch out the lay of the place, and I let Mitch do most of the talking. He had a better feel for it than I did, and since he wasn't going in with us, I got the sense he wanted to do as much to help as he could. I understood the sentiment.

I had to finally release Lucen's hand as discussion turned to strategy, and I hung out on the edges, listening. I was definitely coming off the magical high. A dull ache was starting to throb in my head, and my euphoria was waning. Maybe I could run a 5k at this point, but a marathon was out. There was nothing I could do about it either. Nothing but hope my energy held until we got out of here with the Vessels.

"Everyone clear?" Tom asked.

The Gryphons voiced their assent, and Devon spoke for the satyrs. So far, I'd witnessed little outright hostility between the groups. More questions came to mind, and I pushed them aside, assuming sadly that I'd forget them by the time this was over.

Assuming, also, I lived. But I'd go on assuming that. What else could I do?

One of the foreign Gryphons took the lead, and in pairs and threes, we darted across the open lawn to the door. Secrecy was out. Assuming none of the original furies were around to join the fun, we were close to evenly matched in numbers—if not magical strength—with the regular furies and any remaining addicts. That left surprise and a massive show of force as our best weapons.

Fortunately, though the Gryphons weren't here with a large army, they'd come well-prepared. I'd been assigned to the rear, and I accepted my position grudgingly. I was the only one tagging along who didn't have plenty of experience in these matters. The Gryphons would be well trained, and presumably, so were the handful of satyrs. Lucen could hold his own, and Devon wouldn't have gathered others who couldn't do the same. Of them all, only Devon was as out of place here as I was, but I'd bet he had done his time on the front lines, so to speak. He was plenty old enough to remember an age when fighting for survival was a way of life for preds.

Curse grenades shattered the calm and cleared the way as the Gryphons stormed the building. Taking up the rear, I found little to do. Space was tight. I could hear fighting and shouting ahead, but my sole job was to watch other people's backs.

Slowly, the group lumbered forward, making way to the ritual area. If the Vessels had been moved... The castle was huge. I wouldn't think on it. They'd been in the same room not long ago. I'd have to count on that still being true.

I stepped over an addict, who must have been cursed with some kind of sleeping charm, and kept going. Ahead, Lucen disappeared around a corner, and I wiped sweat from my forehead. Why did he have to be so far in front?

Skittering noises snapped me back to attention, and I spun around, sword ready. But it was only a dragon running across the stones. It disappeared into the next room.

I coughed from the sulfur-stinking curse smoke and waved it away from my nose. Senses on alert, I continued to walk backwards, brushing the wall with my butt for support. We had to be getting close to the area.

I could do no more than think that when it became obvious we'd arrived. I could see nothing around the corner, but I heard the yelling and shocked cursing in both English and French, and the bangs of more curse grenades exploding. Gunshots too. I sucked in a breath, and my grip tightened uselessly around my sword hilt. Fumes from the grenades carried down the drafty corridor.

The Gryphon in front of me sprang as an opening appeared, and I charged after him, no longer looking behind but ahead. Bursting into the ritual space, I found myself in a war zone. Brightly colored smoke clung to the air, obscuring the giant glyph and the farthest Vessel.

"Two more over there!" I pointed in the correct direction for the Gryphon next to me, no idea whether others had already gotten to them.

In case they hadn't, I took off after the Vessels myself. A shudder passed through me as I stepped onto the glowing glyph, and belatedly, I remembered being trapped in part of it. But either the spell was no longer in effect, or it had only worked where Raj had drawn a glyph in my blood. Nothing held me down, so I hurried on.

As I ran, I kept one eye out for Lucen and Devon, and one also for Raj. Two to protect, one to kill. None of whom I could see.

Breathing hard, I paused in what I thought was the right area, and I flung smoke away with my hands. When it cleared in my vicinity, I could make out an empty spot on the floor where the Vessel I'd been aiming for had been. I hoped that meant one of our team had snagged it.

I was about to head for the next one when someone let out a snarling cry behind me. Pure rage flooded my veins. *Fury*, my heart screamed.

I spun around, sword in position, and slashed at the air. The female fury somehow dropped back mid-lunge, her golden eyes glowing.

The red sky flickered above and my blood seemed to flicker with it, but the fury left me little time to recover. Whipping a knife from her belt, she launched a second attack. I wore no armor, but the fury was so tall it hardly mattered. She aimed her attacks for my neck and face. The speed charms the Gryphons had drawn on me tingled with power as I met her blow for blow, dodge for dodge, but I couldn't land a single scratch.

When she backed me against a wall, I raised my blade upward to meet her and used my lack of height to my advantage. Popping out from underneath her raised arm, I turned and kicked her in the back of the knees. She lost her balance and tumbled forward, colliding with the wall.

Before I could raise my blade again, another came down on her neck. Startled—and though I wouldn't admit it, slightly horrified—I spun right and found Devon.

His eyes widened before I could thank him. "Behind you!"

I felt the oncoming attack even as he warned me. It was Raj. The sensation of his magic felt familiar, and it settled within me as though it belonged. The hairs on my neck stood on end. I didn't like that. What kind of creepy connection had he forged between us? How could recognizing his magic be possible?

Alas, this was no time to ask.

My freaked-out thoughts gave me less time to react, and Raj moved fast. Enormous arms yanked me against him, pinning my own arms to my sides. The little magical boost I had left was no match for his strength, and my charms—though they grew warm with power—weren't either. Though I flailed with my blade, I couldn't turn my wrist at the correct angle to use it against him.

Damn it, this was not how I'd envisioned our fight going down.

I kicked and wiggled in his grasp, but the fury was a hulking beast of a man, his grip like iron and no doubt aided by magic of his own. Using me as a shield, he backed away toward an exit.

Devon had raised his blade, but indecision warred on his face. There was no good way to get to Raj without going through me.

I found I didn't much care. Raj's presence heightened my rage. I was sick of being used by him, and fuck it all, I wanted him to pay for everything he'd done. I didn't give a damn if I went out with him so long as he was dead.

"Just kill him," I screamed at Devon. "Do it!"

Raj chuckled in my ear while Devon didn't move.

I yelled at him again, but rather than come after me, Devon took off in the opposite direction. What the ever-loving hell? I growled my frustration.

Raj slammed me into a doorway, on purpose I was certain of it, so my knuckles collided with the rough stone. The shock forced my hand open, and I dropped my sword. Incoherent in my cursing, I continued to struggle, but Raj's grip never faltered. We left the fighting behind, and soon he had a clear path to the outside.

"Damn it, let me go. You've gotten away."

Raj threw open the door with his shoulder, carrying me down the path toward the cars. I could *feel* him smiling in my head, and it made my skin crawl. Why wasn't he out of me completely?

"You are so full of bitterness and resentment, soul swapper. You should have been one of us. The anger just sweats off you. I can taste it." And then he did possibly the most horrible thing to me yet—he leaned forward and licked my cheek.

I cringed, wishing my revulsion would feed my strength, but it only seemed to mess with my head, and that made fighting strategically more difficult. "I'm going to kill you."

Raj laughed harder. "You keep saying that. You probably once told Lucen you wouldn't sleep with him too, didn't you? You did, I can tell from your emotions. People make promises they can't keep all the time. We count on it. So I don't think you're going to kill me, but your hate is fantastic. We'd welcome that. Think, Jessica. The Pit is open. I'm giving you the chance to be on the winning side."

"What?" I momentarily stopped struggling in my surprise.

Raj slowed as we reached the makeshift parking lot. "I told you your power was rare and valuable. If you came to us willingly and let us use it as needed, you'd not only survive, we'd take care of you. Reward you for your service."

"Are you fucking kidding me?"

"Not at all, but this offer isn't going to last forever." He released me at last and shoved me face forward against a sleek, silver two-seater. "Keep in mind, I've got you. You can come willingly or not. You know which I'd enjoy more." He buried his head against mine and inhaled deeply.

Oh, God. Tell me Raj was not getting hard making me this offer. The length of his body was pressed against me, and I could feel the contours of it too well.

"Fuck you. I hate you. There is no way I'm going to willingly help you and yours do anything. Every piece of me you want to use—you're going to have to take it by force."

I could feel his lips on my ear, his breath all the way down my neck. "I have to admit, I was hoping you'd say that. Far more fun for me."

I braced for Raj's next move, but the attack didn't come from him. Gunfire cracked the night. My heart skipped, and all at once Raj let me go. I flipped around, keeping my back to the car until I knew who was shooting and from where.

Another shot, this time from my right. I flattened against the car, gasping. In front of me, Raj staggered. Sweat beaded on his face, and blood spread across his black shirt. But instead of falling over, he grinned like a madman. As though being shot was hilarious.

"Jess!"

Lucen and Devon were charging across the grass. Relief swelled in my chest, and I pushed away from the car. More than ever, I regretted being forced to drop my blade. Raj wasn't dead yet, and if I'd had it, I could have finished him off in his current state.

But wait—did he still have my knife on him? I had a chance.

A hand shot out and snatched my arm before I could check. Raj yanked me backward. "Just a regular bullet. Disappointing, really."

I tore away from him, and he let me go too easily. Out of the corner of my eye I discovered why, but too late. Raj had pulled out a curse grenade. I launched myself at him, but it was already out of his hand.

I screamed as the curse went flying toward the satyrs, and it exploded with a flash. Through the smoke I heard Lucen swear, and I took off toward them. Fear pulsed in my blood.

"Oh, soul swapper!"

Raj's voice caused me to trip over my feet. My knees and palms hit the grass, and I looked up in time to swat away whatever it was he'd thrown at my head. Then a car door slammed, and an engine revved to life. I reached for the object that landed a foot away. My knife. The cocky asshole had returned my knife.

I curled my fingers around the hilt and sprang to my feet. The smoke was clearing ahead. Both satyrs were on the ground, but Lucen was sitting up.

I scrambled over to them as I heard Raj peel out of the driveway, and I threw my arms around Lucen's neck. "You're okay?"

"I'm fine. Devon..." He let me go.

Trembling, I crawled closer to Devon. He hadn't moved yet. My initial relief retreated slightly, and my fear returned, solidifying into an icy terror. "Devon?"

Like Lucen and the Gryphons, he'd dressed in black, and the unnatural sky played havoc with my ability to see detail. But something wasn't right with his clothes and the black scruff on his chin.

Lucen checked his pulse. "He's alive."

I ran a finger over Devon's chest, feeling him breathe but also feeling residue on my skin. Black powder from the curse covered him. "What is it?"

"No idea." Lucen swore. He pulled a generic counter-curse from his pocket, but it didn't help. Devon continued to breathe, but his skin was clammy and unnaturally pale.

Frantically, I brushed the powder from his face, his clothes, wherever I could find it. But nothing we could do would rouse him.

Pressure built in my skull. This night had gone on too long. My magical high had vanished, and I was near my breaking point. "No. Damn it!"

I didn't realize I was smacking Devon's lifeless body until Lucen pulled me away. "Jess, calm down."

"I am calm. I am so fucking calm. I'm going to kill Raj. I could have had him. I could have done it."

Lucen wrapped his arms around me and pinned me against him until I stopped ranting. I think I cried into his chest—angry, frustrated, miserable tears. But Lucen never said a word about it. He held me until the Gryphons emerged from the building and I could pretend I hadn't reached my breaking point.

THIRTY-TWO

"IT ALWAYS TAKES LESS ENERGY TO BREAK SOMETHING THAN to create it." Tom had lined up the four Vessels currently in our possession along a conference room table at World. "Plus the furies are masters of chaos and destruction. I suppose it's not a shock they found out how to do more with less."

Not in retrospect, no. But it never should have gotten this far. We should have figured it out. Even without Olef. There were plenty of magical scholars among the magi and the Gryphons, and assuredly among the satyrs and goblins and harpies. We should have been able to see what the furies were doing.

But we were too busy fighting among ourselves, not trusting each other with our knowledge. The furies had counted on it. We'd formed an alliance, promising to work together, and hadn't kept the promise—as Raj had predicted. Murdering Olef might not even have been necessary to make us fail.

"With the information from the satyrs and the goblins, we might be able to track down the fifth Vessel," Tom was saying to the group. "But time is not on our side."

Dawn had come and gone, brightening the sky but not burning off the red. The Gryphons had destroyed the glyph, for whatever good that might do. Not much, we expected.

The sky continued to flash erratically, and as of this morning, the glowing patch occasionally rumbled too. When I was young, my mother used to tell me thunder was God bowling. I was pretty sure this thunder was demons stirring. *Le Confrérie* theorized that because the originals had had no suffering to feed on in over a thousand years, they'd be tired and weak. It could take time before Earth felt the effects of what had happened. This was why we were back in a race to find the last Vessel and seal the prison once more.

JESS USE KEY

Olef's last message to me burned like a brand in my mind each time I closed my eyes. Once we'd created the prison, we'd need the key to lock it. The key that had been tossed inside the damn Pit.

What else had Olef known that he hadn't been able to tell us? What else had he seen in his visions?

My head throbbed, and I rubbed my eyes.

Across the table, Tom nodded at me. "We can pick up where we left off tomorrow."

Yawning, I peeled myself off the chair. As anticipated, my body was one giant blob of pain. Muscle aches, a headache, I was fairly sure my teeth even ached. Raj's invasion of my head had left me with no residual benefits, not that I'd expected any. I hoped this meant my ability to sense him had also fled.

"Are you sure you don't want something for the pain?" Tom asked as we filed out.

"I'm sticking with ibuprofen. I'm a little magic'd out."

He pressed the elevator button, not looking so healthy himself. A bruise on his cheek was his most noticeable injury, but he walked with a limp. "You're going to be okay—"

"I'll be fine." Lucen was moving into my hotel room for the night, taking Devon's place since Devon was with the local satyr domus.

In a show of solidarity, the Gryphons had offered to let their healers work on the counter-curse, but Lucen had declined. Twelve hours later,

Devon remained in some kind of magical coma. I knew Lucen really wanted to get him home where the Boston domus' own healers could try.

I swallowed hard, unable to shake the feeling that this too was somehow my fault. I'd failed everyone, first by letting Raj play me, then by letting him get away. Worse, I couldn't get Claudius and company's opinion out of my head—if I had died, the furies' plan would have fallen apart.

When I'd mentioned this in front of Lucen and Tom, they'd both been quick to point out that the furies had needed only two people. If they couldn't have used me and Mitch to channel their power, they might have tried Mitch and Grace. And there was a good chance Grace wouldn't have survived. Mitch was far worse off than I was—he was being tended to by Gryphon healers this very moment—and Grace had even less experience using her gift than he did.

It didn't make me feel better. What if using Grace wouldn't have worked because she wasn't as used to channeling power? The furies' plan might have failed.

Of course, Grace might be dead, and I didn't want that. But ugh.

I didn't know what I wanted. To fight, to kill Raj, to undo what had been done. But also to simply crawl into a hole in the ground, cover my eyes and hope someone else could make this nightmare go away. I was tired of being miserable.

"You haven't told me how you found me," I said, stepping into the lobby.

Tom coughed uneasily. "We didn't. We owe the satyrs for being able to track you down."

"How did they?"

"You might want to talk to Lucen about that."

I crossed my arms. "What did he do?"

Tom waved off my question and pushed open the door. "Really, that's a conversation for the two of you. Have a good night."

Was it my imagination, or was he hurrying away? I closed my eyes. Peachy.

Ten minutes later I threw open the hotel room door. Lucen was in the middle of packing, not just my belongings but his and Devon's as well. We were flying back to Boston in the morning.

I tossed my bag on the floor, ignoring the siren call of the bed. Sleep would have to wait. "How did you find me?"

He was freshly showered, hair dripping on his shirt. "No one told you at your meeting?"

"I was told to ask you. That doesn't sound promising."

Lucen threw the shirt he'd been folding in a suitcase and stared me down. "I put a tracking spell on you."

I stared at him a moment while the words penetrated my brain. "You what? When? Did you ever think to tell me about this?" My headache upped the pitch of its shrieking, but I was too damn tired to yell like I wanted to. Intellectually, I knew I was angry, but I couldn't feel the anger, which was strange. Maybe all my anger senses had been burned out by Raj.

"If I'd suggested it, would you have let me do it?"

"Fuck no." Honestly, I wasn't sure if that were true. He might have been able to convince me, but it certainly would have been my first reaction. "I don't need to be tracked like a package in the mail."

Except, apparently, I did. That just made me more annoyed.

"Why didn't you...? How...?" I wasn't even sure what I was asking.

Lucen reached for my hands. I pulled away, and he sighed. "After you were attacked by the sylphs a couple weeks ago, I thought it might be a good idea. Remember when they lured you out of Boston to help an addict?"

"Not likely to forget. Remember how I kicked their asses too?"

"Yes." He sounded as defensive as I did. "But you were able to take them by surprise. It became very clear to me that living in Shadowtown would be more dangerous for you than we thought. So I had the idea to make it easy for me to find you in case you needed help. I should have told you, but I didn't believe you'd be okay with it, and I worried."

He collapsed to the bed and gazed up at me with a pitiful expression. "The more danger you get involved in, little siren, the more you seem to push me away. You're reckless and stubborn and think you can handle whatever life—or the furies—throw at you, but no one can do everything alone. If you wouldn't let me help, I was going to make sure I didn't wait around for you to realize you needed me."

"So you put a tracking charm on me without my knowledge." I glared at him, hands on my hips, but I wasn't feeling the outrage. "If I pushed you away, it's because I was trying to protect you. Damn it. I'm stuck in this mess. You don't have to be."

"We're all stuck in this mess." Lucen raised his hands in either defeat or frustration. "And I'd be stuck in it anyway, no matter what you do, because I go where you go. You should have figured that out after ten years."

My lip trembled. So this was what happened to my indignant wrath. I could feel tears stabbing the back of my eyes. Fuck. "If something happened to you... I mean, look at Devon. At Olef. I can't deal with this."

Lucen tugged me closer, and I fell onto him. Part of me still wanted to smack him a few times for what he'd done, but it was a small part. The rest of me couldn't bear to stop holding him long enough to do it.

"That's just it, Jess. You don't have to deal alone. We will get through this together if you'll stop thinking that everything is on your shoulders." He wrapped his hands through my hair, and I held him tighter. "We all know the risks, and although you might be the only person Olef saw in his visions, this isn't your battle alone. Or if it is, that doesn't mean you won't have an army to support you. And we will break the curse on Devon, and we'll find the last Vessel, and we will end this. Together. Understood?"

I nodded into his neck. Together. Exactly what I'd been criticizing everyone else for failing to do. "Point taken. But one more question— when and where did you put this tracking charm on me?"

Lucen ran a finger down my throat then lifted the pendant he'd given me out from under my shirt. He gave me a sheepish smile. "I'd hoped it would be ready before you left for Phoenix, and after what happened to you there... I'm just glad it worked eventually."

My stomach flopped. "So you weren't giving me jewelry for the sake of being sweet, huh?"

"Hey, I put a lot of thought into this, so yes, I did. It was practical jewelry too. That's all."

I twisted the chain around my finger so I could look at the pendant.

Tracking charm on it or not, it was lovely. "I guess I won't demand you get rid of it then."

"Are you truly angry?"

I let the chain go and pressed my forehead to his. "I'm not sure. What do you think?"

"You know, I'm not sure either. You sounded angry, but I didn't feel it much and I should have."

Chills prickled my spine. Yet I had been angry, hadn't I? I tried to conjure some anger now, not at Lucen, but at Raj.

The emotion was limp and lifeless.

Devon, I told myself. *Olef. How Raj used me.* But it made no difference what I concentrated on. The most I could generate was a bland, stunted feeling.

Raj did something to me. Raj is still in my head.

Fear I felt quite clearly, and I clenched my teeth, refusing to believe it.

"Jess? What is it?"

I leaned over and kissed Lucen chastely on the lips because I wasn't ready to think more about Raj right now. "Nothing. I'm going to shower. I'd offer to let you join me, but it looks like you didn't bother to wait." I flung a lock of his wet hair around.

"It's not a problem," he said as I tossed off my clothes. "I don't expect I'll spend much time getting clean in there."

Olef's funeral was held on a Thursday. In defiance of what should have been the natural order of things, the day was bright and sunny.

I'd never been to a magi's funeral before, and the differences between their customs and human customs might have been interesting to note, but I was too lost in my thoughts and gloom to pay much attention. One of the few things I did notice was that Xander spoke a lot, and he glowered at me when he did.

Birdbrain, I cursed him silently. I'd heard rumors that Xander blamed me, in part, for what happened to Olef. Like it was my fault Olef had visions of me.

Rather petulantly, I thought Olef deserved someone better to speak for him, but it was unfair. Xander did speak eloquently, and he described a far fuller version of Olef than the magi I'd gotten to know. He talked about Olef's charity work within the magi community, his contributions to magical research, his many grandchildren living all over the world, and Olef's own travels to exotic locations.

But while it was fascinating to learn about this side of my friend, I missed the Olef I knew. The one who would stop by the diner where I used to work on a regular basis, and who always had a pleasant word while he paid for his Danish and coffee. The one who'd saved my butt the day I was running from the Gryphons because he believed I'd been framed for Victor Aubrey's murders when few others did. I owed that Olef a debt I'd never had the chance to pay. And I missed the Olef who had a seemingly endless supply of knowledge—and the patience to go with it—whenever I bugged him with questions.

I wished I'd gotten to know those Olefs better. I wished I'd taken more time to ask him about all the things Xander was telling us about—his travels, his grandchildren, his hobbies.

Once, I'd had the time, but it had never occurred to me. Then after life began to throw us together more often, time had been in short supply. I felt like I was always running to or from something.

I sucked on my lip and dug my nails into my palms. I would repay my debt to Olef one way or another. I would take down Raj. Make certain Olef's murder was avenged. And I would use his last message to me to stop the furies. I would ensure Olef hadn't died in vain.

Even if I died trying to do what he'd told me, which I suspected I would.

A surprisingly cool wind whispered through the cemetery, and Xander finished speaking. Someone else took up the role usually reserved for clergy, but magi were typically nonreligious, so I wasn't sure who this person was.

I wasn't religious either, having been brought up in a house where religion played a very minor role. But now I glanced above the heads of the mourners and into the lush maple tree branches around the cemetery and finally into the sky, wishing for a sign. Something to make me believe there was meaning to what happened. That we'd go on, and everything would get better.

Unsurprisingly, I saw nothing.

At least the sky wasn't red. I consoled myself with that. The red spot remained several miles away from a small border town, tucked between the French and Swiss Alps, where the furies had opened the Pit. The Gryphons had commandeered the castle, and a contingent stayed there, waiting for whatever happened next. So far, all was quiet. The longer it stayed that way, the eerier it felt.

Raj, to my knowledge, hadn't returned to Boston. Everyone was on the lookout for him, but a general disaster fatigue had also set in. We were tired, and a daunting task lay ahead.

The Gryphons hadn't taken the news public yet, although they'd been letting more of their own in on it. As well, they'd allegedly broached the topic with certain powerful government officials. Obviously, word of the sky had spread, and rumors abounded. Fierce debates over the public's right to know versus the possibility of mass panic raged within the Gryphons, and within *Le Confrérie* itself. I wasn't sure which side I fell on, so I kept my mouth shut whenever asked for an opinion. These last seventy-two hours had felt like weeks. Maybe when I finally got a good night's sleep again, I'd figure it out.

When the funeral ended, I crept off alone. Well, not entirely alone. I ran a thumb over Lucen's pendant, irked by it yet grateful too. I had so many things to say to Lucen that I hadn't managed to start anywhere.

While you were busy keeping tabs on me, I was trying to find a way to unmake you.

I knew I should confess it, but at the moment, Lucen's need for addicts was so low on my list of concerns that I never thought of it when we were together. Maybe now? I was supposed to see him after the funeral.

Dezzi had called a council meeting, and since I'd been dubbed the official Gryphon-satyr liaison by both groups, I was expected to go. I only hoped Claudius wouldn't show up. Supposedly, he was still hanging around being unhelpful. Just what we all needed.

As I stepped onto the sidewalk, thunder cracked so loudly overhead I jumped. Pausing by the cemetery gate, I checked up but the sky was clear. Not a cloud in sight. The thunder boomed again, and was it my imagination, or did the sky seem to ripple? My skin tingled, and my heartbeat quickened. Magic in the air.

While I gaped, Tom caught up to me. He was putting his phone away, and he pulled me aside to let mourners pass. Like the other Gryphons in attendance, he was wearing his full dress uniform. "We have a problem."

"Another one?" I lifted my head skyward, thinking those weird ripples were not the sign I'd been hoping for earlier.

"No, same one. That was the Brotherhood calling. The magic detectors they set up around the castle were just so overloaded, they broke."

"That doesn't sound good."

"No." Tom took a deep breath and waited for me to meet his gaze. "It's worse. The red sky has started spreading."

Thank you for reading! Did you enjoy? Please add your review because nothing helps an author more and encourages readers to take a chance on a book than a review.

And don't miss more in the final book in the Miss Misery series with MISERY HAPPENS, available now Turn the page for a sneak peek!

Also be sure to sign up for the City Owl Press newsletter to receive notice of all book releases!

SNEAK PEEK OF MISERY HAPPENS

The apocalypse didn't arrive quickly, nor with the ferocity of a punch to the face. Instead, it crept in quietly, a crimson sky oozing over the earth until it blanketed every continent.

Frankly, I'd have preferred a punch to the face. I knew what to do to people who were punching me. I did not know how to handle a world gone mad, bloodthirsty, and irrational. Especially when the real hell had yet to break loose.

"Seems to me that discretion might have been a better choice." Claudius wrinkled his nose at the airport's exhaust-filled terminal and waved a careless hand in the direction of the five Gryphons filing out of their SUVs. "Dezzi and I are the only ones who need to be here. And you, I suppose."

Behind Claudius's back, the long-suffering leader of Boston's satyr domus rolled her dark eyes. She did not, however, contradict him. Preds, regardless of their race, rarely showed their disagreements in front of Gryphons. Also, Claudius outranked her. It was more Dezzi's style to challenge his authority in subtle ways.

I bounced from foot to foot. I was wired on adrenaline and the human anxiety that permanently buzzed throughout the city, and trying to keep my distance from the satyrs' Upper Council member. Claudius had only been bumped from the top of my shitlist because a certain fury had murdered one of my friends. That said, I wouldn't put it past Claudius to reclaim his place at the top if given enough time. The arrogant, flowing-haired jackass had almost gotten *me* killed once already.

"Discretion failed us in Phoenix and Paris," I said, casting a wry glance at Gryphon Agent Tom Kassin. "The fury prison is open, the sky is bleeding, and the time for sneakiness is gone."

Tom nodded in agreement, which was almost as eerie as the crimson sky or the mostly deserted airport terminal. I could probably count the number of things Tom and I agreed on with one hand. Although, unlike with Claudius, I'd recently developed a grudging respect for the blond-haired, baby-faced Gryphon.

It was Tom's fraternity—*Le Confrérie de l'Aile* or the Brotherhood of the Wing—that I wasn't so certain about. Call me petty, but I couldn't entirely get over how they'd performed secret experiments on my teenage self that had turned me into a magical anomaly. Sure, their intentions had been good, but we all knew where good intentions led.

In our case, hell might be more literal than figurative. We'd begun referring to the creatures who had been locked in the magical prison—known as the Pit—as demons, and it was for more reasons than just ease of distinguishing them from the modern furies who'd freed them. Our ancestors had called them the same, and they scared the shit out of super-powerful preds like Claudius.

In the past three days, not only had the red sky spread from its origin above where the furies had opened the Pit, but the frequency of thunder had increased too. We had every reason to believe this was a sign that the Pit's inhabitants were moving about, gaining in power now that they could feed off the negativity and fear generated by the six billion humans on this planet.

Fear, which the preternaturally red sky obviously made worse.

People—be they human, magi, or pred—seemed to have had three types of reactions to the sky changing color. A few were trying to carry on as normal. Others were hunkering down, stocking up on gas, water, ammunition, and—weirdly enough—toilet paper, though not necessarily in that priority. Finally, the most annoying ones were taking to the streets in Boston and cities around the world. This third group was a scary mix of angry conspiracy theorists, religious fanatics, and a rapidly growing segment of the population who were known as anti-magers because they believed any use of magic by any race was evil and the cause of our current problems.

Claudius voiced his skepticism about the need for our Gryphon escort with a grunt. I took my cue from Dezzi and simply rolled my eyes as I wandered away. Ever since I'd had a magical collision with Raj, one of the fury ringleaders and the bastard at the top of my shitlist, my ability to get angry had been muted. I wasn't sure what that meant, but since furies fed on anger and fear, I suspected it wasn't good.

On the other hand, it probably was a boon to my blood pressure given how much time I'd had to spend in Claudius's company lately.

A lone cabbie drove by our spot in the passenger pick-up lot, and the taste of the driver's grapefruit-flavored fear shot over my tongue. It faded as he passed from my sight, but I pulled a stick of gum from my pocket anyway. Lately, I'd taken to chewing a lot of the stuff or munching on breath mints in order to deal with the constant sour taste of that particular emotion.

"You okay?" Lucen came up behind me.

I wanted to snark at him for asking such a ridiculous question, but I held my tongue because he meant well. He knew it wasn't just the situation with the Pit being open that had me on edge. It was being forced to deal with more satyrs from the Upper Council. Alas, Claudius, though a jackass of the highest order, had finally made himself useful and convinced the rest of the highest-ranking satyrs that they'd better help our tentative Boston-based alliance. That was why we were here. After intense political negotiations with the Gryphons, the satyrs had admitted that they held the fifth Vessel of Making.

We had the other four, which meant once we had the satyrs' Vessel too, we could unite all five and relock the Pit, preferably before the creatures inside escaped. Or that's how the theory went. How that would actually work, well, that was something we were struggling with.

I offered Lucen a stick of gum. "I'm fine." Then I wondered if that was a lie, and if so, could my misery-feeding boyfriend detect it?

Lucen declined the gum with an expression of comical distaste. "Sure you are."

"Hey, if you don't like my answers, why ask the question?"

"Habit?" He smiled impishly. The combination of the terminal's yellowish lighting and the ever-present red tinge from above gave everyone a creepy hue, but in that moment his blue-green eyes twinkled as bright as ever.

It was a good thing Lucen's appearance was only the third sexiest thing about him, following his sense of humor and protectiveness. Otherwise, I'd feel pretty shallow for the way I could lust after him no matter what the situation.

Even now, I longed to rest my head on his broad shoulder and breathe deeply of his cinnamon-scented pheromones. The summer night was exceptionally humid, and imagining the taste of the thin layer of sweat on his skin teased me. It wasn't even about sex. I just wanted him to hold me and lie to me and tell me everything was going to be okay. But this was neither the time nor the place. An unfortunate rule of the apocalypse was the more you craved comfort, the less opportunities you had for it.

"You're only asking out of habit?" I pretended to pout. "And here I thought you were genuinely concerned for my mental well-being."

Lucen took my arms in his hands and kissed my forehead. "Always, little siren."

Someone purposely scuffed their shoes against the asphalt as they came up behind us. Since I couldn't detect any emotions, it had to be Dezzi or Claudius. With my luck, the latter.

Indeed, my luck held. Claudius reached out with his power and lightly brushed my mind. Despite my unwillingness, my body reacted to the sensation and I shivered. Lucen could sense my stronger arousal too, and he tightened his grip on my arms.

"You know it's impolite to eat in front of the rest of us." Claudius leered at me.

I clenched my jaw, and Lucen responded before I could. "She is a satyr. Lacking horns doesn't change her race."

"Stop it," I whispered to Lucen. Picking fights with Claudius was more dangerous for him than it was for Dezzi. Claudius already had it in for Lucen, mostly because he thought Lucen was slumming it by being with me, and Lucen rose to the bait every time the topic arose. It was only because Lucen was currently Dezzi's acting lieutenant that he was here tonight. Usually, Dezzi tried to separate the two men.

"Being an abnormal human does not make her one of us. If I can feed on her emotions, if I can addict her"—Claudius's smirk broadened—"then how can she be?"

The memory of Claudius in my head, of how I'd hated him even as I was begging for his touch… It hit me all at once with a searing heat, like a salamander's bite to the brain. Suddenly I was reliving that moment, the way I'd clung to Lucen's railing and spread my legs for the arrogant bastard in front of me.

All the rage I'd felt then exploded inside me. The unnatural calm I'd been experiencing was gone, replaced by a red-hot fire. Damn it, I might not be able to punch the apocalypse, but I could whale on a jackass of a satyr.

I spun around, slipping Misery from the sheath at my hip as I did so. The knife's black salamander fire-forged blade was beautiful in my grip and so easily lethal. Just a single nick would make Claudius bleed out. None of his power could save him from that, and while I held the weapon in my hand, I felt every bit as powerful as he must have when he'd lorded his control over me.

Claudius's eyes opened wide in surprise as I raised the blade toward his annoyingly handsome face. Oh, how I'd love to see it scarred.

Vaguely, I was aware of Lucen calling my name and the Gryphons pausing whatever they were doing and turning my way. But hot blood raced by my ears. I didn't care what they thought, just as I didn't care that threatening an extraordinarily powerful satyr whose help we needed was not a smart idea.

I didn't fucking care about anything except giving in to the fury boiling in my veins. The world had gone mad, bloodthirsty, and irrational, and at last, I'd gone with it.

"Back the hell off." My body was so tense it hurt my jaw to speak. "I don't care what you think I am or what you think of me. But if you ever invade my head that way again, I'm going to tie you up with your own intestines."

Hell, I didn't know why I shouldn't do it anyway. My hand trembled with the urge to drive my blade into Claudius's throat. No satyr healer could close that wound before he bled out, and wouldn't that be oh so satisfying.

Claudius could probably use his magic to force me to drop the knife, but maybe he didn't want to chance that I could move faster than he could mind-fuck me. He kept backing up, and he cast disdainful glances at Dezzi and the Gryphons as he did. "You need to learn to control her."

"Fuck you!" My vehemence echoed off the terminal's filthy concrete walls. "I'm not a satyr or a Gryphon. Nobody gets to claim me or control me, and you certainly don't get to define what I am."

Then I lunged at him.

Don't stop now. Keep reading with your copy of MISERY HAPPENS available now.

And find more from Tracey Martin at www.tracey-martin.com

Don't miss the final book, MISERY HAPPENS, available now, and discover more from Tracey Martin at www.tracey-martin.com

---

Sometimes everything goes to hell. Sometimes hell comes to you.

Jessica Moore has one hell of a to-do list. Number one: Bring the fury who attacked her friends to justice. Number two: Obtain the last item required to re-lock a magical prison. And number three: Save the world by actually re-locking the damn thing before its demonic prisoners escape.

But with a red sky enveloping the earth, humans and nonhumans alike are panicking, and the fanatical fringe is growing violent. Anti-magers— humans who want to destroy all things magical—are waging war on Jess and her friends.

And there's still the problem of the key. It's the last item Jess and her allies are searching for, but legend claims it's trapped within the prison itself. Someone will have to go in there and face down the demons to find it.

Naturally, guess whose strange power is the only thing that might succeed? Even with Lucen at her side and a Gryphon army at her back, this might be too much for a misery junkie to handle.

Please sign up for the City Owl Press newsletter for chances to win special subscriber-only contests and giveaways as well as receiving information on upcoming releases and special excerpts.

All reviews are **welcome** and **appreciated**. Please consider leaving one on your favorite social media and book buying sites.

Escape Your World. Get Lost in Ours! City Owl Press at www.cityowlpress.com.

ACKNOWLEDGMENTS

Thank you to Danielle DeVor, Tina Moss, and all the staff at City Owl Press for making this book happen. As always, thank you to my family, friends, and writing groups for for supporting me on this journey. And thank you to the readers for sticking around with Jess, Lucen, and company for all these books.

ABOUT THE AUTHOR

TRACEY MARTIN lives in New England where she collects pen names, tattoos, and hoodies in shades of gray and black. Under the name Alanna Martin, she's the author of the *Hearts of Alaska* contemporary romance series. If you can't find her online, it's because she's lost in the woods. Send help.

www.tracey-martin.com

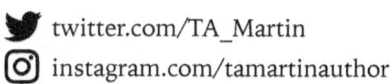

twitter.com/TA_Martin

instagram.com/tamartinauthor

ABOUT THE PUBLISHER

City Owl Press is a cutting edge indie publishing company, bringing the world of romance and speculative fiction to discerning readers.

Escape Your World. Get Lost in Ours!

www.cityowlpress.com

 facebook.com/YourCityOwlPress
 twitter.com/cityowlpress
 instagram.com/cityowlbooks
 pinterest.com/cityowlpress